WHAT YOU *Broke*

SAMANTHA M. THOMAS

Book Cover by Y'all That Graphic

Edits by Emi Janisch

Proofread by Nina Fiegl

First edition 2024

Contents

DEDICATION

To vulnerability: It is not a weakness. Always putting on the strong front gets exhausting and sometimes you just need that one person to lean on. To let you breakdown and feel for once.

Everyone needs an Arlo, even if he's a pain in your ass.

PREVIOUSLY ON BLUEBELL FALLS

These are spoilers for For the Thrill of It. It is recommended to read For the Thrill of It before What You Broke:

Picking up in the direct aftermath of the events in For the Thrill of It, What We broke starts in hospital. Oakley and Tennison faced off as Willow came to save the day. Arlo came into the cabin, rescuing Lennox and rushing him to the hospital in Rosedale. Now, it's time for the Huttons to see the extent of the damage to both Lennox and Oakley.

Content Warning: Mentions of stalking (on page, not between the main characters) and death of parents (off page).

CHAPTER ONE
RINA

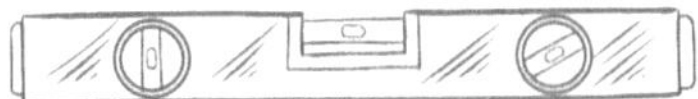

I've never liked hospitals. They remind me of a time when a twenty-year-old and a twenty-two-year-old had to be strong after the loss of their parents, and subsequently transform into parental figures for their two younger siblings.

At the time, it was what I was supposed to do; what my older brother, Ledger, was supposed to do. Neither of us have regrets or any resentment, but it changed the course of both of our lives forever. Instead of experiencing college and then moving on to build his dream landscaping company, Ledger put everything on the back burner, slowly building his company here in Bluebell Falls. It wasn't until very recently that his goals from back then became a reality, thanks to his fiancée, Ainsley.

As for me? I fell back into what I was good at—furniture building. I had greater aspirations once upon a time. I went to trade school to learn the ins and outs of carpentry and such, but I always thought I would do more with it. Sure, I'm pretty in demand lately with my custom furniture builds, but my life changed a lot within only a month's time when my parents died.

Which brings me to why sitting here in the waiting area—waiting to hear any information about our youngest brother, Lennox, and watching our sister, Willow, have a mental breakdown over her man—is literally killing me inside.

It doesn't help that *he's* here.

Sheriff Arlo Steel.

The man who crushed my heart right after my parents died in a car crash.

The man who was supposed to stay away from Bluebell Falls, thanks to his military career.

The man who showed me love is a hoax and not something sacred, like I was led to believe.

It was a hard lesson to learn so young, but I'd like to think I'm all the better for it.

Except now, I see how good Ainsley is for Ledger. How Willow is so desperate to hear good news about her man, Oakley. It has my head wandering into dangerous territories.

And all the while, Arlo, with his stupid, dark brown crew cut, keeps pacing into my periphery. His deep brown eyes keep looking over at me, like he's checking on me.

Well, fuck him. He lost that right long ago.

He doesn't get to act like he gives a shit.

A doctor calling all of us to a room for updates interrupts my angry thoughts.

The update we receive is a good one, albeit still fucking miserable. Lennox was caught in the crosshairs of the Tennison Strangler. He was cut multiple times and had some extreme blood loss, but for the most part, he will physically recover just fine. Emotionally, as the doctor tells us, he's in for an uphill battle. My heart hurts just hearing that. I know, logically, none of this is even remotely on me, but I can't help but feel like I failed Lennox. I'm supposed to keep him safe, and yet he sits in a hospital bed in the ICU after a psychopath took his vendetta against Oakley out on him.

The doctor drones on, but I can barely focus. I catch a few words, like Oakley saying Willow is his fiancée so she can stay updated on his condition, and that Lennox will be here for at least a week.

The walls start to get this weird movement to them and close in on me. Squeezing my eyes closed, I focus on the knowledge that it's just my mind playing tricks on me.

"Do you have any more questions for me?" the doctor asks.

I vigorously shake my head. The claustrophobic feeling is getting worse by the second, and I know I need to get out of this room and away from everyone. I need a place where I can freak out without an audience.

I hear the door shut and slowly open my eyes to see that it's just Ledger, Ainsley, Willow and me left in the room. Everyone looks like they're reeling from the news, but I can't stick around to talk about it.

Slowly, I stand from my chair and walk to the door, shakily heading down the hallway to an area that looks deserted.

Lucking out, I find an empty room with a little table in it and plop down into the chair.

As I bury my head in my hands, the tears start to fall, and it only pisses me off more. I'm not a crier. I'm not one who falls apart. I made a vow a long time ago to always be strong and never let anyone see any weakness. But it sure as hell feels like I have weakness bleeding out of me right now.

And I hate every second of it.

I'll allow myself this moment of fragility before I force myself to get my shit together.

My shoulders shake as the sobs come harder, and I'm barely able to catch my breath. I want to be mad at Oakley, at everyone involved in letting this happen to my baby brother. I want to be able to take Lennox's pain away and have him live his normal life. To go back to being the happy-go-lucky pain in my ass, who names every animal he comes across as a park ranger. For him to bust a hole in Ledger's drywall by throwing open the front door too hard. I don't want him to have to live through this horror, through this trauma, that will probably fundamentally change him.

I'm still trying to catch my breath when I feel a hand on my shoulder.

I turn into the strong body that sits next to me, not even caring when his familiar scent of fresh air and laundry soap hits my nose.

This is my moment of weakness; being fragile enough to take comfort from the one man I swore never to turn to again. *Arlo.*

"Emmerdeur." The anguish in his voice makes the tears fall harder.

The nickname I haven't heard in years breaks my heart all over again. His arms wrap around me, his hand rubbing over my back just like he used to do when we were dumb, young kids. It always soothed me then and it does the same now, much to my infuriation.

"Why" —hiccup— "did this happen?" Hiccup. "Why Lennox?" I whisper.

"I don't know. I've been asking myself the same thing for hours." The hoarseness of his voice catches me off guard. It's not that I think he doesn't care; it's that I don't think he cares about *me*. I know his pain is because of Lennox and not me, but it still throws me off enough to pull back from him.

Wiping my eyes with the sleeves of my hoodie, I sit up straight and clear my throat.

Moment of weakness over.

"Emmerdeur..."

"I'm good." He opens his mouth to say something, but I cut him off. "I'm good, Arlo," I say, firmer.

"I tried to get him out of there as fast as I could," he murmurs. There's that pain in his voice again. It makes me irrationally angry. Mad that he's making me feel bad for him. Pissed that I'm even taking his feelings into consideration when he's never done the same for me.

"You did good. He made it here and is stable. That's all we could ask for." Putting my hand on his forearm, I attempt to assuage him of his guilt. I'm not sure why I'm trying to console him, but I want him to know that we don't blame him for any part of this. Tennison is responsible, no one else.

His eyes shift between mine, looking for God knows what, and before I can get my bearings, he leans forward ever so slowly. I can see it all happening in slow motion, and my logical brain is screaming at me to stop it, but I don't. I watch as he gets closer before he finally presses a kiss to my lips.

My eyes flutter shut with nostalgia. Once upon a time, I thought this man would be my everything. Once upon a time, I thought he was my Prince Charming.

Like a lightning bolt, my body catches up to my brain and I jerk back. I watch as his eyes shutter, the emotion that was so clearly on display now hidden from me. Just like it always is.

"Fuck," he grinds out, scrubbing his hand over his face.

I give myself one second to revel in the feel of his lips on mine again. To imagine those hands all over my body, and then I shut that shit down.

"Fuck!" he says louder as he stands, his chair shoving back with force. I'm sure if he had longer hair, he would be pulling it right now. That's how agitated he looks. It's his own damn fault, though. He's the one who kissed me. He paces in a little circle before beelining for the door.

The sound of the door clicking shut has a finality about it.

I don't know what just happened. I don't know why he followed me in here, comforted me, and then kissed me, but I do know it won't happen again.

I won't let it.

I made myself a promise after the haze of grief cleared all those years ago. Both the grief of losing my parents and losing Arlo. I promised myself I would never give my heart to a man again.

I stand by that, but as I bring my fingertips up to my lips, I can still feel the electricity of his touch. How does he still have this much power over me after more than a decade?

My head feels jumbled with too many thoughts and not enough answers. Between the stressful situation with Lennox and still not really knowing the extent of where he's at mentally, and now fucking Arlo throwing the biggest mixed signal there is, I have no idea where I stand.

Which is not a great place for my head to be. I thrive on having answers, on knowing everything about a given situation. I'm a control freak through and through, born out of necessity and self-preservation.

Leaning forward, pressing the heel of my palms to my eyes, I try to relieve the massive amount of pressure I'm beginning to feel. This is why I don't cry anymore. I suck back any tears I start to feel because I almost always get an instant migraine. And I can't afford to have one at this moment. There's too much going on, and my siblings need me.

That thought reminds me of how distraught Willow was. She probably should be getting looked at too, even if she isn't physically hurt. She was in that cabin, came face to face with the devil himself. Combine that with whatever is going on with Oakley, and I know she's losing it right now, even if she's trying to convince everyone otherwise.

I lift my head up, draw in a deep breath, and count to ten.

Ten seconds to push everything I'm feeling down.

Ten seconds to forget Arlo showed me a glimpse of the man I thought he was.

Ten seconds to pull up my big girl pants and take care of my family.

One more deep breath before I stand up and straighten myself up. Nothing can be done about the beet-red face I'm surely sporting, but I think everyone's focus will be elsewhere.

As I walk out of the door, I spot Arlo no more than twenty feet down the hallway, pacing and looking distressed. I stand up taller as I near him and continue to walk right past him.

It's better for us to get back to hating each other.

CHAPTER TWO
ARLO

I didn't sign up for this shit when I came back here and took over the job as sheriff.

Nowhere in the job description does it say: set up a trap for a prolific torturer and then watch a family, who has already been through too much, fall apart because of it.

I know they'll be okay because they're always okay, but that doesn't make this situation any easier. It certainly doesn't excuse my epic lack of control by kissing Rina. I pound my head against the cement walls of the hospital, begging it to hurt. I deserve it. Hell, I deserve every cold shoulder that spitfire of a woman gives me. And as I watch her walk past me like I don't exist, my heart shrivels up a little more inside my chest.

I'm shocked there's anything left of the stupid organ.

I give myself two minutes to dwell on the fact that I kissed Rina again. The feel of her lips is something I'm not sure I even realized how much I missed.

For years, I've gone about my life acting like the events of fifteen years ago never happened. Pushing down every emotion I felt seeing Rina on a regular basis. But seeing her break down was too much. She's a proud person, rarely showing anyone her emotions, so when I saw her starting to lose control of those carefully closed off feelings, I didn't think. I just followed. She's always so strong for everyone else. I wanted to be the one to help her feel comfortable enough to let it all go. To support her as she fell.

And then it started feeling like the old days, back when she was all I could see. Our future so vivid in my mind, I didn't think anything could tear us apart. Kissing her felt so damn natural. Like more than a decade hasn't passed since we connected.

But it has, and we're no longer teenagers in love. No longer dreaming about a future that never happened—because of me.

Fuck, some days are torture. Being so close to her and not being able to do anything is a fate worse than death.

But this is the life I chose. This is what I thought would be best for Rina. Granted, I never planned on coming back here and making a life, but it doesn't change my choices.

I look at my watch and see my two minutes are long gone. It's time to do my damn job.

To be clear, I love my job. I love being the sheriff in the small town I was born and raised in. Wrangling all the nosy-ass residents comprises a bulk of tasks, but it was never what I was supposed to do. I was supposed to be a career military man. Become an officer in the Marines and see where it took me, retire after I did my time, and then figure out what was next when the time came.

Too bad that time came too soon and not voluntarily. I arch my back to stretch it out, even the memory causing it to ache.

I shake off the phantom pain and head toward Oakley's room. I need to touch base with the U.S. Marshal Task Force that's in charge of the case before I leave, so everyone is on the same page. It may not be my jurisdiction, but it happened in my town, so I'll be damned if I'm not in the know about what's going on. After that, I'm going home. Too much happened today, and I need to decompress and process it all.

It's been three days since shit hit the fan and landed two of the best men I know in the hospital.

The only thing that's happened is the damn media descending on Bluebell Falls, causing me one hell of a headache. The good news is those nosy-ass residents are doing a wonderful job of pissing every single reporter off, so I don't think they'll stick around long.

I'm walking back to my office, flipping my phone in my hand and contemplating something dangerous.

I can't get my mind off of Rina, *my Marina,* and how fucking good it felt to be in her orbit again. Texting her would be so easy; I could pass it off as checking in on Lennox, even though I just talked to Ledger about him.

Flipping my phone once more, I decide to just go for it. What could it hurt? She decides she hates me and never talks to me again? I'm already living in that hell.

Me:

How are things over there? Any news on Lennox?

The ellipses show up almost immediately, and I almost run into the door to my small office.

> Seems like you already know, seeing as you just talked to Ledger.

Busted.

> Okay, you caught me. How are you doing?

The ellipses appear and disappear a couple of times before her message comes through this time.

> Why are you really texting me?

> Truth?

> I think we owe each other that, at the very least.

> I can't stop thinking about the kiss. And I know you still hate me, for good reason. But it just felt so … fucking good.

If it were anyone else, I would never be that honest. But Rina and I were always this way, always blunt and to the point. *Except the one time you lied to her.* Her reply interrupts my self-loathing.

It felt too good.

I sit frozen because, in all honesty, I thought I'd be getting a tongue lashing right now. I'd enjoy every second of it, but I was not expecting this.

What would you say to doing something like that again, except a little more orgasm-centric and less kiss-centric?

Name when and where.

This has certainly taken a turn, but I can't say I'm sorry. Do I know that this is destined for disaster? Absolutely. But does it even matter when the love of my life is asking for orgasms? Hell fucking no.

I'm locked up with a custom order for the next couple of days, but I could be game in a few days. Say, the end of the week?

I'll make myself available.

Of course you will.

I don't reply. There's no need to. It will only lead to a fight. I stretch my legs out in front of me in my office chair and tuck my hands behind my head. Never did I think checking in would lead to this, but damn am I going to take advantage while I can.

"What's wrong with you?" my part-time receptionist, Audrey, asks. She's really more of a "do everything" person, including handling emergency calls while she's on shift, but we haven't come up with a better title for her.

"What?" I sit up.

"You're smiling. You never smile."

"I smile," I tell her in disbelief.

"You absolutely do not smile. I think I can count on one hand the number of times I've seen you smile in the five years I've worked here."

I grumble under my breath because she's probably right. I'm not known for my approachability. Things like that don't matter in the small town you grew up in, though. Everyone knows you and is in your business, regardless of having a *Fuck Off* sign on my forehead.

"Don't you have work to do or something? I'm sure Mabel needs something, especially with these damn news vans everywhere," I deflect.

"Sure do, Boss Man. Just one more thing—whatever made you smile like that, you should do more of." Then she turns around and heads to her small desk outside of my office.

Easy, Audrey. Just keep Rina close. But I know it'll never be more than sex for her. And my heart definitely won't end up crushed by the end of this or anything.

I really wish I didn't have this fucking order to make.

Why is that? Feeling needy?

Jesus, if she wasn't going in that direction, I just proved I'm a horny asshole with one thing on my mind. It wouldn't necessarily be wrong, but damn, a little decorum would be nice.

So. Fucking. Horny.

To be clear: The only reason this is happening is because I need the distraction. It's just sex.

I ignore her second message because, honestly, my shriveled-up heart hurts a little hearing that. Even if I knew the score from the get-go. But I'm down for just sex at this point. Anything that involves Rina is something I'm on board with.

And there's no chance we can get together before the end of the week?

Sadly, no. I really need to finish this.

Where are you right now?

In my workshop, taking a break to tell you how horny I am.

I could always come down there and bend you over your worktable.

You could, I suppose. But that would just prolong getting this done.

I would slide down those leggings you always wear. What color are your panties today? Still fond of lace?

Jesus fuck… Pink lace today…

I adjust myself under my desk, distantly wondering if this is the right move, but it feels far too late to stop.

Me:

I'd slide that pink lace to the side, keeping them on to frame that fucking perfect ass of yours, before sliding my tongue where you really want it.

Rina:

Then what?

I smirk. I've got her right on the edge. And I'd bet all the money in my back account that she has her hand down her pants right now.

Me:

I'd tease the fuck out of you. Not letting you come yet. That would be too easy.

Me:

Is your hand down your pants?

Rina:

Fuck you, you know it is.

Me:

Rub that clit for me, Rina. Get worked up for me.

Rina:

You're so cocky. You talk a big game, Arlo, but how do I know you can actually do all this in real life?

Me:

I seem to remember knowing exactly how to get you off every single time, Marina.

Don't fucking call me that, or I'll call off this arrangement before it starts.

I shift my hand to my hard cock, squeezing in an attempt to stave off my impending orgasm just from her words. She may hate me, but she still knows what I can do to her body.

But then you wouldn't feel my cock inside of you again. Wouldn't feel the stretch as you take all of me while I pinch your clit and make you come all over me. Wouldn't have the most powerful orgasm you've ever had.

Cocky asshole...

You just had a good orgasm, though. Don't even deny it.

It may have been fifteen years, but I know her. I know if she was already horny when she started texting me, it wouldn't take long to get her off.

I'll concede to good… The real thing would have been much better. Don't get a big head about it or anything.

Which head?

I burst out laughing at my stupid joke, which has Audrey peeking her head in, looking at me in utter confusion. I wave her off and turn back to my conversation with Rina. It's a good thing my desk covers my very obvious boner.

Well, thanks for the orgasm. It's been … something. I'll see you on Friday… Maybe.

Oh, you'll be seeing me, Marina.

Fuck off, Arlo.

I just imagine her fake, sugar-sweet voice saying it. I thump my head against my desk, trying to calm my raging boner. It's not like I have a ton to do today, but I can't even begin to work in this state.

Thinking about the last ten minutes, I'm not entirely sure what the fuck just happened, but it was hotter than anything I've done in the last fifteen years. I'm pretty sure I'll do anything this woman asks of me, even if sexting and secret hook-ups are all I get.

Yeah, I'm definitely fucked.

CHAPTER THREE
RINA

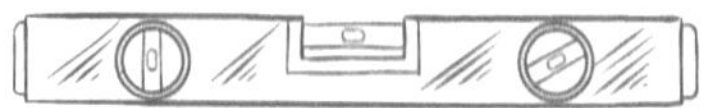

What the fuck am I doing?

My hand is still shoved down my pants, and I'm still panting as I recover from an orgasm that shouldn't have been that good. My brain is having a tough time separating Arlo to just a hook-up, but that's exactly what he is. Our history means nothing, and this is a distraction I'm desperately in need of. It's not like there are a ton of options for a hook-up here in town, not without the gossips knowing everything.

Between everything that happened with Lennox, Willow shacking up with Oakley, the fucking news vans every three feet, and this huge custom order, stress relief in the form of a few orgasms seemed like a great idea. If I'm honest, it still feels like a good idea. I just need to keep my hatred for the man front and center.

It's not like it'll be hard. He deserves every ounce of hate and more from me. When he decided to make a unilateral decision about both of our futures because he was scared, he went from the love of my life to lower than dirt in thirty seconds. Sure, I was heartbroken for a while, but then I took that feeling and turned it into anger. The anger has never really left me. It certainly got stronger when he showed up after five years, like nothing had happened.

And now, here I am, trying to have hate sex with the man in secret.

I'm not going to lie; he may be cocky, but he's right about the orgasm. It's the best I've had in years, and that's just fucking sad. But it fuels my need to get to Friday sooner so I can get the real thing.

I'm just hoping he doesn't open his mouth and talk the usual shit he does. That's a sure-fire way to piss me off and kill my libido.

I rip my hand from my pants and walk over to the little sink I have in my workshop to wash up. Lord knows I don't want the reminder of what just happened every time I use that hand to build this dresser.

Hands on the sink, I bow my head and take a deep breath. I know this is a terrible idea. I know having sex with the man who ripped my heart out of my chest and then stomped on it for good measure is bad news. I also know I'm barely being held together at the seams right now, and this is an escape I desperately need.

Sure, what could possibly go wrong?

It's too late now. Friday feels like the lifeline I need to not fall apart. The thread that will keep me going when everything else feels like it's falling around me.

I'm not sure there's ever been a time in my life where I felt this out of control. Sure, when my parents died, and Ledger taking guardianship of Willow and Lennox when he and I were barely twenty was rough. But we both buckled down and did the damn thing. They've turned out pretty damn good. I didn't even feel this out of control when, less than a month later, *Arlo* decided I was no longer a part of his future. I was no longer the person he wanted to live life with.

The pain in my chest that usually accompanies my thoughts of that time comes in waves, and I shake my head to stop this line of thinking.

Instead, I think about all the work I need to get done.

My custom furniture building business has blown up in the last six months. I've got a huge influx of orders with no end in sight. It's a good thing, exactly what I've been working hard on since I was eighteen and decided to go to trade school. But holy shit are my nerves shot. I've taken on too many orders with a tight-as-fuck timeline that is borderline impossible.

A few days ago, when Lennox was brought to the hospital in Rosedale, I stopped taking new orders. I knew I couldn't keep up this workload and be there for my baby brother when he needed me the most. I still have a ton to catch up on, but once I make it through my existing orders, I can re-evaluate how much work I take on.

I'm to the point now where I'm pretty sought after, so business isn't hard to come by anymore. I can pick and choose when I open up commissions and then close them, with little effect on my overall business. It's something I'm not used to at all. I'm used to hustling for every order, every small piece that costs more to make than I made on the back end. Scraping by and begging for a chance to show my furniture.

This newfound popularity has come at a great time, though, if I need to shut everything down to help Lennox. I'm reminded of the doctor saying that emotionally, he'll have a lot to work through, and I know being more available is the only choice. Family is everything to me, and no obscenely expensive commission will change that.

I take one more deep breath, pushing down all my overwhelming emotions before turning around and making my way back to the dresser I was working on.

It's finally Friday.

Thank whatever deity I need to thank, but I made it. The dresser got done as well as the two nightstands to match, and all I need to do is deliver them tomorrow.

I've been working sixteen-hour days all week to finish this order on time and now my brain can stop thinking. My body can get the release it so desperately wants, and then I can crash for ten hours.

My shoulders slump in relief as I drive the forty minutes to Rosedale to pick up Lennox. I'm breaking him out, and I think everyone is as relieved as he is. Ledger hosted family dinner last night so we could all be on the same page when we brought Lennox home, and it was so nice to get back to our normal routine. It felt like we hadn't done family dinner in months, even though it had only been a couple of weeks. When you do something every single week since we were all babies, it's difficult to not have it. It wasn't quite the same without Lennox, but it was a step in the right direction.

By the time I get Lennox into my truck, he's successfully pissed everyone off in the area. I know he's the free spirit who basically lives in the wild, and being cooped up for so long is wearing on him, but damn. The boy did not need to be an ass to the poor nurse who wheeled him out. Even I know it's hospital policy that you can't just walk out by yourself. It wasn't the nurse's fault. But I know he feels helpless. And if there's anything us Huttons hate, it's being helpless in any way. It's why we've all been so successful in our own careers.

"I know you're dying to get home, but damn, Lenny, what did that poor nurse do to you?"

"I know." He runs his hand over his face. "Fuck. Did you tell her sorry for me?"

"Of course I did. It's not like anyone is blaming you anyway."

"That's not an excuse," he mutters.

I choose not to compound his guilt. He has enough going on at the moment. I look at the clock and realize I'll probably need to drop off Lennox so I can meet Arlo at our allotted time. I pull my phone out quickly and send a text to Willow, asking if she can come meet me at Lennox's house so he isn't alone when I drop him off. It's more of a precaution, and I'm probably a huge bitch for ditching him for sex, but I need this.

The entire drive home, he talks about how we're babying him. When I calmly try to tell him one of us was going to pick him up, he says he could have taken a rideshare. I almost lose what little shred of patience I have. I understand we're all struggling with everything that happened, but shit, does he really think we'd let him take a rideshare home?

It honestly makes me glad Willow will be there when I drop him off. I think I'll probably jump his shit if he keeps up this sullen teenager act, even if he has a good reason for it.

The drop-off is pretty seamless. Oakley is there with Willow, so they get Lennox inside, and I throw up a wave before peeling out of the driveway. I love my brother, and I will gladly drop by tomorrow and listen to him bitch all day long. But today? I'm at the end of my rope. I need sleep and sex—definitely not in that order—to put myself back on equal footing. To clear my head enough to be a good sister and not the asshole I feel like I'm being right now.

Arlo agreed to meet me at my place because it's a little outside of town, with the benefit of no neighbors. I bought the land when my business started to kick off and I needed to make a workshop to house all the furniture I was building. Arlo lives near the center of town, right off of Main Street, so he's close to the "action", I assume. I'll tell you whose house we won't be using for these trysts.

Nope, it'll be one time and nothing more. A one-time distraction, then I'll go back to my normal routine. Go back to ignoring the asshole and actively avoiding him whenever he's nearby.

I pull up to my little slice of Bluebell Falls and think about the last fifteen odd years. Sure, this isn't where I thought my life would go, but as I look at my mid-sized cottage on the couple of acres of land, I feel good about it. I've created a business from scratch, and it may be killing me at the moment, but I'd call myself successful.

Success in business does not equal a fulfilling life.

God, I hate existential thinking. It's not who I am. I'm a realist through and through, and thinking about how things could be or should be is not in my nature.

I'm happy with how my life has turned out. Sure, I'm thirty-six and single as fuck, but being single isn't really the problem. I don't see myself with the whole picket fence and perfect family anymore. The problem is, I need some damn sex once in a while. Sure, vibrators are great, but sometimes I just want the real thing. The intensity, not just the release.

Cue Arlo, hauling ass up my driveway and pulling in next to me. I roll down my window, waving at him to do the same.

"Park behind the barn," I say blandly.

"Are you serious right now?" He sounds appalled, but I don't give a shit. I will not be the talk of this town. I will not have people speculating that there's even a remote chance of something going on between the two of us.

"Deadly. I'm not taking any chances of the meddlesome trio seeing anything."

"Jim, Mabel, and Alice are at bingo right now," he says calmly, but I can see the clench of his jaw.

"Don't care." I stare him down and arch an eyebrow at him that says he either parks behind my workshop or we don't do this at all.

"Fucking pain in my ass," he mumbles, just loud enough for me to hear as he throws his truck in reverse.

"We can just not do this," I offer. I don't need his shit. If he wants to be pissy about something this stupid, he can leave.

He doesn't give me any inflection of what choice he's making, so I watch him pull out of my driveway before taking the little side road that leads to the barn. My shoulders sag in relief. I would have accepted it if he left, but I'm glad he didn't.

Not that I'll ever say that out loud.

It'll take him a minute to walk back up here, so I take that time to dig deep into my hatred for him. I'll need it if I'll ever be able to keep this to sex, as much as I hate myself for admitting that, even internally. It's not that I think I'll cave and just go back to the way things were. I know for a damn fact that'll never happen, but not knowing exactly how my mind will react to being with him again freaks me out a little. I don't want there to be any shred of hope for anything past orgasms.

Because I'll never let him have anything more, ever again.

My wits successfully gathered, I climb out of my truck and head to my front door. By the time I've got it opened and my boots taken off, Arlo is standing just outside of the door.

I don't say a word, not feeling awkward exactly, just wondering why he's hesitating, but I do wave him in as I stand up.

Apparently, that was the password because he doesn't walk in. He aggressively strides to me, sliding his hand into my hair before devouring my lips with his.

Fuck yes. No pussyfooting around, just straight to what I need.

The hand in my hair grips a little tighter, moving my head where he wants it as he rips his lips from mine and trails nips and licks down my neck. A whimper escapes me as the touch of pain from my scalp mixes with the pure pleasure of his mouth on me.

A growl reaches my ears, and I almost lose my footing. Melting into him more, I try to direct him where I want him, but he doesn't relent. Holding my head in place, he continues his mission down my neck and onto my collarbone. He tries to pull down my T-shirt but realizes that won't work, so he pulls away from me, letting go of my hair in the process. I whimper at the loss but immediately feel his hands on my side, dragging up my shirt with less than steady hands.

My hands take on a mind of their own, moving to his belt and undoing it before I lift my arms to help him with my shirt. He moves to my jeans, flicking the button open as I stumble with his. In a blur of movement, we both end up completely naked just inside of my front door.

Arlo steps back, and I watch his eyes leisurely trail down my body. In the fifteen years since he's seen me naked, I've gained a lot of muscle. It's a testament to how physical my job is, but I'm also damn proud of the fact that I can hold my own with most men. And judging by the lust in his eyes, he approves of my bulkier thighs and sculpted arms that lift solid wood furniture on the daily. Then, there are the tattoos that form a sleeve on my right arm and a half sleeve on my left. Multiple others dot my skin randomly. Colorful images that were definitely not there the last time he saw me naked paint a picture on my skin.

While he checks me out, I do the same to him. The years seem to have been even better to him. The height he grew into while he was in the Marines now fits nicely with all the muscle he built onto it. What catches my eye, though, is a scar on his hip. It's just to the left of his impressive dick, distracting me from what we're supposed to be doing.

He must see where I'm looking because, in a flash, he's right up against me, pushing me against the door and ducking his head to take my nipple in his mouth.

It isn't lost on me that we've yet to say a word to each other or that he chose to distract me when I found the prominent scar.

CHAPTER FOUR
ARLO

She saw one of my scars, and I panicked. For the first time since I was discharged from the Marines, I forgot about them. Until her eye pulled to my hip.

I don't even know how to explain everything that happened to earn those scars, or if she even cares to hear it.

What I do know is that she's grown into the sexiest woman I've ever laid eyes on, and I can't wait to fuck her senseless again. I'll deal with the fallout after. Right now, I'm going to enjoy the hell out of it. Pretend I'm not half robotic, and not think about my limitations.

Pushing into her space and taking her delectable nipple into my mouth is both a distraction and a need. The taste of her skin makes me feral, and I don't know where I want to explore next. The muscle she's built while building her business shows, and it turns me on more than I ever thought it would. Back when we were kids, she was always tall and lanky; I'm not quite used to her above average height.

Now? She's grown to that height and is no longer willowy; she's strong and confident in her body. She's so goddamn gorgeous I can barely control myself.

And those tattoos... I've seen them before, obviously, but seeing all the ones she keeps hidden, tucked into sensual spaces, has my head spinning.

My hands slide down her side, gripping her ass in one hand as the other pulls her leg up over my hip. Drawing my nose up her neck, her familiar scent hits me hard. It takes me instantly to when we snuck around behind our parents' backs—hell, behind the whole town's back—to be together.

God, I've missed her.

I know I shouldn't be thinking this way, but I can't help it. She's always been home for me, no matter what the years apart have done to us.

What I have done to us?

Her hand snakes down in between us, gripping me hard and making my knees buckle. Tilting my head back, I breathe out a steady stream of air in an attempt to not come in a minute flat. Once I've let her have her fun, I swat her hand out of the way and move mine to her pussy. Heat and wetness greet me, and it makes me feel ten feet tall. I've still got it; I still turn her on.

Pride hits my chest as I slip a finger inside of her. When she moans, memories bombard my head, sending me back in time. Back when the world was at our feet and I didn't fuck up the greatest thing that ever happened to me.

I shake my head, ridding myself of the depressing thoughts that usually only float around my head in the dead of night. Now is not the time to reminisce; it's time to focus on getting this beautiful woman off and providing a bit of stress relief for her.

And me. True, but my main focus is and will always be Rina.

I tap her clit a couple of times and watch as her head thumps against the front door. Sliding my fingers down, I thrust two in without preamble and watch her almost instantly come apart for me. She wasn't lying when she said she was pent up. It's one of the sexiest things I've ever witnessed, and I let her ride it out before I pull away.

Bending down to get the condom from my pocket, I glance up as I tear it open to see Rina sag against the front door, her head tilted back as she pants. She's a sight to behold. It brings up too many memories, too many thoughts about what could have been. I roll the condom on before stepping back to her and cupping her ass in my hands to hoist her up the door to bring her level with me. Notching my cock at her entrance, I don't hesitate.

In an instant, I'm surrounded by her. It's overwhelming being inside of her again. She fits me too well, and I have to pause to get a fucking grip on myself, especially when I hear her suck in a breath. Her legs wrap around my waist, holding me tight to her, and a wave of nostalgia takes over. Squeezing my eyes tight, I try to tuck all the memories back into the box I usually shove them in. I can't let them take over. Rina wants nothing to do with the past; hell, she barely wants anything to do with me in the present. She made it very clear that my dick is the only thing I'm good for currently, and I need to remember that.

When her legs squeeze against my ass, I take the hint and tune out my over-analyzing thoughts. Moving one of my hands off her ass, I grip the back of her neck, drawing her lips to mine as I pull back and thrust hard. She whimpers into me, and any restraint I had is gone. My hips take on a mind of their own, and I chase our orgasms.

I pour everything I've felt since our kiss in the hospital into our kiss now, hoping she can't see how much being with her again is getting to me. Judging by her moans, she's too focused on the pleasure I'm giving her to notice how fucking conflicted I am.

She breaks the kiss, throwing her head back against the door again as my grip at the base of her neck tightens. I can feel my orgasm just below the surface. My toes are tingling, and my balls draw up, telling me I have very limited time left. But I won't come without her.

I shift my hand to her throat, slightly tightening my fingers to give her the feeling of cutting off her breathing but not actually doing so. She clenches against me and almost sends me over the edge, but it also means she's close.

I feel her swallow against my grip, and it turns me on so much. I want to see her on her back with my cock deep in her throat, my hand resting softly on her throat, feeling her take me.

Her hips start to meet my thrusts, so I release my grip on her ass and shove my hand between us to reach her clit. I need her to come now, or I'll be dangerously close to breaking my rule that she always comes first.

She yelps at first contact and arches her back so hard that I'm worried she'll fall to the floor. I squeeze the hand around her throat a little harder as I push deep to pin her to the door.

Gasping, she pulses around me, and the relief of feeling her come is almost too much. I thrust a few more times and tilt my head back, releasing her neck and slamming my hand against the door as I come inside of the woman I've always loved but whose heart I'll never have again.

The intense relief is over too fast. I gently lower her to the ground as I pull out and watch as she refuses to make eye contact with me.

I knew. God, *I knew* this would happen. But it doesn't lessen the pain in my chest at seeing her avoid my eyes. Ripping off the condom and shoving it into my pocket, I move to pull up my pants and grab my shirt. I don't even bother putting it on because I know if I spend more time here, I'll lose it completely. I'll tell her how badly I fucked up, how my eyes always find her in town. I'll tell her it's always been her. And I know with every fiber of my being that she doesn't want that.

She shuffles to the side, and I pause before storming out. Tilting my head to the ceiling, I breathe through the hurt before leaning down and pressing a kiss to her cheek. No words are needed. As phenomenal as that just was, it doesn't change things between us, no matter how much I wish it did.

She sucks in a breath when my lips touch her cheek. My heart pounds in my chest, instantly filled with regret, and I hate it.

I step away, opening the front door just enough to slip out before slowly closing the door and heading to my truck.

Once I'm finally alone in the cab, I let everything that just happened sink in.

So many thoughts swirl in my head, but the one that sticks out is that no matter how much it hurts me, if she asked me to do this again, I would in a heartbeat. Just the chance to be close to her in any capacity is worth all the pain I feel as a result.

Turning on the ignition, I take one last look at Rina's house, seeing the curtain shift before I pull out and head home.

My head is a fucking mess.

I came home and jumped in the shower before flopping on my bed. I haven't moved an inch, and judging by the moon shining through my window, it's been a few hours.

The self-loathing and guilt hit almost instantly on the drive home and have done nothing but grow. I don't know why I agreed to go over to Rina's house. I knew it would wreck me, knew it would just give her more reason to hate me, but damn was the temptation too strong.

I just wanted to be with her one last time.

Too bad all it did was make me want her more. Once was never going to be enough, and I fucking knew that driving over there. Yet I seem to be a glutton for punishment.

Yep, my head is fucked.

I think about the little piece of paper sitting in my safe. The piece of paper that would change everything if Rina knew about it. Or maybe she would just hate me more if that's possible.

Another mistake on my end. Something I was in charge of figuring out yet didn't.

And then there's Lennox and the whole Hutton family, who have to deal with the aftermath of the Tennison Strangler infiltrating our little slice of Texas. Hell, I still have to deal with the aftermath. I'm sure the paperwork is going to be never-ending, and the Fugitive Task Force won't just let things go so easily. Not with everything that happened.

Maybe I needed this night with Rina as much as she did. A moment to just forget about everything that happened. A moment to release all the built-up tension and be able to think again.

My phone rings on my bedside table, and I blow out a breath. Of course, my phone rings right now. Can't possibly lie here in my misery without interruption.

"Sheriff Arlo," I grunt out.

"Sheriff, I'm so glad you answered. I have a concern about the cabin in the park where … everything happened. Are we condemning it? We couldn't possibly keep it standing, correct?" Alice's voice grates on every single frayed nerve I have.

"It's" —I pull my phone away and check the time— "four in the morning, and you thought it urgent enough to call me? You couldn't just stop by in the morning, Alice?"

I'm not known for my coddling when it comes to the nosy residents of Bluebell Falls.

"My word, Sheriff. I am concerned, and I felt it was important to ask."

"At four a.m.," I droll.

"Well, I am an early riser. I just assumed you would be as well since you are the sheriff, after all." Her hurt tone does nothing to lessen my annoyance.

"Well, I enjoy sleeping. I don't have an answer for you at the moment, but when I do, I'll be sure to call you." *Preferably when you are sleeping, to piss you off.*

"Well, I suppose that works. Thank you, Sheriff." The click of her hanging up hits my ear, and I throw my phone onto the bed.

What a clusterfuck.

Scrubbing my hand over my face, I relegate myself to another night of no sleep. Might as well get up and head into the office to get a jump start on more paperwork. It's not like I have a life outside of my job anyway.

At least it will take my mind off of Rina for a while.

CHAPTER FIVE
RINA

Last night was a mistake.

I knew it the second I came down from my orgasm and watched Arlo walk out the door.

Did it help relieve everything I was hoping it would? Sure, but it also made me remember, and that's the last thing I want to do.

Remembering means thinking about the good times and not about every minute after he broke my heart. It means thinking about how good we were together instead of thinking about how easily he threw us away when I needed him the most. And I can't afford to remember. My heart can't handle remembering.

So, I did what any woman avoiding the man who gave her two spectacular orgasms would do: buried myself in work.

For me, that means working on this fucking custom order that's testing every ounce of my skill and capability.

I'm sweaty, annoyed, and stressed—a dangerous combination for my current state. When my phone pings as I'm mapping out a daybed, I take it as a sign to take a break.

Ledger:

Anyone heard from Lennox yet today?

No, and I doubt we will.

He promised me he would communicate
through the group chat, so I think if we check in,
he'll respond. He just needs some time, though.

I'm going to add Ainsley and Oakley to this chat
so we can all be on the same page, and keep our
usual family chat to just us four.

If Lennox finds out, he'll be even more annoyed
that we're creating a group chat to talk about
him behind his back.

He may, but I don't think that's a huge concern
for him at the moment. I was going to text him
and see if he wanted to shoot the shit with a beer
or something later.

I think we should just do a quick check-in.

Arguing with my siblings and their significant others over how to handle Lennox is starting to piss me off more than this damn furniture. Lenny may have annoyed the shit out of me yesterday, but I also know giving him some time to cope with what happened to him is probably our best option. I will say, Oakley might be our biggest asset in helping him since he knows the most about what actually happened to him. I'm not holding my breath that anything we do will magically make him better, though.

Me:

I'm with Willow. Turning things into a big deal is going to piss him off. He knows we plan to check in, and at least for now, let's keep to that. If he's still in the recluse stage in a week, we can send Oakley in.

Ledger:

I hate this.

Ainsley:

We all do, but taking over and bombarding him will probably make things worse right now. I'm with Rina and Willow.

Oakley:

Looks like the women have it. I'll do a drive-by when Grind Time closes and make sure things look okay at his house.

Ledger:

Thanks, Oakley.

I open up our family chat because I'm over talking behind Lennox's back at the moment.

Me:

Just checking in, Len. If you need anything, let us know. Love you.

Short and to the point. Lennox is simple. He doesn't need this long, thought-out message. Keeping things simple so he doesn't feel guilty is the best option.

> Doing okay. Just changed my bandages, and things are looking good.

Leaning against my workbench, all the emotions of the last week hits me square in my chest. I slept with Arlo. Lennox just went through hell, and our family is walking on eggshells because we don't know how to help him. Everything feels out of control, and I hate feeling this way. I like control; I like knowing how to handle situations. And suddenly, I have zero control over anything. My phone pings again.

> You have enough food?

> Yes, Dad.

Laughter bursts from my chest. It's nice to see some resemblance of normalcy. He has a long way to go, but this is a great step.

> Oakley said he can drop off a panini later if you want one. Just text him.

Lennox:

> Will do. Thanks, guys. I think I'm just going to binge-watch some shows and crash early tonight.

I set my phone down, hopeful that Lennox isn't feeling smothered. Looking around my workshop, I mentally catalog every piece I still have to complete, and the stress starts to build again. My organization of my commissions has been severely lacking, and I need to get a hold of it sooner rather than later.

A clamoring sound draws my attention outside, and my brows furrow. No one ever comes here unless they're invited. I've made it perfectly clear what happens if someone shows up unannounced. I don't like showing my barn to anyone, and the lovely people of Bluebell Falls stopped questioning why when I lost my shit on Old Man Walter when he showed up unannounced and wanted to watch me work because he was bored.

There are times that I still feel inadequate with my work. I know I'm good at what I do, logically, but having an audience makes me nervous and, in turn, makes me mess up.

I let out a sigh, annoyed that I'm probably going to need to live up to my bitchy reputation. I'm not in the mood to deal with more shit right now, but I don't have a choice.

Walking out of the door, I look around and don't see anything.

"I know you're out here. Might as well just come talk to me," I say in exasperation.

Silence greets me, and I start getting pissed. Stomping my way around the exterior of my building, I look in all directions for who could be fucking around on my property. Walking to the back, I see a wood pile—that was neatly stacked earlier—strewn across the ground.

What the fuck?

"You could at least own up to your mistake, ass," I mutter out to the void. Whoever did this is long gone because I would have seen them.

Under normal circumstances, I would make a call to the sheriff's office, just to have a report on file. However, that's not going to happen now. Not after what we did last night. I need to distance myself from Arlo and act like nothing ever happened, not call him to tell him I suspect someone was messing around on my property.

Tilting my head up to the sky, I blow out a breath, preparing myself to clean up the mess and taking more time away from working on the damn daybed.

Time to get to work.

Two hours.

That's how long it took to fix the damn wood pile. It was a mess, and I'm not sure how someone messed everything up that badly and so fast, but the whole thing had to be re-organized.

Now, I'm driving to Grind Time because I need a pick-me-up since I'll be working well into the night to catch up.

The bell dings above my head as I walk in, and Oakley looks up with a smile on his face. Behind him, Willow is concentrating hard on a cup of coffee I assume she's trying to make.

A genuine smile takes over my face as I watch these two together. They had a rough road, but it looks like things are going to be just fine for them.

"Hey, Rina, what'll it be today?" Oakley asks. I might be the only person in Bluebell Falls that doesn't have a regular coffee order for him to memorize, and I think he sees it as a challenge some days to guess what I'm in the mood for.

"I need all the caffeine today, my man. Largest iced americano you can give me, please."

"Everything okay?" Willow asks as she finishes whatever coffee she was making. She sips it and makes a face, telling me she doesn't love what she created.

"It's fine. Just someone or an animal trashing shit at my place. A whole pile of wood knocked over."

"You think someone did that?" Oakley's protective instinct kicks in.

I don't want to tell him I think it was a person because he'll go all U.S. Marshal on me, and I don't have time to have a shadow checking to make sure no one's messing with me.

"It was probably an animal, honestly. I didn't see anything that would suggest otherwise." I shrug as he moves over to start making my drink.

He arches an eyebrow at me, and I do the same, challenging him to disagree with me. I am definitely not in the mood to deal with any more wannabe cops in this town.

He backs down as he hands me my coffee, and I instantly feel bad comparing him to Arlo in any way. Oakley's not a wannabe cop; he's my sister's boyfriend, who saved my brother. He doesn't deserve my annoyance, especially when it's directed at Arlo, not him.

"Sorry, I've just been on edge a lot lately. Obviously," I add because if anyone is dealing with shit outside of Lennox, it's these two.

"All good. We're all trying to figure out how to get back to normal," Willow says.

"How are you both doing?" I ask.

"Not bad. Healing is fine. We're just happy to open back up and have a regular workday. Yesterday was … a shitshow," Oakley says with a chuckle.

"Did the nosy trio bombard you immediately?"

"Oh yeah, asking Will a bunch of invasive questions, so I kicked everyone out and we closed up. I think everyone got the message, though," Oakley says as he looks around at the calm coffee shop.

"You fit right into this family already." I laugh.

"You sure do." Willow leans into his side.

He presses a kiss to her temple, and I feel the sudden urge to flee. I'm happy for Will, more than happy, but I'm struggling not to compare my life to hers at the moment.

"Well, thanks for the pick-me-up. I'll see you both for family dinner?" I ask.

"We'll be there," Willow says.

I head back out to my truck and prepare myself for a long-ass night.

CHAPTER SIX
ARLO

It's been a few days since ... everything happened with Rina, and it's still all I can think about. I'm distracted and no amount of work, working out, or avoidance provides any clarity for me.

My head is a mess, and Audrey has been giving me concerned looks. Apparently, it's possible to look grumpier than I usually do, according to her.

I drop my head to my desk in a lame attempt to clear my head and focus on shit that needs to get done.

"Knock, knock. Bad time?" Oakley's voice disrupts my self-loathing.

"Nope. How can I help you?" I sigh as I lift my head up.

"You okay?" he asks with a tilt of his head.

"Peachy. What's going on?" I hear the bluntness of my words, but my brain is too muddled to address it.

His eyebrow arches before he walks in and takes a seat in front of my desk.

"I meant to get over here earlier, but the shop's been busy as hell since we re-opened. A couple of days ago, Rina came in telling Will and me about a knocked-over pile of wood on her property. She's claiming it's probably an animal, but it hasn't been sitting right with me. I've been on her property and know how high some of her stacks are, and it would take one hell of a huge animal to do any damage to it."

"It could have been an animal," I grumble. Inside, I'm trying to figure out how quickly I can go check out her property for myself while doing it covertly enough that she doesn't know. My heart rate has skyrocketed, thinking the worst.

"We both know that's bullshit, Sheriff."

"Arlo," I say automatically.

"Whatever. I just wanted you to be aware. I plan to keep an eye out if I see anything suspicious."

"Thank you for that," I concede, even though my head is spiraling with thoughts of anything happening to Rina.

"Have you talked with Lennox recently?" Oakley thankfully changes the subject.

"I haven't. I was going to finish up stuff here and then maybe stop by and check on him." Lennox has been weighing on me too. I pulled him from that cabin, and I can't help but wonder if I did enough, moved fast enough to get him to the hospital. He has extensive injuries. Even though it's illogical, I feel some of the blame lands on me.

"I texted him earlier, seeing if he wanted a panini. I've been doing it every other day or so to not piss him off and annoy him too much, but he said he would be okay with food and visiting tomorrow. You want to join me?" Oakley asks.

"Do you think he would even want that?" I cringe at my uncertainty. I haven't seen Lennox since I first dropped him off at the hospital. Didn't feel like it was my place to encroach on family time to check on him. I've gotten updates, sure, but nothing from the man himself.

"I think he would appreciate some non-pressured guy time without the family around. He seems to be doing well enough, but that makes me more worried, honestly. He's putting on a good face around his siblings, but..."

"But he won't talk about what happened with anyone, and now he's internalizing it."

"It has to eat him up inside. Hell, he seems too well-adjusted compared to every other victim we encountered. Maybe it's because he wasn't branded, or-or strangled" —he visibly swallows— "but he still went through too much to just brush it under the rug." His words are only a whisper toward the end.

I take a minute to really look at Oakley. He's been through a lot, just like everyone else, except Tennison coming to Bluebell Falls was all about him. A vendetta if you will. The guilt has to be all-encompassing. His head is bowed, his shirt is a little rumpled, but otherwise, he looks okay. Probably more worried about Lennox if my hunch about the man is right. It's why I've been subtly recruiting him since I found out he was an ex-U.S. Marshal. It's why, a week ago, I asked him point blank to come work with me. He turned me down but agreed to help if needed. Coming in here to tell me about what's going on with Rina tells me he'll be a good asset to the department.

Now, I just need to curb my reaction so I'm able to check in on Lennox.

"I think stopping by would be a good idea. No pressure on Lennox, and if he's uncomfortable, we can leave."

"Agreed. I close up shop around three and can meet you here tomorrow?" he asks.

"Perfect. I'll be ready to go."

He stands up and leaves without further conversation. I like that about him. He doesn't try to prolong shit for no reason. Lord knows my attention span for long-winded conversations is reserved for the elders of this town.

Turning to my computer, I see it's just after three p.m., which means Audrey is getting ready to leave for the day. I'm not sure if that's a good thing or not, seeing as I can't focus at all. I need to get my head on straight, but between the constant worry about Lennox and now wondering what the hell is going on at Rina's place, my nerves are a little more than shot.

"I'm heading out. Maybe you should too. Keep your phone on, but call it early today." Audrey sticks her head in right on time.

"Thank you for continuing to point out how much I look like shit today. It's truly appreciated."

"Anytime, Boss. Seriously, though, go home. It's quiet today, and everyone knows to call your cell if there's an emergency. Paperwork can wait."

Wise, wise Audrey. She may be young, but she's got a good head on her shoulders.

"You may be onto something." I sigh, relenting to the fact that I'm completely useless right now. "I'll be right behind you. Have a good evening, Audrey."

She smiles one of her overly large ones that takes over her entire face and bounces out the front door.

Stretching my arms over my head in an attempt to release the painful tension in my back, I contemplate taking some work home with me but decide against it. A fresh start tomorrow will probably do me better.

Locking up as I leave, I walk the two blocks to my house. I pass by the house I spent most of my youth in and stop in my tracks.

This house holds a lot of memories, both good and bad. There's a reason I joined the military, and it's because of the former owner of this house, my uncle Charlie. My mom passed away when I was six, and I never knew my dad. Uncle Charlie was my mom's brother and took me in without a moment's hesitation.

He was a marine for a good portion of his life and then came back here to be close to my mom and me. He worked random jobs, mostly handyman stuff, and never complained about anything. I wanted to be just like him. He was always happy, always willing to help a person out, no matter what it entailed. I decided in high school to follow in his footsteps and go into the Marines. I think it's the proudest I'd ever seen him when I told him I was going into the Marines. He's also where I got my nickname for Rina, *Emmerdeur*. He used to say it so endearingly, and it just stuck. I'm not even sure what it means, but it's been what I've called her since we were eighteen.

Then, four years into my service, he was murdered by a traveler who was looking for some quick cash. He took advantage of Charlie's good nature and killed him for his service. When my injury happened just over a year later, it felt like the right move to come back here and take over the sheriff's duties. Old Man Walter was beyond ready to retire, and I wanted to ensure nothing like what happened to Uncle Charlie ever happened again.

And look what happened to Lennox and Oakley on your watch.

Shaking my head from the memories, I continue on to my little bungalow. I could have just moved into Charlie's house when I moved back, but it felt tainted. Instead, I'm in a little two-bedroom right off of downtown, so I'm available to everyone. Funny that I'm never actually here, it seems, always sitting in the office or patrolling.

Real full life you're living here.

Finally reaching my house, I stomp up the steps and unlock the door before stepping in and slamming the door shut. I wasn't expecting to analyze everything that feels wrong in my life at the moment, and I don't feel equipped enough to actually do it.

Sitting on my hand-me-down couch, I feel restless. My fingers are tapping my thigh, and I'm starting to feel the subtle onset of pain radiating from my back. Ever since I got Lennox out of that damn cabin, my back has been hurting more than usual, and I know I probably tweaked something in it. The problem is, I haven't had time to go get it checked out. And if I'm honest with myself, I don't want more bad news about it, so I'm avoiding it altogether.

I close my eyes and try to focus on something other than the pain I know is coming. Having three burst fractures on your vertebrae and then having a spinal fusion to fix them means the pain only grows throughout the day. Tilting my head back, I take a few practiced deep breaths.

In for the count of ten.

Out for the count of ten.

Repeat a million times.

It doesn't help my back pain, but it does help my head focus on something else. Once I'm in that floaty stage where my brain feels like it's over-oxygenated, I lift my head up and focus on what my plans are for the rest of the day.

I look at my watch and see just over an hour has passed, which is mildly ridiculous. This just means Audrey was right. I was useless at work today.

Leaning forward, I prop my hands on my knees and prepare for the inevitable slice of pain that will shoot down my back and legs when I stand up. This is the only place I can let the pain show. Everywhere else, I just ignore it and act like everything is perfectly normal. I think that's why I freaked out so much when Rina saw my damn scar on my hip. No one knows why I came back here after I was dead set on being a career Marine, and I prefer to keep it that way.

I put all my effort into standing up, swaying on my feet once I'm finally there before stabilizing myself on the back of the couch. I fucking hate this shit. It makes me feel like half of a man, even though I know I'm fully capable of normal activities.

Walking the ten steps to my small kitchen feels like a chore, but once I'm finally there, I'm able to pre-heat the oven and toss in a pizza.

Fifteen minutes later, I'm still standing in my kitchen, pulling out the now cooked cardboard pizza. I realize I only have so much strength left in my back and hip today, so I quickly cut up the pizza and plate it, taking it to the bathroom with me.

The only thing that helps when the pain gets to be too much is an Epsom bath, so it looks like dinner is in the bathtub tonight. Placing my scalding hot dinner on the vanity, I turn on the water as hot as I can stand it and dump in an obscene amount of Epsom salt. I eat two slices of pizza while I wait for the tub to fill up before stripping out of my work clothes. Dipping a toe in, I hiss at the depths of hell that is the hot water, but I know it'll be good for my body. I slowly lower myself into the water, gritting my teeth the entire time. Once my body adjusts to the temperature, I relax against the tub wall. Closing my eyes, I take a few deep breaths as the worst of the pain finally eases.

Stretching my hand out, I grab a slice of pizza. Everything is small in this house, so the vanity is within reach of the tub, making it easy to reach without opening my eyes. The water finally hits my chest, and I slowly lean forward to shut it off before collapsing back.

While the pain in my hip and back seems to be mellowing, my head is bombarded with everything that's happened in the last week. What a clusterfuck things are. I don't even know how to make things better for Lennox, for Oakley, and mostly for Rina. Hell, I'll be lucky if she even acknowledges my presence after what happened Friday night. I fully expect her hatred for me to grow, not diminish.

I rub the spot on my ribcage, just small enough to not be noticed in the dim light that was Rina's entryway. Thank God, too, because if I didn't want to explain my scar, I sure as hell don't want to explain my tattoo.

Not to the person it was for.

Being with Rina again makes me remember why we went through hell to be together in the first place. Makes me remember why I got a tattoo for her. Makes me realize I'd still do anything for that woman.

I pick up my phone sitting next to my plate of mostly eaten pizza and scroll through to her name. I pull up our text thread and foolishly start typing.

~~I miss you.~~

~~I know I fucked up.~~

I erase everything I'm tempted to write because it doesn't matter. I did fuck up, and now I get to deal with the consequences of those actions.

The actions of a scared young man who didn't know what else to do. One who thought he was doing the right thing.

My phone dings in my hand, scaring the shit out of me, so much so that I almost drop it in the tub.

Rina:

What are you doing currently?

CHAPTER SEVEN
RINA

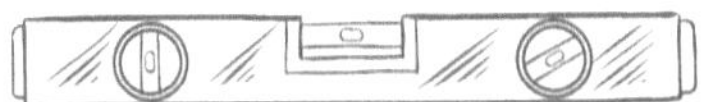

*S*tupid. *This is such a stupid idea.*

I can blame it on being overtired, overworked, and completely running on empty. That's the only thing I can think of that would lead to me texting Arlo.

This week has been hell. I have a huge delivery tomorrow, so I had no choice but to work around the clock to get three pieces of furniture done. I think I've slept a grand total of six hours all week, and I'm officially losing my damn mind. It's the only logical explanation.

The Asshole:

Currently, I'm relaxing at home. Why?

I'm the one that texted him, and now I freeze up? Lovely.

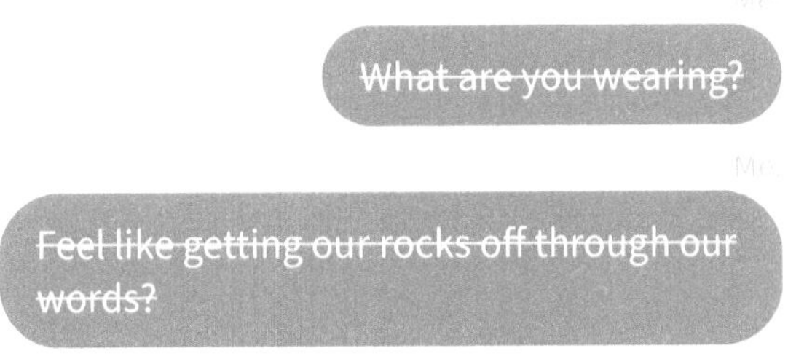

Awful, just terrible. Who even talks like that? To make it worse, I would put money down that he's just watching those little ellipses pop up every time I attempt to write something.

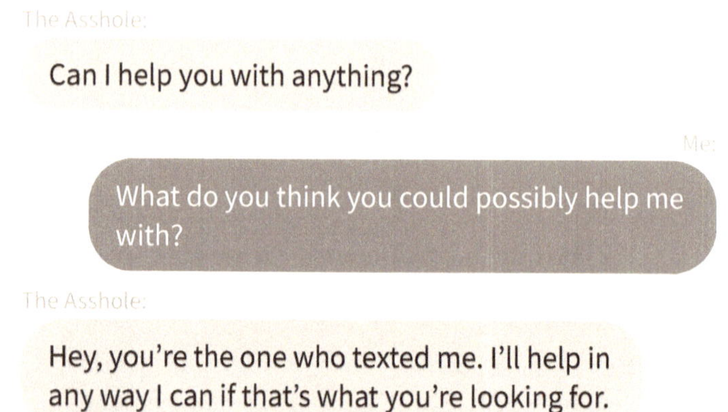

I'm standing in my bathroom, so I take a long look in the mirror and think about what I want and why I chose to text Arlo in the first place.

Because I wanted an orgasm before I crashed for the night and Arlo was the first thought that popped into my head.

Grabbing my phone, I walk to my bedroom and strip out of my clothes before crawling under the covers. Direct and to the point is the way to handle this.

Slide that free hand down your stomach, but
don't touch that pussy. Just touch your body.

I do as I'm told, and as frustrated as I am that he isn't getting straight
to the point, my body lights up as I comply with his simple directions.

Bring that hand up and circle your breast, but
don't touch your nipple.

You're being a fucking tease.

I am because you came to me for an orgasm. Not
a random video, not a book—me.

I'm currently re-thinking that strategy.

No, you aren't. Squeeze that hand for me, and
switch to the other breast and do the same
thing.

Slide that hand up to your throat, imagine it's
mine, and add just a little pressure.

Whimpering at the feeling, I've never been into the whole choking thing, but obviously that's changed for me. I don't even have the brainpower to text him back, but he doesn't seem to mind as his texts continue to come through.

The Asshole:

> Now, move that hand straight to your clit, circle it a few times before you pinch it, then tell me how wet you are for me.

I do as he says and then dip my fingers down to feel the slickness everywhere. I move my fingers up to spread it around my clit before I text him back with my other hand. One-handed texting has never been so difficult.

Me:

> Too wet. It's annoying that I'm this turned on.

The Asshole:

> Fight it all you want, but I'll still get you there and you know that. Dip those fingers down and get them nice and wet for me. Move them to your nipple and circle that wetness all around. Get them nice and hard before you pinch it too. Then switch to the other side.

Again, I follow directions like the good girl I am. He's right; I'm fighting on principle only, but damn do I want this. I've never been this turned on while playing on my own. His words are doing all sorts of good things for me, and I really should stop fighting it. I'll deal with how I feel about it all after the fact. Or tomorrow. Or never.

God, I love your breasts. I wonder if I could make you come just from playing with them. Move that hand back to your clit and circle it nice and slow. Don't go too fast.

Since when have you been a tits man?

I freeze as soon as I send it. Talking about the past, acknowledging it in any form is like eating the forbidden fruit. I don't talk about it. And I just opened the crack on our past in a few mindless words.

Are you naked? Or is this one-sided?

There, redirection.

I'm in the bathtub, so yes, I'm naked.

Mister "I only take showers" is in the bathtub? What the hell? Nope, not going there. I'm going to focus on his nakedness. His lean muscled body that his stupid *Sheriff* shirts do nothing to hide.

And is your dick hard?

Of course it is. I'm imagining doing all of this to you and stroking it. I'll be honest, though; I may come faster than you do.

Me:

Well, it's not a competition as long as you get me off.

The Asshole:

Do you have a vibrator or dildo close by?

A rush of arousal hits me hard. I think it's more about the fact that he's not shying away from toys.

Me:

Pick your poison. I have options.

The Asshole:

Dildo. A vibrator will get you there too fast.

I reach over to my bedside table and grab the very standard six-inch dildo I have. I rarely use it, but this seems like the perfect application.

Me:

Done.

The Asshole:

Lube it up for me then. Thrust just the tip in. Keep circling that clit while you're doing it.

Fuck, that feels good. I lean my head back and moan as I slide the toy in. It's hard to follow directions and not thrust the entire thing in, but I want to see what he does next.

> Rock your hips. Act like you're meeting me thrust for thrust.

I do as I'm told, and it feels so damn good that I decide it's my turn to have a little fun.

> Grip that cock tight. Bring your other hand down to your balls and tug on them gently. Imagine it's me on my knees for you.

> Jesus fuck, Marina, you can't say shit like that and not warn a guy. I almost came all over myself.

> You've got me so close I thought I'd give you a taste of your own medicine.

His reaction makes me feel giddy, like I still hold some power even if it doesn't feel like I do. Even if I feel like I've lost all control since I let him in at the hospital.

> Mission fucking accomplished. Slide that toy all the way in and hit that spot on your clit that gets

you every single time. I'm so fucking close, but I
need you to come with me.

I'm feeling the build-up of my orgasm. It's so close I can taste it when a ping from my phone interrupts me. A video from Arlo pops up, and I click on it.

My jaw drops. Arlo, in the bathtub, stroking his sexy-as-fuck cock and coming all over his abs. A faint groan of my name sounding through the speakers sends shockwaves through my body as I rub my clit hard with his motion. I whimper out my orgasm before I'm completely out of breath and collapse against my bed.

Holy shit, that was hot as fuck. Who knew he had it in him?

The Asshole:

Did you come with me?

I take a second to catch my breath because not only did I come, but it rivals the orgasms he gave me on Friday.

Me:

Yes, yes, I did.

Me:

I didn't know you had that in you. That was sexy
as hell.

Will I regret telling him that in the morning? Most likely, but I don't care. That was by far the hottest thing I've seen by a mile. Screw dick pics. I want a video of a guy coming from now on.

It would have been better in person, but it'll do for tonight.

For tonight?

Why, oh why, am I even asking? This is supposed to be a one-off, just like Friday was. *Yep, doing a great job at keeping it a one-off, Rina.*

Logic can suck it for once.

I'm here whenever you need some relief, so how about we keep it open-ended?

Can I do that? Keep anything with Arlo open-ended and not lose my heart to him again? I'm not one hundred percent sure, but I do know my business isn't slowing down any time soon, and having guaranteed orgasms on top of everything isn't a bad thing.

I could be amenable to that.

I swear I can feel him smiling from here, and my hackles raise just enough to second-guess things. But then, he texts me again.

There's no pressure, ever, Rina.

Feeling myself start to crash, I toss my toy on the floor so I remember to clean it in the morning. I plug my phone in as my eyes feel heavy and send one last text before I crash for the night.

Me:

> Thank you. Good night, Arlo.

CHAPTER EIGHT
ARLO

Daydreaming about phone sex with Rina was not on my bingo card this year.

Keeping our ... activities open-ended was one hell of a surprise too. I'm not sure what's changed for Rina, but I'm not questioning things right now. If it means I get a little more of her, I'll take it, even if I know it'll eventually break my heart.

The office is quiet today because I gave Audrey the day off. Oakley should be here soon so we can head to Lennox's house, and I've actually gotten some of the paperwork I've been procrastinating on finished.

I take a peek at my clothes and see my standard uniform of jeans and a gray *Sheriff* T-shirt is looking a little worse for wear, but it's not like Lennox will give a shit. It's suitable for a guys' night or whatever we're calling this.

Can we call it a guys' night when our primary connection is Tennison? It feels wrong somehow.

"Hey, man, you ready?" Oakley's voice startles me, and he grins like he knows exactly why I was distracted. Joke's on him. No one would know a certain Hutton who hates me has my mind spiraling through a million possibilities.

"Yep. Do we need to pick anything up on the way?" I ask.

He holds up a six-pack and a paper bag, and I'm happy he didn't get any more. I rarely drink because I'm essentially always on duty, and I'm not sure if Lennox is drinking at all because of any pain medication he's still on.

"Alright, let's go." I lead him out to my truck, and we climb in to head to Lennox's cabin.

Oakley knocks on the door without preamble as I stand back and shift on my feet.

Lennox cracks the door before opening it just wide enough for us to walk through.

"Brought the sheriff. Hope that's okay. Thought we could do a sort of guys' night." Oakley chuckles.

"What do you know about a guys' night?" Lennox asks as we walk through the door.

"Not a damn thing, but there's a first for everything. This one's been bugging me about getting more friends, so that's why I dragged him here." Oakley tips his thumb over his shoulder to me as I grunt in reply.

He's not wrong, but this wasn't exactly what I had in mind when I told him to start forging friendships.

"Well, grab a seat. You want anything to drink?" Lennox asks as he hobbles to the couch.

"I can grab a water. Oakley brought some beer." Walking to the kitchen, I grab a glass after searching through the cabinets and fill it up. I hear the crack of beer cans as I join the two of them in the living room.

I've been to Lennox's cabin a few times, but I never realized how much space he has out here. His little cabin isn't so little, with what looks to be a couple of bedrooms and a roomy living area and kitchen. He's made quite the home here. Everything is updated and modern, and somehow still feels lived in and homie.

"I'll get the elephant in the room out of the way. How are you doing, Lennox?" Oakley asks.

"I honestly don't know." He sighs. "I'm still processing shit."

I nod at his vague answer. The whole reason we came over here was to not bring up all the shit he's been through, so I'm not shocked at his lack of an answer.

"Sweet. Now that that's out of the way, I brought food." He sets down a bag I now realize is paninis, and my mouth starts to water. I recall I haven't eaten since my protein shake this morning.

I reach out, and snag the one Oakley offers me and practically inhale it.

"Jesus, do I need to feed you as well as Willow?" Oakley asks with a chuckle.

"It's been busy lately. Got a lot on my mind," I say.

"A lot on your mind. Wouldn't have anything to do with a certain Hutton sister, would it?" Oakley asks, and my head snaps up as soon as he says it. Lennox and Oakley laugh at my reaction, and it's good to hear Lennox laugh, even if it is at my expense.

"I didn't say anything," I mumble.

"You didn't have to. It's in your reaction," Lennox says as he takes a sip of beer.

"So, how's Grind Time been since it re-opened?" I redirect the conversation.

"So fucking busy. I don't even understand how because it's not like we have a huge influx of people in town. I saw Kelly when I stopped at Sal's Diner the other day, and she was giving me shit for stealing all her customers."

"She's just giving you a hard time. Sal's is still as busy as ever." I roll my eyes.

Lennox slowly starts eating his sandwich, and relief hits my chest. The guilt is a little less heavy knowing he's interacting with us. He's still covering up the worst of his cuts with a long-sleeved shirt, but hopefully those are healing as well. I'm going to have to talk to Oakley about making this a weekly or bi-weekly thing. It's good for Lennox and probably for me as well.

Who knew I'd ever want to continue guys' night willingly?

Headlights shine through the front window, and Lennox's brow furrows as his shoulders stiffen. I unilaterally decide to have a chat with whomever it is and tell them to fuck off so Lennox can have a little peace. I'll do it nicely, of course.

Heaving my stiff back up from the couch, I walk to the front door and open it just as Rina walks up the front steps.

"Umm."

"What are you doing here?" I ask at the same time.

"Checking in on my brother, asshole. What are you doing here?" Her normal snark hits me square in the chest.

"Guys' night with Oakley."

"You? At a guys' night?" She smirks, and a smile cracks my face.

"I know, hard to believe, but here I am." I open up my arms.

"You going to let her in or just stand there in this weird version of flirting you guys do?" Lennox calls out.

"You're busy. I just thought I'd check in," Rina says awkwardly, rocking back on her heels as her cheeks turn a subtle pink.

"I'm good, Marina. I promise," Lennox says.

Rina's eyes narrow at his use of her full name, and I see the instant her fire gears up.

"Well, *Lenny,* excuse me for wanting to be a good sister and check in on you. I was going to see if you needed a grocery stock-up, but you're on your own now." She crosses her arms. I know if Lennox said he needed anything, she'd drop the act in a heartbeat, but it's wonderful to see the two of them bantering, considering how unsure we all are around Lennox. This normalcy is needed for everyone.

"Aww, Rina, you know I'm fucking with you," Lennox says in his best "annoying little brother" voice.

"I know. Seriously, I was just making sure you were stocked up. Since you've got 'the boys' here," she air quotes, "I'll be on my way. Text me if you need me to pick up any groceries, though." She spins on her heel and throws up a hand as she skips down to her truck.

I stand in the doorway, watching as she climbs in and reverses down Lennox's driveway.

"Damn. He's whipped already," Oakley murmurs.

"Another one bites the dust." Lennox sighs.

"Shut the fuck up," I grumble as I join them back on the couch.

We spend the rest of the evening watching a hockey game and talking about nothing of consequence. Oakley may have been onto something with this.

Too bad my next decision negates all the good I'm feeling.

On my way home from Lennox's, I pull up Rina's number and hit dial. After seeing her at Lennox's, I know I need more of her today. This time, I want to see if we can have an actual conversation before we fuck each other's brains out.

"What?" she asks.

"Meet me in an hour?" I ask without preamble. We both know the current score, even if I wish it were different.

"Where?" she clips, and I get the feeling she's mad about something. At least she's intrigued enough to meet me.

"The falls," I say impulsively. The falls—or Bluebell Falls—is our spot. It's where we snuck away when we were younger. Hidden from the town, it was where we were allowed to just be us. It's where we fell in love.

Her quick inhalation of breath tells me I might have made a mistake, but it's too late. The words are already out.

Opening my mouth and closing it a couple of times, I try to think of something to say or somewhere else to go, but I come up empty. Anywhere in town will be noticed by the townspeople. We could do her house again, but I want a more equal footing. I'm constantly on the back foot with Rina—it's always been that way—but the falls are probably the worst option for that. It brings up too much of the past.

"Fine," she says before the line clicks, telling me she hung up.

I flip a U-turn and head to the falls instead of my empty house. Now, I just need to think about how to get her talking to me more instead of just using me for sex.

Baby steps.

CHAPTER NINE
RINA

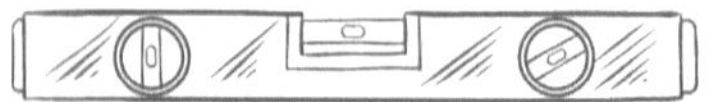

I can do this. I can separate the falls from our past. I can be here and not think about a deeper connection to the man who shattered my heart and dreams all those years ago.

It's just sex.

As long as I remember that, I'll be good.

I park my truck and proceed to make the twenty-minute walk to the falls. Once they finally come into view, I see Arlo standing stock still with his hands in his pocket, gazing out into the forest.

Taking a moment to observe him, I realize how dangerous this entire situation is. In a moment of weakness, I kissed him. In a moment of need, I let him so easily back into my life. I've agreed to keep this to just sex, but if I really analyze things, is my heart able to stay locked up nice and tight? I'm not sure, which means I need to be cautious. I need to keep his actions fifteen years ago in the back of my head and take to heart that people rarely change.

Clearing my throat, he spins around and gives me a small smile.

"I haven't been back here since..." He trails off.

"Me either." I couldn't. Not when it's tied to some of my worst and best memories.

"You know, I am sorry for how everything happened," he says softly.

I scoff at his audacity.

"Just not sorry enough to give me the real reason you ditched me faster than a Tinder date."

"Rina..."

"No, you don't get to just throw a bullshit apology at me and think it'll just magically help everything. We were fucking married, Arlo!" I scream at him.

His head bows, but I couldn't care less about how he's feeling right now.

"You don't get to come here, in our fucking spot, and say you're sorry for how things happened. Be sorry about breaking my heart into a million pieces. Be sorry for not being there when my parents died. Be sorry that you didn't have the balls to take our relationship public because you were scared of judgment or Ledger's reaction. You know what? Sorry won't ever cut it." My volume is too loud, and my frustration is at a breaking point. I can feel the pressure behind my eyes signaling I'm on the verge of crying, and I refuse to cry over this man ever again.

I go to turn around, but he grabs my elbow lightly, stopping me in place.

"I thought I was doing the right thing, Rina. You have to understand—"

"I don't have to understand shit. You had time to make things right. You had time to tell me the truth. In fifteen years, you've never once attempted to explain things to me. My fucking parents died, and when I needed you the most, you abandoned me." Tears spill from my eyes as I whisper the last part.

"I know I did, and I'm so fucking sorry."

"No. You aren't sorry. You have a false hope that, after what happened this week, you can turn it into more and go back to how things were. You're a delusional fucking coward, Arlo. And I wouldn't let you back into my life for anything other than meaningless sex. And because of this little stunt, that's now over too." I rip my arm from his grip and stomp back the way I came.

"You're just as much a coward as I am, Marina. You know we're good together; you're just too scared to admit it. You'd rather drown in your anger than hear me out," he yells at me as I walk away.

"Fuck you, Arlo!" I yell back.

"Fuck you too, Rina!"

I pick up my pace and make it to my truck in record time.

Fuck him for trying to apologize. The time for that was fifteen years ago.

I knew letting him into my bed was a mistake.

I've shed so many tears, it's pissing me off.

I've been in my workshop all night, and these damn tears are making things take twice as long. The good news is that the daybed I've been working on is finally done and I can deliver it in a couple of days.

The distraction has barely helped, and all I've thought about is our past.

How I always had a crush on Arlo. When he and Ledger were best friends in high school, I tagged along whenever I could, just to spend time with Arlo. Our senior year, we got closer but chose to keep it a secret because we didn't want the attention or Ledger's wrath, and it just kind of became the way we did things.

When Arlo went into the Marines, I realized quickly how much I loved him and wanted to be with him. We talked about our options, especially because he wouldn't be stationary and I would only have privileges if we made things more permanent. Getting married felt like the perfect progression. So, when he was home from basic training, we went into Rosedale and got married at the courthouse. No one knew. We didn't have a plan for how to tell people, so we just didn't. We both figured we had time.

Then my parents died in the crash. He was overseas, and I was devastated. Instead of coming home and consoling me, two weeks later, he broke things off with me, saying the distance was too hard. Nothing more, nothing less. I signed the divorce papers he sent two months later and never looked back.

Of course, it took years to recover, but having to step in and help Ledger take care of Willow and Lennox helped. It made me realize that family is more important than anything, and I wouldn't subject myself to putting my heart on the line ever again.

I'm not even sad he hasn't given me a real reason as to why he randomly decided one day I wasn't worth it. I'm fucking angry.

And then he has the audacity to try to talk to me about things now? Like a couple of orgasms negate all the hurt he caused. It's insulting and, frankly, makes me happy this happened when it did. I can't imagine if we had been hooking up for longer than a week when shit hit the fan. My already pieced together heart would have never recovered.

This just reinforces the need to keep that organ locked up tighter than a bank vault.

I walk over to the table by the door and check my phone. Twenty plus texts from the family group chat feels overwhelming, so I swipe the notification away. I see a text from Arlo, and I'm so tempted to just delete it, but morbid curiosity tugs at my gut.

The Asshole:

> One day, I would like to explain things to you. If you ever get to a point where you are open to hearing that, let me know. Otherwise, I'll see you around, Marina.

Condescending asshole. He acts like I'm in the wrong here, and although I probably could have checked my emotions more, I'm not the bad guy. Poor Arlo; his ex-wife won't hear him out after he proved to her that he is a selfish prick who only thinks about himself.

It sure doesn't feel like much has changed in the last fifteen years.

I shut off my phone screen and tuck it into my back pocket before leaving my workshop and heading to the house.

Collapsing on my bed, I don't even have the energy to change, which is a big deal. I always change out of my clothes after working because they're covered in sawdust and wood stain. I'll just add washing the sheets to my never-ending list of shit to do.

Sleep doesn't come, even though I'm exhausted. Instead, thoughts of Arlo fill every recess of my brain.

Him holding my hands with a beautiful smile on his face as we said, "I do." The sheer love on his face when we both thought we'd be together forever. The feeling of excitement for our future was so vast, I thought the best days were to come.

Then, the crushing hurt of not only losing my parents but my husband in the span of two weeks. Tears trail down my face as I revisit the black hole of my life. I rarely think about it because it's so fucking painful. How does someone continue with their life when they lose their entire support system? Sure, Ledger has always been here for me, but he took on so much responsibility that my goal was to hide all of my hurt and not add more burden to him.

It became a way of life for me. I pushed all the pain and hurt down until I completely ignored them. And now it's all rushing to the surface, and I'm unprepared for the pain of it all.

Burying my head into my pillow, I scream in agony. It physically hurts to dig up all these memories. I never wanted to relive any of this, and somehow, letting Arlo have my body again has turned into a broken dam.

I cry until the tears run dry and my eyes hurt so badly I can't open them. And somewhere along the way, I fall into a fitful sleep.

I'm disoriented when I wake up, unsure of how long I slept for. The good news is I did get some sleep, so I feel semi-human again.

Except my entire face is swollen and tight from crying so hard. I swing my arm over to my nightstand and slap the surface in search of my phone.

I knock over a tissue box and god knows what else, but I finally find it. Squinting as I turn it on, I see that it's almost three in the afternoon.

Shit. I'm supposed to deliver a bed today. Luckily, I gave them a timeframe and said I would call them when I was on my way. It looks like I have just enough time to shower and attempt to turn myself into a real human again.

The drive to Rosedale is an easy one. Traffic is non-existent, and my head is blissfully blank. I decide to stop for a coffee, though, so I can feel less like a zombie and more like a business owner when I deliver this bed.

Pulling into the only other place I get coffee from besides Grind Time, I walk in and get in line. Looking around, my eyes catch on a pair of green eyes already staring at me. The man attached is pretty handsome—in a classic sense, I suppose. Not like I'm looking for an actual relationship, but he's easy enough on the eyes.

He smiles, and a pair of dimples greets me as I tilt my head in acknowledgment. I'm in no place to entertain flirting today, but that doesn't mean I'm not thinking about some possibilities to get Arlo out of my head for good.

Yeah, good luck with that.

"Next!" the barista calls, and I jolt before moving forward to put my order in.

While I move over to the side, the green-eyed man continues to stare, and I wipe my face, hoping it's not because of something on my face instead of interest in me.

Yeah, I need to get out of here quickly because I am in no fit place to even remotely be thinking about a man showing interest in me. Knowing my luck, there's probably a huge stain on my shirt somewhere that I didn't see when I threw some clothes on. Whatever, it's not like it matters anyway.

"Rina!" I turn to see the barista sliding my coffee my way, and I take it gratefully before heading to the front doors. I feel Dimple's stare the entire time it takes me to leave, but I don't look back. Today is not the day to be playing with fire.

CHAPTER TEN
RINA

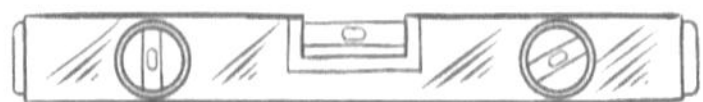

Three days after delivering a bed to Rosedale, I'm making the drive again to deliver the daybed I finished this week.

I've successfully distracted myself from thoughts of the past and Arlo, along with my entire family, as I've buried myself in the workshop and worked non-stop.

The good news is that I'm damn near caught up on custom orders. The ostrich act of mine has really helped my business, so I guess that's a bonus.

I'll admit I'm worn out, though. Emotionally and physically, I feel close to my breaking point. Again. That's why after this delivery, I'm taking the entire day off. I'm going to lounge on the couch, watch *Friends*, and eat all my favorite junk food.

A lazy day is well past due.

Pulling up to Elise Irvine's house, I'm met with her sheer excitement.

"Good morning, Elise. We ready to install this gorgeous bed?" I ask, as chipper as I can.

"So ready! We've kept the whole project from my daughter, so she's going to freak when she gets home from school."

"Well, that's adorable. Do you want to show me where the room is first, and then I'll work on bringing in the pieces and putting the whole thing together?" I ask.

"Sure, follow me."

She leads me to the most adorable little girls' room I think I've ever seen. A unicorn mural covers the wall, and the rest of the room is a blank slate, ready for the daybed to make everything else work.

"I think I would have died and gone to heaven if this was my room as a kid."

"Thanks! I can't wait to see everything come together in here." Her excitement permeates my worn-out brain, and I jump into action.

It takes me a little over an hour to bring all the pieces in and build it. Installing is easy, but since I'm only one person, I usually break the larger pieces down to manageable sizes so I can carry them on my own. Eventually, I'll need to hire some helpers for deliveries. But today, I got it done.

"Oh my gosh, this is incredible," Elise's awed voice sounds from the doorway.

"I'm so glad you like it! Will you send me pictures after you add all the decorations? I would love to see the finished product."

"Oh, absolutely! Thank you so much again, Rina. This is more than I could have ever imagined." She abruptly gives me a hug, and I pull away slightly before hugging her back. This stranger's comfort almost breaks me, but I hold strong. Instead, leaning into the hug, I try to hold back my emotions. A client sure as hell doesn't need to see me break down. And I'm nothing if not the queen of shoving emotions down.

"Well, I'm glad you like it! I hope your daughter loves it, and call if you need anything else."

She walks me out, and I wave as I drive away.

Driving through the downtown area of Rosedale, I see the coffee shop and take a detour. If I go to Grind Time, I'll have to talk to everyone. If I go to this coffee shop, I can just enjoy my solitude while being surrounded by people. A contradiction, but I don't think I want to be alone at the moment.

Sipping my black coffee, I look around and people-watch. I wonder if anyone else feels like their world is crashing down around them. If anyone is so exhausted by their past that they just need a damn break.

The bell dings over the door, drawing my attention to it. Green eyes flash to mine, and I immediately recognize him from earlier in the week. I watch as he orders his coffee. He's tall—not as tall as Arlo, but still taller than my own five eight. His blond hair is perfectly swooped to the side, and he's wearing a T-shirt and jeans. He's got a clean-cut surfer guy look to him, and it's not unattractive.

He grabs his coffee and makes his way over to my table.

"Care for some company?" he asks in a gentle voice.

I offer up the spare chair wordlessly. I think about how much Arlo has and continues to hurt me, and suddenly this stranger doesn't seem so bad.

"I've seen you in here before," I say. Speaking first gives me the edge. I'm not even sure what I want from this man, but I do know I need control, regardless of the outcome.

"And I've seen you. Name's Tyler." He holds out his hand for me to shake, and I take it cautiously.

"Rina."

"Pretty name."

I roll my eyes at him. The blatant line won't fly with me.

"What do you do that you're able to just shoot the shit with a random woman in the middle of the day on a Thursday?" I ask in a bored tone.

"I'm a freelance illustrator. Make my own hours, so I can get coffee anytime I want." He winks.

"Sounds interesting." I take a sip of my coffee.

"It's creatively fun, and it pays the bills. What do you do?"

"I build custom wood furniture."

He arches an eyebrow, impressed, I'm assuming. Usually when I tell a man what I do, I count to five to see the second he gets intimidated and falls back from the conversation. It's laughable, honestly. But Tyler seems more intrigued than anything.

"That's unique." I chuckle at his response. "How many pieces do you do in an average month?" he asks.

I tilt my head, trying to figure out what his angle is. "Depends on the pieces, but I'd say around ten."

"Very impressive." He sips his coffee.

"Thanks?" Maybe I've just been out of the flirting game for too long. Or maybe I'm too suspicious because of everything that just went down with Arlo.

"Listen, I'm just going to cut the bullshit. I think you're gorgeous and would love to take you out on a date to learn more about you."

I sit back, a little stunned at his blunt approach. I'm not sure if it's him being straightforward or my need to throw Arlo a big fuck you, but I make a reckless decision.

"Dinner tomorrow night?" I ask.

"I know a great steakhouse on the outskirts of town," he says.

"Great, I'll meet you there."

He pulls out his phone and hands it to me with a new contact screen open. I add my details before texting myself from his phone.

"I look forward to tomorrow, Rina." He stands as he smiles. A smile that tells me I responded exactly how he wanted me to.

I watch him walk out the door before pulling out my phone and adding his name to my contacts. *The Rebound.*

It takes a minute for what just happened to really hit me. I just got asked out... And I said yes.

What the fuck am I thinking? I'm not in any position to date. *It's one date, Rina, hardly a commitment.* That may be true, but going out with a man because of a reaction to another is probably not a healthy way to cope with my shit.

Letting out a sigh, I stand up and make my way to my truck to head home. My lazy day needs a healthy dose of solitude, it seems.

I've had a successful lazy day. I've only gotten up to pee; everything else is piled up conveniently on my coffee table.

My phone pings, and I groan at whomever is interrupting my day. It's not like they know, but it's an inconvenience I'm not thrilled about, nonetheless.

Ledger:

Family dinner on Sunday? Whose house?

I have to give big bro credit. Lennox doesn't want to leave his cabin currently, so leaving it open gives Lennox the option to invite us over. I doubt he will, but it's worth a try.

We have options now?

I'm taking my house out of the mix, so that narrows it down for you.

Why do you hate people in your space? You have a huge house. Why did you buy it if you are there all by yourself?

Well, big bro, thank you so much for asking. I bought it because I could. I bought it so that I had space to do whatever the hell I wanted without all the busybodies in my business, including you.

Am I irrationally angry at the question purely because my head is still a mess because of Arlo? Possibly, but I don't need this shit from my family, whatever the reason. I busted my ass for my land, house, and workshop. I don't need to give anyone a reason why I need this much space. The simple answer is because I wanted it and I could.

Sorry. Overstepped on that one.

I'm being a dick, sorry.

Lennox:

You guys can come here if you bring the food.

Little bro breaking up Ledger and me by doing something he really doesn't want to do hurts my heart a little. I know he wants normalcy, but I also feel like shit that we're fighting over stupid shit when he has real battles to fight.

Willow:

You sure? You don't have to. Hell, you don't even have to come to family dinner if you don't want to. I can always drop a plate off afterwards.

Lennox:

That's sweet, Will, but I'm sure. There's space, and it's time to rejoin the chaos.

I chuckle at that. He absolutely doesn't want to join the chaos, but hopefully getting back into a routine, even if he's still staying in his cabin, will help him in some way. God, I hope it helps him.

Ledger:

Ainsley and I will bring the food. Thanks for hosting, Lenny.

Maybe this weekend is turning into something eventful. A date and family dinner with Lennox again? What else could possibly happen in my normally mundane life?

CHAPTER ELEVEN
ARLO

Oakley's old U.S. Marshal partner, Kellen Woodcroft, called me this morning, letting me know he was sending over the last of the paperwork and statements that needed signing off on. What he didn't say was that I needed to sign off on every single statement that was given by anyone involved, including hospital staff that treated Lennox, Oakley, and Willow.

I've been buried in paperwork all day in an attempt to finish this shit today, and I haven't looked at my phone or the clock since I started. Audrey promised to only bug me if it was an emergency.

At least it's been a distraction from my constant thoughts of Rina and how we left things the other day.

I should have known things wouldn't be as easy as apologizing. I'm honestly not sure what I expected, but Rina completely lashing out was a surprise. And I reacted. I said shit I shouldn't have, and now I don't know how to fix it.

Or if I even can.

She was absolutely right. In the fifteen years since we were together, not once did I try to tell her why I did what I did. I didn't even attempt to be there for her when her parents died; instead I broke her heart and forced her to handle the tragedy on her own.

God, I'm an asshole. I wouldn't hear me out either.

And she doesn't even know about the worst of it.

"We need to talk to him, Audrey. It's important, practically an emergency," a voice sounds from the lobby area.

"Practically does not mean it actually *is* an emergency, Alice." Audrey's voice sounds exhausted.

I sigh and shove the last of the papers to the side.

"Let them in, Audrey," I call out.

"Oh, thank you, Sheriff," Alice overdoes the theatrics of gratitude.

Jim and Mabel trail in behind her, and I have to refrain from rolling my eyes.

"We had a thought about security in town we wanted to run by you," Jim says when he sees I'm not going to actively engage in this conversation.

"And that's an emergency?" I ask.

"Well, since the influx of reporters the other week, we thought we could create a barrier system blocking off Main Street if something like that ever happened again," Mabel says.

I sit frozen. *Are they fucking serious with this shit?* Sure, let's just block off our entire main thoroughfare on the off chance that the one-off with Tennison and Lennox happens again.

"Let me get this straight. You want me to spend our already non-existent budget on a removable barrier, on the rare chance that something like what happened with Lennox happens again?" I ask in disbelief.

"Exactly!" Alice nods with enthusiasm. Meanwhile, Jim and Mabel seem to have caught on to what an asinine idea it is if their frowns are anything to go by.

"No."

"No?" Alice asks.

"No. I'm not wasting funds on something that will most likely never happen again."

I pull the papers I was working on before they interrupted me towards me and start working through them as the trio stands silent in my office.

I let them stew in my bluntness for a couple of minutes before I look up. "You can go. I've got things to catch up on. If there is a real emergency, feel free to call or stop by. Otherwise, I will talk to you three tomorrow."

They shuffle their way out the front door, and Audrey's laughter tinkles through the office.

"Most days, I think you need to lighten up. Today is not one of those days. Maybe those three will finally learn what an emergency is," she says.

"They won't." I sigh. "They live for the gossip. I just don't have the time to babysit them today."

"Well, regardless, that was entertaining as hell."

"Glad I can be of service." I chuckle.

"Well, I'm leaving in a half an hour, so if you need anything else today, let me know. I can stay later if need be."

"Nah, we should be good. I'm just going to get all of this done, then call it a day. Go enjoy your Friday afternoon."

She nods and then heads back to her desk as I try to get back into the groove I was in before the trio interrupted.

I'm just finding my flow again when my phone pings.

Frustration makes me groan as I pick up my phone and check my message.

Oakley:

Heard a little rumor just now.

Definitely credible. Willow just talked to Rina.

He's being cryptic, but the second he mentions Rina, I'm on high alert.

And?

And she told Willow she has a date tonight.

What the actual fuck? Jealousy like I've never felt before takes over my body. My vision goes hazy with rage for a minute.

Some guy in Rosedale. They met in a coffee shop while she was over there delivering some furniture.

Thirty minutes later, I'm still waiting for a response, and finishing up this paperwork is not happening. I'm antsy as hell, my knee is bouncing, and I'm drumming my fingers on the desk. My brain is coming up with every scenario, and none of them are good for me. I'm about to walk my ass over to Grind Time when my phone finally pings.

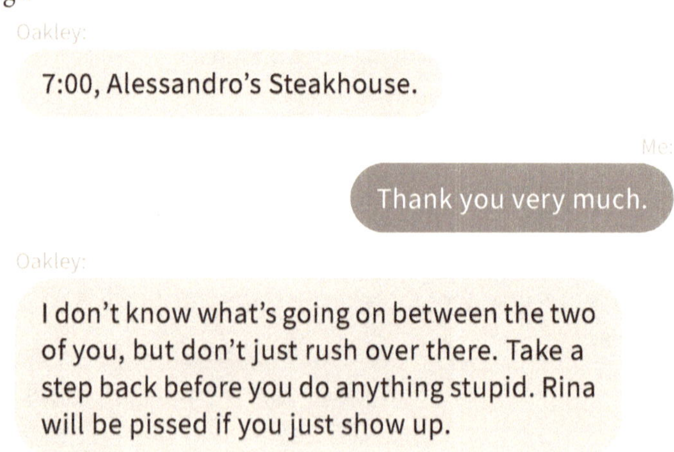

She'll be pissed off either way, but he doesn't know that. All I know is I need a plan because there is no way in hell she's going out with another man. Even if I have no right to demand it, I'll drag her ass from that restaurant before she goes out with anyone else.

> I will try. Thanks for looking out, Oakley.

Don't make me regret it. Willow will skin me alive if this goes south.

The Hutton sisters are not to be messed with, and it's good Oakley realizes that already. I don't bother with a reply. Instead, I focus my attention on the remaining paperwork. I have enough time to finish this and think about what I'm going to do about this date situation.

Can I do anything? I don't really know. If I asked Rina, I bet she would say I have no right to feel this intense jealousy. And she's probably right, honestly. I know she's dated since we split up, but if it was anything serious, I would have figured something out. One good thing about all the gossip in this town is staying updated on Rina's extracurriculars, however fucked up that is.

Being faced with my failure is eye-opening. Of course, I've harbored guilt over how things went down with Rina. I've never forgotten her, and I sure as shit never wanted to give her up. And up to this point, I've never physically seen her out with anyone. She's been too busy building her business, and that worked for me. If she went on a date, it was a one-off and everyone moved on.

I can see now how fucked up and selfish that is. I want to believe she's doing this shit out of spite for me. Especially after our conversation at the falls. But there's a voice in the back of my head that says I need to step up and figure out how to make her mine again. In my mind, she's always been mine; however, that's not actual reality. If I really want a shot at this, I need to figure out how to get her to hear me out. That's the first step. There are about a million more steps to get us to a place where we can move forward, but I can't think about that. I need to figure out this step first because nothing happens without that being successful.

If only there was a way to google: How to get your girl back after you abandoned her and broke her heart while also trying to deal with your own shit, like an injury you've never really come to peace with.

The answer is probably therapy. I did the mandatory appointments needed to be medically discharged but never followed through after. Maybe I was too stubborn, and I need to think about going back to being the kind of person Rina should have in her life. It just feels ... impossible and scary. Analyzing why I did what I did when the end result destroyed my world is something I don't willingly want to do. Why bring up all the pain when it's easier to just bury it deep in the recesses of my brain?

I sit back in my chair and think about that statement. Yeah, I need to work on that. Having this mindset will get me nowhere with Rina fast, and I know it.

However, I can't let her just go out on this date tonight. I think a huge chunk of my already bruised and battered heart will break off if I do.

Scrubbing my hand over my face, I contemplate my options. Anything I do will have Rina pissed off at me, but am I willing to dig the hole a little deeper to stop her from dating? As fucked up as it is, yes.

I cringe, but the possessive side of me can't let it happen. Ever since I felt her come around my cock again, it triggered the voice that screams *mine* every single time I think about the woman.

Fuck. I lean my head back, looking at the ceiling.

I'm about to make a very stupid and impulsive decision. I know it will bite me in the ass, but my rational brain is nowhere to be found right now.

I look at the clock and see I've spent the last two hours alternating between work and self-reflection. If I'm going to do anything about this fucking date of hers, I need to leave now. I hastily shuffle all the paperwork on my desk together and slide it into a drawer before locking it. I'll just have to deal with it tomorrow. Jumping up, I smooth a hand down my chest and stomach, making sure my shirt isn't wrinkled before wrinkling my nose at my attire. It's not really steakhouse appropriate, but I doubt I'll be staying long. It'll have to do.

Rina can yell at me about it later when I'm fucking her to exhaustion. Hopefully.

CHAPTER TWELVE
RINA

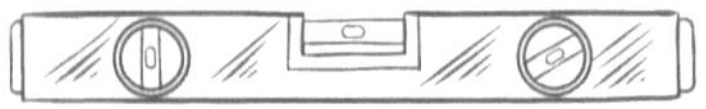

This was a terrible idea.

I don't want to go out on a fucking date. An impulsive and spiteful decision is biting me in the ass right now. I lost all sense of confidence in this plan about three hours ago when I was trying to find something to wear.

But I feel like I have something to prove to myself.

Now, I'm walking up to Allesandro's in a pair of black jeans and flowy, sleeveless, maroon shirt with my hair in a ponytail and no makeup. The lack of effort is blinding, but it feels like a test. If Tyler can't handle me like this, then he can't handle me at all. Because this is technically dressed up for me, even if it is a shallow attempt.

Screw Arlo for making me feel like I need to go out of my comfort zone just to prove something to both of us.

The closer I get to the front doors, the more I want to turn right around and ditch Tyler.

"Rina." His voice pulls me out of my musings.

"Tyler, hey." I stop in front of him. He's dressed in dark jeans, a blue polo shirt, and a blazer. His blond hair is perfectly coiffed, like it was at the coffee shop. *Jeez, he's like a Ken doll.*

"You look sexy as hell." He smirks, and I can't hold back the eye roll. He actively chose sexy, not beautiful or gorgeous, to describe me on the first date. I don't have high hopes for the rest of this evening.

"You ready to go inside?" I deflect.

"Absolutely." He puts his hand on my lower back and leads me in, and I'm glad he can't see the cringe on my face.

God, this was a terrible idea. The instant regret pisses me off. This was supposed to be my "fuck you" to Arlo, and I can't even do that right. It's becoming very clear to me that I've never actually worked through my feelings for the man. I just ignored everything to do with him and moved on like it didn't bother me. It was mostly because of the responsibility I felt for Willow and Lennox, but it's very clear I haven't worked through things as well as I thought I had.

"Reservation. Roberts," he throws out to the host without a please, thank you, or hello.

Off to a wonderful start.

"Of course, right this way." The host throws a look my way, and I nod in acknowledgment. Her subtle warning makes me both annoyed and thankful for the unspoken girl code.

We get seated easily, Tyler pulling up the menu to cover his face, so I do the same. I'm not even looking at the menu. I'm thinking about how to get out of this situation. Suddenly uncomfortable, I have this off feeling about Tyler I can't quite place. He hasn't done anything wrong, per se, but his charisma from the coffee shop doesn't seem to be here today.

"I can't believe what they charge for steaks at restaurants nowadays. It's highway robbery," he says with disgust.

Definitely time for an exit strategy.

"Yeah, it's a high-end product, though," I mumble.

"Well, I won't be supporting that. Maybe the chicken," he ponders.

Who the hell suggests a steakhouse only to boycott ordering actual steak? You can bet my ass is ordering the largest steak I can out of spite now.

A shadow falls over the table, and I put my menu down, excited to piss off Tyler and order a steak, when I see it isn't a server.

It's Arlo fucking Steel.

"Can we get a bottle of the Zapata Malbec? And for my entrée, I'll have the roast chicken with a Caesar salad." Tyler doesn't even look at the man as he orders, and I sit there in shock, mouth open and everything. It's when Tyler hands Arlo the menu that the giggles start.

What an actual shitshow. My date, however horrible he is, is handing my ex-husband a menu and treating him like a server. Arlo's entire body is clenched tight. I can see the tick in his stubbled jaw as he stares down Tyler.

"Rina, can I talk to you for a moment?" Arlo grits out.

My laughter gains more traction at how ridiculous this all is. Tyler finally takes a look at Arlo and arches his eyebrow.

"Is there a problem?"

"There will be if Rina doesn't come with me," Arlo says, and my laughter stops at once.

How dare he come in here and order me around? How the fuck did he even find me?

"We're on a date, so you can talk to her later," Tyler says before going back to ignoring him.

"You're no longer on a date," Arlo counters.

"I'm right here. You don't need to talk around me. No need for the dick-measuring contest." I roll my eyes before standing up from my chair. "I'll be right back," I tell Tyler. I know Arlo will stand here the entire time if I don't figure out why the hell he's here, so this is the only choice.

"Are you kidding me right now?" Tyler practically yells.

"It'll just take a minute." I grab Arlo's arm and don't give in to Tyler's outrage. Yes, this is not normal, but it's a first date. He doesn't have any say over what I do either.

Dragging Arlo away from the table and outside, I pull us around the side of the restaurant and out of sight for anyone to see or overhear us.

I spin around after I drop his arm. "What the actual fuck, Arlo?"

"You can't go on a date with that asshole."

I stare at him in disbelief. He's got to be kidding right now.

"How in the world do you think you have any say in what I do?"

"Rina..."

"No. We're settling this right now. How dare you think you have any say over what I can and can't do? And how did you even know I was here?"

He has the decency to look shameful as his head bows.

"I can't stand to see you with someone else," he murmurs.

"Then you should have thought about that fifteen years ago!" I yell. "I'm not having this conversation again. You know exactly what you did and exactly how badly you hurt me. We may have fucked, but that does not mean we are anything more, Arlo Steel," I say at a calmer level. I'm proud of myself for standing my ground. The date with Tyler was almost immediately a wash, but Arlo didn't need to know that. He needs to know he doesn't have access to me anymore.

"I know!" he yells, attempting to pull at his hair. "I know. But my chest..." He pounds it with his fist, right where his heart is. "It fucking hurts thinking of you out with someone. I can't breathe, I can't think, and I sure as hell can't work. I can't pretend to be okay without you anymore." The strain in his voice almost has me. It's like I can see the pain over every inch of his body, and it makes me soften toward him.

"Why now? I just don't understand why *now*? It's been years since you came back, and you've treated me like just another citizen. You've never shown an ounce of interest, so what the fuck is going on?" His emotion is breaking through my walls, and I hate it. I hear it in my voice, this ache, letting me know I'm not as far removed as I'd like to be.

"I don't know, and I know I need to work on that, and figure out all of this shit and why I've done what I have. But I couldn't sit by, knowing you were on a date. I couldn't sit by, knowing you're meant to be mine. For God's sake, Rina, my cock was inside of you less than a week ago!"

Just hearing the words makes my legs clench together. *No, I should not be turned on right now.*

"And that gives you the right to just come in here and pull me away from a date?" I hold strong.

We stare at each other. The tension, the sparks, are always so prevalent. My skin tingles, the hair standing on end, and the need in his eyes probably matches mine. It pisses me off. I'm not supposed to be feeling this with him still. I'm supposed to hate him—I *do* hate him—but I can't deny he does something to my body that no man ever has.

In a flash, his hands wrap around my jaw, and he pushes me against the side of the building as he kisses me. I grip his biceps and do the only thing I can at the moment—hold on tight.

I don't know why I don't shove him away.

No, that's not true. I don't shove him away because deep down I want what only he can give my body. He can give me the release I have craved since the last time we were together. But that's all this is, nothing more, nothing less.

It has to be just this, I plead with myself, begging me to not fall for him.

He kisses me like he's starving for it, like he's been dying for me, and I melt into it. My brain rebels and I bite his lip hard, just to piss him off. He growls in response as he jerks back. His tongue swipes over the broken skin, and I smirk as his eyes flash to mine.

"Dirty play, Marina."

"Don't fucking call me that," I whisper with less heat than I want.

He leans forward and whispers in my ear, "I'll call you anything I want while I'm buried deep inside of you."

Fuck it.

My hands frantically reach for his jeans and pop the button. He shoves my hands and spins me around.

"Hands on the wall." His voice deepens as I comply subconsciously.

He wrenches my ass back before sliding a hand to my stomach. He skillfully pops the button on my jeans and shoves his hand inside as I moan in anticipation.

The loss of his hands has me pushing my ass back for any touch, but then, this man shocks the shit out of me by yanking my jeans and panties down just low enough to expose me.

I should probably worry that we're out in the open, that anyone could see us, but if anything, it turns me on more. My clit pulses with need right as his hand smacks my ass. The sting is delicious and melts into pure pleasure. I hear moaning, and I don't realize it's me until Arlo leans over my back and puts his mouth right next to my ear.

"Keep moaning my name, Marina. It only makes me harder."

"Shut up and fuck me." I push my ass out again.

His deep chuckle reaches my ear as he straightens, the crinkle of a condom the only other sound.

The anticipation of his touch while simultaneously having my legs immobile and my hands on the brick wall of the building makes me crazy.

But he makes me wait.

CHAPTER THIRTEEN
ARLO

I'm out of control. I can feel it. But seeing Rina splayed out in front of me makes me want to be wild.

Seeing her sitting with that preppy asshole had me seeing red, and I know I overstepped. It felt like I was watching it all as a movie; I stepped into the restaurant and watched myself get this red haze over my vision before stomping over there and inserting myself. I almost laughed when he thought I was a server, and then wanted to punch him in his dick when he acted all high and mighty. He's not right for Rina. I know that in my bones.

I didn't mean for things to go this far, though. I had no intention of fucking her where anyone can see us, but damn it, her fiery attitude and calling me on my shit just does it for me. I know it's unhealthy and that I need to find a way to get her to hear me out, but all the blood and oxygen are currently vacant from my brain.

There's a red handprint on her ass from my hand, and I wish I could pepper her pretty porcelain skin more, but I know, realistically, we don't have a lot of time.

Gripping my dick, I slide it through her opening, not quite penetrating before sliding down to her clit. Rina's back arches, and a whimper sounds out in the warm evening air.

Her skin pebbles with goosebumps, and my hand moves down my cock and squeezes hard. I need to get a grip, or I'm going to come before I ever get inside of her.

I palm her ass before spanking her harder than the last time, and when she pushes back, causing my tip to slip inside of her, I lose what very little control I had.

I slam into her as she braces against the wall. Gripping her hips tight, I set a fast, punishing pace right from the word go. She's feels too fucking good, and this unexpected development has my orgasm too close to the surface. Tilting my head up as my hips keep pumping, I think about the stupid request from the meddling trio earlier, and it takes just enough of the edge off to make sure I get Rina taken care of.

Her hand slaps the brick, and I internally cringe at how much that probably hurt. I'll be sure to check it out after we finish. I shift one of my hands around her hip and down to her clit, feeling her clench around me.

"Oh God," she moans out.

I pinch it hard, causing her to tip over the edge, and I follow after her. Her whole body sags as I collapse on top of her to catch my breath. It may have been a quickie, but it was still mind-altering.

Fuck, why can't I keep my hands to myself around her? I did so well for the last decade, but now it's like the dam burst. One touch was all it took to fall right back to her. Back to the feeling of rightness she's always unknowingly brought to my life.

I know we need to sit down and talk. Ignoring what's happening with us is just causing everything to go to shit. And fucking her every time we're within two feet of each other is not doing me any favors at the moment.

"Get off me," she says as she starts to stand up.

I reluctantly pull out of her, taking off the condom and shoving it in my pocket to toss later. She scrambles to pull her underwear and pants up, and I can feel the shift around us.

Fastening up my jeans, I wait her out. If she's in her head, I don't want to push her and get her more pissed off at me.

"I need to leave," she says. Her voice cracks, and I reach out to spin her around. The tears I see in her eyes crack my heart into a million pieces.

What did I just do?

"Emmerdeur…"

"Don't! Don't you dare call me that, Arlo! You lost that right, and you will never have it again," she all but screams, shoving me away from her.

"I'm sorry—"

"No. No more apologies. I can't do this anymore." Her whispered statement is followed by the tears finally falling, and I feel like the biggest asshole alive.

"I fucked up. I shouldn't have come here and crashed your date. And this… I shouldn't have done this either," I try to explain.

Her more forceful shove makes me step back.

"Why are you doing this to me?" she cries. "Why couldn't you just leave me alone, like you have been since you came back? Why now?"

I can feel the pain in her words, and I know nothing I say will help. But I need to try. I can't leave things like we did at the falls.

"In the hospital, I couldn't just sit by and watch you go through that. I had to go to you. What happened after was not intended, and I know we agreed to just sex, but it's never that with you for me. I can't keep things to just sex between us. I can't watch you go out on a date knowing it should be me. I'm not claiming to be making good decisions because

I know I'm not. Hell, I'm making the worst decisions when it comes to you, but that hasn't really changed over the years."

"You don't have an opinion on my life anymore!" she yells. "Those are just excuses, Arlo. Whatever your reasoning is doesn't really matter because, at the end of the day, I can't trust you. And that won't ever change." She tones down her volume and gently pushes me to the side. The tears fall faster on her face, and I want nothing more than to wipe them from her face and tell her everything will be okay. That we'll work things out.

But I can't say that because she's right. I broke her trust, and I'm not even close to piecing it back together. Tonight definitely hindered any progress I've made.

She walks away with her head down, and I try to think of anything to say to make her come back to me, but I come up empty.

I watch her walk to her truck, climb in, and pull out of the parking lot. Rubbing my chest, I know I need to figure my shit out. Confusing both of us with this back and forth isn't doing either of us any favors. Hurting her any more isn't an option.

The drive home was long, my head too muddled with just how much I've fucked with Rina's life. When I got home, I went straight to my safe and pulled out the piece of paper that could change everything, and probably not for the better.

Our marriage license.

Behind that, the divorce papers that she sent back to me that I never signed.

I just couldn't. When I received them, I knew they were coming, but seeing how easily she signed them broke a part of me that will never heal. Which is a contradiction since I was the one that asked for it in the first place.

It's a secret I've held for fifteen years, and I'm not even sure why. It's possibly my biggest fuck-up, and that's saying something considering everything I've done to Rina.

If Rina had gotten serious with someone, I would have figured out how to make sure the divorce went through, even if I had to tell her about it. But she never did. And being married, even if it was in name only, gave me hope. It gave me strength when I had my injury. When I was all alone in the hospital recovering. Through the thousands of hours of physical therapy to learn to walk again. I continued through all of it because of this piece of paper.

I remember the courthouse wedding, how gorgeous she looked in her white sundress. I couldn't believe that was my life, that Marina Hutton chose to marry me. Just an orphan, with a plan to be career military. I was nothing special, but Rina? Rina was everything. Hell, she still is.

I may have kept my distance from her prior to the last few weeks, but I've always looked after her. When I knew she was working late, I'd drive by her workshop to check on her. When I knew she was doing a delivery, I would follow her to make sure everything went smoothly.

And I know, without a doubt, she would kill me if she ever found out about any of it.

Setting the marriage license on my bed, I flip through the divorce papers until I find the sticky note on the last page.

This was never what I wanted. I'm not sure what's happening with you,
but know that you will always be the love of my life.
Whatever is going on, I hope one day you'll tell me about it. I hope you
know, no matter how hurt I am, that I'm always on your side.
I'll love you always.

She signed it with a heart, nothing more. I rub my ribcage where the same heart is tattooed, along with an outline of the falls we loved so much.

It's time I start being the man she deserves, even if I never get to have her again.

Picking up my phone, I send a text that will hopefully be the first step in a long line to be the man I always should have been.

Me:

> Can I have the number of your therapist?

Oakley:

> Of course, man.

He sends it with no hesitation and no questions, and I couldn't be more grateful for his presence in my life.

It's time to work through my past in order to have any chance at a future.

CHAPTER FOURTEEN
RINA

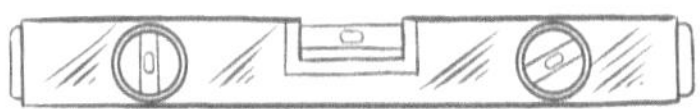

I sent a text to Tyler, letting him know I wasn't feeling well and needed to leave.

He responded asking if there was anything I needed to let him know.

Unless he can replace all my memories with Arlo, there isn't a lot anyone can do. The drive home exhausted me, and by the time I got there, I collapsed on my bed and slept for hours.

Waking up, I feel like I'm currently experiencing the worst hangover of my life. I have the worst migraine, and my mouth is dry as hell. This is why I don't like to cry. Rolling over, I groan as the events from last night slam back into my brain.

I went on a date. Then I fucked Arlo, who was absolutely not my date. And in public, where anyone could have seen.

What the fuck is wrong with me?

I don't have an answer, but I probably should take a long, hard look at my decision-making process lately. Because this cannot continue. My head and heart are a mess around Arlo, and I need to figure out why. I've hated him for far longer than I was with him, so I don't understand why I keep going back to him, even if it is just sex.

It's not just sex.

Shut up. I don't need to think about that at the moment.

Sitting up, I figure a shower might be just enough to help my migraine and clear my head so I can really figure things out.

Stripping out of my jeans and blouse that I slept in last night, I cringe at wearing outside clothes in my bed yet again, so it'll be a laundry day again because that's just gross.

I walk to the bathroom and turn the water as hot as I can stand it before waiting for it to fully heat up.

Why can't I stay away from that infuriating man? I turn to look at myself in the mirror. I look like the same person I've been for the last decade, but somehow, I look hollow. Ever since Lennox and Willow landed in the hospital, I feel out of control. Vulnerability hit hard in the hospital, and I let the comfort of Arlo hold me together.

And it snowballed from there.

I've been shoving my emotions down since my parents died, and apparently, my head and heart decided it was time to let them all start coming out. It tells me that I need to actually deal with shit in my life instead of acting like I'm unaffected by it all.

My normal bright blue eyes stare back at me, duller than I remember, and I know I need to face my demons in order to figure out what I really want in my life. Having my business is wonderful, no doubt there, but is that all I want?

The dream was always to find the love of my life. I never thought much past that, but once Arlo and I got together, I thought life would be perfect.

I gave up on that dream after I signed the divorce papers and never looked back. But seeing Ledger and Willow find their significant others has my mind reeling with longing. A longing I thought I was well and truly over.

Maybe that's why I'm having a hard time separating myself from Arlo again.

I shake my head and move to the scalding shower. It feels like a cleansing of sorts.

Maybe I just need to suck it up and go talk to Arlo. Truly hear him out, say my peace, and be done with it all. Avoidance clearly isn't working for me, so hopefully this will.

Decision made. I stay in the shower long after I wash up and until the water turns cold. The blast of freezing water centers me and hardens my resolve.

I'll go after family dinner tomorrow at Lennox's cabin. Today, I want to attempt to finally get ahead on some commissions.

I technically don't have anything scheduled and I was supposed to take off this weekend since I finally finished that daybed, but getting ahead and occupying my mind sounds like a much better idea.

Dressing in my usual uniform of worn-out leggings and a long-sleeved shirt, I don my steel-toed boots and head to my barn.

Family dinner at Lennox's cabin is upon us.

It feels like a huge milestone for Lennox, even if he is reluctantly hosting to make us less worried about him. Judging by the line of cars, I'm the last one here today. I grab the craft beer I picked up in Rosedale the other day and head inside.

"Knock, knock!" I call out.

"Out back!" Ledger yells from the sliders at the back of the house.

It's a cooler day now that Texas's version of fall has entered the picture, so hanging out on the back deck sounds perfect.

"Good evening, family," I greet everyone. Ainsley and Willow stand up and rush to me with hugs. I'm not the most touchy-feely of people, but I'll always accept hugs from these two. Ainsley started dating Ledger, and I might have interfered, but I knew the second I showed up at her house uninvited that we would be friends for life. Having her as almost a sister-in-law at this point is the cherry on top of the sundae.

"You've been working too hard. I feel like I haven't seen you in weeks," Ainsley faux scolds.

"I know. I have been, but I finally caught up, so hopefully, we can get back to our weekly lunch dates," I say.

"Good."

I disengage from the girls and head toward Lennox, who is sitting quietly in a rocking chair I built for him when he moved in.

"Got some fancy beer. Want one?" I ask as I sit next to him.

"Sure, thanks."

I inspect him, and he looks pretty good. The overgrown beard is starting to look rough, but he's looking pretty healthy. A change from the first couple of weeks he was home.

We both crack our beers as the surrounding conversation continues. I catch snippets of conversation but don't really have anything to add. I've been disconnected from everyone except Arlo lately, it seems.

"How are you?" Lennox asks quietly.

I sigh. "I'm ... unsettled," I finally say.

"Unsettled?"

"A lot has happened recently, as you know." I look over at him with a smile. "And it's made me think about a lot of things."

He nods but doesn't say anything.

We both silently watch Willow and Oakley hugging as he whispers in her ear. Ainsley hugs Ledger from behind as he cooks burgers on the grill, with the most content smile on her face.

"Do you think it's possible to be that happy?" I ask Lennox quietly.

"For you? Totally. For me?" He pauses, thinking. "I'm not so sure. Maybe I'll always be this fucked up, and then I can't see a happy ending happening."

My heart cracks in two, but I also have no clue what to say to make any of this better. I can only assume the events with Tennison are still very fresh for him. Nothing I say will make any of that better right now. But I try anyway because that's what our family does.

"You may not see it now, but in time, things won't look so bleak. If anyone can be that happy, it's you, Lenny."

He reaches over and grabs my hand, squeezing it as I look down and see the pink scars on his hand. I flip my hand over and squeeze his back. It's a sort of promise that we'll make it through this hard time. That we'll be there for each other through it all, no matter what it takes.

"Love you, Rina," he says softly.

"Love you too, Lenny."

"Let's eat!" Ledger's powerful voice interrupts our moment as he sets a plate of burgers down on the table. Someone already put all the fixings on the table, so now all we have left is to eat.

We gather around the outdoor table and start making our plates before we go around in our usual routine.

"Okay, this week, my favorite thing was planning our vacation for this summer," Ledger says.

"Rude. Way to steal it." Ainsley rolls her eyes. "My favorite thing was seeing the forest behind the house start to change colors."

"My favorite thing this week was Oakley and me agreeing to move in together," Willow says with the biggest smile on her face.

"Oh my god! Congrats, you guys!" I clap my hands with sheer excitement for them.

The rounds of congratulations last a couple of minutes before we all settle back down.

"Mine's that too. I don't care if it's supposed to be different." Oakley chuckles, and we all join him in laughter.

"I think we can let it slide this time," Ledger says.

"My favorite thing this week is this family dinner. Sorry I've been absent for a hot minute," Lennox cuts in and attempts to joke.

We all sit frozen, not sure how to respond, when Oakley steps in. God bless Oakley. He seems to be the only one who understands how Lennox is feeling at the moment.

"We're just glad you're feeling up to it. No need to apologize."

Lennox bows his head in thanks before all eyes turn to me.

"Umm, my favorite thing about this week is..." I draw out the last word because the first thing that popped into my head was fucking Arlo and lord knows I can't say that. "Finishing up some projects and actually being ahead for a change," I throw out once I push all thoughts of Arlo down.

"Kicking ass as always, Rina," Ledger says.

I smile at him, but I know it doesn't reach my eyes. That's all I seem to do: work, kick ass, repeat. It's more prevalent after my self-reflection earlier than ever before.

The rest of dinner is the usual combination of talking over each other, learning what new gossip is floating around town, and just spending time with each other.

Before I know it, dinner is done and I'm in my truck, driving to Arlo's house.

Parking on the street a little further down where Sal's is, I climb out of my truck and walk up to his front door. My phone buzzes in my back pocket, and I pull it out before knocking on his door.

Unknown:

You looked gorgeous the other night, in that maroon top. Maybe you can wear it with a skirt sometime.

What the fuck? I'm staring at my phone, both confused and creeped out.

"Rina?" Arlo's voice scares the hell out of me. I startle with my hand on my chest and almost drop my phone.

"Arlo. Hey. Hi." My racing heart is having a hard time catching up with seeing Arlo, even though it's why I came over here. The cryptic text is completely throwing me off.

"Umm, do you want to come in?" he asks, clearly confused, and why wouldn't he be? The last time we talked, I screamed at him, yet again, and left things worse off than before.

"Yes, please." I step in as he ushers me in, and I take a minute to look around his house. I've never been here, obviously, and I'm suddenly desperate for insight into who he is now.

I guess I was expecting something more, but his house—although nice—is barren. Only the basics of a couch and a television fill the living room.

"Take a seat. Can I get you something to drink? Water? That's all I really have," he says shyly. It would be adorable if I weren't here to crack my heart open.

"I'm good, thanks."

"Okay. So, what brings you here?" he asks out of pure curiosity, and I would feel the same. I've yelled at him more than I've talked, so what expectation does he have that it's changed?

"I wanted to clear the air." I hold my breath and wait for his response.

His brows furrow, and he looks torn. "Okay."

"I want to let go of this anger. I don't think I can ever be anything more than a friend or acquaintance to you, but I want to at least have closure." There, quick and to the point.

I stare at him, strong and unflinching. I have no illusions about this being an easy conversation or that it'll magically heal every single wound he's made, but it's a start and that's all I can ask for.

He looks sad and accepting, all at the same time.

"Where should I start?" he says softly as he sits on the opposite edge of the couch.

"From the beginning. Things were going so well..." I trail off.

"Things were going well. And the first few major missions after basic were eye-opening. We lost good people, and I saw firsthand what the possibilities were for the loved ones of those that choose to put their lives on the line every single day.

"The mission right before ... everything happened, I lost one of my best friends on my team. I called his widow, and it all crashed into me. It wasn't the life I wanted for you, for us. I knew that I wanted you to have everything in your life, and a dead husband wasn't in those plans."

"So, you made a unilateral decision for your wife instead of just talking to me? It's not like I didn't know what I signed up for," I say, exasperated.

"I know that now. But at the time, it seemed like the best thing to do. I just wanted what was best for you."

"*You* were what was best for me! How didn't you see that?" I try to lower my volume, but it's hard. Logically, I see where his head was at, but I don't understand why he couldn't just talk to me instead of thinking this was the best move.

"I just didn't," he says with his head bowed.

"And what happened when my parents died? You just doubled down and decided I was fine without you, so why would I need any type of support." My tone is bitter. I can hear it, but I can't soften it to save my life. The old hurt is flooding my veins, and I'm unprepared for how painful it is all over again.

"Rina, it's one of my biggest regrets not being there for you when you lost them. I was lost in my own shit, and I know that's not an excuse, but at the time, it was all I had. I wish I had done things differently."

"You've had fifteen years to make things right. If you really regretted it so much, why didn't you even try to talk to me?" I ask, hurt seeping into every word.

"I did!" He jolts up at my question and yells his response. "I did, and every single time I tried to talk to you, you either ignored me or wouldn't hear me out. And I'm not blaming you; if the roles were reversed, I don't think I would have heard me out either."

I think about his words, and he's right. I haven't let him tell me anything since he's been back. I just couldn't. It was too hard. I think about everything he told me, and although it doesn't change the way I feel about how he handled things, having answers is a bit of closure I didn't think I needed.

The one thing that still bothers me is why he came back here. He was supposed to be a career Marine, and five years in, he shows up here like nothing happened.

"What happened to make you come back here?" I impulsively ask. This isn't something he owes me an explanation to, but it's something I've wondered about more times than I'll admit to anyone.

He heaves a sigh before he settles his elbows on his knees, with his head in his hands.

"It was supposed to be a straightforward mission. Get in, get out, come back home with the newly freed hostage, and everyone would cheer us as American heroes. Not that I gave a shit about that. I can't tell you where we were, but I can tell you we were rappelling from a helicopter when things took a turn." He sits stock still for a second, and I have the strongest urge to comfort him. To hold him and let him know I was an asshole for even asking. The pain is still so prevalent in his voice it makes me think he's never dealt with this, or hell, even talked about it.

"The helo was under attack before we realized what was happening. They swung around to avoid being hit, and while it was mostly fine since everyone else on the team was already on the ground, I was still on the rope, rappelling down."

I gasp in shock.

"I was smashed into a tree where it shattered my hip, then I rolled as the chopper shifted again and smashed my back too."

I don't realize I'm crying until Arlo shifts on the couch and tentatively puts an arm around me. All I can think about is the scar on his hip that I saw not long ago. Where I once thought it was some funny or crazy story, the truth is a million times more heartbreaking. I wasn't prepared to hear how hurt he was.

I wasn't prepared for it to bring up all these protective feelings for him.

CHAPTER FIFTEEN
ARLO

I made her cry.

She's crying because she pities me and this fucking injury. This is why I've never told anyone, especially her. I didn't want the tears, the looks of sadness. I wanted to pretend it never happened.

But if there's anything I've learned, it's that the past doesn't stay where you want it to, especially when the woman you love asks you about it point blank.

I don't want to lie to her, to keep things from her anymore.

Then now is probably a great time to let her know you never actually filed the divorce papers.

Nope. That's the one thing I can't tell her yet. Her coming to me, to really hear me out, is a massive step in moving forward, and I can't jeopardize that. Not yet.

I need to wait until she's ready to hear it, and after all that I just dropped on her, this isn't the time.

I do the only thing I feel is right and put my arm around her to try to comfort her. I'm not sure if she'll pull away, hit me, or lean into me, but I can't stand to see her crying.

"Why didn't you tell me?" She hiccups.

"I didn't tell anyone. No one knows about any of it. When I got hurt and landed in the hospital, I realized I had no one. Uncle Charlie passed away a year earlier, so there was no one left to call. I knew you hated me, and I just wanted to move on from the whole thing. So, I did."

"You could have told me," she admonishes. I know she believes that with her whole heart right this second, but I couldn't tell her when it all went down.

I remember the look in her eyes the first time she saw me when I came back home. The agonizing hurt and confusion mixed with pure hatred made it clear where I stood. And I couldn't hurt her more than I already had.

"You know I couldn't, Rina," I say softly.

She leans into my hold and buries herself into my chest as she cries for an injury I grieved years ago.

But you haven't gone to the doctor in forever, even though the pain has gotten worse.

Now is not the time for my brain to point out just how much I've avoided everything in my life except my job.

I let her get all her tears out, even though it kills me to see. She shouldn't be crying for me. I sure as hell don't deserve it. But feeling her in my arms again is something I'm going to hold on to, even if it makes me selfish.

Even if it won't last.

She clears her throat, wiping away her tears as she sits up.

"Thank you for telling me." I see the second she puts her armor back up. Her eyes shutter, and I see the Rina I've known since I came back to Bluebell Falls, not the one I knew before I left. That brief glimpse of the woman I married is enough to make me question a lot of things, though.

She abruptly stands up, scrubbing her hands on her pants, and I start to panic.

"Stay. Please, we can talk more," I rush out.

"I can't, Arlo. I needed to know why, and you told me, but that's all it can ever be. I can't do more. I can't continue to do what we have been. I needed to hear you out because I need to finally move on from this all. I promise to try to be nicer to you when I see you out around town, but that's it, Arlo."

No. *No, this can't be all there is between us.*

I try to think of any response that will make her stay, but I come up empty. Finally telling her everything has worn me out, and mentally, I can't think of a single thing that would help my case here.

"I'm sorry you've had to deal with so much alone, and I'm sorry I wasn't there for you," she whispers before she walks out the front door.

I'm left reeling and surer than ever that going back to therapy and getting my overall health back in order is top priority.

I also feel a huge sense of relief. Rina finally knows most of what happened, and it's as if a huge weight has lifted off my chest. The constant guilt and longing warring in my heart have taken their toll, and it's freeing to finally have it out in the open, even if it's only with Rina for now.

I take a long look around at the place I've called home since I moved back after my accident. Shame, that's the overriding emotion I feel. I moved back here and focused solely on work, and it's very clear by looking at my living environment that everything else has been put on hold.

I wonder what Rina saw when she looked around. Did she feel sorry for me? Feel a sense of victory that she's clearly doing better than I am without her? I wouldn't blame her if she did.

What would I do now if I was the man worthy of Rina's heart? What would I do now if I faced everything I've been avoiding as I let Rina walk out my door?

I'd go after her and show her that regardless of how we left things, regardless of how much I've fucked up things, I will always be her support. I'll always put her as a priority.

Without a second thought, I grab my phone and keys and head to my truck. I can't leave things the way they are right now. I don't care if I have to sit on Rina's porch and talk to her through the door. I need to be there for her.

Pounding on the door of Rina's house, I wait impatiently for her to open the door. Or to yell at me. I'll take either one, honestly.

The door swings open, and a red, blotchy face greets me.

I don't think; I don't consider what my actions broadcast. I just act. As I pull her to me, she sinks her head against my chest and wraps her arms around my middle. She isn't crying anymore, thank God, and she's gripping me like she's afraid she'll lose me if she lets go. I bury my face into her hair and smell that now familiar sawdust and citrus, and I'm instantly soothed.

I softly press a kiss to the crown of her head, and she steps back and wordlessly walks to her bedroom. I close up, kicking off my shoes next to hers, and follow her unspoken invitation. By the time I walk into the bedroom, Rina is just climbing under the covers, wearing an oversized sleep shirt and boy shorts.

I look around and see a chair in the corner of her room with a throw blanket on it. Quickly grabbing it, I lay it on the bed next to her and proceed to take my pants off. As long as I've known her, she's had a strict rule about outside clothes in the bed, but this isn't a "get naked and fuck" type of situation. No, this is a "let me hold you on a night that was hard on both of us and then most likely pretend none of it happened tomorrow". So, a throw blanket is the best I can do with what I have right now.

She's facing away from me as I climb in next to her, wearing my T-shirt and boxer briefs. We both lie there, not moving an inch and not speaking. I'm wondering if this was even a good idea, if maybe I overstepped, but then I remember she let me in with no hesitation. The tension in my body leeches out of me as I shift toward her at the same time she turns to me. Her head lands on my chest as my arm wraps around her shoulder like a practiced dance.

"This is a one-time thing," her whisper-voice breaks the silence. "It doesn't change anything. You leave in the morning, and this never happens again."

"Whatever you want, Emmerdeur," I murmur into her hair.

I have no idea where we go from here, but I do know finally opening up to her about what happened all those years ago was the first step.

The first step in healing.

The first step in living.

The first step in getting my wife back.

CHAPTER SIXTEEN
RINA

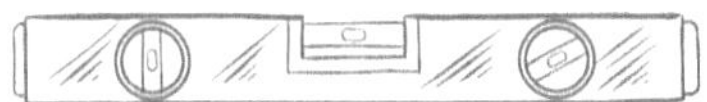

When I wake up, Arlo is gone. It's as much a relief as it is crushingly disappointing. I know I told him it was a one-time thing, but damn if I wish it could be more, no matter how illogical that is.

I'm still not sure how to react to all the information he told me last night. Answers I've always craved suddenly don't feel like closure. Instead, I just feel heartbroken that he went through so much with nobody by his side. I'm starting to regret the anger I've held onto for so many years.

I stretch out before slowly getting out of bed to start my day. I pull the blanket from the side Arlo slept on, and a smile blooms on my face. *He remembered.* I have a lot of quirks, none of which are particularly interesting, but the fact that he remembered something so mundane has my ice-cold heart thawing ever so slightly.

I toss it in the washing machine as an erratic pounding on my door starts.

I practically sprint to it and find it locked, which is not something I do. Sheriff Arlo would absolutely lock my damn door, though. He just can't help himself, apparently.

I rip the door open to find Ainsley standing there with her fist up.

"Why the hell is your door locked?" She tilts her head.

"Must have blacked out." I move aside to let her in.

"Did you forget?"

"Forget what?" I ask as I walk to the kitchen and start a big-ass pot of coffee.

"That we were supposed to go hang out at Sal's and talk shit about what crazy new rumors have popped up this weekend?" She eyes me up and down, and I realize I'm still in my underwear and oversized shirt I slept in. It's not like I care. We've had girls' nights, but I've never actually forgotten a get-together with Ainsley before.

The asshole Arlo makes me lose my damn head. *Damnit, I don't even know if I can call him an asshole anymore. Not after what he's been through.*

"I'm sorry. I..." I am trying my very hardest to come up with an explanation that doesn't involve the name Arlo. "I came back after family dinner and went to work. Lost track of time and slept through my alarm."

She arches an eyebrow and crosses her arms. "You better go get some clothes on. I'll pour the coffee. I feel like we have a lot to talk about." She turns without a word and grabs two coffee mugs from my cabinet.

Shit, I forget sometimes that I can't bullshit Ainsley like I can everyone else. I kind of forced my friendship on her when she came back to town, and while she's my best friend, I have undeniably kept a lot of secrets from her. I spin around on my heel and book it to my bedroom, shutting the door behind me and taking a deep breath.

If I want to keep everything that's happened recently with Arlo a secret, I need to be way more convincing than I just was. But I also think about the possibility of talking about everything.

Ainsley grew up here, sure, but she kept to herself in high school and then left immediately. She's as much of an outsider as you get in Bluebell Falls and might have a perspective I've been too blinded by anger to see.

I contemplate my options as I change into my standard uniform of black leggings and a razorback tank top, this one forest green. I decide that if I really want to move on, I need to talk things out. I'm not so sure I've ever had a clear head when thinking about anything involving Arlo.

Opening my door, I plaster a smile on my face.

"Oh, stop. Don't fake smile around me. It's just insulting." She shakes her head with a smirk.

I sigh as I collapse onto the couch next to her and pick up the coffee she made me. The fortifying sip gives me the boost I need to open up.

"You're right, sorry."

"What's going on? You're usually the one pounding on my door for our morning girl time," she says with nothing but concern.

"You have to promise that none of this leaves this room. Ledger can't know; Bluebell Falls can't find out, okay?" I know Ainsley, and she would never gossip or tell my business to anyone, but this is huge and would be a shockwave throughout our small town.

"Oh shit, this is serious." She puts her mug down and shifts her left leg under her right as she turns to me. "It doesn't leave this room, I promise."

"God, I don't even know where to start." Understatement of the century. Between our past and our recent hook-ups, there is no easy place to start explaining things. "Arlo and I ... have a complicated history."

"I fucking knew it!" Ainsley yells with a fist pump. "Sorry, sorry. That was rude. Carry on."

I snort at her reaction. "What gave it away?"

"You hate him just a little too hard for there not to be something going on there, sorry." She cringes, but I love her honesty. It's exactly why talking this out with her might help my very scrambled brain.

"No need to apologize. This is a long-ass story, so bear with me." She nods, and I proceed to tell her about our whirlwind romance when we were barely out of high school. How we had this grand plan for our life together, and then I drop the biggest bombshell of it all. "And then we got married."

She stares at me blankly as the confession finally sinks in. "What the fuck? You married Arlo? How did I not know this?"

"No one knows. We kept the whole thing a secret. Back then, he and Ledger were best friends, and Arlo was scared of his reaction. Arlo was going to basic, and our plan was to figure out the military life thing before telling our families."

"Holy shit," she whispers.

My phone pings, but I ignore it.

I chuckle. "Oh, it gets worse." I tell her how he had to almost immediately leave for a deployment or a mission and how it changed things for him. "I didn't know any of this until last night. He blindsided me with divorce papers, and I never knew why." I explain his reasoning ,and although saying it out loud makes my heart hurt for him all over again, my anger is simmering just below the surface still.

"That's so tough. Not going to lie, I completely understand the animosity toward him now. Did hearing his explanation help at all?" she very astutely asks.

"Yes. No." I sigh. "I'm not sure, honestly. I feel for him and everything he went through, but I still don't really understand why I wasn't enough, you know? Why couldn't he just talk to me about his concerns and fears, and let us work through things together?" It's the biggest question I still have. I would have run through fire to help him, to be there for him, and I just can't comprehend how his head went to divorce so easily.

"I'm going to look at this objectively. You were both extremely young, right? Both had huge changes happening. Maybe he thought it was his only option. No one would claim that twenty-year-olds make great decisions. That's not excusing his behavior, but I think it explains more about why he made such a shit choice."

I choke out a laugh because she has a valid point. "I think the reason I couldn't—and still can't—fully forgive him is because he did it two weeks after my parents died. I needed him more than ever, and instead, he just threw everything we had away."

"Can I ask you a question?"

"Absolutely," I say.

"Do you want to forgive him? Is that something you are even interested in?"

I try to find the answer, but I'm no closer than I was when I knocked on Arlo's door last night.

"I'm not entirely sure. I want to move past the anger, move past hating him, but I don't know that it includes forgiveness."

"I can understand that. What happened recently that allowed you both to talk about things and get to this point?"

My fucking phone pings again, and I turn the ringer off without even looking at it.

I almost completely forgot about all the events of the last few weeks. "Well, when Lennox was in the hospital, I snuck off to just … feel it all. I needed to break down, and I didn't want to do it in front of you all because you needed the strength. Arlo followed me, comforted me, and

I forgot about all the reasons why being together was a bad idea." I go on to explain the kiss and subsequent hook-ups, and I internally cringe at how quickly I fell back into his arms.

"There's a lot to unpack there. First, why did you think you needed to hide from us? Everyone was crushed when Lennox was in the hospital. You should feel comfortable leaning on your family when you need support too. It's not all on you and Ledger to hold strong in every shitty scenario."

"I have a feeling you've given Ledger the same lecture." I chuckle.

"You'd be right. It was hard for him, seeing Lennox in the hospital. He took it really hard but hid it from everyone. I swear, you elder Huttons are too damn stubborn for your own good." She rolls her eyes. "Now, back to you. How did being with him again feel?"

I sit back against the arm of the couch and think about her question. The first word that comes to mind is safe, and it sends my mind reeling.

"What did you think just now?" Ainsley asks.

"That it felt safe. I felt safe to just be, to feel." Pressure in the back of my eyes tells me I'm dangerously close to full-blown tears, but I need to talk this out.

"I feel that's more telling than anything else you've said. You still feel safe with Arlo, even if you wish you didn't."

I contemplate her words, and she's not wrong.

"Then what do I do?" I whisper.

"Do you feel like it's possible to forgive him, truly forgive him, and move forward? I'm not saying this needs to happen now or even this year, but in the future, do you think you can forgive him?"

My thumb scratches the seam on my leggings, and I chew on my bottom lip, thinking about her question.

"I feel like I can forgive him eventually, but I'm not sure I can move forward as anything more than friends. It feels too easy to fall right back into his orbit, and that scares me more than anything," I finally admit.

"And that's perfectly okay. You don't owe him anything more than you can give him willingly. Take things slow and make sure you are open with Arlo about your expectations between the two of you. You're allowed to be scared, but I think you owe it to yourself to be completely honest with how you feel about him and what you want for *your* future." She reaches over and grabs my hand, squeezing it in support. I am so thankful she came back to Bluebell Falls and joined our family.

"Thank you," I say softly, "for helping me talk through all of this."

"Oh, Rina, you know I'm always here for you. We should come up with a secret code if you need to talk about things in the future, though. Ledger would shit a brick if he accidentally saw a text involving anything Arlo and you related," she says, breaking the seriousness of our conversation.

I burst out laughing. "You have a point."

She rubs her hands together, eager to come up with a secret spy name, I'm sure.

"What about Operation Tight Jeans?"

I laugh so hard I have tears streaming down my cheeks. "What the hell?" I wheeze out.

"What? He always wears those tight jeans. I may be with Ledger, but I'm not fucking blind, girl." She giggles.

"We cannot name it that. Oh my God." I clutch my chest, trying to catch my breath.

"Fine," she huffs. "What about ... a-a code like, 'I need to talk about the bed I'm making.' Get it? It's like a double meaning, making your bed and lying in it, but you're also sleeping with him." She looks so pleased with herself I almost don't have the heart to nix it.

"What about, 'I need girl chat'? Straight and to the point and not something Ledger will question."

"I still like the bed one, but fine. It's your code anyway," she grumbles.

"Well, thank you for allowing me to pick my own special code word so that we can talk about Arlo behind my brother's back."

"Anytime! I wonder if this is how Oakley felt being all secret spy agent," she ponders seriously.

"I doubt it, but I still love you," I tell her through my laughter.

"Buzzkill. Let me have this," she says in faux indignation. "On that note, I need to get back to the office. We're supposed to have a meeting with all our contractors, and Ledger is making me lead it."

"The joys of working together." I stand up with her and give her a crushing hug. "Seriously, thank you. I needed this more than you know."

"Anytime, and keep me updated!" She heads to the front door and throws a wave over her head.

I plop back down on the couch. Ainsley gave me a lot to think about. It's only once I grab my phone to check my schedule for the day that I see the multiple texts that came during our conversation.

Unknown:

> You shouldn't be sleeping with men that aren't me.

Unknown:

> Ignore me all you want. One day, you won't be able to just ignore a message that comes through.

My face drains at the messages. I have no clue what this person is playing at, but I need to be cautious. Ignoring the messages is probably the best course of action, but I need to keep an eye out if it escalates. If it gets more serious, I'll have to go to Arlo.

CHAPTER SEVENTEEN
ARLO

It's been a mostly uneventful few weeks.

I finally finished all the paperwork dealing with Tennison, so I can officially put it behind me. Thank God too, because the constant reminder of the case keeps the image of carrying Lennox out of that fucking cabin fresh in my head. Between that and whatever is going on with Rina, I'm not sleeping and am grumpier than usual, according to Audrey.

Today is a big day, though. It's been about a month in the making, between making sure the whole damn town knew I had the day off and not to bug me, to finding a doctor in Rosedale. It's taken far longer than I wanted.

My back pain has been steadily growing worse, and it's time to get it checked out to see if there is further damage than what was already there. The nice thing about my hip injury is they just replaced the whole damn thing. So, while I have some achiness when it rains or gets cold, it doesn't give me trouble like my back does.

The forty-minute drive gives me too much time to think about Rina, though. Ever since the night I told her why I did what I did and then spent the entire night holding her, it's been radio silence. I've only seen her around town a handful of times, and I don't know if she's avoiding me completely or just working through her own shit. What I do know is I fucking miss her.

That night also prompted me to start taking care of myself. I had already gotten Oakley's therapist's number, but I actually called and scheduled an intake appointment when I got home from Rina's that day. Of course, they didn't have availability for almost a month, so while I wait for that, I figured out things with the doctor's appointments I've been putting off.

Pulling into the medical center, the nerves start to get to me. I had three burst fractures in my back from the accident, and the only thing they could do to fix them was to do a spinal fusion. I was told I could live a perfectly normal life with no pain, or I could live with constant pain. I've never lived pain free since the surgery, but it also wasn't anything more than a dull ache when I overworked it.

This pain, though? Completely different. Sharp, shooting pains along with a near constant ache throughout my entire back and random numbness in my extremities have become the norm. I'm just hoping I didn't do something that can't be fixed.

Getting checked in goes smoothly enough. The office is nice, and the receptionist put my nerves at ease while I was filling out the pages and pages of paperwork.

"Mr. Steel?" a nurse calls from the side door, and I groan as I use my hands to push up out of the chair. "Are you good to walk? I can grab a wheelchair if that would ease the pain a little." Her voice is sweet and non-judgmental, but it makes me feel weak and I can't handle feeling weak right now.

"I'm good," I grunt out, trying extremely hard to not take my terrible attitude out on this poor nurse who is just trying to do her job.

She nods but follows behind me closely to make sure I'm okay. "We'll be in room three today."

I walk a little slower than normal until I get to room three and take a seat in the chair off to the side of the medical bed. The nurse gets the usual information, and then I'm left with every possibility of what could be wrong.

A knock sounds at the door, and I abruptly straighten, causing my damn back to lock up again.

"Good morning, Mr. Steel. I'm Dr. Vincent." He holds out his hand to shake.

"Arlo works perfectly, thanks, sir."

"Then Brian works perfectly for me as well. What's going on today, Arlo?" He takes a seat on a rolling stool and sits right in front of me, giving me his full attention. He doesn't look at his paperwork like most do, and it throws me for a loop.

"Umm, I have back pain," I stumble to get out before clearing my throat and continuing. "I was in the Marines, and I had a repel go bad. It smashed up my back and hip, and I had a spinal fusion to correct the burst fractures."

"That's a lot of trauma to your body. I'm glad you were relatively okay. How long ago was this?" he asks.

"About a decade ago. My back was re-aggravated after I carried a guy to my truck. Long story and mostly confidential, sorry," I throw out. "And it's been shooting pain and periodic numbness ever since."

"What do you do now for work?"

"I'm the sheriff in Bluebell Falls," I say with that little hint of pride.

"Well, thank you for your service in both the Marines and as sheriff." He bows his head in thanks. "Do you mind if we do a physical exam?"

"Not at all." I get situated on the bed and take my shirt off. His hands gently trace the scars long ago healed. The same scars I avoid looking at all costs.

He asks me a million questions about where the pain is and how it feels before he tells me I can put my shirt back on.

"So, it could be a few things, but I feel like two are the most likely. We'll need to do a couple of scans to narrow it down, but I feel confident it's either arthritis or ASD, which is adjacent segment disease. Both are treatable. However, they both don't have a cure."

I nod slowly, not really coming to terms with the fact that this may never get better.

"I don't want to give you a treatment plan until we narrow down which it is; however, we have a CT machine in house and can get it in while you're here if you have time," he offers, and my shoulders release all their tension. No waiting for answers; I'll get them today.

"I have nowhere to be until four this afternoon."

"Perfect. Let me go grab Sandra, and she'll get you set up. I promise to answer any and all questions once we get an actual diagnosis." He holds out his hand to shake, and I take it. I've never had a doctor be so ... human before, and I'm more than glad I found him. It also makes me a little depressed I waited so long to get it checked out.

Sandra, the nurse, comes in and takes me to the area where the CT machine is, and in the matter of an hour, I'm back in room three, waiting for Dr. Brian Vincent to come in and tell me what's going on.

He doesn't make me wait long and comes in with a file in his hand. He sets it on the counter before taking a seat on the stool again.

"Well, good news. We have a diagnosis." I nod, holding my breath, expecting the worst. "It's ASD, like I thought. It basically means the areas above and below your fusions are getting overloaded. I assume when you carried the man to your truck, it was a little too much strain on your back, and because you have three fusions, it's giving you exponentially more pain than I would expect. Now, like I said, there is really no cure for this. However, we are able to do injections from some good stuff in your platelets to help promote a higher level of healing, and you should be feeling great within a few months."

I breathe out and let his words really soak in. It's not terrible news, and it's treatable. That's the best-case scenario.

"Okay. How many injections?" I honestly don't have a lot of questions because he's done a really great job of explaining it at a level I understand.

"Well, I don't have a definite number because I would want to see how you react to the first two or three. I'd want to spread them out to do one a month, and then do a scan after the second one and see how things are looking. We'll do a lot of rinse and repeat until you feel better and I'm happy with how things are looking around your fusion sites. If we see a lack of progress, we have other options to look at, but I don't want to get into those unless we absolutely need to."

"How soon can we start?"

He chuckles and directs me to the front to get everything scheduled. Because the injections are a bit of a process, I'm driving back here in a few days to get the ball rolling.

I finally end up back in my truck, and I take a minute to process the entire appointment. The overwhelming calmness that settles over me almost brings tears to my eyes. Being stubborn is a part of my DNA, and suddenly it all feels stupid as hell. I could have been more proactive and not let my back get so bad; instead, I let it get to a point where I can barely get out of bed in the morning.

This first step in taking care of myself, in order to be the man Rina always deserved, is officially complete. Now, I just need to drive home in time for my first therapy appointment.

Well, therapy fucking sucks.

For an intake appointment, I didn't expect to get into a lot of things, but holy shit was I wrong.

I've been sitting on my couch for God knows how long, just staring at the wall, ever since I hung up on our virtual session.

We only got through my childhood, but apparently, I don't talk about things often enough because it all rushed out once I got started. Now, I just feel empty, but not in a bad or negative way; more like a cleanse.

I think about what the therapist said, about taking the time to reflect and think about what's truly important in my life, and I decide today is as good as any to start. I get up slowly, looking forward to the day when those injections start working, and go to the kitchen to make a sandwich. Once that's done, I head to my truck and drive out to the falls.

It's still the one place I feel I can come to that clears my head and allows me to just think. It's the best place to attempt to figure out what's important to me. I may not have come here before I invited Rina not all that long ago, but breaking that barrier makes it seem like a safe space again.

The twenty-minute hike has my back screaming, but I know working through the stiffness in my hip will help me sleep later.

I end up sitting on one of my favorite large stones right on the edge of the water, and I unwrap my sandwich to eat while I start thinking.

What's important to me?

Obviously, Bluebell Falls and my job as sheriff. I take pride in making sure everyone is taken care of and babysitting the gossip crew. They keep life fun even if I pretend to act annoyed most of the time. It may not have been where I saw my life going when I was younger, but now I can't imagine doing anything else.

Rina.

This is the big one. Rina is important to me—always has been, always will be, regardless of how things go between us. I will continue to watch over her, to be there for her in the background, no matter what.

It brings me to what I *want* in life.

This is what's hard. I've been a soldier most of my life in one form or another; it's never been about what I want. If it was, I would never have broken Rina's and my heart. I wouldn't have taken every ounce of her hatred instead of just talking to her.

I sit back with a jolt before groaning at the sharp pain in my back. But the thought I have is like a lightning strike.

What I want is Rina.

I thought I did what was best, saving her from a life of unknowns and an absentee partner. I made a decision based on my job, which I didn't have a choice in at the time.

What I wanted and what I did were two completely different things.

I swear it's like a rainbow sprouting from the waterfall, and this huge revelation seals my fate.

All of this work I'm doing to better myself is for me, yes, but it's also for Rina, for the life I would do anything for us to have. I'm under no illusion that winning Rina back will be easy or possible, but am I even really living if I don't try?

Just as I think this, my phone pings in my pocket. I fish it out and see the message is from the very woman I was just pondering.

Hey, are you busy tonight? Could you stop by after work?

Absolutely.

It's time to go get my woman.

CHAPTER EIGHTEEN
RINA

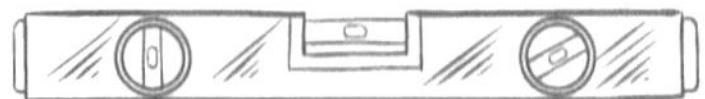

I'm nervous. Texting Arlo to come over is a risk, but I know we need to talk more. I heard his version of how things went, but we didn't dive into anything more, and I think I want to.

This doesn't necessarily mean I'm willing to forgive him or move forward with him as anything other than a friend, but I need to talk it out with someone and he's the only one with the answers I need.

Half an hour after I text him, there's a knock on my door.

I brush my hands down my shirt, checking to make sure I look presentable and then immediately chastise myself because it doesn't matter what I look like. Arlo sure as hell doesn't care if I'm in a paper bag or dressed to the nines.

I crack the front door and see his stubbled face, deep brown eyes, and a beat-up Bluebell Falls Landscaping baseball hat.

Shit. He looks good. Too good. This is the first time I've seen him in a baseball hat in years, and it was always my favorite look on him.

"You okay?" he asks, concern etched all over his attractive face.

"Yep, yep, great." I hold the door open and usher him inside. "Drink?" I ask after I close the door.

"I'm good. Everything okay?" he asks, and I realize I didn't tell him why I wanted him to come over.

"Do you want to sit down?" I suddenly feel extremely awkward, which irritates me because I never feel this way.

"Whatever you want." He takes a seat on my couch as I debate getting some water.

I pivot on my heel and grab a bottle from the refrigerator. Joining him on the couch, I sit down next to him before cracking open the water bottle and downing a couple of swallows. I see Arlo out of the corner of my eye, and he's wearing a smirk like it's his job, and I realize he sees how nervous I am.

"Okay, I want to pick up where we left off the last time we talked about things. I was … shocked, hearing everything you went through, and it took me a while to process. I still think I'm processing, honestly, but I'd like to talk about it all," I tell him as my hands wring together.

"I can do that." He says it so simply, and I can see in his eyes that he'll answer any questions I have.

God, I don't even know how to start, and it makes me more frustrated with myself.

Sighing, I relax back into the couch and say what's truly on my mind. "I feel like I don't know how to act around you anymore. I've been mad—no, angry. So damn angry for so long, and I don't really know how to move on from that. This awkwardness I'm feeling is not me at all, and I hate it. I don't want to be awkward around you, but I don't know if I'm ready to let go of the anger either."

He nods, and I appreciate that he doesn't just attempt to placate me immediately.

"I didn't really expect your anger toward me to just go away when I told you everything. I'm honestly a little shocked that you aren't holding on to it a hell of a lot harder."

I chuckle at his words because he's not wrong. I expected my resentment to last until I died, but it just … isn't.

"Same, honestly, but after everything you told me, it just feels silly to hold on to it when you went through so much."

"Rina, don't forgive me or act like everything is okay because you pity me. I don't want it or need it. I did a horrible thing to you, and I don't think what I went through with my injury negates that. I know saying sorry again won't help, but I need you to know hurting you was the worst thing I've ever done in my life. I never wanted to let you down, and I know I should have explained things before now, but I was scared. You had so much going on in your life, and I didn't want to add any stress to your already busy life. It's a sad excuse, but at the time it's all I had." It's basically a reiteration of everything he told me the first time, but the sadness and pain in his eyes make me want to figure this out. Move past the sorrys and the fuck-ups.

"No more apologies. Please. I really want to move past this, and I don't want this weird space we're in to continue. I want to be able to see you in Sal's and say hi without feeling this stabbing in my heart. I want to be able to text you randomly and not scroll through my phone to 'The Asshole.'" His bark of laughter at that makes me smile. "I just want to get to a place where things feel normal." I know I'm not making a ton of sense, but that's why I wanted him to come over, so I could make sense of how I feel about him and figure out if moving past all the hurt is a real possibility.

"Am I really 'The Asshole' in your phone?" he asks, and I pull up my phone and show him, biting my lip to hide my smile. "Fitting. Can I be one hundred percent honest here, with absolutely no pressure or expectation from you?"

"Always."

"For me, it's always been you. When I think about marriage or babies or my future, it always has you in it. That hasn't changed to this day, and it won't change anytime in the future. My ideal is that we aren't just friends or neighbors who wave as they pass each other on Main Street."

His words send a rush of warmth to my heart, and I know with every inch of my scarred heart that if it isn't Arlo, it's no one. The problem is, I don't forgive him, at least not right now, and no matter how we both feel, we both have too much to work on at the moment.

"I'm going to ask something really unfair, but it's the one thing I haven't been able to get past since we talked," I tell him instead of addressing his declaration.

"Ask me anything, Emmerdeur." I want to shove him for using that name because he knows it does things to me.

"Why wasn't I enough? You made a decision because you thought I wouldn't want to be lonely with you gone all the time, but you didn't even talk to me. You didn't talk to me then, and you waited fifteen years to talk to me after. Why wasn't I good enough to just talk to?" My voice is barely above a whisper as vulnerability pours out of my soul.

"You were everything, and I was a coward. It's every bit the reflection of me and not you." He scoots forward and wipes the tears falling. "I was scared shitless on that mission, and when one of my best friends died, I talked to his widow and I panicked. I didn't want that for you; hell, I wanted literally anything else for you other than an officer knocking on your door telling you your husband died. I fully admit it was the wrong decision, but then I got hurt and I thought about them calling you with me in the hospital on the other side of the world. It reinforced my thought process and when I came home, you hated me anyway, so I just … let you hate me. At the time, it felt like more than I deserved."

"You punished yourself," I murmur.

"In a way, I guess I did. Until recently, I didn't really have a reason to shift that way of thinking," he says.

"What happened recently?" I ask.

"I realized that no matter what happens between the two of us, I haven't been a man I can say I'm proud of. I'm not a man deserving of you, and I decided it was time to make a change."

"What does that mean?"

He takes a deep breath before sliding his hand over to mine. He grips it tight as he starts talking. "I went to the doctor finally. My back has been bothering me a lot since I pulled Lennox out of the cabin, and I've been avoiding getting it looked at. I also started therapy."

Woah, not what I was expecting at all.

"And how is your back?"

"Fucked, but not as bad as I thought." He laughs.

I slap his shoulder. "That's not even remotely funny!"

"Okay, sorry." He chuckles. "I basically have a disease in my back around my spinal fusions, where it's overworked."

"Fusions, as in multiple?" He told me he smashed his back, but shit, I don't think I really realized what that meant.

"Three, and my hip is completely replaced and full of metal. So, airports are a good time."

"How can you even joke about that?" I ask, appalled.

"I've lived with it for a decade. I've come to terms with everything both injuries entail."

Right, and I'm only just now learning about it. I'm sure he doesn't need or want my panic over an old injury he's mostly healed from. Except he now has some disease in his back that is causing him pain.

"What did the doctor say about your back? Can you do something to help it? Reverse it?"

"We're doing injections. Think stem cells but a little different, once a month to try to regenerate the area and promote better healing. It's really fucking cool, actually."

"You're ridiculous, but I'm glad there's a treatment. And that you are getting help," I add.

He's still holding my hand as we both get quiet. There's so much running through my head, but the one voice that's yelling the loudest is that I want to move forward.

"I don't know that we can be anything more than friends," I tell him. "I want to be friends—well, I want to try—but we need to stop sleeping together. It's muddling my head and my feelings, and I want to be one hundred percent sure if we choose to move past friendship, in the long future, that it's because our friendship is strong enough. I know we're banging in the bedroom." He bursts out laughing, and I join him.

"I get your point," he says. "Friends would be amazing, honestly. And I'll follow your lead on everything." His eagerness tells me I need to keep my head on straight and not get distracted by his Arlo-ness.

"Well, I should try to get to bed early. I've got a lot to work on tomorrow." I not-so-slyly attempt to end the entire conversation.

"Right, of course. Thank you. For everything." He leans forward and presses a chaste kiss to my cheek, squeezing the hand he's still holding before standing up.

He doesn't turn around as he walks to the door, just locks it before he shuts it behind him. I listen to the sound of his truck leaving before the ping of my phone distracts me.

Unknown:

What did I tell you about being with other men?

A picture of Arlo kissing me on the cheek no more than five minutes ago accompanies the text, and sheer panic hits my chest.

I screenshot everything before blocking the number, my hands shaking the entire time. I know better than to antagonize someone like that, but my impulsive reaction to being scared took over. The two-second sense of control felt good before I realized I probably did more harm than anything.

Shit, I'm going to have to tell Arlo about this if whoever it is escalates.

CHAPTER NINETEEN
ARLO

I t's been three days since Rina and I decided to work on our friend-ship—well, she decided, and I was willing to go along with anything if it meant having her in my life again.

We haven't seen each other since, and I'm jonesing for some time with her.

"I'll be back after lunch," I tell Audrey as I walk out of the office and head across the street to Grind Time.

"Arlo! Where have you been hiding?" Willow asks from behind the counter as Oakley looks up when she calls my name.

"Sheriff." He nods, and I roll my eyes. It's now a game that he doesn't call me Arlo. An argument we've had since he moved here. It's like pulling teeth to get him to call me Arlo. After the Lennox incident, he conceded but now calls me Sheriff to piss me off.

"Your usual today?" Willow asks, chipper as ever, and it starts to grate on my nerves. It's not her fault I had a rough therapy session last night and everything seems to be getting to me today.

"Umm, yeah, and whatever Rina usually gets." I should know what she drinks, but avoiding each other for a decade only allows for so much information.

Willow arches an eyebrow at me with a smirk on her face.

"Not a word, Will," I quip.

She mimes zipping her lips as she rolls them inward, and I look over at Oakley as the same smirk graces his face while he makes our coffee.

Should have known I'd get shit from a simple coffee order.

Oakley hands me our coffees and meets my eye. "Any update on what you brought to my attention?" My eyes shift over to Willow to make sure he knows what I'm talking about. Rina hasn't told me about anything happening at her place, but that doesn't mean it isn't.

"Nothing more, but I'm keeping my ears open. You'll be the first to know if there's a new development."

"God, I hate it when you two talk in code. So annoying," Willow grumbles as she walks by, and Oakley follows her with love-struck eyes.

And that's my cue to leave.

I toss a ten on the counter and grab our coffees before leaving.

The drive to Rina's house only takes about fifteen minutes, and when I pull into her driveway, I glance at her barn, seeing the main door wide open.

Climbing out, for the first time in a long time, my back doesn't immediately lock up. One injection in, and I'm already seeing a difference. I don't know why I waited so long.

Walking the long path, I hear a table saw as I get closer. I stop in the open doorway and watch her as she works.

Her usual leggings are wrapped around her long, toned legs. A long-sleeved Sam Houston National Park shirt covers her body, and safety glasses cover her gorgeous blue eyes. I'm transfixed observing her work. I don't think I've ever had the pleasure of just watching her in action, and it's incredible to witness. The way she confidently makes cuts and knows exactly how a stack of wood can turn into a beautiful piece of furniture is nothing short of impressive.

When she decided this was what she wanted to do with her life in high school, I couldn't have imagined it would turn into the booming business it has. That's not because she isn't fully capable; she absolutely is. She just had a different plan back then.

I've always wanted a Rina Hutton piece, but it's not something you ask your wife who doesn't know you're still married for. Plus, my house is not the place for something so meaningful; it's basically a glorified bachelor pad. Her pieces deserve to be cherished and in a house filled with love.

"You just going to stand there like a creeper all day?" Rina's voice jolts me out of my reverie, and I almost drop both our coffees.

I feel my cheeks heat as I clear my throat. "Sorry, I didn't want to startle you."

Smooth, real smooth, Steel. I internally roll my eyes at myself.

"Well, thank you for that. Is one of those for me?" She nods at the coffee in my hand.

"It is. I don't know what you usually drink, but Oakley gave me your usual."

She smirks. "I don't have a usual." Stepping forward, she grabs the drink intended for her and takes a sip. The moan after the sip damn near makes me audibly gulp. Maybe this was a bad idea. I'm not sure my body has gotten the message that we're just friends, and going slow with everything at that.

I take a sip of my own drink just to give myself something to do. She's so close to me I could just reach out and pull her to me, kiss the hell out of her before she knows what's hit her. I want to do all of that and more, but I won't because I'm not a total asshole. Probably still a small one, though.

"So, Sheriff, what brings you by? Just bringing me coffee out of the goodness of your heart?"

My cock twitches when she says Sheriff like that, and I didn't know that was something that could get me going.

"Noticed you've been busy, so I thought I'd stop by and check in. That's what friends do, right?" I'm honestly asking at this point because I don't have a fucking clue. All I know is that I wanted to see her, so I made up a reason to.

"Normally, Ainsley just lets herself into my house and starts making me breakfast, but I don't think the same thing can fly for you." Her grin grows, and I look back and forth at her eyes.

Is she flirting with me?

It's apparently been so long since I've flirted that I can't even recognize it. A sad realization that reinforces my poor decisions from the past.

"I'll ... not be doing that," I finally say. Would I love to eventually? Hell yes, but I'd also like to go to sleep with her at night and wake up with her every morning, so just bursting into her house doesn't really feel like the end goal for me here.

"Would you like to sit down outside?" She barely hides her laugh.

Nodding, I follow her as she leads us out of a side door I never knew was here, to a small porch overlooking part of the stream on the outskirts of town. It's gorgeous out here, and I can see why she wanted to live out here. It's peaceful and hidden away.

Two rocking Adirondack chairs flank a small side table I assume she built. We both take a seat, and I start rocking without a thought.

"I'm not sure if this was the right thing to do. I don't really know how to do the whole friend thing, but I wanted to see you. Even if it was for something stupid like coffee," I say. Hiding behind my coffee won't really move us forward, so being honest feels like the right move.

"Coffee is never stupid, especially from Grind Time."

I shoot her a look that says 'you know what I mean'.

She sighs. "I don't exactly know how to do this either, but I like this. It was a nice surprise."

We sit quietly, drinking our coffee and looking out at the creek. I've been everywhere in this town, and yet somehow, this little piece of Bluebell Falls Rina has claimed is almost as soothing as our spot at the falls. I wouldn't ever leave if this was my house.

"It's gorgeous out here," I murmur.

"It is. Ever since Willow and Lennox graduated high school, I had my eye on this plot of land. It's the perfect mix of 'close enough to town' and 'has enough space to build my shop on'. And then the creek, being close to the water, it's what sold me."

"You've done amazing things, Rina," I tell her earnestly.

"Why, thank you. I think so too. Although, lately, I've been taking on too many jobs. I never really thought about what would happen if I started getting more than steady jobs. I mean, I'm only one person, and I think I forget that sometimes when I take on commissions," she muses.

I make a mental note to figure out how to help her with that if I can.

"What about you?" she asks. "What made you come back here and take over the job of sheriff?"

"Felt like the right thing to do. After Uncle Charlie died, I had no plans to come back, but Old Man Walters heard through some obscure grapevine that I was out and offered me the job since he was long past wanting to retire. It all just naturally fell into place."

"And do you like it?" A simple question, but one I've never actually asked myself.

"I do," I say after I mull it over. "I didn't think I would, mainly because I always expected to retire an officer, but there's never a dull day here." She laughs in agreement. "I honestly didn't expect to be so busy all the time." It's true. I expected small town problems, not a town full of talkers who make up problems every single day.

"I don't think I ever thanked you for getting Lennox out of that cabin." Her voice softens as my spine stiffens.

"No thanks needed." I can hear the shift in my tone, but this isn't something I want or expected to talk about.

"I think it's needed. It rocked our world and continues to do so, but you got him out when things could have gone downhill fast. And now, knowing about your back, I just ... need you to know how much I see what you did."

"What brought this on?" I deflect.

"Self-examination?" she asks like she's unsure if it's the right answer. "I realized I have a tendency to shove all of my emotions down, so I've been working on that. It also made me realize that we've talked to Oakley and Lennox about all things Tennison, but I don't think anyone has told you how thankful we are that you were there. I wanted to change that."

Stunned. I feel stunned, and I'm having trouble accepting her thanks. I didn't do enough so her thanks feels ... misplaced.

Another thing to work on in therapy, I suppose.

"Thank you," I whisper. It's a positive step for me, although I still am uncomfortable with any praise relating to what went down in that cabin.

"What are you working on right now?" Moving on to a less serious topic helps me save face. If we continue talking about Lennox and Tennison, I know I'll break, or worse, take my insecurities out on her and I refuse to do that.

Her audible sigh sounds tired. "Let's see... This week, I'm finishing up a dining room set for a sweet couple in Rosedale. I also started this super adorable picnic table with a matching kid-sized one for a family all the way in Austin. They're coming to pick that up, though, so at least I don't have to stress about delivery."

"If you ever need help on deliveries, let me know, or if you don't want to be alone doing it for whatever reason." I offer more for myself because I hate not knowing who she's delivering to. It could be anyone, and anything could happen to her.

"Gee, thanks, *Sheriff.*" She smirks.

"I'm serious, Rina. If you ever feel the slightest bit unsafe or unsure, just call me."

"I will," she concedes. "Are you this over-protective with all of your friends?"

I shoot her an annoyed look. "What friends?" I joke, but the truth of the statement hits me hard.

We stare at each other. The sadness in her eyes makes me wish I didn't say that. My hand slides over to hers, and I hold it in a firm grip. Her eyes dart to our hands, and when they look back up at me, the heat I see throws me, but I can't say I'm upset about it.

"You could stop by again and bring me coffee whenever you want to get away from the office," she offers with a twinkle in her eye.

"Oh, could I? And what do I get out of this generous gift?" I smirk, still holding her hand.

"Hmm, that's a tough one," she muses. "There are quite a lot of options. I could … teach you how to use some power tools."

Shocked laughter escapes me. Her innuendo does not go unnoticed.

"Your power tools? What makes you think I need any help with that?"

"I don't know. Maybe there's some new way I do things that would really work for you." She bursts out laughing like she's shocked she even said that.

I still don't stand a chance with this woman. Somehow, we can go from serious conversation to sexual innuendos at the drop of a hat, and I fucking love it.

"I like your versions of friends," I chuckle.

Her smile drops a little, and I internally curse myself for saying it.

"We already established I don't know how to do this, and although I firmly believe we need to work on our friendship before anything happens—if anything else happens—you're really good in bed and sometimes my brain wanders, and we land on shitty sexual overtones." She cringes, but I love her blunt honesty.

"Friendship is whatever we say it is, Rina. And lucky for you, I happen to love sexual innuendos." I wink.

She squeezes the hand that's still holding hers before letting go and taking a final swig from her coffee cup.

"Well, I think this is a sign that I need to get back to work before that moves from suggestive jokes to fucking me over my workbench." She stands up, but I stay seated, shocked and picturing the exact image she just put in my head. My dick hardens in my jeans, and I adjust without a second thought. When I look up, her eyes are where my hand was, and I tip my head back and groan.

"I'm going. You can't say shit like that and then not expect me to react, Marina." I groan, scrubbing my hand over my face.

"Yep, you know how to get to your truck." She turns on her heel then calls over her shoulder, "Thanks for the coffee and the ... conversation."

I watch her walk through the side door, a mumbled, "Keep your head off his penis, Rina. Jesus," reaching my ear before I chuckle.

Dear God, friendship with my wife just might be the death of me.

CHAPTER TWENTY
RINA

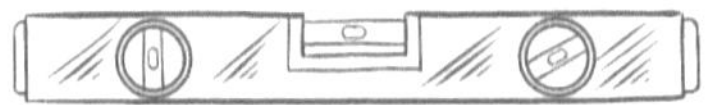

This is a terrible idea.

I haven't seen Arlo since last week when he brought me coffee, but my head sure as hell has been stuck on him.

The dichotomy of our conversation that day haunts all my free time. The serious stuff needed to be said, but the sexual? I have no clue why I couldn't keep my thoughts to myself, but I haven't been able to think of much else since. What's stuck the most was his reaction to it.

So, here I am, loading up a dining room set into my truck carefully while I wait for him to show up.

I called him yesterday and asked if he wanted to help me with a delivery. Because I *missed* him. And being stuck in the truck with him for an hour and a half round trip doesn't sound like a terrible decision in the making at all.

I just need to keep my libido in check. We're working on our friendship, and we certainly don't need me muddling everything with sex again.

I'm wrapping the chairs with some moving blankets when I hear his truck pull up. I glance his way as he jumps out, and my head tips back toward the heavens.

Of fucking course he's wearing a baseball hat and a threadbare Marines T-shirt, *and* jeans that wrap around his muscled thighs too perfectly.

Have mercy on a woman, damn. How the fuck am I supposed to focus with him looking like a literal piece of meat I want to nibble on?

"Here, let me help." I hear him jog up next to me, and I take a deep breath to calm myself down. It's going to be a long-ass day if I can't keep my shit locked down.

I straighten and turn to tell him all that's left is to load it into the truck, but I hit his hard chest instead.

His hands grab my upper arms to keep me steady, and the jolt it sends down my spine is bad news. He's just touching my arms; I cannot turn every touch into something sexual.

Maybe I just need to start having regular orgasms. It could combat this insane reaction to him. Of course, I'd have to work less in order not to collapse into bed every night with barely another thought to make that happen.

Shaking my head, disrupting my thoughts, I pull away with a muttered, "Thanks."

Together, we get the truck loaded up in no time, and it's glaringly obvious that I need to start hiring people to help me. Loading and delivering is the bane of my existence lately, and having Arlo's help shows me how much time I could really be saving myself. I tuck that away to work on later.

For now, I have to focus on keeping my cool for the next forty minutes.

We end up talking about everything under the sun but nothing of actual substance. Maybe we're both tiptoeing around each other, but I'm thankful for the bit of reprieve.

We're about five minutes out from the house when Arlo points out the window.

"That's where my doctor is for my back."

"How's that going? Do you feel like it's helping?" I don't really know the ins and outs of his treatment, but if he's feeling relief from the pain, that's a win in my book.

"I do, actually. I've only had the one injection so far, but the pain has already lessened. The next injection, they'll do another scan and see if there is any regeneration, and go from there. I assume I'll need a few to get to a good place, whatever that means."

"Do they hurt?" I ask, heart already aching that these injections could be causing him even more pain, regardless of whether they are helping in the long run.

"Like a bitch." He chuckles, but my heart clenches. "They offered to numb everything up, but I declined."

"You're such a stubborn ass. Why wouldn't you get it numbed if it hurts?" I'm not one to lecture on being stubborn because Lord knows I'm the worst of the bunch, but hearing he's in any more pain is something I'm not okay with.

"Aww, Marina, are you worried about me?" he teases.

"Well, let's see... You go off on crazy missions that I'm not privy to thanks to reasons I won't bring up, end up smashing your back and hip, and have surgery on both without telling anyone. Then, you fuck it up again by being a hero to my brother, which lands you in more pain. Forgive me if I don't particularly think you're a good judge of injury decisions." I roll my eyes. What I said registers in my head, and I realize I may have given away more of my feelings about him than I wanted to.

I do worry about him all the damn time. Usually, it's a fleeting thought, but ever since Tennison, I realize this small-town sheriff job isn't all that much safer than being in the damn Marines.

And it scares me to think about. Because I don't want to be worried about him. I don't want him to burrow deeper into my head and heart than he has been for years. It feels like the last fifteen years of anger are non-existent half the time, and my stubborn little heart just wants to hold on with both hands.

I'm not ready to let the hurt go; the anger maybe, but not the hurt.

The conflicting emotions have been exhausting me for weeks.

"I know. I'm trying," he says softly. I glance over at him and see a somber look on his face.

"I know you are. That was a dick move from me. I'm sorry," I say as I pull into my client's driveway. I'm glad I need to work because this line of conversation will show him too much.

I park and see the husband-and-wife duo stepping onto their front porch, and I throw a little wave.

Climbing out of my truck, I hear Arlo follow my lead.

"Good morning. You guys ready to see it?" I say in my best *Price Is Right* voice.

"We're so excited!"

Unloading is just as easy, and Arlo helps me set it up too. The couple obsesses over the dining set, and I swear—as much as I hate delivering things—this is the best part. Seeing their reactions in person to something I poured so much time and love into is simply the best. Pride hits my chest as I accept their appreciation before leaving just as fast as we came.

Wordlessly, we walk to the truck before climbing in.

"That looked fucking perfect in their house," Arlo says in awe as soon as his door is shut.

"It really did."

"You are so ridiculously talented," he says, not allowing me to brush off his praise.

Listen, I know I do awesome work. Arrogant or not, I've busted my ass at my craft, and the number of commissions I get tells me it's all paid off. But there's something to be said about Arlo recognizing it and not letting me shove things down. That's what I'm trying to work on, after all.

"Thank you. While not one of my favorite pieces, it did look really good with their style."

I put the truck in reverse and start driving back to Bluebell Falls. Being away from anyone that could "catch us" feels dangerous. Like I could just get my taste of him without consequences. It's complete bullshit, but my body doesn't get the message. It's pleasantly warm from his admiration, and the libido I tried to shove down is peeking its head out, seeing if the coast is clear.

We're on the road for about ten minutes before the silence between us is broken.

"I've always wanted one of your pieces," he says like he's talking about what he wants for dinner.

I've never been shy about building furniture for the people in my life. I've built half of the shit in Ainsley and Ledger's house. Lennox has a couple of things he really wanted, and there's a smattering of my work throughout the entire town.

If he had asked, I'd have made him something in a heartbeat.

That's not true. You would have told him to fuck off if it was before a couple of months ago.

Yeah, bitch of reason, you might have a point.

"What would you want?" I ask instead of the logical response of "send me a commission inquiry". We're just friends, and barely at that. I should be trying to keep it that way.

"I honestly have no clue. It's not like my tiny house is something I've put a lot of thought into. If I had one of your pieces, I'd want it to be a focal point in my house, you know? Build the whole damn thing around it."

"The whole house?" I ask, thinking surely not. It's just a piece of furniture. I could see decorating a room around a custom piece, but not a whole-ass house.

"Oh yeah. I wouldn't even know how to narrow it down to one piece," he muses, completely unaware of what his words are doing to me.

Vulnerable.

I'm torn between changing the subject entirely, fleeing before I get any deeper, and leaning into this feeling. Letting the desire to be something to him again take over.

My thoughts are all over the place, confused as hell and wondering how I can even be thinking about anything other than friendship with the man who broke my heart.

Yes, remember what he did and steel yourself against it.

But that's a problem in and of itself, isn't it? I said I don't forgive him completely yet, but that I wanted to grow our relationship. If that's truly what I meant, then I need to stop holding our past over his head, even if it's only in my thoughts.

It's not healthy and doesn't actually help me grow as a person like I'm trying really hard to do.

"Hey." His deep voice startles me as much as his hand on my thigh does. "I'm sorry. If I took that too far, I apologize."

"No, no, it's absolutely not you. I ... overthought the shit out of your statement." I let out a self-deprecating chuckle. "I'm a bit of a mess. I'm sorry. I keep thinking about taking things slow and working on our friendship again, but then you say things like that and I just..."

"Just what, Emmerdeur?"

That nickname gets me every single time.

"Just want to say fuck it all and jump into the free fall."

His hand squeezes my leg, and I realize I've been so lost in our conversation that we're almost back to my house.

He says nothing as I pull into the driveway in front of my barn, hand still on my thigh.

I turn to face him, trying desperately to think of something to say, or hell, a direction to go with him.

His eyes, that gorgeous brown like a perfectly stained piece of walnut, heat as they trail over every inch of my face.

Desire spikes in my veins.

I don't know who moves first, but it doesn't matter anyway. All that matters is our lips touching as his hand slides into my hair, holding me to him.

All that matters is that his kiss silences the loudness in my head, giving me a clarity I haven't had since he left.

CHAPTER TWENTY-ONE
RINA

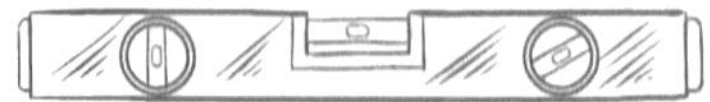

The door slams behind us as we wrestle with our clothes, mouths still connected in a wild mess of limbs. He spins me around, my back slamming against the hip-high workbench as I whimper in pain.

"Oh shit, I'm sorry," Arlo mumbles as his kisses trail down my neck.

Somehow, my shirt is already off, and I move my hands to his side to even things up. Sliding my hands up, I take my time feeling his muscles—the notch at the start of the V that leads directly to his dick, the subtle bumps of the edge of his abs. The man is built even after everything he's been through. With all the pain he's been suffering through, he still manages to keep himself in peak condition. It's ridiculously sexy.

I don't even notice the hard, metal bench digging into my lower back; not when I drag his shirt up and over his head, revealing a literal piece of art. I push him back a little so I can just look at him. Every time we've been together, it's been rushed and to the point. I'm not sure what exactly shifted, but I don't want that right now. I want to see him, see the man who seems to be wiggling his way back into my life like I don't have a say in the matter.

Honestly, I'm not sure I want a say. I'll just overthink it.

My fingernails scrape against his skin, sending goosebumps over his body. I study him as my eyes follow every inch of skin I touch. I see a touch of black on his side; a tattoo I never knew he had. Forcefully twisting his body so I can get a better look, I suck in a breath at what I see.

My eyes flit to his, unsure if I'm seeing what I think I am.

"The falls," he whispers, and my heart clenches in my chest. He got a tattoo of a place that only means something to us. I don't know when he did it, but it certainly wasn't when we were together.

What does this mean?

Before I can contemplate the answer to that question, I see that it isn't just an outline of the falls we both love too much. There's a shape that flows seamlessly into the design, something you might miss if you aren't looking at it like I am.

A heart.

It doesn't look like just any heart. It looks familiar, but I can't figure out where I've seen it before. Maybe it has to do with us. It would make sense since it ties in with the falls. It's not perfect, almost like it's handwritten. I trace it as if by memory.

My fingers freeze on the heart when the realization slams into me.

It's the heart I drew in the note I sent back with the divorce papers.

I look up at him, confusion no doubt written all over my face.

Pain shows all over his.

"I ... I needed a piece of you. Despite everything, I needed you close. Always." His gravelly voice mixed with his words sends a baffling combination of want and panic through my system.

Emotions I don't want to face right now war with the fact that I just want to jump him. At the most basic level, he branded me on his skin, and it's sexier than I want to admit.

My finger is still tracing the image as I think about my next move. I have two options. Shut shit down right here and now, and really figure out what I'm doing with him. Or say fuck it and pretend this revelation doesn't fuck with everything I knew about him.

I look up at him and see him patiently waiting for me. I know with every fiber of my being he'll do whatever I want. If I walk away, he'll respect that, but if I don't?

Impulsive.

Needy.

Loved.

I feel it all in a matter of seconds, and the overwhelming feeling of being loved overrules any logic I desperately try to hold on to.

My hands move to the band of his jeans, barely dipping inside as I move toward the button.

"Is this okay?" I ask because it's a two-way street. He may go with anything I say, but that doesn't mean how he feels doesn't matter. If anything, that means it matters a hell of a lot more.

"God, yes. Touch me, Emmerdeur." He groans as his arms encircle my waist and hoists me up onto the bench. His hands shift to my leggings, trying to pull them off before realizing my position makes things complicated.

He lifts me back up, placing me on the ground as I hold on tight to his shoulders.

"Fucking pants," he mutters. "Strip me," he says more firmly as he rips my leggings and panties down my legs.

I step out of everything, including my shoes, as I fumble with the button of his jeans before it finally pops through the little hole. I waste no time unzipping and shoving them down, catching his boxers with my thumbs as I do. He clumsily kicks off his tennis shoes before using his feet to get his pants the rest of the way off. Never once do his hands leave my waist.

Once he's completely naked, his attention shifts back to me as he picks me up and places me back on the workbench. His thumb shifting back and forth on my skin sends a wave of longing through me.

Even though he's right here, even though we're doing this, it doesn't change things outside of sex. I wish we could cut to the end where we've somehow made it through all the work we need to put in, all the hurt, and come out the other side together like we always should have been.

But I don't want to focus on that. I want to focus on the heat turning his brown eyes nearly black. The tension in his muscles tells me he's barely restraining himself.

"Fuck me," I whisper, and it's like the tether snaps.

His body engulfs mine as his lips crush against mine. I feel him everywhere, and yet it's not enough. My short nails dig into his ribcage, right where the tattoo is, pulling him impossibly closer.

One hand on my ass, he yanks me to the edge of the bench where I feel the fingers of his other hand slip down to my pussy. As he circles my clit a few times, I moan into his mouth, grinding my hips against his hand.

I want more. I want it all.

A pinch to the clit sends a jolt through me, making me pull back from our kiss and narrow my eyes at him.

He licks his lower lip with a smirk on his face, and my mind screams, *Danger!*

Two fingers glide through the wetness already building before pushing inside of me. My head tilts back on another moan.

"Eyes on me, Marina. I won't ask again."

My head jerks up as he pulls his fingers out. I whimper at the loss, on the verge of begging, when the hand on my ass squeezes tight and I feel his cock notch at my entrance.

My breathing is erratic with anticipation, but he just stares at me, making me wait.

"Arlo..." I breathe.

His hips shove forward until he's fully seated, and his jaw is clenched. My hands move up to cup it, and he looks deep into my eyes as he stands stock still.

Everything shifts at that moment. I see things I thought were impossible for so long, a future I had given up on.

His head tips forward, resting against mine.

"You're mine. You've always been mine, and you will always be mine. I don't care what it takes to get there. I will do it all." He grinds against me, making me whimper. "Say it, Emmerdeur. Say you're mine."

"I'm yours, Arlo," I whisper. His eyes close as his hips flex.

His eyes open, and I can tell immediately the switch has flipped. Sweet, almost unsure Arlo is nowhere to be found.

And I am so ready for it.

He pulls all the way out before thrusting deep inside of me. The friction is everything as I feel my orgasm building. The grip on my ass tightens, and I know there'll be little fingerprint bruises there tomorrow.

His very own mark on me.

His pace picks up, and I'm lost in pure feeling. The tingle in my toes. The heartbeat in my clit begging to be touched. The warmth of his breath on my neck as he bites that tender spot where my shoulder starts.

I cry out at the same time as I feel his hand shove in between us, wedged with no way to move, but it doesn't matter. The tip of his finger presses down on my clit with perfect precision, and I detonate.

The whooshing in my ears makes everything sound far away, but I vaguely hear my screams as I come.

"That's it, Emmerdeur, come all over me," Arlo grunts through my orgasm haze.

Before I can register what's happening, he pulls out of me completely and yanks me off of the bench. I barely have the strength to stand up, but he spins me around and pushes on my back, folding me over the bench.

I whimper at the loss of him, but he wastes no time.

He slams back into me, and my hips jolt into the metal bench. The pain mixed with this dominating version of Arlo has my lower stomach tightening.

Moaning, I slap my hand against the table.

"You are so goddamn beautiful." He groans as he grips my hips, pulling them back a little so they don't slam against the table with every thrust. "Your pretty pussy was made for me. Say it," he demands.

"My pussy was made for you." I cry out as he hits a spot I've only heard of.

"No one else will fuck you like I do. You hear me? No one else will give you what you need." He grunts as his grip tightens, and I know he's close.

The words mixed with him hitting the spot that feels so damn good lift me on my toes as I come again.

"God, yes," he grinds out before he pulls out, and I feel wetness coating my clit and the surrounding area.

It's then I realize he wasn't wearing a condom like he has been, and a brief moment of disappointment that he didn't come inside of me hits me out of nowhere.

It feels like he comes forever, and it's just as sexy as him actually fucking me.

He collapses over my back, sliding his hand up my arm and intertwining our fingers.

Pressing a kiss to my shoulder blade, he pants until his breathing finally settles.

"I didn't intend for this to happen," he murmurs against my skin.

"Me neither, but I can't say I'm mad about it." I chuckle as much as I can with his weight pressing down on me.

He sighs like he's reluctant to say something, and I decide to wait him out.

"I didn't bring a condom with me. I'm sorry I put you in that position," he says softly after a few minutes.

"Don't wear one," I say simply. "There's nothing to worry about on my end." I don't know where this is all coming from, but I know this entire day changed everything for me somehow.

I want Arlo.

I know it will take more than spontaneous sexcapades in the middle of the day to get us to a point where we can move forward.

But I'm ready to forgive him.

I'm ready to move forward with him.

"Rina..." he draws out.

"You wouldn't have put me in a dangerous position if there was something to worry about. And I..." I pause, attempting to figure out how to put how I'm feeling in words. "I don't want anyone else. Things won't change overnight, but I just want you." My words are whispered at the end, scared of how he'll respond.

He abruptly stands up, dragging me with him before spinning me around.

"You mean that?" The hope in his eyes makes my answer easier than I could have ever imagined.

"With every beat of my brittle heart."

He cups my jaw with his callused palms and kisses me like I just made all his dreams come true.

CHAPTER TWENTY-TWO
ARLO

The last two weeks have been, dare I say, quiet?

Rina took on a last-minute custom piece for some restaurant in Rosedale, so she's been tucked away in her lair for much of that time. After what happened in her workshop the last time I was there, we both decided it was best to give her space to actually work and not be distracted.

What that time apart has done, though, is give me time to throw myself into therapy and really think about what I want moving forward with Rina.

Two weeks ago, everything changed. I could feel the physical shift between us, and it wasn't just the sex. We wordlessly decided we wanted more than friendship.

That's not to say that we're jumping right in to where we were before I fucked things up. God knows I wouldn't expect that, but we're both wanting to make the effort to try.

That's why, today, I'm asking her on a date. A proper one.

We've never actually been on a proper date. Everything we did was in secret, and I want a way to show this time would be different. This time, I will shout to the world that Rina Hutton—Steel—is finally mine.

Hopefully.

Maybe this is too much for her but it's worth the attempt, at the very least.

I'm currently sitting in my office, mulling over how to ask her out while sipping coffee. The gossip committee has been strangely quiet of late, and I'm not expecting that to last for too much longer. Audrey has the day off, and the silence has allowed me to think about a lot of things.

I had my second injection a couple of days ago, and my scan is scheduled in two days and we'll be able to really see if things are helping. I'm scared but hopeful. My back has been feeling light years better, so hopefully, that means things are progressing how they should.

It still makes me nervous, but I'm trying not to stress until I get definitive answers from the scan.

"Knock, knock." I look up, confused by the voice I'm hearing.

"Hey," I say softly as my eyes confirm it is indeed the woman I'm in love with.

"Long time, no see. Thought I'd stop by and check on you." She gives me a cheeky grin, and I love that she took the initiative. She's never been shy, per se, but this grown-up, assertive Rina has my heart pounding and my dick hardening.

"How sweet of you, Marina." The use of her full name always pisses her off a little, and that fire in her eyes gets me hot every single time. That probably says more about me than it does her, but I'll own it.

Her eyes narrow on mine, and I chuckle at the exact reaction I was hoping to get.

"Anyway, it's shockingly quiet in here. What are you up to?" she asks.

"Oh, you know, the usual. Trying to avoid Alice and Mabel, drinking some coffee, relaxing," I say casually.

"Sounds boring as fuck" —she shoots me a look I can't decipher— "and I'm jealous." It's then that I really look at her. Dark circles under her eyes let me know she's been working too hard. They make me want to take care of her, scold her for working too hard, and find a way to carry some of her load all at once.

"How's the table coming along?" I ask instead of saying what I really want to. Something like, *Come home with me. Let's snuggle and binge-watch TV so you can sleep without judgement or stressing about what job is next.*

"Done. Thank God. I finished it about" —she pulls her phone out to check the time— "Twenty minutes ago."

And her first stop was here.

I want to analyze that more, but I'm not sure she really wants to scrutinize it. I need to remember to take things slow.

"What's on your agenda the rest of the day?" Do I sound nonchalant? God, I hope so.

"I ... have no idea," she says, sounding lost, and I decide it's the perfect time to move forward with my plan.

"Would you, maybe, want to go out to lunch? Together?" Jesus, I sound so unsure of myself, and I hate it. I hate that I've put myself in this position with her, but gaining back her trust is more important than feeling uncomfortable.

Her head tilts in question. "Like a date?"

"Exactly like a date."

I let the concept seep into her brain. I wonder if she's coming to the same realization I had about never actually going on a date before.

"Where?"

"Sal's?" It's the only place outside of Grind Time and Mullin's Pizza, and neither of those seems like enough of a date.

"You're sure about this?" she asks.

I'm entirely unsure if the hesitation in her eyes is anything to go by.

"I think this is the surest I've been in a very long time," I say. I hope she can see the honesty on my face.

She bites her bottom lip, gnawing on it as she thinks. I'll wait for her all day if that's what it takes for her to say yes.

"If we do this, we'll be the talk of Bluebell Falls for the foreseeable future," she offers like that's something that would change my mind.

"Yep."

She studies me like I have some wild ulterior motive, but she won't find anything but the truth there.

Letting out a heavy sigh, her whole body seems to decompress. "Okay, let's do this."

I scramble from behind my desk, not wanting to give her a moment to change her mind. I bang my hip on the edge of my desk, cursing as the pain radiates through my leg. I'm usually more careful around that hip, but apparently this woman makes me reckless.

"Oh shit, are you okay?" She rushes over to me and bends over to check my denim-covered hip. I'm not sure what she's expecting to see, but her worry for me causes warmth to bloom in my body.

"I'm good, just got a little too eager." I chuckle, but the look on her face tells me she doesn't find it amusing.

"Now that I know about your injuries, I swear you stress me out with shit like this." She shakes her head.

"I'm fine, I promise. I'm a lot tougher than I look," I joke.

"Don't I fucking know it," she mutters, and I have to hide my smirk by biting my lip.

"Let's go eat." I grab her hand as I stand to my full height once more and pull her out of my office, through the front door and into the warm Texas air.

Immediately, Jim Mathews catches my eye before looking down at our connected hands. An arched eyebrow looks back up at me, but I give him no response. This means the entire town will know in about ten minutes.

"Wow, that's got to be a record," Rina says quietly as she watches Jim scamper away into Grind Time, presumably to tell whomever he finds there about this new development.

I'm sure anything having to do with me is news around here since usually they can't get any information out of me. And given Rina's well-known dislike for me, this is definitely news-worthy.

Making our way to Sal's, we walk in and it's like a scene from a movie. A hush falls over the entire dining room, and everyone turns to stare at us. *Fuck, maybe this was a terrible idea.*

"Booth in the back is open," Kelly Adams, the owner of Sal's, calls from behind the counter.

"Thanks Kelly," Rina says and then drags me to the open booth. She plops down on one side, and I slowly take my seat opposite her, trying to figure out if leaving is the best option here. I expected the gossip; I didn't expect the gawking.

"We can—"

"Geez, it's like we're the next coming attraction," she says at the same time.

"We can leave if you want. I didn't expect it to be this bad."

"Hell no. If we're really going to do this—and I want to—we need to face the peanut gallery, however annoying it is. Now, if they come over here and try to interrupt our lunch, I will have a talking to with the whole damn town."

God, I love her.

"Yes, ma'am," I say with the biggest smile on my face.

She rolls her eyes and picks up the menu by the window so she can look at it. I'm not entirely sure why since we've all had the menu memorized since we were in high school. Maybe it's nervous energy. If that's the case, she's hiding it extremely well.

"Alright, kids, the burger and the club?" Kelly asks as she comes over.

I nod, telling her wordlessly that my usual is fine. At the same time Rina sighs, tossing the menu down, and taps her finger on the table.

"Yep, thanks, Kelly."

I almost laugh at how annoyed she seems to be at the menu, or rather the lack of needing it, but I wisely don't. I'm trying to stay on her good side today.

She glances at me before shifting her eyes, then quickly looks back. The double take makes me absolutely sure that I'm smiling like a loon at her.

"Why are you smiling like that?" she asks accusingly.

"Like what?"

She waves at my face. "Like you're enjoying this!" she says, exasperated.

I do laugh then. "Because I am. I mean, not how uncomfortable you look right now, but the date overall? Best day ever." I lean back in the booth and watch the emotions scuttle across her face.

"I'm sorry. I just realized how very little of these I've actually been on, and it freaked me out, and then I got super nervous, and I looked at the fucking menu I've known from memory for too many years to count, and then I just looked stupid." She sighs before slumping back.

I won't touch on the fact she just told me she rarely dates. The confirmation is something I didn't even realize my caveman ass needed to hear, but damn does it make me happy.

"You didn't look stupid. Look, there is no pressure, no expectations, none of it. Although this aspect is new, we've known each other for years. That hasn't changed in the walk over here. This isn't an average first date, but we're still just us, okay?"

She tips her head back onto the booth's back and lets out a breath. "I know. This just feels so ... huge, you know? Like, yes, it's a date, but it's a date with *you* and that feels so much more monumental."

It *is* monumental. It's nothing short of miraculous that my wife is willingly sitting across from me, wanting to give things a try, showing off our new relationship to our small town.

Shit, I really need to tell her about not filing the divorce papers.

Not now; this moment feels too fragile.

"I get what you're saying. Let me try something." I clear my throat, straighten my seat, and prepare to hopefully make her laugh. "I'm so glad you agreed to our date. What do you do for work?"

Her eyebrows furrow. "You know what I do for work. What the hell?"

"That sounds super interesting. Did you always know you were going to go into furniture building?" I plow through her confusion, hoping she catches on.

The twinkle in her eye transforms into a bright smile. "I actually took a woodworking class in high school, and it changed the course of my life.

I found I was not only good at it but that I loved it as well, and I just ran with it."

"Fascinating," I murmur. And it is. Even though I know this story, she tells it with the same excitement she did when she decided to really lean into her love of working with wood and went to college for it. I've never known anyone who loves what they do as much as Rina does, and it's still inspiring to this day.

"What about you? You're in law enforcement?" She plays along, and I already see the tension in her shoulders lessening.

"I am the sheriff of the lovely Bluebell Falls. I had intended to be career military, but that fell through." I keep it light, mainly because I don't want to talk about it. Therapy is helping me with that, but this isn't something I want to bring up at the moment.

"Alright, folks, club and a burger," Kelly interrupts and sets down our food. We say our thanks and wait for her to walk away before continuing our first date narrative.

"Do you miss it?" she says softly.

I exhale. "Not as much as I thought I would, if I'm being honest." This is something I've been really trying to isolate with my therapist, and I concluded that I miss the idea of being a career Marine more than I miss what that actually entails.

"Can I break this really cute thing you did to get me out of my head?"

"Absolutely," I say.

"I think you were always meant to be our sheriff." She takes a bite of her burger like she didn't just blow my world apart with her thoughtful words.

"I—" I try to come up with a response, but I honestly don't have one.

"Everyone loves you." She wipes her mouth quickly. "You go above and beyond for every single person, even the really annoying ones. Do you know how many times I've delivered something to someone in town and they brag about something you did? Maybe that's a huge part of why I was so angry with you too. It was like you were always being talked about; but not just talked about, raved on. You do so much damn good, and I just wanted you to be an asshole to everyone. Sure, your surly attitude is one thing, but your actions show a different side of you."

"Rina..." I'm speechless. I've never once thought about my job as sheriff like that. I just do what I've always thought I was supposed to do for the job.

"Sorry, that was probably a little much. I just wanted you to see yourself how the town does."

"And what about you? How do you see me?"

She puts her burger back down on the plate, wiping her hands on a napkin before giving me her full attention.

"I see a grown-up version of the man I loved all those years ago. A man I'm scared shitless to fall for again. But I really want to give this a real try."

I reach across the Formica table and grab of her hand.

"I know none of this is going to be easy, Emmerdeur, but I'm going to try like hell to get you back." It's as much of a promise as any truth I've ever spoken.

CHAPTER TWENTY-THREE
RINA

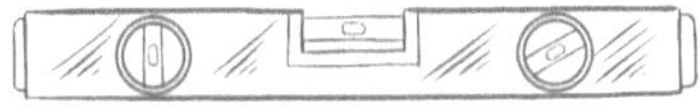

Today has been ... life-affirming. Is that too much? Possibly, but going on a proper date with Arlo feels like it changed my brain chemistry.

It was all so normal, like we hadn't even been ignoring each other for the past fifteen years. I wouldn't say it was like we were, back when we were together, because hiding our entire relationship from everyone was certainly nothing like a date at Sal's for all of Bluebell Falls to see.

And the craziest part? Once I got out of my head, I enjoyed the hell out of it. I didn't focus on what all the nosy people would say. I just got to know Arlo, as a first date usually does. God bless him for the quick thinking to pull me out of my nervousness.

We're now walking to my truck, bumping each other's shoulders every so often, and the anticipation is killing me.

"We should do this again sometime," Arlo breaks the silence. I smile at his continuation of the first date narrative.

"We should. You have my number. Just let me know when you're free," I offer, playing along.

We stop in front of my truck and I rock on my heels, suddenly feeling very shy, which is highly unlike me.

He grabs one of my hands, the heat and calluses causing me to melt in a puddle at his feet.

"I had a great time, Rina." Leaning forward, he places a kiss on my cheek before shifting to my lips and placing the most tender kiss I think I've ever had in my life. I reach out to steady myself on him, but he pulls away from the kiss before it continues. I sway forward, finally finding his forearm in my Arlo haze as he lightly grabs my hips to stabilize me. He presses his forehead to mine, closes his eyes, and just *smiles.* The brightest, happiest smile I've seen grace his face since we got married at the courthouse.

"I have to get back to work, but I'll talk to you later," he murmurs.

"Perfect," I whisper. I don't want to part ways. I want to invite him home and possibly have a repeat of the workbench fun we had, but I also know walking away is the smart decision. We need the time to figure out who we are now as a couple, not who we were back when it felt like we could work through any obstacle that came our way.

He pulls away and walks back to the sidewalk, watching me as I climb into my truck. His eyes track me the entire time as I drive away from downtown. I feel the heat of his gaze on me long after he disappears in my rearview.

A crash startles me awake.

I look at my phone and see it's just after eleven at night, and in my sleep-confused brain, I'm trying to figure out what's happened.

Another crash sounds and I jump out of bed, phone in hand, racing outside without another thought. I don't immediately see anything, but I run to my workshop to see if something fell in here.

What I see when I open the door stops me dead in my tracks.

Wood chunks, splintered and *destroyed* pieces cover every inch of the large space. My eyes look everywhere and nowhere at the same time, not believing what is clearly in front of my face.

Everything I had in here is destroyed.

I feel my shoulders shaking before I realize I'm crying. Not just crying, full-on hysterics. Sinking down against the doorframe, I hug my knees to my chest and let the worst of my sobs out.

The phone I just remembered I brought with me lies on the floor and I pick it up gingerly, realizing I must have dropped it, judging by the shattered screen.

I can still navigate around it, but I'll have to figure that out tomorrow too. Pulling up Arlo's number, I don't hesitate to call.

"Rina?" he answers almost immediately. I can already hear the worry in his voice, and I lose it, barely able to get the words out.

"Please come," I gasp out. "I'm at the workshop." It'll probably freak him out more, but I can't talk through the borderline hyper-ventilation.

"Shit, okay. I'll be right there. Stay with me on the phone, okay? Are you hurt?" I hear shuffling around in the background, and I know he's rushing like hell to get to me.

"Not hurt," I say through the tears.

"Okay, that's good. Can you tell me what happened?" His calm tone immediately centers me, but not enough for me to tell him what I walked into.

Shaking my head, I realize I didn't verbally give him an answer. "N-n-n-no." I put the phone on speaker and set it on the floor so I can wrap my arms around myself.

"That's fine. Are you safe right now? Is there any threat there?" One day, I'll think about how good under pressure he is and appreciate his entire demeanor in what feels like one of the worst moments I've had since my parents died.

"Safe. No, I don't think so." Basic answers seem to be the only thing I can do through my panic.

"Good, that's good, Emmerdeur. I'm less than five minutes away. You're doing so good."

I nod again, incapable of anything more. The rush of tears takes over again as I think about the bunk bed that was almost done, the coffee table sitting off to the side waiting for pick-up, and the picnic tables. *All of them gone.* Not one scrap looks recognizable. I randomly think about how I slept through most of this destruction, and it freaks me out more than I'd like to admit.

How do you just sleep through this? Sure, it's not super close to my house, but I should have heard this. I should have been able to stop it.

Truck tires barrel down my driveway, but I don't look up. I'm hypnotized by my livelihood being ripped to shreds. I turn my head to look at the space where I keep a smallish table that holds all the things, like plans and contracts, and I see something odd. What looks like blank paper covers the tabletop, and I frantically get up off the floor to figure out what it is. Maybe the asshole that did this left something.

Somewhere in the distance, I hear my name being called, but I don't detour from my mission. It takes all of ten steps to see there's something written on the papers.

I warned you. You are mine, and you've been very bad by allowing another to touch you. Remember when I said you couldn't always ignore me? This is just the start.

I've got eyes everywhere, Marina.

XO,

Yours

"Rina!" Arlo yells and wraps his arms around me.

The tears flow freely and a chill sets in. The words replay in my mind even though he's dragging me out of the building.

What the hell is happening? And why me? I keep to myself; no one in town would do something like this, so how is this happening to me?

Arlo rubs his hands up and down my arms in an attempt to soothe me, saying words that I don't hear but that are presumably to try to calm me down.

"What the fuck happened?" a voice not belonging to Arlo yells, and I jolt away from Arlo's warmth.

Ledger is stomping away from his truck toward us, looking between us like we've both grown two heads. I don't miss the question in his eyes, but I don't have the brainpower to even consider talking to him about what's going on between me and Arlo.

"I just got here. I know as much as you," Arlo calmly tells him. "Let me get her inside the house. Can you call Oakley and see if he'll come down here too?" he asks—or rather orders—Ledger, and it's ridiculous considering the circumstances, but I have to hold back my laugh.

Arlo walks me back to the house using the walkway I have between the two, and once we're inside, he immediately cups my jaw in his hands.

"Are you okay?"

"Yes. No. I have no fucking clue. My whole workshop, Arlo." My bottom lip trembles as images flash through my head.

"I know. I'll figure it out, okay? I'll make it all okay." It's not something he can promise. I know that as sure as the sun will rise tomorrow, but damn, I want to believe him.

I think I nod as his thumbs wipe the tears from my cheeks. "Can you stay here, go take a bath or just cuddle up in bed? I need to really look through everything, and it's probably going to take me a while. I'll check in periodically, though."

I nod again, wishing he could just stay with me, but I'm abundantly thankful that he knows what to do in this situation because I'm so lost.

Nodding—God, I feel like all I'm doing is nodding—I step back, letting my arms hang lifelessly as he presses a kiss to my forehead and walks out the door.

I somehow find my way back to my bedroom, where I proceed to crumble, crying every tear I've fought against the last decade and finally falling asleep somewhere along the way.

CHAPTER TWENTY-FOUR
ARLO

Never in my life have I been more scared than getting a call from Rina in the middle of the night, sobbing so much I could barely understand her.

Thank God for all the years in the Marines. My work brain kicked in, and I immediately went to her. The fact that my wife was basically traumatized needed to be put on the back burner as much as I fucking hated it. At least I got a second alone with her to make sure she was okay. I know I'll be checking on her throughout the night because you couldn't bind me tight enough to stay away.

When I return to the workshop, Ledger's looking at me like he's trying to solve a crossword puzzle.

"What—"

"Not now, Ledge, please," I all but beg. Telling a guy who used to be like a brother to me, whom I cut out of my life along with everyone else, that I not only married his sister in secret but picked things back up fifteen years later is absolutely not something I want to get into right now. My concern is Rina and the fucker who did this. Everything else can wait.

He holds his hands up, but I don't miss the flash of anger. It's something I'll have to deal with eventually, but not right now.

"

I walk gingerly around the space, careful not to touch anything yet and look for anything obvious: a shirt, candy wrapper, anything that the asshole could have left.

"Holy shit." Oakley's voice startles me enough. I have to steady myself on the wall to my side.

"It's bad," I confirm.

"She slept through all of this?" He looks around, cringing every time he sees a pile of basically scrap wood now.

His concern is something I immediately thought of and already have a plan for. I won't let her work out here without protection again.

"Apparently. I don't know when exactly she woke up, but when she came in, whoever did this was already gone." My head flashes to the fact Rina was dressed in a tank top and boy shorts when she came running in here, completely unprotected and exposed. My fists clench so hard my knuckles crack before I give my head a small shake to focus on the task at hand.

"Hey, man, thanks for calling me in. I think Arlo and I have it if you want to head home. We'll keep you updated on anything we find out." Oakley turns to Ledger, and I'm more than happy he took the lead on that one because if I would have had to do it, I have a feeling a lot of information about Rina and me would come bubbling to the surface.

"I'd rather stay and help." Ledger doesn't concede.

"Seriously, we need to take pictures, look at the scene, all the police work, you know? It's going to take all night too, so no reason for us all to be here and get no sleep." Oakley says it casually, but my skin is itching.

Ledger looks between the two of us, but I look toward the ground. I can't be positive that my face doesn't give me completely away with how I feel about his sister, and although we aren't hiding things anymore, this is not the time to get into it with her big brother and my teenage best friend.

"Okay, I guess." He still looks confused, but maybe the cop card worked. "Arlo, thanks for texting me on the way. I think Ainsley and I have a pretty mellow day tomorrow, so call me if anything else happens. I mean it." His serious tone leaves me feeling like an awkward teen again, afraid to upset my friend. But he breezes out just as fast as he came.

A throat clears, and I turn my attention to Oakley, who has a shit-eating grin on his face.

"He know about you and Rina yet?"

"I'm guessing no because I don't have a black eye. Thanks for sending him home."

"You're so fucked." He chuckles. "Okay, what do we know so far?" He moves on, and I choose not to address his words. I'm more fucked than he knows considering the woman of the hour is still technically my wife.

"Not a lot so far. There's a note on the desk over there, but I haven't found anything else." The note I briefly got to read as I was pulling Rina out of the workshop turns my veins into fire. A new level of anger hits me hard, and all I want to do is strangle whomever this asshole is. I watch Oakley walk over to the desk, read the note, and jolt back as he does.

"Jesus. A stalker?" He looks at me with his eyebrows raised so high they're almost in his hairline.

"My best guess." I grind my teeth. "She hasn't told me anything about a stalker, so I'm not sure if this is the first time or if he's escalated."

"If this is his first contact, we need to figure this out ASAP because I don't want to know what his escalation looks like."

"Agreed. I'm going to take pictures, and then we can start going through everything if that's okay with you?" I ask before I realize he probably needs sleep if he's opening up Grind Time in a few hours. "Or I can take handle it, so you can sleep before opening."

"Nah, Willow's going to open, so I can hang out as long as needed."

"Thanks, man." I get everything photographed within fifteen minutes, and then my skin starts to itch. "I'm going to go check on Rina, then I'll be back and start clean-up." Oakley nods but doesn't look up from the pile he's shifting through.

I race up to the house and see she isn't in the living room before heading to the bedroom. Rina curled up in the bed, tear tracks still fresh on her cheeks as she breathes softly, makes my heart hurt. I'm glad she's finally asleep, but seeing her breakdown was so fucking hard for me. I'm torn between taking care of her and figuring out what the hell is going on with this stalker situation. I knew handling the workshop would be better in the long run, but all I wanted to do was hold her all night long. Take away her fears, and prove to her that I would be here for her and take care of any shit that pops up in her life.

Kneeling on the floor next to her, I softly run my fingertips over her temple, down her cheek, and across her lips. I lean forward, pressing a kiss so gently that she doesn't feel it to her forehead before pulling back an inch.

"I'll fix this, Emmerdeur. I'll make sure you're always safe and taken care of," I whisper before slowly getting off the floor and getting back to the workshop.

Oakley and I made good progress into the early hours of the morning. By the time we called it, we'd gotten most of the space cleared and all the destroyed wood thrown out. I didn't even have the energy to drive home; instead, I crashed on Rina's couch, hoping I wouldn't scare the shit out of her when she eventually woke up.

It's where I find myself currently stretching after being woken up by the smell of coffee.

"Coffee?" Rina's voice pulls me out of my sleep haze.

"Please." She places a Grind Time mug on the table in front of me, and I smirk. "Steal this one?" I ask as I take a sip.

"I would never," she gasps, with her hand over her chest in faux indignation. Dropping her hands, she chuckles. "I took it after I asked Oakley, thank you very much. Even offered to pay, but he turned me down."

A genuine smile graces my face, one I haven't felt since this whole thing started, but it drops just as fast.

"Are you okay?" I ask.

She sighs in response, and I put my coffee down and motion her over to me. Once she's close enough to touch, I pull her into my lap. I realize she's in nothing but a tank top and boy shorts, and I'm in only my boxers, but I'm determined to not let my dick run the show right now.

"I-I have no idea, honestly." She sinks into me.

"Is this the first time something like this has happened?" I want to be gentle and not push her, but I also need answers.

The tension in her body is instant, and I know the answer before she opens her mouth.

"I've been getting texts..."

"Rina," I scold before reeling myself back in. "Why didn't you tell me?" I try so hard to soften my tone, but I know I fail.

"I don't need to tell you everything, Arlo. Hell, we just started" —she gestures between the two of us— "whatever this is. And it seemed harmless. I just blocked the texts and moved on."

"Texts, as in multiple?" Definitely having a hard time staying level-headed and not freaking the fuck out right now.

She sighs and leans into me. "Look, I was going to tell you if whoever this is had texted me again, but it has been radio silence for a couple of weeks, so I thought I was in the clear. The texts weren't anything super crazy, but they were worrisome. I promise I was going to bring it to you with the next contact."

I rub my hand up her back as she talks, hoping the sheer anger and fear I'm feeling right now aren't translating into my movements. She doesn't need to know how much this is affecting me. I need to take care of this, take care of her, and not let my emotions get in the way.

But they will always be in the way because she's the love of your life. There's no changing that.

Well, I need to try to stay rational because I won't be any help to her if I don't.

"Do you still have the texts?" I ask.

"I deleted them and blocked the number, but I took screenshots," she says weakly.

"Good, that's really good, Emmerdeur," I whisper into her hair. "Can you send those to me?" She nods, sinking further into my hold.

"Who would do something like this?" Her voice has a slight tremor in it, and I know right this second I'll do anything to make her feel safe again.

"I have no clue, but I'll figure it out, okay? I think it's a good idea to just stay in today, email your clients and tell them about the delay, and then regroup and start fresh tomorrow. Take the day to just be fucking pissed, and then we'll get you back on track. I'll handle everything else, okay?"

"Okay. Can we just sit here for a few minutes before I tackle all of that?" She sounds exhausted, and I wish there was more that I could do, but this will have to be enough for now.

"Of course. We can stay here as long as you want." She snuggles into me more, and I pull the blanket I slept with over us both.

This feels like the calm before the storm, and I'm determined to weather it with her.

An hour later, I've gotten Rina settled back in bed, with her laptop and a shit-ton of snacks. My goal is to keep her there through the day so I can get some work done without her knowing or interfering.

Oakley texted me not too long ago and said he did as much clean-up as he could before Willow texted him for the morning rush at Grind Time.

Honestly, I'm thankful he showed up at the drop of a hat and that he stuck around for clean-up. It saves me some hours that I'll need to get everything else set up.

Now, I may not know exactly what Rina needs in her workshop, but I took pictures of the wreckage, so I'm hoping the lumber yard in Rosedale can help me piecemeal everything together.

The guy at the yard was pretty helpful overall. I showed him the pictures, gave him a generalized version of why I needed to replace everything, and he seemed cool with that. He seemed to know Rina well because he asked if she was okay without me telling him it was her workshop. My jealousy reared up instantly before I remembered he probably has delivered to her before.

This whole damn situation has me more on edge than I like, and I'll own the fact that I looked at him like a suspect for a minute longer than I probably needed to. That's not to say I won't be looking into him just to be sure later.

When I got back to Rina's house, she was sound asleep again in bed. Her exhaustion won over her need to feel useful, and I was grateful for it. The time it gave me allowed me to clear out the rest of the now scrap wood and bring in all the new boards I got. I attempted to organize it all how she had it, but I know I fucked a bunch of things up. She's going to be pissed as hell at me for taking the initiative. She'll focus on the money, attempt to pay me back because that's just who she is.

I'm not taking the bait, though. I've saved, been frugal as hell since we got married, and if I'm able to put a smile back on her face, I'd spend it ten times over. I have never seen her more broken, and I want to do everything in my power to ensure it never happens again.

The only thing I can't do, much to my annoyance, is build any of her pieces.

"Umm…" My head whips around at the small voice.

"Hey. I didn't know you were up." I internally cringe, knowing I need to explain what she's seeing but coming up empty-handed.

"How?"

I look around and try to see it from her eyes. It looks like nothing happened. No broken glass, no shards of wood, and no tools out of place. You'd never know a crime took place here. I even managed to find her a new desk to put in the corner.

"I…" I suddenly don't know how to explain all of this. Sure, helping with clean-up and getting things set back up is a natural step, but taking it upon myself to do it all before she even stepped foot back in here was probably a little extreme, even for me.

Before I can register her movements, her body slams into mine. Legs tangle around my waist as her arms wrap around my shoulders.

Home. This is exactly where I'm supposed to be.

"Thank you," she breathes into my neck.

"I couldn't rebuild anything, although I did think about it."

"Shut up. I can only take so much hotness, and it's wildly attractive you even thought about doing all of this, let alone actually accomplished it."

I chuckle into her neck as I hold her close to me.

"I'll try to be less attractive, then. Sorry."

"No, you're not." She laughs.

"You're right, I'm not. I had to do something, and this was the only thing I really could do." My tone shifts to reflect the seriousness of the situation. We could beat around the bush and act like nothing happened since it looks like nothing happened, but we both know that's not realistic.

I gently place her down on her feet and press a kiss to her cheek.

"Well, I told all my clients it would take me a month to get back on track, and this exponentially speeds up that timeline. Do you want to see if Willow will bring us some food and talk?" she asks as she pulls back from me.

"Sounds perfect."

CHAPTER TWENTY-FIVE
RINA

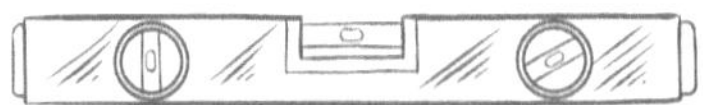

Willow drops off paninis within twenty minutes, and I'm happy she brought extra because I eat my weight in them, realizing I haven't eaten at all today.

I think I'm still a little in shock that Arlo fixed my entire workshop in less than a day while I was freaking out, emailing customers, and sleeping. I may still be in shock that the place got trashed in the first place.

I wouldn't have believed the mysterious texter was the same person who did this if not for the creepy-as-hell note left behind.

The sensation of whiplash feels like an apt description for the latest day of my life. Whatever good Arlo has brought into my life currently feels like it's being quickly ripped out from underneath me by this sleazeball. It's one thing to send anonymous texts but another entirely to destroy someone's property because of some misguided thoughts of ownership. For God's sake, what fucking century are we in anyway?

"You want to talk about it?" Arlo asks as we finish our food.

"Not really, but hiding from things has never really solved anything." I wince as I hear the words I said back, not realizing I just inadvertently called out Arlo. "That wasn't directed at you," I add quickly.

"I know, but you're also not wrong. I looked over everything you sent me, and I'm really struggling with the fact you didn't think to come to me about it, regardless of where we stand together. This is something serious that you should have taken to the police, to me, not brushed aside because you thought it was harmless." He's getting worked up; I can tell by the vein slightly popping in his neck.

"As I already explained, *Sheriff Arlo,* I blocked it and moved on. They didn't attempt to contact me again, and I wasn't worried. I clearly should have been, but I didn't think it would escalate to..." I gesture over to the workshop, and my head fills with images of my work demolished. Everything I've built and worked so damn hard on gone in an instant, and the tears rush out once again.

"Shit, I'm sorry. I'm not trying to lecture you." He scoots over next to me and pulls me into him. "I have never been as scared as I was when I picked up that phone. I would smash into ten more trees, fuck up my back twenty times over, rather than hear you sobbing on the phone again." His words are soft, but his meaning is loud, and it shakes me to my core.

My shoulders shake, and I can barely keep another breakdown at bay. I haven't cried this much in fifteen years, and I'm beyond over it. I know a massive migraine is waiting for me once the dust settles, but that's a problem for later.

"Please don't cry anymore. I promise I'll handle it all. I'll find this asshole; I'll take care of him and make sure he never does this to you or any other person again." The anger in his voice shocks me. As the sheriff, I fully expect him to arrest someone like this if he gets enough evidence and all that, but this feels different. This is specific to me.

I shift so I can run my hand along his back, and for once he doesn't stiffen. "Why are you so worked up about this? We can figure out who it is, and then you do your police thing and arrest him. Nothing more, nothing less. This overprotective act is a bit much, even for you," I joke.

He looks at me then, staring deep into my eyes like he's seeing into my soul. I'm so lost in his gaze I almost miss what he says in his whispered tone.

"It's different because you're my wife, and I need to protect you."

I jolt back before stumbling to stand.

"What did you just say?"

The pain I see in his eyes has my heart cracking in two. I don't understand what this means, and my confusion must be written all over my face.

"Sit. Let me explain please," he pleads.

"I'll stand. Talk," I clip.

"Fuck." He runs his hand over his buzzed head. "This is not how I wanted you to find out."

"Find out what?!" I'm bordering on hysterics, and I can't do anything to stop it. He can't mean what he said, right? I signed the fucking papers. Sure, he tattooed the heart I signed the note with on his skin, but that doesn't mean we're married still … right?

"I never filed the papers." It's so quiet, yet it's as loud as a train whistle.

"You *what*? You have two minutes to explain, so talk fast." I'm losing every ounce of my rational brain at an alarming rate, and I know I need the full story before I completely blow up on him, but I'm so close to kicking him out of my house forever, regardless of what he says.

"When you sent the papers back, I knew it was what was best for you, but I second-guessed it every minute. It was like I knew letting go was the right thing, but I just … couldn't do it. And I know that's so fucked up, but I couldn't force myself to submit them, even though I knew it was wrong." He sounds ashamed, but it does nothing to soothe my shattered heart.

Physical pain radiates from the stupid, gullible organ deep within my chest. At the moment, I don't know what to trust, but I do know I need him out of my house. I can't think about anything logical with him sitting nearby.

"Get out," the strangely calm voice I realize is mine says.

"Rina…"

"Get out Arlo. Don't come back unless you are explicitly invited." I turn on my heel, walk up to my house, then to my bedroom, and slam the door before heading to the bathroom. Turning on the shower, I walk in fully clothed. Collapsing on the floor in a mess of tears and confusion, I sit, soaking wet, until the water makes me shiver, forcing me out in order to warm back up.

Betrayed.

All I feel is the betrayal of Arlo's actions. It's been like this all night, and I can't even get out of bed now that it's morning.

The thought still ringing loud and clear in my head is, *How the fuck are we still married?*

It's a thought that I just can't wrap my head around.

A cherry on top of an already fucked-up sundae.

Turning over in bed, I check my phone to see it's ten in the morning, later than I've slept in far too many years. I also notice an influx of text notifications. A few from Arlo, which isn't altogether shocking but not something I want to deal with right now, and the rest from the family group chat.

I open it up to hopefully distract myself for a few minutes.

> **Whose house are we doing family dinner at tonight?**

> **I think I'm out tonight, guys, sorry. I tried to go for a little hike through the park, and I'm exhausted. I definitely overdid it.**

The mix of feeling so damn happy he got out of the house and heartbroken he didn't call any of us to help him is too much for my already heavily confused heart. I know this is a tremendous step, regardless of if I think it was right or wrong to go out by himself, and I need to count this as a huge win.

> **Look at you, getting out early and grabbing life by its balls.**

I try to go for my usual sarcasm in the hopes my siblings don't pick up on anything. I know, realistically, at dinner, I'm going to get grilled because there is no way the news of Arlo and me together at Sal's hasn't gotten around by then.

Lennox:

Yeah, it sounded good on principle, but now I'm paying for the lack of physical activity I've had in over a month.

Ledger:

No worries, if you change your mind, we can always bring the party to you. Just let us know.

Lennox:

Will do, thanks.

Willow:

Sorry, sorry! Got caught up writing a scene. Oakley and I will be there tonight. Lenny, awesome job! Proud of you! Now, get some sleep. We'll drop off a sandwich on the way to dinner.

I flip the phone over, glad everyone is taken care of because I need a minute to figure out what's in my head. The things I currently know are:

Arlo and I are technically still married.

I want to date Arlo.

I lost all my work in my workshop.

The trust I was starting to get back with Arlo feels completely broken.

And I have no idea where to go from here in my personal or professional life.

I don't think I've felt this lost since my parents died and Arlo broke my heart fifteen years ago, which isn't surprising. I assumed I wouldn't ever be put in a position like this again. That I would close myself off to this feeling, and I had, until Arlo broke that down too.

Fucking Arlo.

Who the fuck files for divorce, sends the papers, and then doesn't actually submit them? And doesn't once have a conversation with me about it? I mean, shit, even for how young we were, that's just appalling. I don't understand his reasoning—not that I really heard him out if he had more of an explanation—but I'm honestly not sure any clarification would help me come to terms with all of this.

The worst part of all of this is that I can't just pretend he doesn't exist again. I can't shove him back into that tiny little box of hatred because I know he's not going to leave me alone with this stalker situation. And I maybe started to *like* being around him again, and I don't know how to shut that off now that the spout is open.

What a mess.

Rolling over in bed, I punch the pillow a couple of times, trying to get my aggression out or get comfortable. Who knows at this point. But all it serves to do is remind me I can't bury myself in work today. Arlo told me he would let me know when he was done investigating, and as much as I want to ignore him just to be defiant, I know it's not the best course of action.

I figure I have two, maybe three options to kill time before family dinner. I could just head over to Ledger and Ainsley's early and spend the day there, but their overly lovey ways might make me lose my mind. I could lie here and wallow in my too many thoughts and nurse my migraine, which honestly sounds horrible. Or I could go hike through the park. Sam Houston National Park has acres of paths to get lost in and fresh air that might just allow me to figure out how to move forward with Arlo.

The fresh air felt refreshing.

But it didn't help my tumultuous thoughts at all. My hopes of clearing my head before family dinner were dashed as fast as they came, and now I'm on my way to Ledger's house, hoping I can keep my emotions under wraps.

"Rinaaaaaaaa," Ainsley drawls from a rocking chair on the porch as I climb out of my truck.

"Ainsleyyyyyy," I mimic.

"Ledger is forcing me not to work, even though we have a huge project coming up, and I'm bored. You should have come over earlier," she whines.

"You could have texted me if it was that dire," I titter as I sit in the rocker next to her.

"I got Ledger to keep me company." She winks, and I can't hold back the gag.

"Please don't... We had a deal—no sex talk about my brother." I groan.

Her giggle sounds out around me, and I have to laugh with her.

We talk about how our weeks have been, and before we know it, Willow and Oakley are pulling up, signaling the start of family dinner.

"How'd Lenny look?" I ask Oakley as we follow Ainsley inside.

"Tired but good, honestly. He got a little sun on his face, and it seemed really good for him. He's just annoyed he's so out of shape."

"Yeah, slowing down is his nightmare, so I'm sure he's grumpy as shit."

"Don't let him hear you say that." He chuckles.

"Whose favorite are you making?" Willow asks Ledger once we're all in the kitchen.

"Burgers," he yells over his shoulder as he takes a plate out to the back patio to the grill.

Yes, my favorite. I almost fist bump but choose to play it cool. After the last couple of days, something as simple as this is bumping my spirits exponentially.

It takes no time to cook dinner while we're all talking about nothing of consequence. Ledger and Oakley keep giving me looks like they are checking to make sure I'm okay, and it's skyrocketing my blood pressure. I've been able to push my thoughts on the stalker to the side a little, thanks to Arlo's bombshell confession, and now their concerned looks are bringing it to the forefront of my mind.

Dinner starts off well enough. We go around saying what our favorite thing about the week was, but when it's my turn, it all goes downhill.

"My favorite thing this week is..." I think and try to come up with something, but my brain is blank. All I can think about is everything that went wrong. "My favorite thing is..." I try again, but the pressure behind my eyes is signaling that I'm two seconds away from another breakdown.

"Oh shit," I distantly hear Ainsley say, and before I realize what's happening, she and Willow are wrapped around me as I cry over my burger.

"I'm ruining family dinner!" I wail because, somehow, it feels like just another blow.

"You are not. You've had a lot happen this week, and it's completely acceptable to still be feeling all of that," Willow says.

I take a couple of deep breaths in an attempt to calm myself down, and everyone takes it as a hint to finish dinner. I barely hear the rest of the conversation as we finish dinner, but once the plates are cleared and everyone has a drink in hand, all attention turns back to me.

"So... You and Arlo?" Ledger asks in a tone I can quite decipher.

Sighing, I put my drink down, knowing this is a conversation that needs to happen but one I'm not ready for.

"Me and Arlo."

"I thought you hated each other," he continues like me being uncomfortable doesn't matter.

I glance at Ainsley, and she nods in encouragement.

"Arlo and I dated before he went to the Marines, and then when he came home from basic training, we got married." The silence that greets me suddenly blows up in loud voices trying to talk over each other.

I hold up my hand for them to stop. "I'll tell you guys everything, but you have to shut up. I can't handle the million questions right now. My head is pounding." Ledger's jaw clenches, but he nods as everyone else follows suit.

I tell them about our history and how we have managed to reconnect, if that's what we want to call it, but I keep the fact we're still married to myself. I feel like I need a better handle on it before I start talking about it.

"I'm not saying this all makes perfect sense, buttttt this makes perfect sense," Willow says as she smirks over at Oakley.

"Why do you say that?" I ask.

"Because there's no way you hate someone as much as you hated Arlo without a huge reason, and I'd say getting dumped without an explanation after our parents died is the best kind of reason. Although, I always thought there was some tension there," Willow says.

I roll my eyes. "You're delusional."

"Am I, though? Are you not currently hooking up with your ex-husband?" She giggles. "God, that's weird to say."

I could tell her it's weirder because he's still my husband, but I refrain.

"Not currently, no." I go for some form of the truth. I don't know what the future holds for Arlo and me, but I do know we won't be hooking up anytime soon.

"And what's going on with this stalker? Arlo texted Ledger about a break-in, and now it's a stalker?" Ainsley asks, hurt poking through her words. She's my best friend, and it sure seems like I've hidden a lot from her.

"I don't really know what's going on with that. I've gotten a few texts that were creepy, but I didn't think much of them. Then he trashed my workshop and left a note on my desk, leading Arlo to think it's all connected."

"It is. Did you give Arlo all the texts? It'll help him try to figure out a connection. We were talking earlier about how to trace some leads," Oakley adds.

"Yes, I gave him everything," I snark. I almost feel bad, but everyone is acting like I'm a child and it's pissing me off.

"Good, I'll get with him later, then."

Rolling my eyes again, I pick up my drink and down half of the can in one go.

"Are you okay?" Ainsley asks.

I look around at most of my family looking at me with concern, and it breaks me once more.

"No, I don't think I am," I hiccup.

Willow and Ainsley surround me once more before sitting on either side of me as I attempt to work through my thoughts.

Oakley looks on awkwardly and Ledger just looks pissed, but I'm more worried that I'll never be able to figure out how to move forward. These mental block and insane emotions are wreaking havoc on my life.

"If there was nothing else going on, what do you want with Arlo? Is this something you want to continue to explore?" Ainsley asks.

Instead of over-analyzing it to death, I say the first thing that comes to my mind.

"Yes."

As soon as the word is out there, I know it's the truth. It doesn't mean we don't have a ton to work through, or that I forgive him for not sending in the divorce papers and lying to me this entire time. But it does mean I think it's worth trying to work through. It's worth putting in the work because I'm never as happy as I am with Arlo Steel.

I look around at my siblings and their partners, and realize the dream of finding what they have never really went away. I have a chance to get that again with Arlo, and I think I'd hate myself if I didn't try. If we make it through the storm, maybe I can have everything I've always wanted.

My phone dings, distracting me, and I check it, expecting another text from Arlo.

Unknown:

I'll be seeing you soon, Marina.

CHAPTER TWENTY-SIX
ARLO

A week and a half.

That's how long it's been since Rina kicked me out of her house. I can't even blame her; I deserved a hell of a lot worse. That's not to say I've just left her alone. I've done the exact opposite, actually. Trading sleep for naps so I can park my ass in front of her house at night and keep watch. Leaving Audrey in charge of our office while I go Sherlock Holmes on the texts Rina's sent me from the stalker.

I haven't gotten anywhere, though, and it's pissing me off.

This can't be a case of wait and see. I need to be proactive.

Today, however, I'm on my way to Rosedale and feel more anxiety over it than I want. It's time to get results of my scans and possibly another round of shots, depending on those results. Overall, I'm feeling better, but the pain isn't completely gone.

As I walk into the medical center, all I can think is how much I wish Rina was here with me. Her presence calms me, and I could use that right now. It's not that I think anything bad is going to come back from the scan; it's just that I've rarely had good news at the doctor's, and that fear is a hard habit to break.

It takes them no time to call me back before I'm waiting in a room, nervous as hell.

"Good afternoon, Arlo. How are you today?" Dr. Vincent asks as he walks in.

"Doing okay. How are you?"

"Really good, especially after seeing these results."

My heart rate rises. Logically, I know that's a good thing, but it doesn't stop the anxiety from hitting me full force. Now, I wish more than ever that Rina was here with me.

"It looks like things are progressing the way we want them to. The inflammation has gone down a lot, and the pressure on the areas surrounding your fusions looks like it's slowly healing, right along the timeline I would expect. So, I think we should stay the course, do a total of six months of treatment and reassess, but if things improve the way they are, we should be able to be done with the injections for a while. So, three more treatments after today?"

I nod, a little dazed that everything is working the way it should.

"It's a lot to take in. I apologize. How are you feeling about all of this?" he asks, sensing my anxiety.

"Honestly, I feel great about it, but it's just hard to believe. This has been such a long-ass process it's strange that things are finally working, you know?"

"Totally understand that. I'm glad you took a chance and came in, though. You aren't always forced to stay in pain, and now you can see the results of coming in." He's not condescending; he's just saying exactly how my thought process went. Getting out of this mindset that you're forced to deal with pain is hard to shift from, but I'm glad I did.

"I appreciate you working with me," I tell him. This has changed my life more than I thought it would, and I'll forever be grateful to Dr. Vincent because of it.

"Anytime. Now, injection today. I'll have the nurse come in and do all the good blood draws and such, and then we'll pull the stem cells and inject them again. You should be out of here in an hour if we're lucky. Any other questions for me?"

"None that I can think of." I'm still a little shell-shocked things are this easy.

"Alright, well, I'll send the nurse in, and I'll see you in a little bit."

The rest of the appointment goes as it usually does, and before I know it, I'm walking back out to my truck.

As I climb in, my phone pings with a text, so I pull it out and see it's from Oakley.

> Rina texted me. She got another message from the stalker.

He forwards her message, and it stabs me in the chest. *She texted Oakley, not me.*

> Any new leads? I've got nothing, but I'll buckle down today when I get back and see if I can figure out where the messages are coming from at least. I have a therapy appointment in a few, but after that, I'm on it.

> I'm already at your office, trying to look stuff up.

> And you just happen to know the login to my computer?

Oakley:

> … Arlo … it's not hard to figure out…

I curse under my breath. Of course, all my passwords have Rina in them, and I'm sure it wasn't hard to narrow down from there. Stupid ex-U.S. Marshal. He's too good at his damn job.

Me:

> We don't talk about it … ever. Did you find anything?

Oakley:

> The phone number pings in Rosedale, but that's all I've got. That doesn't really narrow things down all that much.

Me:

> It's more than we had. Can you write all of that down and leave it on my desk? I'll stop by after therapy and see what I can connect, if anything.

Oakley:

> Sounds good. Sorry I didn't get more information, but I promised I'd take Willow out tonight and I can't cancel.

Me:

> No worries. I'll keep you updated if I find anything.

The drive home is long, and my thoughts bounce between the progress with my back, my therapy session, and all things Rina. I know I need to give her time, but fuck if it's not the hardest thing I've done in a long while. I'd do therapy every single day over not talking to Rina again.

The problem is, she has every right to never speak to me again. I beyond messed up, and not only was it a shock to her system, but she had just started to trust me again and I blew that all to hell too. I seem to be good at doing that.

I have to remember things won't change in an instant. I'm working toward being the best man for Rina, but that doesn't guarantee I get her in the end. It doesn't make this journey any less important; it just adds a certain level of stress to my shoulders. A need to figure out how to make things right has definitely taken over my brain power over the last week, but now that the stalker has reached out again, that needs to shift too.

Never has Bluebell Falls been as busy and crime-riddled as it has in the last few months. I don't know what the fuck is happening, but I will end it. This doesn't happen on my watch. Tennison was a special case, not something many people see in their lifetime, let alone in their town, so I don't put that on my shoulders.

This shit with Rina, though? One hundred percent my responsibility. No one should feel unsafe here. Hell, we haven't had a break-in since I took over as sheriff, and the fact that it happened to Rina kills me on a level I don't know how to move on from. I guess that's why it's a good thing I go to therapy now.

I finally get home, get my laptop set up, and dial my therapist.

"Good afternoon, Arlo. How's it going today?"

"Hey, Doc. It's going." Dr. Ames pulls zero punches, and my very generic answer doesn't go unnoticed.

"You want to talk about it?"

I sigh, knowing it's better to just get it off my chest than keep it bottled up. "I just got home from the back doctor and things are going well there, so that's positive. But when I was leaving, I got a text about some shit happening in town that I need to put an end to." I keep it vague, knowing I'll eventually get all the information out, even if he drags it out of me.

"Put an end to how? Violently?" He's more curious than accusing.

If it comes to that. "No, nothing like that. There's a stalker bothering one of the women here, and I don't like how it's escalating."

"That's a hard one to deal with, no doubt. You said someone had told you about this? Do you have help finally?"

I chuckle. "Kind of. It's more of an as needed basis."

"Well, that's still good progress. Takes a little of load off your shoulders."

"That's true. It's Oakley," I decide to tell him, although I'm not sure why. It's not like he'll share deep, dark secrets from their therapy sessions, but I also want him to see how seriously I'm taking things and that Oakley has played a large part in helping me do that.

"Ah, that makes sense. He's a good guy, smart as hell."

"Bluebell Falls is lucky he decided to hide away and then stay. He's been a tremendous help, and he doesn't even realize it."

"Do you feel as though you don't contribute enough to the town?"

"No, why do you ask?" A knee-jerk reaction, no doubt.

"I've never heard you talk about your job the way you just talked about Oakley helping out. He's not even a full employee, and yet you don't give yourself the same curtesy."

I hum, thinking about his words.

"He caught Tennison—well technically, Willow did, but Oakley did a large bulk of the work. I just got Lennox out when we busted in. I didn't stay and help out. I didn't prevent Lennox from being taken."

"You feel you failed."

"Yes," I whisper.

"Remind me of what the doctor told you about Lennox and how fast you got him to the hospital."

I know where he's going with this, and I understand his point, but it doesn't lessen the useless feeling in my chest.

"He said if I had gotten him there ten minutes later, he would have lost too much blood. If I waited for an ambulance, he would have died." The words are still so hard to say. I don't even think most of the Huttons know that, but I do, and it doesn't bring me any comfort to what happened.

"And why does that mean anything less than what Oakley and Willow did?"

"In theory, it doesn't."

"But it does to you. Why?"

"Because I was supposed to do more, be better."

"With the Tennison case or your career?" he asks, so very astutely.

"Hit the nail on the head, Doc."

"What made you want to come to therapy? Don't give me a canned answer. Really think about your reasons."

I do as told, and I decide it's time to stop hiding behind whatever life I thought I should have and face the one I do.

"Rina. There's a lot that we've already talked about, us getting married young and everything that I did after her parents died. After the Tennison case, I ran into her in a quiet room at the hospital. I was looking for a place to wallow, to feel like the failure I was, and instead I found Rina breaking down. I just reacted, needed to be her comfort, and I didn't think about the consequences. We started hanging out." I cough into my hand, not wanting to say what hanging out actually looked like. "And I realized she's always been it for me. It didn't matter if she took me back or if she forgave me. What mattered was that I was the man she always thought I was. I never really took a hard look at what the injury cost me and how it made me feel. I just shoved it all down. Just like I did with everything else in my life, and she deserves better than that."

"*You* deserve better than that too, Arlo."

I nod, knowing he's right but still having a hard time getting over that feeling of failure.

"I'm trying. With this stalker shit, it's bringing up all the usual insecurities, and the fact it's Rina getting stalked has me acting like a damn fool around her."

"Rina is the one getting stalked?"

"Yeah. He trashed her workshop about a week ago. He's getting bold, and I don't like it. I'm scared I won't be able to catch him before he does something really drastic, though."

"I understand that. Even when you feel you've worked through a lot of your issues, that doesn't mean these doubts will just magically disappear. It's about finding coping mechanisms and leaning on people you trust to help you when you need them. Asking Oakley for help is a huge step for you," he observes.

"I know, but what if it's not enough?"

"I don't think for a minute you'd let anything happen to Rina. You may be working through how to move forward with your life after everything you've been through, but even I can see with what limited information you've told me that you'd protect her with your life. If you think about it, it's not so far off from your mission statement in the Marines," he contemplates.

I sit back on my couch and think about his words. Are my doubt and hesitation because it's Rina? Or do I feel this way because my injury dashed my dream of being career military? If I'm truthful with myself, which is the goal after all, I'd say it probably goes all the way back to my injury and not fulfilling my commitment to the Marines. If I go back further, not keeping my word, my vows, to Rina is probably the start of all this.

"How do I move past the doubt?" I ask softly.

"The short answer is you don't, really. The long answer is you learn to take things one step at a time and focus on the facts. You don't focus on the what-ifs or the possibility of something happening. You throw all your focus into what steps you need to take to accomplish what you need to. Lists are a great tool to stay on task. It's simple but effective."

"A list?" I ask skeptically.

"Look, it doesn't work for everything. It's more a tool to start using so your brain starts looking at things that way, so you're able to catastrophize less."

"Makes sense," I grumble.

"Listen, we're closing in on our session, but I want you to make a list every time your mind starts to wander when you have a task. It can be anything, checking your email, making the rounds through town. Just start the habit. If you need another session before our next one, you know you can always call me and I'll fit you in, okay?"

"Will do. Thanks, Doc. I'll see you next time." I shut my laptop, slumping back into my couch.

He always gives me a lot to think about, but for some reason, today feels more overwhelming than usual. Leaning forward, I grab the pen and paper I usually have out during therapy so I can write things down.

Opening a new page, I start a list before going back to the office.

Find the stalker.

I leave it blank before turning the page and starting another one.

Make things right with Rina.

CHAPTER TWENTY-SEVEN
RINA

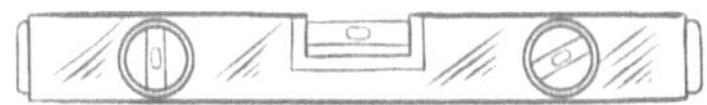

Was it a chickenshit move to text Oakley about the new message instead of Arlo? Absolutely. Even though I've told myself time and time again that I'll pull on my big girl pants and be a grown-up who can talk to Arlo without my feelings taking over, doing so is a completely different story.

I'm still so mad at him.

But I also think I'm ready to hear him out. I kicked him out before he could tell me anything past us still being married.

He gave me the all-clear to go back to work the day after the bombshell hit. Since then, I've done nothing but work and sleep. By the time I call it a day, I barely have the energy to shower and change before collapsing into bed. I know this isn't sustainable, though. Playing catch-up gave me the excuse to push everything I'm feeling to the side, and now that I'm on top of things, all I can do is think about what still being married to Arlo means.

I'm wrapping up the picnic tables, happy to have them complete and ready to be picked up once again.

I finish the stain on the kids' table and clean up before calling it a day and heading up to my house.

Something catches my eye, and I stop in my tracks when I see a box sitting at the side door. If this was a normal delivery, it would be at my front door. Everyone, including our mailman, knows to put things at my front door, not the side door.

Tipping my head back, I blow out a steady breath, preparing myself for what I know I have to do. Pulling out my phone, I snap a picture and then pull up my messages to Arlo.

Me:

Picture attached I found this when I finished up work. No one I know would drop off a package to the side door.

The Liar:

Go back to your workshop and lock the door. Don't come out until I get there and leave the package alone.

I roll my eyes at what I know is his stern tone, even through a text message.

Me:

Yes, Sheriff.

Shoving my phone in my pocket, I hurry back to my workshop. I lock everything up, double-checking the back door too, before settling at my desk. Taking a deep breath seems like the easiest thing to do to calm my nerves, and it works to an extent until I see the letter sitting in the middle of my desk.

My heart drops to my stomach, and my blood runs cold.

How was I so caught up in my thoughts that I missed someone lurking around? That they not only had time to leave a package by the side door but also a letter in here? What the fuck is happening?

I've locked up my shop, but please hurry.

I attach a picture of the untouched letter and send it to Arlo as I continue to freak out. He doesn't text me back—not that I expect him to, especially if he's driving. But what I don't expect is, no more than two minutes later, a pounding on my door that scares the shit out of me. A scream leaves me as Arlo's voice sounds through the barrier.

"It's me, Rina. Just me."

My forehead thumps on the desk as I catch my breath. "Jesus, I don't know how much more of this I can handle," I mutter before standing up and rushing to the door before Arlo breaks it down.

Unlocking the deadbolt, I rip the door open as he rushes in without preamble. He beelines it to my desk and grabs the envelope carefully, looking at it in every direction. Squeezing my hands together, I hope it'll help stop the shaking as I watch him analyze everything. He drops it back onto the desk, turning to me, and I can see him gearing up.

"How did you not see anyone?" His voice is loud, but it's the hint of fear I hear that stops me from yelling back at him.

"I just didn't, Arlo," I say softly.

I step up to him, wrap my arms around his waist, and lean into him. The air seems to release from him all at once as his arms come around me.

"What the fuck is going on?" he asks.

"I wish I knew. I don't know who is doing this or who I pissed off, but I don't want to live like this."

"You won't. I'll be by your side from now on."

I pull back from his hold. "No, you will not."

"Oh, hell yes, I will. I'm not letting you out of my sight."

"I don't need a babysitter, Arlo," I scoff.

His grip on me tightens. "I can't let anything happen to you, okay? Just … let me figure this out how I need to."

Sighing, I lean into him once again. We take a minute to let the adrenaline mellow out and for both of us to be a little more level-headed.

"Sorry," Arlo finally murmurs against the crown of my head.

"I get it. I'm just not good at accepting help, especially from someone I'm used to hating."

"Does that mean you don't hate me anymore?" he asks.

"It means we have some talking to do." I pull back and look up into his eyes. I still see the underlying fear, but I also see determination.

"Let me grab the stuff that was left, and then we'll head to the house." His sheriff voice is present, and it almost makes me laugh. Until I realize he wants me to go back into my house, and just the thought has my anxiety ramping up.

"Umm, do you think we can, maybe, go to your place?"

His head whips around after he grabs the letter, and his eyes soften as he looks at me.

"Of course. Let me grab the package and put it in my truck, and then we can head to my house." He grabs my hand and leads us out to the side door, before heading to his truck and carefully dropping the package off in the back. He opens the passenger door, lifting me up into the truck before buckling me in and shutting the door.

Once he climbs in the driver's side, I feel a little of my defiant self return. "I can get myself safely into a truck, you know."

"Not now, Marina. I need you safe, and I know you're just trying to get under my skin."

"Is it working?" I barely hold in my chuckle.

"Unfortunately." He sighs.

I slide my hand over the center console to take his hand in mine. His thumb grazes over mine as he pulls out of my driveway. We're both quiet as we make our way to his house. I'm trying to figure out exactly how I want things to go once we get there. I know we need to talk, but I hadn't planned on this psycho stalker encroaching on my time with Arlo. Or scaring me more than ever before.

Too soon, we pull into his driveway, and I'm no closer to knowing how I'm feeling than I was when he first showed up.

"I need to call Oakley and hand off this package. I'll meet you inside?" he asks.

"Sure." I jump on the chance for a few minutes alone. He opens the front door for me, and I try to walk inside, but he grabs me around my waist and presses a kiss to my temple.

"I'll be two minutes," he whispers.

As he goes to meet Oakley, I pace around his sparse living room. I know I want to talk to him about why we're still married, but this stalker situation is distracting me from that goal. I've racked my brain trying to figure out why me and what I did to make someone think this behavior is okay. I've come up empty at every turn, and now my only hope is that Arlo and Oakley can find this asshole before things get even worse.

Grabbing a blanket off the back of the couch, I kick off my shoes and curl up on the corner of his couch. The ivy chill I've felt since I saw the package has only deepened.

"Hey, Emmerdeur, you doing okay?" Arlo's soft voice reaches me.

"I—" I think about how I want to move forward with Arlo and brushing my feelings to the side won't help accomplish that. "I don't think so."

Arlo kicks his shoes off before picking me up off the couch and settling in my spot, placing me in his lap and wrapping his arms around me.

"Why me? What did I do?" I ask, even though I know he doesn't have an answer.

"You didn't do anything. I promise I'll work my ass off to find this guy and stop him from doing this again."

"I know, but you aren't a superhero, Arlo. You can't promise anything, especially when we have no idea who this guy is."

"Oh, Rina, you underestimate me." He chuckles.

"I'm serious." I pull back and look at him. "We have no clue who this is, and you can't make promises like that. And you can't be with me twenty-four seven. That's not feasible for anyone."

"You sure about that?"

"Yes! You have a job and a town to take care of! I have furniture to make and don't need a shadow for a just-in-case scenario here." I throw my hands up, trying to keep my thoughts logical.

"Rina... You are more important than anything," he says softly.

I look back and forth between his eyes, unsure of what to say or how I'm feeling about his statement.

"Am I?" It comes out without my consent. "If I'm so important, how did we land ourselves here?"

He sighs. "Do you want to a take a shower or bath? Get more comfortable for this conversation in bed?"

"We can go to the bedroom, but I'm not getting naked around you before we talk. We can't be trusted naked together." His booming laughter makes me join in.

"Fair enough. I'll let you borrow one of my shirts to sleep in."

"Who says I'm sleeping here?" I ask, but the look he gives me tells me I'm not fooling him. "Just sleeping, Arlo. Nothing more."

"Whatever you say, Marina." His smile is infectious, and I kind of want to punch him. Even after all these years of distance, all these years of anger, he still somehow knows me better than anyone.

He stands up with me still in his hold, and I smack his shoulder. "Are you kidding me? You're going to hurt your back!" I yell at him.

"My back is fine." He continues to walk to the bedroom, setting me down next to his dresser before pulling out an old Marines shirt and tossing it at me.

"You can't just toss me around and throw shirts at me and expect me to just go along with everything." My need to be rebellious, to not cave too quickly to him overrules any logic.

"Just trying to get you comfortable," he says, so nonchalantly it grates on my nerves.

"Liar," I snip as I snag the shirt and head to the bathroom.

"Where are you going?" he calls out.

"To the bathroom to change," I say over my shoulder.

"Seriously? Like I haven't seen you naked?" His confusion is kind of adorable, but I refuse to focus on that.

"We need to talk. Seeing me naked will distract you, and I need you to focus."

"What makes you think I won't think about you naked either way?"

"You're ridiculous."

"And you're gorgeous." He shrugs.

"Arlo!"

"Rina!"

I laugh at his response. "I'm changing," I say before walking into the bathroom and shutting the door. Leaning against the door, my chief concern is that he'll keep this playfulness and make me forget that we have a very real conversation to have.

I strip out of my jeans and tank top, tossing on the oversized shit, and leave my legs bare. Staring at myself in the mirror, I vow to myself to figure out where we stand before things go further between us. Sex comes easily, but if I really want to move forward with him, then a long, hard talk is in order first.

Cautiously opening the door, I peek out and see him in basketball shorts, lying on top of the bed. I really wish he wasn't so damn hot or that the tattoo on his ribcage wasn't a glaring sign that we were never quite done with each other.

It's time to grow up and deal with the past.

As I softly walk to the bed, his eyes follow my every step. Climbing into the bed, I quickly get under the covers to help with the temptation that is Arlo.

Turning toward him, I tuck one hand under my head as the other trails over his tattoo.

I take a deep breath and ask the question that's been bothering me for almost two weeks.

"Why didn't you sign the papers?" I can hear the shakiness in my voice, the fear that the answer will be too much for me to handle.

His heavy exhale draws my attention, and I watch as he slides down and mimics my pose, facing me.

"Logically, I knew it was the right decision. I saw so many guys die on missions, men who had families and kids. When one of my closest friends died, I visited his wife while I was on leave. Seeing her devastation was something I never wanted for you. At the time, it felt ... merciful. Not saddling you with the life of being married to a Marine who may not come back from a mission or might not come back the same man. We were so young..." He trails off, his voice betraying the pain caused by his decisions.

"Did it ever cross your mind to just talk to me?" The pressure of unshed tears and a tightening throat send me right back down the depressive spiral from all those years ago. I've asked this question what feels like a million times, and somehow, I still don't understand it.

"This is where I sound like an asshole, but no. I knew you would never agree, and I didn't think you understood how tragic things could be."

"So why go through the trouble of sending papers? At the same time my parents died, I might add, and then not actually filing them? I still don't understand any of this." I'm not trying to guilt-trip him, but I do want him to understand how broken I was. Hell, probably still am because of his solo decision.

"When you sent them back, it was like my heart smashed in my chest. The pieces were just carnage left behind in my body. And I know that doesn't make sense, but I couldn't even look at them for weeks. Every time I tried, it stole my breath and I started to panic. It took me a few months to look through them, and that's when I found your note." His hand goes to his ribs, and the pain in his eyes almost makes me forgive him, but we both need to work through this if we're to move forward.

"When did you decide you weren't going to file them?"

"I honestly don't know. I said I would do it the next time I was on leave, and then I would put it off and just repeat the process, and then I got hurt and it got brushed to the side while I figured out how to recover and deal with a life outside of the Marines."

"Can I just spew my thoughts, even if they're shitty and don't make sense?" I ask, knowing I have many, many thoughts that I need to get out.

"Please."

"God, I don't even know where to start. I was pissed as fuck when you told me we were still married. It was such a shock that I didn't even know how to act. When I got home, this weird sense of relief hit, and that just made me angrier. You crushed me, plain and simple. I feel like I'm lucky everything with my parents happened at the same time because no one questioned why I was so broken, and that's super shitty to say, but I didn't want to explain anything to do with us to anyone.

"I was over you. I thought I was over you..." I feel wetness on my cheeks, but I don't stop because I need to get this out. "But it still hurts so fucking much. And you're the asshole who never left my heart, and I'm so mad at you for that. I was so mad when you moved back here. It was easier to be angry at you than to analyze how I actually felt when you came back. I honestly don't know if I can move past all of this, but I really want to. And that makes me even more annoyed with myself because I shouldn't want you still, but I do." I heave out a breath and look over at him.

"I'm so sorry I put you through all of that. And I know I don't deserve another chance with you, but fuck, I want one, Emmerdeur. It's always been you; it will only ever be you. If it takes you years to forgive me, I'll be here waiting for you."

"You're not allowed to say things like that." I let out a watery chuckle.

His hand reaches up, fingers grazing my cheeks to wipe away the tears.

"I know I did everything wrong with you, with us, but I'm trying to be better, to be someone worthy of you every single day. Even if at the end of the day you decide I'm not what you want, I'll continue to try to be worthy of you."

A make-or-break moment. That's what this feels like. And I want to make it.

Grabbing the hand that's on my cheek, I pull it away and kiss his palm, subtly telling him I'm ready to move past all the heartache.

CHAPTER TWENTY-EIGHT
ARLO

I don't know how I got this lucky, but I'm not second-guessing a thing. That's not to say we're completely good. I know we still have a lot to work on, but she's taking a chance again. It's better than I could have hoped for. The merry-go-round we've been on finally feels like it's coming to a stop.

I lean forward, resting my forehead on hers.

"Thank you," I whisper before pressing my lips to hers. An overwhelming feeling of rightness surrounds me. This is where I'm supposed to be, with Rina, always.

Our kiss grows deeper, tongues tangling as I grip her jaw in my palm. I can't remember the last time I just kissed her, and it's glorious. I think I could live the rest of my life only kissing this woman and be totally complete.

I break the kiss, Rina gasping as I move to her jaw and down her neck. The sudden urge to mark her, to show anyone who looks at her that she's finally mine after all this time, is too strong to ignore. I nip her neck before moving to that spot where her shoulder meets it. My teeth sink into her. A breathless moan greets my ears as I lick the abused flesh.

"Fuck, I missed you so much," I murmur into her skin. "I'm never letting you go again. You're mine, Emmerdeur."

"Show me," she moans as her hips lift against my thigh to get friction.

"You want me to show you how hard you get me? Show you exactly how little it takes to work me up around you? Or do you want me to show you I still know exactly how to work your body? Coax out every ounce of pleasure from your bones before finally giving you what you really want?"

"Jesus, where did your mouth come from?" She groans as her nails rake down my chest.

"You didn't want more than sex before. It was safer to stay quiet." I shove my borrowed T-shirt up as she arches against my chest, not caring if I have to rip it off her damn body. I need her naked now.

Leaning back on my knees, my fingertips feather from the bite mark I just gave her down to breasts. Gently circling her nipple before cupping her, I take a minute to just look at her. Tattoos cover more of her body than not. It's not that I hadn't noticed them—obviously I had, especially the colorful sleeves she has—but I've never gotten the time to just look at them.

A vine of thorns forms the curve under both breasts. Words line her ribcage, causing me to lean in closer to read them.

The strongest hearts are the ones that have been broken.

"Tattoos became a way to ease the pain, to release it," she whispers.

"Maybe one day, I can be the cause of a happy tattoo instead of a sad one." I kiss along the words, vowing to make that a reality.

My tongue drags along her stomach, feeling it contract under my touch as I slip my fingers into her panties. Dragging them down her smooth legs is an erotic dance that makes me glad my basketball shorts are still on.

Leaning back once more with her completely naked, I tip my head back and thank whomever I need to for letting me be with Rina in this moment. My hand reaches for her foot before bringing it up to my lips. Pressing soft kisses to every inch of skin I can reach, I drift up her leg.

"What are you doing?" she asks with a shuttering breath.

"Savoring." I continue my path until I can't reach any further from my stance and then switch legs.

"You're killing me."

"It's been fifteen years since I got to taste every inch of you. I'll be damned if I wait another second to do it again. You know I'll take care of you," I murmur between kisses on her other leg.

"After you torture me to death," she whines, her hips trying to arch up before I pin them down with my hand.

"Keep complaining, Marina, and it'll only make me take longer."

"God, I fucking hate when you call me that."

"You love it. Insults are practically your love language at this point." I smirk.

"And yet, you're into that," she quips.

"So fucking into it." I groan as I drop her leg and collapse between her legs. Her giggle fills the room but abruptly stops when I nibble the inside of her thigh. Switching sides, I barely hold off devouring her pretty pussy until I've explored every inch of her body. But this feels like a new beginning, and I'm taking advantage of that.

Her hands land on my head, groping for a grip but finding none in my crew cut.

"Damnit, grow your hair out," she growls, frustrated.

"No." I nip her clit before sliding up her body and coming face to face with her.

Her gaze catches mine. "You're different."

"How so?" I ask, pressing a kiss to her lips.

"You seem lighter, happier."

"I have you in my bed. What more could I want?" Her eyes glitter, and I get the sense I'm overwhelming her. I grab her hand, kissing my way up her colorful skin before switching to the other. My hips take on a mind of their own, grinding into her to relieve a little of the tension.

"If you don't take your damn shorts off, I'm going to scream." She grips my shoulders.

I lean back with a smirk. "You're just begging me to take longer, aren't you?"

"It's ridiculous that I'm begging for your cock right now and you're denying me." She huffs.

"I'm not denying you, Emmerdeur. I'm loving you."

She stares at me for a long minute, and I feel frozen in her gaze.

"Kiss me," she whispers.

Who am I to refuse my wife?

My wife.

That could be a real possibility in the future, not just wishful thinking.

Our kiss turns heated within a second. Her hands scrape down my side and hook into my shorts before I feel her hips shift. She's wiggling all over the place, and I finally release her lips to figure out what she's doing.

Her feet hook into my shorts as I pull back, and they shove the offending material down my legs. I chuckle. I can't help it.

"Easy, girl, you could have just asked." I grin.

"I fucking did! So, excuse me for taking it upon myself." Her outrage just turns me on.

"Keep talking dirty, Rina. It's doing it for me." I kick off my shorts completely before shifting close to her.

Her laughter shakes her chest, and I get distracted for a second. "You're ridiculous."

"Ridiculously happy," I offer.

"And cheesy as hell." She rolls her eyes.

"You love it," I murmur against her lips as I drag my cock through her wetness.

"I honestly do, and it's only mildly irritating." She hooks a heel around my ass and pulls me in.

"I'm not done yet." I bite her shoulder again before shuffling down her body, kissing as I move. Once I'm between her legs again, I shove her legs open and press a kiss to her clit.

"Yesss," she hisses.

As much as I want to continue this sweet torture, I'm about to lose all of my control, and getting her an orgasm before that point is my number one priority.

I nip at her clit before I lick everywhere I can touch. Her hands grip my head and shove me closer. Her moans are a symphony I need to hear more of. I snake my hand up her leg, sliding one finger inside of her, causing her back to arch and her screams to fill the room. My dick grinds into the mattress on the verge of losing my shit like a teenager, but I barely hold on. I slip another finger insider, crooking my finger to hit the spot I know will send her to the moon in minutes.

"Arlo!" Her chant is the only thing I hear as her thighs close in around my head and her body tightens up with her orgasm. I wait for her to come down, and once her thighs release me from the greatest prison there is, I move up, gripping her neck as I kiss her like my life depends on it.

Ripping my lips from hers, we both pant as we catch our breath, but I barely give us time to do so before I notch my cock at her entrance and slide in with one smooth stroke.

"Holy shit," Rina breathes.

"God, you feel good. So fucking good. I just want to bury myself inside of you and never leave." I grunt as I thrust hard, shifting us up the bed.

She wraps her body around me, making sure every possible inch of skin is touching. Her gasps fuel a part of me I didn't realize I had. This need to own her, to ravage her so she knows I'm the only man that makes her feel this way takes over.

"Tell me it's only me. Tell me we'll make it through everything together," I whisper as I roll my hips.

"It's you, Arlo. It's always you." She's breathless, barely able to get the words out, but I hear them and it sends me spiraling.

My teeth find that spot at the junction of her neck and shoulder again, clamping down as my thrusts pick up and I grind against her clit.

Her legs and arms squeeze me as tight as possible as she grips me and pulses as she comes. The feeling of her coming around me, knowing we can overcome anything, sends me over the edge.

She collapses under me, and I thrust hard once more as I come.

A crash sounds around us as the mattress drops us to the ground. Rina's tinkling laughter tightens her around my dick. I groan, still trying to figure out what just happened through the haze of my orgasm.

"What the fuck?" I breathe as I pull back from our entanglement and look around.

CHAPTER TWENTY-NINE
RINA

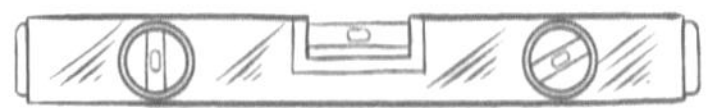

We broke the bed.

We broke the fucking bed, and I can't stop laughing.

"My builds would never break," I gasp out through my laughter.

"How the hell did we break a bed?" Arlo sounds like he's in shock, and it only cracks me up more. I can't say I've ever broken a bed while having sex, but it's definitely one for the records books.

"You were a little aggressive," I offer with a giggle.

He rolls off of me, and I immediately feel the loss. I'm not sure what just happened outside of the bed breaking, but this felt like the start of something special. It wasn't just sex; it was pouring our love into each other. It was showing each other that we're all in.

"Was I too rough?"

His concerned tone has my head rolling to the side to look at him. "No. Hell no, that was ... the best," I say wistfully. He turns his head to look at me, and I'm blown away by the depth of feeling I see in his eyes. It makes me wonder if he sees the same within mine.

"I'll make you a deal," he says.

"Oh, yeah?"

"You make me a new bed that I will pay for, obviously, when we're serious. Like, 'move in, ready for the whole life together' serious."

I stare at him, not knowing how to respond. Mainly because after tonight, it feels like we're already kind of there, which is scary as hell.

"Deal," I whisper.

His smile starts small, then grows to take over his entire face. He looks gorgeous like this, happy and full of hope. I just want to keep that look on his face. But I can't guarantee anything right now as much as I want to. I still need time with him, time to learn if we can really be together, if I can trust him with my heart again.

But I'm dangerously close to that point already.

He reaches for my waist, dragging me over his body as I laugh at his playfulness. It's such a change of pace for both of us that I don't know how to act.

"I don't think I've ever heard you laugh this much, Emmerdeur," he murmurs as he nuzzles my neck. His scruff scrapping deliciously against my skin makes me want round two before I've recovered from round one.

"What does that mean? You've always called me that, yet I've never looked it up," I ponder. It always sounded so romantic; I didn't even question it. It was just what he called me, and I loved it.

"I'm not even sure. Uncle Charlie used to say it all the time, and I always thought it was said with reverence, so I just stole it from him."

"You gave me a nickname, and you don't know what it means?" I laugh.

"Correct." He nips at my neck.

"Give me a phone. We're looking this up." I swat at his shoulder. He reaches over to his nightstand, grabbing his phone, unlocking it, and handing it to me.

"How do you spell it?"

"E-M-M-E-R-D-E-U-R," Arlo says in between kisses. I barely focus enough to type it into the search engine.

"Shut up." I laugh as the long curious question gets answered on the screen.

"What?" He pulls back.

"It's the masculine version of annoying in French." I bite my bottom lip to stop from laughing. It's the most ridiculous and perfect thing I've ever seen. It fits us to a T, even when it was supposed to be romantic.

"No, it doesn't." He gasps. He looks horrified as I show him the screen. "Oh my god, I've been calling you annoying this whole time."

Laugher bursts out of me.

"Stop, this is so far from funny," he groans into my neck.

"This is literally the best thing ever," I say through my laughter. "How fucking perfect is it?"

"You can't tell anyone."

"I'm telling everyone! You can't make this up, Arlo." I giggle. "I've gone around hating you for the last fifteen years, and your nickname for me is 'annoying'. If that doesn't explain our relationship, I don't know what does."

"How fucking embarrassing," he groans into my neck. "You're going to tell people about us? About my terribly picked nickname that's lasted longer than I want to admit?" he asks, sounding all kinds of hopeful.

"Well, we did go on a date at Sal's. It feels fitting to tell everyone how bad you are at picking nicknames too." I giggle.

"I lied. Emmerdeur fits you perfectly." He nips my neck again before kissing the same spot.

Wrapping my arms around his neck, I sigh and can't help but think about how perfect everything feels. I just hope it lasts.

For now, though, I think round two is in order.

I finally made it home after round two, a shower, and a very long kiss goodbye.

An attempt was made to sleep, but I found myself standing in my workshop wide awake and needing to do something. My computer shows a couple of new inquiries for builds, which I promptly email back to work out more details.

I inventory all the projects I'm currently working on or that are coming up, as well as materials, and set my calendar accordingly so I can stay on track, but my head is still firmly distracted by a certain sheriff.

Things have changed, and although I'm still not sure what to do with the fact that we're still married, being together feels more right than anything has in the last decade. It's terrifying, exciting, and downright perfect all at the same time. My head is all over the place, and the only thing that will clear it is working.

My computer pings with an incoming email, and I'm thankful for the timing. I just finished everything organizational I had available.

Thanks for the quick reply. Ideally, I'd want you to do whatever you want. Whatever your perfect bed is, that's what I want. Money is no object.

-T

I stare at the email, getting a weird feeling about it. It's not uncommon for people to defer to my expertise, but they all still have some idea of what they want. It's strange that a client wants "my perfect bed" when it's their furniture and in their house. Something grates in my head, this sense of unease, and I'm not sure what to do about it. I rarely turn down clients if the build is feasible for me, but I'm questioning this one.

> *This sounds interesting. Would you mind giving me more information, like if you're able to pick up or if it's for delivery? Where you are located and general size specifications for the project. And wood preferences. Also, a good number to reach you at.*
>
> *Thanks,*
>
> *Rina Hutton*
>
> *Hutton Custom Furniture*

It may not lead anywhere, but at least I'll have more information and I can pass it along to Arlo to look into. This stalker situation is causing me to want to be more thorough with everything.

Since they wrote back so quickly the last time, I decide to stay at my desk while I wait for their reply.

My mind wanders to Arlo's bed that we broke, and I pull out my notebook with all my plans in it. Opening to a fresh sheet, I start sketching the bed I'll eventually make for him, for us. God, that feels weird to say, but my pencil starts moving before my mind can catch up.

I've got the basics down before my laptop pings again. Opening up the email, I shudder runs through me at the response.

I will be picking it up from your workshop. A king is perfect unless you prefer a queen. Wood preference is whatever your favorite wood to work with is, and my number is 555-1845.

I look forward to seeing the progress,

-T

I stare at the email and immediately know something is up. The wording is too much to ignore, and I internally start to panic. What if this is the stalker? What if I start making this and it ends up being the way he really gets to me?

Just send everything to Arlo and Oakley, and let them take over. Don't do anything else.

Logically, it makes sense, but I'm having a hard time separating that voice from the one that hustles for business, that treats every client like their family. Shutting my laptop, I decide I'll deal with this mysterious T character tomorrow. For the rest of the night, I sketch out not just a bed for Arlo but furniture to fill a whole house.

CHAPTER THIRTY
ARLO

I t's been a week since we broke my bed and decided to make a real go of things. Of course, that was the same day that some creeper decided to ask Rina to make her a bed. Ever since she forwarded the email thread, I've been her silent shadow. She doesn't know I've been following her and basically living out of my truck. If she did, she'd probably kill me.

But her instinct was right. There was something wrong with whomever sent the inquiry, and I couldn't leave her by herself until I figured it out. Audrey's been up my ass about working out of the office, and Oakley's annoyed he can't just walk across the street to brainstorm and come up with a plan to catch whoever is stalking Rina.

We did finally have a breakthrough with the damn box that was left on Rina's doorstep.

A scrapbook of pictures, date ideas, and house plans were inside, and it made my stomach physically roll when I dug deeper. Combining that with this new furniture inquiry, Oakley and I are ninety-five percent sure they're connected. The number he gave was a dead end, but we're working on getting through the red tape to locate the IP address, so hopefully that narrows things down for us.

Thank God Oakley decided to help out on a case-by-case basis because his connections and knowledge have eased me off the edge with Rina's case. I think I'd be losing my mind every day if I didn't have his help.

Rina and I have been going at a much slower pace as well. I think the other night freaked her out, and I understand her reasoning for wanting to take things slower. She may have mostly forgiven me, but that doesn't mean we can just pick up where we left off. We've been talking, texting mostly, about everyday life, but nothing past that. No other mentions of the past, of us being married, or the future. However, tonight, we're going on a date.

And I'm nervous as hell.

One wrong move could topple this carefully held together truce, and that's the last thing I want to happen.

My phone pings, and I sigh as I pull it out, expecting it to be Audrey again, yelling at me that the meddlesome trio is bothering her about my whereabouts again.

How long are we going to pretend you aren't sitting outside in your truck all day, every day?

Busted.

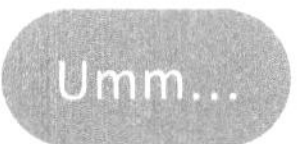

You should just come work at the desk in my workshop. That's if you can deal with the sounds of power tools… On second thought, that's

Adorable; she's completely adorable when she rambles.

Me:

I would pay good money to have my workday be in the same building as Rina. I probably wouldn't get much done, but the life of a small-town sheriff isn't all that busy to begin with. Watching my wife work her magic on some planks of wood? Definitely sounds like a great day to me.

I grab my laptop, phone, and bottle of water before heading to her barn workshop. When I step through the door, my teeth grate at the knowledge that anyone could just walk in here. Closing the door and locking it behind me, I finally take in the view in front of me.

Rina's wearing dark purple leggings and a grey tank top. Her hair's plopped on the top of her head, and she's wearing safety glasses that somehow look endearing on her. There's also a sexy-as-fuck smirk on her face that I would give anything to wipe off her face with a couple of orgasms, but work needs to come first right now.

"How long would you have kept up your watch dog act?"

"As long as it takes to make sure you're safe," I say. "Although, I'm disappointed I wasn't more discreet."

"You were. I just seem to have an innate sense of you whenever you're close by." She shrugs.

Warmth blooms in my chest at her words. It's starting to feel like we aren't as far away from my ultimate end goal as it seems. That's not to say I won't continue to work my ass off to be deserving of her because I know it will take continual work on my end. But her words, no matter how much of a smartass she tries to be, give me endless hope about the future.

"Good to know if I ever want to surprise you," I say quietly.

Rina clears her throat. "I don't have a ton of work left, but I will be sanding a ton and ripping some larger pieces of wood. Is that going to be okay?"

"Absolutely. Pretend I'm not even here." I set down my stuff at her desk as she stares at me with a look I can't decipher.

"Yeah, super easy. I'll just ignore the tight jeans and baseball hat. Let's not even mention the tights-as-fuck sheriff shirt that shows all your muscles." Her murmured tone is almost too low for me to hear but not quiet enough.

I grin. I can't help it. "What was that?" I ask like the asshole I am.

"Oh, shut up. You heard me. If I cut myself today because I'm distracted, it's all your fault."

"I can take the T-shirt off if it's too distracting," I offer with laughter.

She narrows her eyes at me before spinning on her heel and going to the opposite end of the building.

Within twenty minutes, she's working away like I'm not even here while I'm stuck staring at her, mesmerized by her capabilities. Seeing the end product is so much different from seeing her actually build them. Logically, I know she's good at her job and she makes beautiful things, but watching her process and how she can turn raw wood into works of art is truly something to behold. I don't think I'll ever get over it.

Our deal about building me a bed pops into my head, and I can't wait to see what she comes up with. Although, I'll sleep on a mattress on the floor for as long as it takes to get to that point. With the injections, my back isn't totally fucked in the mornings anymore, so getting up off the floor no longer poses the challenge it would have a few months ago.

I start thinking about what I want our life to look like. Things like moving into this house with her, getting a dog, run like a motion picture through my head. The land she has here is perfect, but I would want to add to the house. Really turn it into something that works for both of us and possibly any additions we bring home.

I'm so caught up in my daydreams that I don't realize the power tools have stopped and the gorgeous woman I can't stop thinking about is standing right in front of me.

"Must be thinking about something really good," she observes with a small smile on her face.

"You have no idea, Emmerdeur," I whisper.

"I'd love to hear all about it at dinner. I need to change, and I didn't know if you did as well." She gestures to my "distracting outfit".

"I do. We could stop by my place on the way out if that works for you."

"Since you aren't leaving my side, apparently, that works."

"Don't act like you don't love it," I tell her as I get up and walk around the desk.

"I do, but I can't let you know that. You'll just get a big head, and Lord knows, it doesn't need to get any bigger."

I lean down and press a kiss to the side of her mouth. "You like my big head. Who else will you spar with every day?"

"I've done well on my own so far," she snarks, but it hits a cord for me.

"Have you? Are you living the way you want to?" I ask softly as I wrap my arms around her waist.

"I-I don't know. You make things complicated, make me question a lot of things, and I'm still trying to figure out what that all means."

"Well, we've got all the time in the world, and I plan to be right by your side as we figure it out together." I press another kiss to her temple before stepping back and tapping her ass. "Go get ready. We've got a date to get to."

I happen to know Rina hasn't been to the new bistro that opened up in Rosedale yet, so I thought it would be the perfect date night spot tonight.

Somehow, we didn't end up getting distracted as we changed, so we made it on time for the reservations I called in a couple of days ago. She changed into a dress I've never seen her wear, her long hair floating down around her shoulders with just the hint of makeup around her eyes. I tossed on a button-down black shirt and the only pair of nice slacks that I have when we stopped by my house. Although technically not our first date, I wanted to make sure it felt like I was still courting her, still putting in effort to show her how important being with her is to me.

The hostess walks us to a table near the back, and I pull out Rina's chair once we get there before I sit down.

"I feel out of place," she leans forward and whispers.

My heart drops, and I start to backpedal. "We can go. If you don't feel comfortable, we can go somewhere else."

"No! God no, what I mean is, I live in leggings and usually have a layer of sawdust on me at all times, and this is fancy and normal. I'm used to not being put together enough to go somewhere like this, but I love it. I love the change of pace, I promise." She places her hand on mine and gives it a soft squeeze. "And you look hot as hell in a button-up, not going to lie." She smirks.

A surprised laugh leaves me. "If I had known all I needed to do was dress up occasionally, I would have done it sooner."

"Oh please, you look good in anything. It's insulting, honestly. I look like an overworked science experiment most of the time, and you just stroll in looking sexy as hell every single day." She rolls her eyes.

"You know you could be in a burlap sack and I'd still want to fuck you, right? You are literally the sexiest thing I've ever seen, especially when you're covered in sawdust. Never doubt for a second that you are anything short of gorgeous, every single day." I grab her hand and press a kiss to the top.

"Did you learn how to be poetic from Oakley? Because you're damn good at it, and I need someone to thank for it."

"Why do you think I would learn it from Oakley?"

"Because he's dating Willow, and she's the resident writer; it makes sense that they would both be decent with words, and I've heard the way he talks to her sometimes... Poetic, I'm telling you."

And I'm suddenly in competition with Oakley.

"This is all me, Emmerdeur," I tell her with a sternness that I only let out in the bedroom. The arch of her eyebrow tells me she didn't miss it.

A throat clears next to us, and we see a young man holding a notepad ready to take our order. We both jerk back, Rina's face turning red as I roll my lips to keep from laughing.

"Good evening. How are we doing today?"

"Great, how about yourself?" I ask.

"Good, thanks for asking. Can I get you something to drink?"

I defer to Rina.

"I'll have the grapefruit gin and tonic, please." She places her menu down and looks at me.

"I'll just have an iced tea, thank you." He nods before leaving and leaving us on our own once again.

"Not drinking?"

"I haven't been much of a drinker since my accident. It and pain meds didn't mix well, so I just stopped drinking altogether and never looked back. I'm also almost always on call, so drinking doesn't really lend itself to that either."

"Makes sense. So, why are you parking in front of my house every day? I never asked you."

I sigh, not really wanting to get into this on our date but knowing she will keep pressing until I do. "Between the box that was left and the furniture inquiry, I don't feel comfortable leaving you alone."

"It's that bad?" she asks, fear in the undercurrent of her voice.

"It's not necessarily bad; it's just unknown, and sometimes that's worse. If I'm able to protect you and take away the chance that this person gets close to you, I'll do it. Oakley and I are still working to narrow down some firmer leads, so I don't have much to tell you at the moment." It kills me to admit that.

She nods, looking pensive. "What if we speed things along?"

I already know I'll hate whatever direction her thoughts are going. "How?"

"By being bait. Draw them out somehow."

"Absolutely not."

"Arlo! We're not any closer, and this is starting to rule my life. I don't like living this way, looking over my shoulder, wondering what's coming next. If there's a chance that I can do something to help, I want to do it."

"No."

"You're a stubborn mule," she mutters.

"But you're safe, and that's all that matters."

She gives me a death stare as our waiter delivers our drinks. I thank him before ordering my food and then turning my stare to Rina. She confidently orders her meal, and he leaves just as quickly as he came. She turns her hard stare back at me.

"Be mad at me all you want. It's not happening." I bring my iced tea to my lips and take a sip as she rolls her eyes.

"I'll just talk to Oakley." She smirks.

"Like hell you will," I growl. Pinching the bridge of my nose, I realize she's just trying to goad me, but damn, it's working. "Please, just give me time to figure this out."

"I'll try, okay? That's all I can give you because it can't be like this forever."

"I know. It won't be. I just need a little more time," I beg. I know she hates this whole situation. She's freaked out more than she wants to let on, but I absolutely can't let her take things into her own hands.

A throat clears from behind me as whoever it is scoots back in their chair, bumping into mine in the process. I roll my eyes, but my eyes snag on Rina's facial expression. She looks uncomfortable, and I start to turn around before she grabs my hand and shakes her head subtly.

"Fancy seeing you here," a man's voice sounds from behind me, presumably the man who bumped into me.

"Tyler, hi. Looks like things are going well for you," Rina says with faux friendliness.

Tyler. Why does that sound familiar?

"Apparently for you as well." The slight anger in his tone has my back straightening.

Rina cringes but doesn't say anything.

"Well, I was just running to the bathroom," he mocks. "Before going back to my date."

I have never wanted to punch a condescending asshole as much as I do right now. I think this is the guy Rina was on a date with that I interrupted. I'm especially not sorry now that I know he's a total dickhead.

Rina throws a little salute as I watch him walk to the back of the restaurant. So much for a nice, easy date.

CHAPTER THIRTY-ONE
RINA

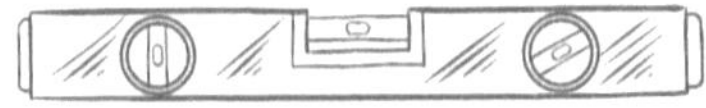

Of fucking course, we run into Tyler here. The second I realized it was him, I was hoping he would just do a little wave and then move on, but nope. I'm now in the middle of a dick measuring contest. I can see Arlo about to lose his shit, but luckily, Tyler walks away before things get out of hand.

"Was that the prick you tried to make me jealous with?" Arlo asks quietly, contentious of Tyler's date still behind us.

"Jesus. First, it was weeks ago; second, it was never really going to go anywhere, and you know that, so chill out." This is turning out to be a great date.

"He sure didn't sound like he felt it was going nowhere."

"Well, I can't speak for him. For me, it was going nowhere as evidence of where I ended up that night," I calmly counter.

Arlo's head tips back as he takes a deep breath. This is not how I saw tonight going, especially after the verbal foreplay we've been doing all day. Is this some kind of sign that we're trying too hard at something that was never meant to be? I know that's bullshit, but damn, every time we start to really make progress together, something pops up and pushes us ten steps back.

"I'm sorry," he says as he refocuses on me. "There was no reason to react to any of that when he's basically inconsequential. I was just jealous ... again."

His honesty and quick assessment of the situation makes it clear as day how much work he's really put in. Although, I'll say his jealousy is kind of hot.

"It's okay. He was super aggressive for no real reason. I mean, we went on half of a date if you can even call it that." I roll my eyes as I laugh, hoping to brush the whole situation to the side. I also peek over Arlo's shoulder to see what his new date looks like and maybe to throw her a quick warning, but footsteps sound next to me, signaling either our waiter or Tyler. Looking up, I see it's the latter, and he has a sneer on his face fully directed at me.

Geez, what did I ever see in that asshole? People flake on dates all the time. It's not like we were set to get married and live all our days together. This feels extreme for the situation, and it's making me feel super uneasy.

Arlo's eyes follow him as he passes and then sits down with his date. Poor woman has no idea what she's getting into with that one. Or maybe she does and she into the whole asshole thing, who knows.

"Okay, back to our date," I say as I pick up my drink and take a healthy sip, hoping the liquor somehow saves how awkward everything has turned, thanks to Tyler.

"Good plan."

We stare at each other silently as we try to think about what to talk about.

"So, I think I'm finally caught up with orders again. Everyone was super understanding when I had to adjust delivery dates and such, but you, cleaning everything up and restocking everything I could ever need, really helped."

"Good. I'm glad I could help get you back on track." His tone is almost clinical and I snap, wanting to break the tension so badly.

"For fuck's sake," I mutter. "I'm dating you. I want to be with you. Fuck everything else, okay?"

"God, I love this feisty side of you. It's so fucking sexy," he whispers. And just like that, the awkwardness breaks.

"It's a damn good thing you like it because it's seventy percent of my personality." I take another sip of my drink.

Waiters come with our food, placing our plates in front of us before disappearing without a word. This is one of the fancy bistros where they don't ask a lot of questions but still somehow have impeccable service. I wasn't lying when I said I felt out of place earlier. This isn't my usual style, but I love that he's putting in the extra effort for me. For us.

We both dig in, moaning at how delicious the steaks we both got are, and before I know it, we're both finishing our meals without having said much of anything to each other.

"Damn, that was phenomenal. Sorry, I lost track of all thoughts outside of how good the steak was," Arlo says, putting his napkin down on the table.

"Don't be sorry. We might have to come here once a month to get our fix."

"I can make that happen." He smiles.

Planning for the future. Who knew that was something I would actually look forward to, and with Arlo of all people? But I feel like me, not the me I had to be when my parents died but the me I always wanted to be. As much as Arlo has made changes for himself, I hope he can see I'm trying to do the same. I'm trying to step out of my comfort zone to really jump in with both feet, even if it scares the shit out of me.

"I'd like that very much. What do you say we grab the check and head out of here? Maybe go back to my house." I don't even try to be seductive, but my meaning is clear as day.

"I'd say that sounds like the best idea yet." He flags down our waiter for the check, and within ten minutes we're back in his truck, heading back home.

Arlo's asleep next to me after our very vigorous activities tonight. I should be fast asleep too, but my brain won't be quiet.

I keep thinking about how weird Tyler was at dinner. About how the last few months have garnered more change than I think I was ready for. About this damn stalker. And oddly enough, I'm thinking about Lennox and how he's coping when all we see is the face he puts on around us all. It makes me realize I'm not as well-adjusted as I want to be when it comes to what happened to him or what is currently happening to me.

I reach over to my nightstand and grab my phone, opening up a text thread and sliding out of bed to head to the bathroom.

Are you awake?

I am. Why are you?

Me:

Couldn't sleep. My brain is thinking about … everything.

Lenny:

Well, that's always a shitty option.

Me:

How are you doing? I mean, like how are you just moving on and living?

Lenny:

I'm … not really? I know you guys all see that I'm not 100% there at family dinners, but I appreciate you all for not bringing attention to it. It's strange because I know logically what happened to me, but it's like I have a mental block where I don't think about what specifically happened. Does that make sense?

Me:

It does. But that doesn't really help me right now, ha ha.

Lenny:

What's going on?

Lenny:

I'm not trying to throw my shit at you because we need to move forward as a family, and I'll be okay eventually. I know that.

I sniffle as his last texts comes in because I feel like I've failed him. He's going through so much, and none of us knows how to help him. We may be hindering him more than anything, and that breaks my heart. But I also texted him for a reason. He's always been pretty point blank with any advice, and I need that now more than ever, even if it makes me feel like a shitty sister.

> Things with Arlo are progressing, and it's scary. It's good. I know that, but…

I realize he wasn't at family dinner when I filled in a lot of the blanks, and I hesitate.

But what?

> You tell no one what I'm about to say…

rolls eyes Who the fuck do I talk to anymore?

Well, now I just feel selfish. But I'm about to tell him more than what the rest of the family knows, and I just need to cover my bases.

Arlo and I were a thing back in the day before Mom and Dad died. And it ended … badly. I've never really wanted anyone else, but now that things are kind of coming full circle, it scares me that he's going to crush my heart again, and I don't think I can survive it again. And then there's this asshole who keeps texting me and sending me shit. My nerves are frayed, and you always shoot straight and I need that blunt honesty right now, even if it means I'm selfish as hell. I am sorry about that; I promise I'll bring you a steak from the bistro we went to tonight to make up for it.

Lenny:

That's a lot to unpack… Give me a second to write it all out.

Lenny:

I won't pretend to know what happened between you two, but I do know that you've never dated, never shown an interest in anyone since Mom and Dad died. That's not a way to live. If Arlo is showing up now, and his actions—not his words—show you he's serious, then it's worth risking a broken heart for. I may be basically a recluse now, but when I do see you, you're happier than I've ever seen you. If shit with Tennison taught me anything, it's that life doesn't give you time. It doesn't care if you're scared or second-guessing things. It can all disappear at the drop of a hat. Keeping Arlo at arm's length will only hurt you both more in the long run. It's okay to be cautious, but don't let good things slip through your fingers if they make you happy.

Lenny

And what the fuck is this about a guy that's basically stalking you? Does Ledger know?

I cringe at his second message. I didn't think that one through, and with Arlo up my ass and basically babysitting me, the last thing I want is either brother to join in the fun. His other advice, however, calms my thoughts and sends clarity crashing through all my confusion. It also doesn't lessen my sisterly guilt that he's struggling more than any of us really know.

Big bro doesn't know the new developments, and I'd like to keep it that way. Arlo is always overprotective enough for everyone. And you make some good points there, little brother. Thank you for talking me off a ledge and somehow making things clearer than they have been in years. It must be some kind of superpower you have.

Lenny:

No superpowers here, unfortunately. I'm glad it helped, though. You and Arlo are pretty good together, I guess.

I laugh at what I assume is a sullen tone and quickly quiet down, so I don't wake up Arlo.

Me:

If you need anything, please, please call me, text me, send a letter, whatever. I know things are hard and it will take time, but we're all here for you with whatever you need.

Lenny:

I know. I'm just not there yet, I think. You'll be there first I bug when I'm ready, though, because this was dangerously close to girl talk.

Laughter bursts out of me, and I slap my hand over my mouth.

"What is going on over there?" Arlo's groggy voice sounds out in the quiet room, loud enough for me to hear him.

"Sorry," I whisper. "Go back to bed," I say as I walk out of the bathroom and put my phone back on the nightstand as I get back into bed and snuggle against Arlo's side, feeling more hopeful for the future than I have in fifteen years.

CHAPTER THIRTY-TWO
ARLO

I've been up for an hour, my mind running a million miles a minute as I watch Rina sleep. Her little snores are so endearing it makes me fall in love with her more by the second. Not that I'd ever tell her about the snoring. I'd like to not get punched this morning.

My thoughts turn back to the situation at dinner last night, and I can't get my head off of this Tyler guy. There was something about him that didn't sit right with me, and at this point, we have no other leads, so it's worth checking out on the off chance we find something. Picking up my phone, I send Oakley a text to see if he can come to Rina's house so we can game plan since I don't plan on leaving her alone anytime soon. He agrees and lets me know he'll bring breakfast and coffee as well. For a man who claimed to not want friends, he's a very good one without even trying. I do feel bad that Willow has to run Grind Time because of my insecurities with leaving Rina, but I'll figure out a way to make it up to her.

"What time is it?" Rina's sleep-riddled voice interrupts my chaotic thoughts.

"Six-thirty."

"Jesus, is this normal for you?" She rolls over, rubbing her eyes.

"Waking up early? Usually." I try very hard to hide my amusement.

"This is never going to work. I can't be with someone who is this peppy in the morning. You were never this way when we first got together," she groans.

I do laugh this time because she's too fucking adorable.

"It's a deal breaker?" I ask, not doing a good job of covering my laughter.

"Ugh, shut up. My brain doesn't work this early." She throws her arm over her eyes as I slide down into the bed, pressing a kiss to her forearm then her shoulder as a breathy moan comes from her.

"What if I wake you up in a different way?" I murmur against her skin.

"Yeah, that's probably okay," she drawls.

I chuckle into her neck before I pull away. "Good to know. I'll keep that in mind. Unfortunately, we'll have company in about twenty minutes, so it'll have to wait for another day."

"That's cruel," she whines. Dropping her arm from her face, she sends me a death stare that makes me smile.

"If it helps, he's bringing breakfast and coffee." I dangle the hope of sustenance in front of her.

"You're lucky Oakley somehow always knows what I want to drink, or this would be an entirely different conversation." She rolls to face me, and I can't help myself. My fingers trail along her cheek, across her plump bottom lip and down her jaw before cupping it. I lean in and press my lips to hers, wanting to savor this quiet moment before real life takes over again.

As I pull away, she follows me with an unhappy groan.

"You should have started with that; I'd probably wake up happy every day if you did."

It's not supposed to be a meaningful statement, but to me, it means everything. The thought of being able to kiss her every morning, to make her happy every day, sends warmth through my chest. It's all I've ever wanted, and right this second, it feels attainable.

"That can be arranged," I hum before pulling back completely and flipping the covers off of me. I wish we had more time, but I know Oakley will be here any minute, and I have to physically remove myself from Rina's side in order to get ready for him.

"Take your time getting up," I tell her as I pull on my slacks from last night and throw on my button-up shirt. I have a gym bag in my truck, but it feels like too much effort to go get right now. I do make a mental note to pack a bag to leave here.

Walking out the front door, I sit in one of the rockers and wait for Oakley. I'm desperately trying to shift my head to work mode and not love on Rina mode, but it's harder than I anticipated.

A truck comes down the drive, and I throw a wave up as Oakley parks. I stand up to meet him and grab the coffee he brought.

"Rina says you always know what she drinks, so I hope that's true because she's grumpy as shit this morning."

"I heard that!" Rina yells from the porch.

"Shit," I whisper as Oakley starts laughing.

"Oh-ho, this is a good time." He walks toward Rina, handing her a bag of food. "Good morning, lovely Rina. How are you this morning?" His sweet tone makes me want to punch him, but I know he's just goading me.

"Wonderful now that you're here," she says sweetly.

"Are you two done? Trying to rile me up is not going to help what we need to accomplish today," I grumble.

"Your americano is in your left hand, and there's breakfast in the bag for you too. Stop complaining," Oakley jokes as he walks into Rina's house.

Rina smirks as I walk up the steps of the porch.

"You two are *Emmerdeur* together," I snark.

"Mr. Grumpy, not loving a taste of his own medicine? Also, I don't think you're using that right still," she adds.

"I'll spank your ass later for that comment," I say as I pass her.

"Don't threaten me with a good time." The door clicks closed behind her, and I have to take a steadying breath with the turn in conversation. Rina's tinkling laughter as she passes me makes my dick hard, and now is not the time to indulge.

"So, what's on the agenda?" Oakley asks as we all sit at the dining room table, Rina dishing out food as we do.

"We were out last night and ran into an old flame of Rina's—"

"He wasn't an old flame, and your jealousy is still showing. I had a half a date with him before *someone* crashed it, and I haven't seen him since. He was acting super aggressive last night when we talked, and then that was it."

Oakley starts laughing. "Is this what your foreplay looks like?"

"You know what? Maybe we don't need your help." I side-eye Oakley.

His booming laughter is apparently contagious because Rina joins him.

"Alright, you've both had your fun. Can we start working now?"

"Yes, sir." Rina salutes with a smirk, and I arch my eyebrow at her. Yeah, we're going to have fun later.

"So, you're wanting to look into this guy?"

"Yeah, if we can. He raised all the red flags and if nothing else, I'd like to just rule him out."

"Okay, does this guy have a name?" He looks at Rina as he pulls out a small notebook from his back pocket. I have to smirk at his action because, as much as he resisted the idea of working with me, he's falling into the role with ease.

"Tyler … umm, let me see if I have his last name anywhere," Rina says as she pops up from her chair and goes to the bedroom, presumably to grab her phone.

"You really think it could be this guy?" Oakley asks quietly.

"I honestly don't know, but we don't really have another lead right now, and the way he acted last night was … too much for how much interaction they had." I don't know how to tell him it's a gut feeling more than anything. Maybe it's desperation to find this guy or maybe it really is just jealousy, but I don't want to take any chances.

"Okay, Tyler No Last Name, but I have a phone number that you can do your cop thing and check out who it's registered to, right?"

Oakley and I stare at her with blank faces.

"Is that not how things work? Is it just on TV?" she asks, looking between the two of us.

I crack first, chuckling as Oakley joins in. "It's not that fancy, but we can call the cellular company and ask nicely. Possibly make it seem like we need the info for an investigation that's of highest importance and see where it goes. Otherwise, we need a warrant."

"Well, shit. What happens if we don't get the information?" she asks.

"We'll figure something out," Oakley reassures her.

"And we don't have any more information on the IP address, right?" I ask Oakley, knowing he would have told me if he had it.

"Not yet, but my guy at the Marshals said he should have it in the next day or two."

"Okay, that's good."

"Can I ask a question?" Rina asks as she puts her Danish down.

"Go for it," I say.

"What happens when we figure out who's behind all of this?"

"We go arrest him." I shrug as Oakley looks at me, knowing it's not quite that simple.

"Liar," she says, rolling her eyes. "What if we figure out a way to use me as bait?"

"No."

"No, listen. I don't want this to continue longer than it already is. If we use me to draw them out, this all ends faster. It's not like I'll be unprotected. Lord knows you won't leave my side, but we could end this."

"No."

"Sheriff..." Oakley draws out.

"You can't seriously think this is a good idea." I throw my hands up in exasperation.

"I don't necessarily think it's a good idea, but it would streamline things. Less red tape to work through."

"No. End of discussion."

Rina rolls her eyes as Oakley eyes me, with more curiosity than anything.

"You're being ridiculous," Rina says.

"Let me do my damn job, Marina. I don't tell you how to do yours, so don't tell me how to do mine," I say in frustration.

"I'm going to let that slide because I know you're stressed, but that's the only time you get to say that to me." She looks at me, irritated.

I sigh. "I'm sorry. This whole situation stresses me out, and I don't like that you're in the line of fire. I need to do something, but I can't risk you in the process. Please understand that," I beg.

"I do, but it doesn't make me less annoyed," she grumbles.

"And with that, I think it's time I head out and call my friend for an update." Oakley stands up.

I sigh and pinch the bridge of my nose, frustrated that things have taken such a turn. But I should have expected it from Rina. She's hard-headed and independent as hell.

"Keep him updated!" Rina calls as Oakley chuckles in response.

"You're a pain in my ass," I mumble.

"I know, but you wouldn't like me if I wasn't this way. I meant what I said, though. Don't take your frustrations out on me, please."

"I won't. I'm sorry I was a dick."

"Hey, guys!" Oakley calls from the front door.

"Yeah?" Rina asks.

"You might want to come see this."

Rina and I look at each other before abruptly standing and meeting Oakley by the door.

The box wrapped on the porch sends a chill down my spine.

"Do you have gloves?" Oakley asks Rina, who is standing stock still next to me.

"Umm, yeah, there's some by the side door and some in my work-shop," she whispers.

"Hey, come here." I pull her to me as Oakley disappears to grab a pair of gloves.

"I don't understand why this is happening. What did I do?"

"You didn't do anything, and Oakley and I will figure out who's doing this, I promise," I tell her before pressing a kiss to her temple.

"You can't promise that, and you know it."

"I can, and I will," I counter.

"Okay, let's check this out." Oakley interrupts us as he takes a couple of pictures with his phone before bringing the package inside.

We stand around the dining room table as he carefully unwraps it and takes pictures as he goes. Once it's finally open, he peeks in and furrows his eyebrows in confusion.

"Umm, I'm not sure what I'm looking at. I mean, I know what it is but not its significance," he says, looking at both me and Rina.

"Show me," Rina says, strong and firm.

Oakley sighs as he shifts to the side, taking a picture before he pulls whatever it is out. Rina may be prepared, but I know I'm fully unprepared for what's inside. Anything at this point could send me over the edge.

Oakley reaches in and pulls out fabric, but I can't make out what it is until he holds it up fully. Rina's gasp combined with what I'm feeling makes me feel dizzy, and the panic starts to close in on me.

Rina's dress that she wore to dinner last night is a stark reminder of how serious this guy is. How much he's escalating, and how close he really is.

What he doesn't know is I'll do anything to protect my wife, and he just signed his death warrant.

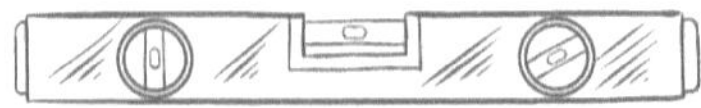

I'm still shaken from the box that landed on my doorstep yesterday.

After it showed up, Oakley took it back to Arlo's office and called his friends at the Marshals. There was a lot of talking and a lot of information flying around, but I zoned out pretty quickly.

All I could think was that this person was in my house. Not only that, but was in my house while both Arlo and I slept. My house now feels like a tainted place, somewhere I'm no longer safe. And I'm truly scared for the first time since this whole thing started.

Arlo spent the day by my side, helping me—rather terribly, I'll add—finish up some pieces before we headed to his office so he could work.

Today has been a day of avoidance. We're held up in Arlo's house, doing a whole lot of nothing, but our time to hide is about to come to an end.

It's family dinner night, and I've just decided I want to bring Arlo with me. It's a huge step, and everyone in the family knows you don't bring someone to family dinner unless you're serious about them. And I feel very serious about Arlo.

I still feel conflicted about us being married, but I've put that on the back burner in my head. We've been married all these years, and it hasn't affected anything. What's a few more weeks or months until I come to terms with what I want in the long run with him?

Yeah, you're not in denial at all, are you?

I roll my eyes at myself, not wanting to analyze how far deep I am with him already. I know Lennox talked about not waiting, but getting this stalker situation figured out feels like the priority in my life. After that, I can focus on Arlo and me.

"What's got you thinking so hard over there?" Arlo's voice pulls me out of my thoughts.

"It's family dinner tonight. And I'd like..." Here goes nothing. "I'd like for you to come." I hold my breath, dreading his reaction. I know I don't have reason to think he'll say no, but there's always a possibility we're not on the same page.

"Really?" His astonishment draws my attention.

"Only if you want to," I hurriedly say before cringing. I'm giving him every out instead of telling him that I really want him to go. It's childish, but the fear of getting my heart broken again weighs heavily on my chest.

"Hey, look at me," he says softly.

We're sitting on the couch, so I turn my body toward him, tucking my foot underneath me as he grabs my hands in his.

"I want nothing more than to be included in your life, including family dinner. My endgame is you as my wife, and not just because of a piece of paper. I don't want you to ever doubt that I'm all in with you. You are who I want to spend the rest of my life with, Emmerdeur. I understand things will take more time for you, and I'm fine with that, but know that you're it for me."

The honesty in his eyes breaks down the last of my barriers. It's like my heart cracks open and all the possibilities, all the dreams I put in a locked box, are suddenly available again. These hopes and dreams I gave up on are no longer a distant memory.

Leaning forward, I press a kiss to his lips. I don't think I have words to tell him how I feel, and the impulse to tell him I love him is too damn strong right now.

He cups my jaw, angling me the way he wants me as he shifts forward, covering my body with his. Making room for his body, I spread my legs and wrap them around his torso. He rips his lips from mine with a growl.

"We need to get ready for family dinner, and yet you tempt me to skip one of the most important things I've done in a long while."

"I was about to suggest skipping it," I breathe.

"Not a chance, *Marina*. This is my first invite to family dinner, and you can bet I'm not missing it for anything."

He lifts off of me and stands next to me on the couch, where I'm still a little breathless and a whole lot horny.

"Not even for sex? What man turns down sex?" I mumble the last part.

"I do, because I know you're coming home with me at the end of the day and that I can tease the shit out of you at family dinner."

"You're a cruel man, Mr. Steel. Do you enjoy torturing me?" I arch an eyebrow at him.

"Like you wouldn't believe." His devilish grin shouldn't be so attractive, but I must be a glutton for punishment because Arlo teasing me during family dinner sounds like sweet, delicious torment, and I can't wait.

"Ugh, let's get dressed, then. Ledger could use the help cooking." I roll off the couch unceremoniously and plop onto the floor before shifting to my knees, doing a version of downward dog before standing up.

"Jesus, have a mercy on a man, Emmerdeur." Arlo scrubs his face with his head tipped back, and I smirk, knowing this family dinner is going to be rough for both of us.

Half an hour later, we're walking into Ledger and Ainsley's house.

"Where is everyone?" I yell as we walk toward the kitchen.

"Ledg's out back," Ainsley replies from the kitchen as she chops up some vegetables.

"What can I help with?" I ask, saddling up next to her.

"You can grab potatoes from the—" She stops abruptly as she looks up and sees Arlo standing across the kitchen island. "Damnit, I owe Ledger twenty bucks," she whispers, stunned.

"What the hell?" I cannot believe these assholes were betting on me. Well, that's not true; it's completely believable. It's usually just me making the bets. And I thought I had a better handle on all things Arlo, which I evidently didn't.

Arlo's booming laughter fills the kitchen as Ainsley's cheeks turn pink.

"Shit, I shouldn't have said that."

"Oh no, please tell me more." I cock my hip against the island.

"Ains, did you pull the—" Ledger stops in his tracks as he walks in from the back porch. He looks pointedly at Ainsley. "You owe me twenty bucks."

"Oh, for fuck's sake." I throw my hands up as Arlo is still laughing. "It's not funny! You should be just as mad as I am!"

"You aren't mad; you're just annoyed you weren't as smooth as you thought you were." He smirks.

"Shut it, *Sheriff*," I snark.

His wink takes away the sting out of my brother and best friend betting on me, but only just.

"So, what's for dinner?" I deflect and decide moving on is the best option. Giving Ainsley and Ledger more ammunition is not something I want to do right now.

"To be fair, we knew you were together, or whatever you're calling it since you already told us. The bet was when you were going to bring him to family dinner." Ledger shrugs like it's not just as bad.

"Moving on!" I say loudly as everyone else in the room laughs.

"Dinner is grilled chicken with baked potatoes and random veggies on top of the chicken, like a sauce but not." Ainsley thankfully helps me out. She can still be called my best friend, I guess.

"Sounds delicious. How can I help?" Arlo asks.

"Oh, just sit and enjoy yourself. You're a guest. Do you want something to drink?" Ainsley asks sweetly like she doesn't interact with Arlo on a semi-regular basis.

"I'll get it," I jump in, feeling inadequate as a girlfriend already.

Am I his girlfriend? I mean, technically, I'm his wife, but am I considered girlfriend level now? Yes, you overthinking mess of a woman, especially if the conversation before we came here is anything to go by.

I grab him some iced tea from the refrigerator and grab myself a seltzer. Ainsley and Ledger look at each other, eyebrows raised, and I roll my eyes at their antics.

"Why, thank you, *Marina,*" Arlo jokes.

"Stop. You're giving them more to work with." I chuckle as I set his drink down and take a healthy gulp of mine.

"Knock, knock!" Oakley yells as he enters the house.

"Hi, we're here! Sorry, I got distracted writing," Willow says, looking rather frazzled.

They both stop the second they enter the kitchen, and Oakley's smirk is bigger than I've ever seen.

"Not you two as well," I groan. "It's not even fair since Oakley knows too much." I bury my head in Arlo's neck as he laughs.

"It was just about when you'd bring him to family dinner!" Oakley protests.

"And who won?" Arlo asks. He grunts as I slap his chest.

"I did, of course," Oakley says.

"Barely." Willow rolls her eyes. "And what's this about insider knowledge? I call a mulligan because that's cheating, my dear James." She smirks.

"Okay, that's enough of that. I can already see the heart eyes happening, and making out is never far away from that." I gesture to them wildly.

Everyone laughs as I groan.

"I'm so happy we could provide tonight's entertainment," I say sarcastically.

Arlo chuckles as he pulls me back to his side. "How can we help?" he asks.

"I think we're good. Just going to pop the potatoes in the microwave because we were running late—" I gasp. "I know, I know, don't give me shit. I'll crisp up the skin in the oven, I promise." I wipe my brow in relief as she points her knife at me. "And then the chicken and veg will go on the grill. Nothing else really to do."

Arlo leans in next to my ear as the rest of the family starts talking about business. "I don't think I told you, but you look beautiful tonight," he whispers.

I lean back and look at my usual outfit of leggings and a tank top with skepticism. He yanks me back to him and leans in. "It's not your outfit; it's your whole demeanor. I know your family gives you a hard time, but you're playful and so damn sexy right now."

I move closer to his chest and soak in his words. He may be onto something. Just like when I talked to Lennox, it feels like little pieces of me are changing for the better. Like I'm less bitter, less beaten down by life. The constant grind that I'm always on doesn't seem so appealing anymore. And it's because of this man.

"Can we leave immediately after dinner?" I ask quietly.

I feel his smirk even though I can't see it. "We can do whatever you want, Emmerdeur." He presses a kiss to my temple.

"Eww, get a room. Is this how you normally feel around us?" Willow says in a little sister tone I haven't heard in years.

"Yep, this is payback," I say smoothly, still buried in Arlo's chest.

"You and Oakley are the worst of us all. I wouldn't be one to talk, Will," Ledger says as he walks out the patio doors.

Willow gasps, "We are not! Are we?" She turns to Oakley, who just laughs. "Whatever, I'm not apologizing." She shrugs and drops her indignation act.

Shortly after the usual shenanigans of the Hutton siblings—minus Lennox—dinner is served, although we leave an open seat for him.

"Alright, I'm going first," Ainsley says. "I think my favorite part of the week was taking a half day on Friday. Work has been so busy it was nice to just come home and do absolutely nothing for a couple of hours."

"I'm glad you did that," Ledger says. "My favorite part was hiring a new contractor that will take over the day-to-day details of our projects. I'm officially handing over the reins of every single job at Bluebell Landscaping."

"Holy shit, that's huge!" I say in shock. Never in my life did I think my big brother would give up any control of his company.

"It is, but it feels good. It'll free up more time for me to help Ains out with the bigger picture stuff. Give us more time together."

"That's awesome. Congrats, guys," Arlo chimes in.

"My favorite part was seeing these two finally figure their shit out," Oakley says, gesturing to me and Arlo.

I don't bother with a response; I just roll my eyes as Willow picks up the trail.

"My favorite part was figuring out this damn plot hole in my book. Piece of shit took forever, and I finally figured it out." We all clap as Willow does a little bow with a laugh.

Arlo clears his throat, looking at me, and I nod. "My favorite thing was being invited to the illustrious Hutton family dinner."

"We're happy to have you," Ainsley says happily.

"My favorite part was being forced out of my house and spending more time with Arlo," I blurt out, not even thinking about the repercussions of what I'm saying. The entire table freezes, and a cold silence takes over. I look over at Arlo and see him visibly cringing. Well, shit.

"What do you mean, forced out of your house?" Ledger's tone is one that was common in our house when he had to raise Willow and Lennox when our parents died, and I've never really had it directed at me.

"Umm, well ..." I look at Arlo again, not sure what to tell them.

"Someone has been texting Rina some creepy shit. It's escalated to stuff being left at her house, and I thought it was safer for her to not be there for the time being until I can get things figured out," Arlo says, strong and clear.

"Excuse me?" Ledger's voice gets louder. "This is related to the wrecked workshop?"

"I've called in a friend from my old job, and we're looking to track down the culprit," Oakley adds.

"You fucking knew about the escalation too? Jesus, who doesn't know about this?" Ledger's outrage is obvious.

"Just the three of us know," Arlo says, placating Ledger.

"Are you safe?"

"How the fuck do I know you're safe with him?"

"You knew this whole time!"

"We've got it handled!"

Everyone except Arlo and me talk over each other.

"*Enough!*" I yell, finally silencing the panic. "We didn't tell you because we knew you would freak out." I gesture to everyone. "Arlo and Oakley have things handled, and I'm staying with Arlo as a precaution and nothing else. They're close to figuring out who it is, and things will go back to normal."

It's close enough to the truth, and if the looks of Arlo and Oakley are anything to go by, they see right through my white lie. Who knows, they could be close, could figure this whole thing out tomorrow.

"I don't like this," Ledger says.

"Well, I don't either, but it's happening, and we have the best guys handling things," I tell him, getting more and more irritated by the second by his big brother act. I know it's because he cares, but it also feels like he doesn't trust my judgement or trust Arlo to protect me.

Ainsley puts her hand on his forearm, dousing the fire spewing from his head. Oakley looks like he's caught in the middle of something he didn't willingly volunteer for, and Arlo looks like he's about to go toe to toe with Ledger. I don't know what happened between those two, but the distance between them seems larger than ever. They used to be friends in school, but who knows what happened with that? I'll have to ask Arlo sometime.

"Let's just all calm down and enjoy dinner. Take the night to process everything, and we can get together tomorrow, calmly, to talk about it if you want." Ainsley takes control, just like she usually does. Her badass self can tame a group of rowdy men with just a few words, and I admire the shit out of her for it.

The men grumble in what can barely be considered agreement, and Willow looks like she's plotting an entire book in her head. I breathe out a sigh of relief that this conversation is at least on pause for the moment. Fighting with my family is the last thing I want to do right now.

Dinner slowly returns to our normal routine, and I'm thankful for the reprieve. What I'm not thankful for, or what I'm affronted by, is how subtly handsy Arlo has become as the meal has wound down.

The horniness that sat idle during most of dinner has returned with a vengeance, and I'm ready to get the hell out of here.

It takes ten more minutes of chatting about things I'm not paying attention to, Arlo's hand sliding between my thighs and grazing my clit every so often to make me lose my mind.

"Well." I abruptly stand. "This was great, as usual. Dinner was delicious. If y'all want to get together tomorrow, let me know. We're going to head out." I reach out and grab Arlo's hand, pulling him up as he stutters out a thanks.

Oakley hides his laughter behind his hand. Ainsley and Willow have dreamy looks on their faces, and Ledger looks like he doesn't know what to think.

I drag him to his truck, but he spins me around as we come up to it, pinning me against the side.

"Need something, Emmerdeur?" he asks, ducking his head to press a kiss to my neck.

"You know what you were doing. Whether you were distracting me or not, I don't care. Take me home."

"Done." He opens the door and lifts me into the seat like it's nothing, and I instantly worry about his back. I open my mouth to say something, but he cuts me with a look. "I'm fine, I promise. My back is fine."

"Then show me what you're working with," I say with a smirk. He slams the door and runs around to the driver's side. I can't wait to see what he has in store for me tonight.

CHAPTER THIRTY-FOUR
RINA

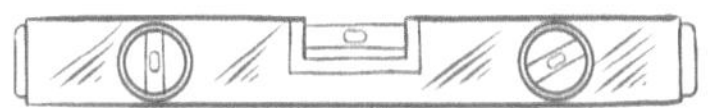

He slams the front door behind him, hands slipping under my shirt and ripping it off over my head. His lips are everywhere and my head dizzy with lust.

I try to reciprocate, but he bends down, pressing his shoulder to my stomach and hoisting me in the air over his shoulder.

"You're going to hurt yourself," I grumble as I smack his ass.

"Quiet, Marina," he growls as he stomps to the bedroom. He gently lowers me down onto the mattress that's on the floor, and I can't help but laugh every time I see it.

"I'll make you a bedframe, I promise," I say in between my laughter.

"Nope. We had a deal, and I'm standing by it." He reaches behind his neck, pulling his shirt off by the collar, and there's something about that move that has me squirming. He quickly kicks off his shoes as he unbuttons his jeans and shoves them down with his boxers.

With him completely naked in front of me, my hands move to my breasts of their own accord. I pinch and roll my nipples as my legs clench together to find some relief.

"You are so fucking sexy," he whispers as his hand glides up and down his cock while he watches me.

My hands move to my leggings, hooking my thumbs in the waistband, and I lift my hips to get them off. Arlo smirks the whole time, not helping me. I'm just watching as he swipes a bead of pre-cum from the head and glides it down.

"So, Mr. Steel, what's on the agenda tonight?" I ask.

"Get on your knees."

Moving without thought, I scramble to my knees in front of him. The bed on the floor is the perfect height for what I assume he's alluding to, and with the added cushion on my knees, it makes me think a floor bed isn't such a terrible idea after all.

His free hand cups my jaw, his thumb trailing along my bottom lip before gently pushing it into my mouth.

"Suck," he commands.

I groan as his thumb pushes against my tongue. His demanding presence awakens something in me I never knew I wanted. Swirling my tongue around his thumb before I suck it, I imagine it's his dick instead. He curses under his breath before ripping it from my mouth.

He takes a step forward, guiding his cock to my lips, and I open greedily.

"You want my cock, Emmerdeur? Does it make you wet to suck me like you own me?"

I moan against his skin, closing my eyes and squeezing my legs together.

"Look at me. I want to see how you feel, how turned on you are, and when you reach the point where you can't take it anymore. I want to see you gag on me as you try to take me all the way." His thumb brushes against my cheek in a sweet gesture that doesn't reflect his words, but the dichotomy makes my clit pulse.

My eyes hold his gaze as his hand threads through my hair and he guides himself further into my mouth. He pauses, wordlessly checking to see if I'm okay, and I give him the slightest nod. It flips a switch for him as he pulls back before thrusting further in, hard and setting a punishing pace. I can only kneel here and take what he gives me, and somehow, it's one of the hottest things I've ever done.

"That's it, you're doing so good, Emmerdeur," he praises. The words make me moan around him as my hands move to my breasts once again. He pushes to the back of my throat, just to my gag reflex, but he goes too fast, triggering the response. Drool pools in my mouth, and I can feel it trailing down my chin as I try to breathe through my nose.

"God, you look gorgeous like this. I wish I wasn't so fucking close already so I could push you to your limit and watch you swallow all my cum." He groans as he pulls out. I suck in a deep breath, trying to regulate my breathing as he steps forward and gives me a soft nudge, causing me to fall onto the mattress. He follows me down, his hands touching every inch of skin he can as he shoves my legs apart. His movements stop as he leans back, and I open my eyes, not even realizing I closed them.

"I can't believe you're mine," he whispers, his eyes touching every inch of skin. When they meet mine again, he looks so vulnerable. "You are mine, right, Emmerdeur?"

"Only yours, Arlo," I murmur.

He settles between my legs, draping his body over mine as he cups my face. "There's never any pressure with me, okay? I would wait forever for you to be mine, and I will continue to wait until you are sure this is what you want. Because I'm all in." He hesitates for a moment, emotions vivid in his eyes. "I'm in love with you. I've always been in love with you, and I will always be in love with you." He presses a soft kiss to my lips as I feel wetness trail down my temples.

I want so badly to reciprocate, and I feel like I'm so damn close, but the fear still stops me. I'd hate myself for it, but telling him I love him before I'm ready wouldn't be right either.

"I mean it, Rina, no pressure. I can see it written all over your face, but I don't say that to push you. I say that because I physically can't hold it in anymore." He kisses the tears away, and I can only hold on to his shoulders like a lifeline. He effortlessly notches himself at my entrance before pressing forward in a smooth, steady thrust.

"You are my everything, Emmerdeur," he whispers in my ear before pulling out and slowly pressing back in.

I feel *everything*. Every emotion I try to run from, every fear I want to ignore, and every inch of him sliding inside of me, giving me pleasure only he can. And for once, I stop thinking. I stop every what-if in my head, and I just *feel*.

His languid thrusts somehow feel better than our usual intense hook-ups, and I know it's because this means something. We mean something, and for the first time since I was handed divorce papers, I want to fight for us. Because I know deep down, it was always supposed to be Arlo.

"Oh god," I moan at both the bliss and the realization.

"Why do you always feel so damn good?" he grunts, and I can tell he's just as lost in the emotion of everything as I am.

"It's because my pussy is perfect, obviously," I throw out as levity, a way to lighten the intensity I'm not sure I can handle more of.

He pulls back from my back abruptly with a grin. "You would be a hundred percent right about that, Marina."

I smirk at his nickname use, and I know no matter how serious things get, we're still us underneath it all. We can joke and be smartasses in the middle of overwhelming emotions, and it somehow doesn't deter from anything. It makes it feel more real.

His thrusts leisurely keep pace. For how long, I'm not sure. All I know is a million years could have passed and it still wouldn't be enough time. This moment is a moment I'll remember for as long as I live, no matter what happens between us.

His hand reaches in between us and circles my clit a couple of times as I throw my head back with a whimper.

"That's right, come for me." His gentle yet demanding tone seals my fate.

The force of my orgasm is so strong it catches me off guard, and it sends Arlo over the edge with me. The sound of his moan is so damn sexy, I swear it sets off another orgasm.

We collapse in a heap on the mattress on the floor as we catch our breath. My blissfully blank brain snags on everything he's said, and my heart pounds in my chest. Doubts persist, and I wonder if things were said in the heat of the moment. It's like I'm just waiting for the other shoe to drop, and I hate that my head goes to that. I don't know how to just shut it off, move on, and stop re-running every single doubt I have.

"Hey, you okay?" his soft voice breaches my slight panic.

"Did you mean it?" I whisper.

He lifts his head so he can look at me. "Every word, Emmerdeur. And I will tell you every single day until you believe it. Until I show you how much I mean it."

The earnestness in his voice almost breaks me. He doesn't realize he already does. He doesn't realize how close I am to reciprocating, and for whatever reason, that bit of control makes the panic recede. He told me no pressure, and I have to take him at his word. No decisions need to be made right this second.

But I know it's only a matter of time before he owns my heart completely again.

CHAPTER THIRTY-FIVE
ARLO

Waking up with Rina in my arms is everything.

I know I overwhelmed her last night, but it was like the truth just bubbled out of me. I couldn't stop it. I don't regret it, per se. I just don't know if bearing my soul will be a setback in what has been significant progress between us.

The sun is just starting to rise, and with it a new day to show I meant every word I said. The buzzing on the makeshift nightstand I have makes me sigh. The downside to being the sheriff in a small town is always being on call.

I carefully slip my arm from a still sleeping Rina and roll over to see who it is. When I see *Oakley* flashing across the screen, I'm instantly hit with a shot of adrenaline.

Rolling off the bed and carefully standing up, I swipe to answer even though it takes me a minute to get up off the floor. Once I walk to the living room, I bring the phone up to my ear.

"Hey."

"Sorry if I woke you," he says.

"I was awake. What's up?"

"I have a lead." The silence is deafening. I'm simultaneously excited, worried, and anxious. "We got a hit on the IP address, and it conveniently lines up with one Tyler Ramsey."

"No shit?" I'm shocked. It feels easy, and I know things like this are never easy.

"The problem is it has to run through Rosedale's system to get a warrant. I'm not sure how long that'll take, and if his escalations are anything to go by…"

"We don't have much time," I finish.

"There's also no guarantee that it is Tyler. It could all be some insane coincidence."

"It's not." I know it's not. Ever since we ran into him at the bistro, I knew something was wrong with him.

"We have to let this go through proper channels," Oakley says like he knows my thoughts are turning to how I can go get this asshole.

"Sure," I clip.

"Arlo…"

"Just let me handle this."

"You're the one who asked me for help, man. I'm not going to let you get yourself into trouble if I can help it."

I sigh, knowing I'm being an overbearing dick right now. "You're right." I think about what I can do to expedite things, and the only logical thing is to go check out Tyler's house and tail him if I'm able to. "Can I ask another favor?"

"Anything." He offers it so freely. It's such a change from when he first moved here.

"I need someone to be with Rina while I'm … out. Can she stay at Grind Time while I go check things out?"

"What exactly are you checking out?" he asks.

"I won't do anything stupid. You're right, it needs to go through proper channels. I just want to check out his house and see if I can get anything. If I'm able to follow him, I'll do that as well, but I won't be noticed."

"I gotta be honest; I'm not loving this plan, but I also know men do stupid shit for the women they love." I laugh at his response because he isn't wrong, although Willow ended up saving his ass in the end.

"Can Rina stay with you? You're the only one I trust with this." A vulnerable truth I wouldn't have admitted a few months ago.

"I can't force her to stay, but I will keep an eye on her as best as I can, even if she leaves," he concedes.

"That's all I ask. Thanks, man. I'll keep you updated." I hang up without preamble. We don't need to harp on shit, and I need to figure out exactly what my plan is.

"Who am I apparently staying with?" Rina's annoyed tone startles me.

I turn to look at her and see her standing in my bedroom doorway wearing nothing but one of my *Sheriff* shirts. It's sexy as fuck, and if I didn't just get the phone call I did, I'd drag her back to bed.

Sighing, I know being one hundred percent honest is the only way she'll do what I tell her.

"Oakley found a lead, and I want to investigate it today. The problem is, I need to know you're safe."

"You can't watch me twenty-four seven, Arlo."

"I know, but right now? With everything that's happened, I need to know you're safe at all times. I know that's irrational, but I'm not apologizing for it. I can't let anything happen to you, and if that takes eyes on you all the time, so be it. I won't change my mind on this." My words are stern.

Her shoulders slump as she walks to where I'm seated on the couch, leaning into me so my head is on her stomach. I wrap my arms around her, running my thumb back and forth on her lower back. "I don't like it, but I understand it. Where am I going today?"

"Grind Time. I know it's not ideal for working, but hopefully I won't be gone long."

Her fingers softly scratch my head, and I can feel the moment she caves. It settles my heart more than I thought it would. This entire stalker situation has me so on edge, but I'm trying to hide it from Rina so she doesn't freak out more than she already is.

"I'm going to need unlimited food and coffee."

My shoulders shake with my laughter. "Tell Oakley to put it on my tab."

"Be careful giving me that power. I'll be buying shit for everyone," she quips.

"If it keeps you safe, buy the whole damn town breakfast." I chuckle. She doesn't join me; instead, she leans back so she can look at my face.

"This whole thing is making you really nervous." A statement, not a question.

"Truthfully? Yeah. Stalkers are unpredictable, and the fact that you are the one being targeted is ... fucking scary for me," I admit. Her eyes hold mine before she nods.

"Okay. If it makes things easier for you, I will try very hard not to be my usual stubborn self."

"Be stubborn, but just do it at Grind Time with Oakley around, okay?"

"I can do that," she whispers before leaning down and pressing a kiss to my lips. Relief hits me hard, and I take the moment to just hold her.

She has no idea how much relief her concession gives me, and I mentally make a note to find some way to make it up to her. To show her how thankful I am that she didn't fight me on this.

Walking back from dropping off Rina and having a quick conversation with Oakley is only giving me too much time to think. I also have a forty-minute drive with nothing but the open road to do more thinking. I'm not sure my anxious mind can handle it, honestly, but I don't have much of a choice. It will be the ultimate test in using what my therapist has been helping me with. Coping with the stress, the self-doubt, and trusting myself.

Way easier said than done, but here goes nothing.

I'm ten minutes into the drive when the panic starts to override logic. The what-ifs, the thoughts of this stalker actually getting to Rina, become overwhelming.

All I can picture is finding Rina how I found Lennox, tied up in the dilapidated cabin with blood everywhere.

My knuckles turn white as my grip on the steering wheel tightens. My chest feels too tight, like I can't get enough air.

I breathe in deep, holding it to the count of five before blowing it out slowly. I repeat this process until the tightness in my chest lessens.

I consciously stretch my fingers, attempting to get the blood flow back into them as I start to feel more focused.

It won't get to that point because I'll keep Rina safe. I can do this; I can figure out who this person is and take care of him before it gets to any of that. Thanks to Oakley, I have more resources at my disposal than I ever have. The panic subsides, bringing resolution to the forefront. Failure isn't an option, not when Rina is at stake. If I remember that and hold the fear at bay, I can catch this guy. I know I can.

I turn my thoughts to what I need to do today. There isn't a ton I can really do since I technically don't have a warrant and we're mostly working off of hunches at this point. Checking out Tyler's house and possibly tailing him are the best I can do, but you can learn a lot about someone's everyday habits, and I'm hoping he fucks up, missteps just enough to give me the in I need.

Pulling up in front of one of his neighbor's houses, in perfect view of his, I'm impressed with the neighborhood. It's nicer than I anticipated, more of a family neighborhood and less of a place that screams "a stalker lives here". Although, I'm not sure what a place like that would look like.

I park, grab my notepad from the passenger seat, open to a fresh page, and poise my pen at the ready. A list starts to form, first with license plates, then descriptors of people I see. It adds up to a few pages of notes, and I haven't even gotten a glimpse of Tyler yet.

A sigh escapes me as I toss the notepad onto the dash. Picking up my phone, I shoot a message to check in with Oakley, and he reassures me everything is good. I know if I text Rina, I'll get distracted, so I have to be happy with his vague reassurance.

I glance up and glimpse of movement in front of Tyler's house, doing a double take before I realize it's him. Scrambling to grab my notepad, I write down everything I see. His clothes, his demeanor, and his activity. Any tiny detail may prove to be the thing that solves everything. You never know.

He moseys around his property, not overtly looking for anything or doing much of anything, and it's strange. I get a tingle in the back of my neck, and my gut says he's our guy. I have exactly zero evidence to prove that, but there's something about him that makes me uncomfortable. He disappears into the backyard, and I wish I had a fucking warrant to just bust into his house. This waiting and observing when I'm so sure he has something to do with all of this is quite possibly one of the hardest challenges I've had in a while.

Fifteen minutes later, there's no movement and I'm losing my mind. I seriously contemplate just busting in, the law be damned, but I know that's irrational. Drumming my fingers on the steering wheel, I try to calm myself. Being antsy won't help anything, and staying level-headed is key. As I'm talking myself down, his garage door opens and his car pulls out.

It's showtime.

Tailing him is simple. I don't get too close, conscious of looking suspicious, as he drives to the center of town. He pulls into the on-street parking of a smaller Greek restaurant. I luck out and find a spot that has a good view of the front door and his car, so I can watch where he goes. He calmly gets out of the car, stepping onto the sidewalk and walking up to a woman who's standing in front of the restaurant.

She turns, and the excitement on her face is obvious. The hug she gives him even more so. It's not a familial hug but intimate, and it just creates more confusion in my head. He presses a kiss to her lips, and I see her melt into him.

What the actual fuck? I snap a quick picture with my phone before I lose the chance to.

They enter the Greek restaurant, and I contemplate going in and grabbing a table, but he may recognize me from dinner at the bistro, so I choose to play it safe. This also means I have some time to go back to his house and see what I can find through the windows. Maybe not my smartest idea, but I need something to work with.

I quickly drive back to his house and make sure there's no one walking around, and double-check for any security cameras he may have before I walk the same route he did not that long ago. Every window in the front is closed up, and I'm starting to think I'm not going to get lucky today.

And then I walk around to the back. Technically, I'm illegally entering his property, but I'll deal with the repercussions if they arise.

I slowly peek around the back, making sure I don't run into anything like a dog before releasing my breath at being alone. His backyard is pretty unkempt. Lots of dirt and overgrown grass, but no dogs, thankfully. I look at the backside of the house and see no covering on his slider, and the blinds are open on all the back-facing rooms.

Jackpot.

Taking my phone out, I carefully walk up to each window and take pictures of what I see. The first window, along with the sliding glass door, doesn't really show me much outside of normal living spaces. However, the last window has my teeth grinding so hard I feel like they may crack with the force.

A desk sits as the lone piece of furniture, but that's now what draws my attention. It's the walls covered in pictures that send me into a panic. It's hard to make out who the women are, but I catch a glimpse of familiar brown hair. She seems to be the main focus on one wall, but the other three walls are other women.

Is he stalking more than just Rina?

I snap pictures as best as I can, knowing they aren't going to be super clear and nothing we can use to gain a warrant, but it's more information.

I take one last look at the room before I flee to my truck and head back to Bluebell Falls. I need to talk to Oakley, and then I need to go stand under the waterfall and let the water pound out all of my anxiety and fear from seeing that room.

Then, I'll regroup and figure out how to catch this bastard once and for all.

CHAPTER THIRTY-SIX
RINA

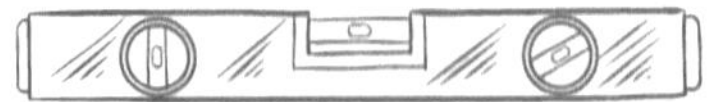

As much as I love Oakley and Willow, and as much as I know this is helping Arlo's sanity, sitting in a coffee shop all day and not working is going to make me lose it.

I'm ahead with commissions so it's not like I can't afford the day off, but just sitting here knowing Arlo is doing God knows what in Rosedale has me on edge. I wish I could do more, honestly, and I feel useless. I hate feeling useless.

"How are you doing, Rina?" Oakley says as he sits next to me, placing a fresh coffee on the tabletop.

I guess that's the good part of today. Arlo told Oakley to keep the food and drinks coming, and I'm not even pretending to play coy about it.

"Oh, swell," I snark, then instantly feel bad. It's not Oakley's fault I'm bored out of my damn mind. "Sorry, I'm not used to just sitting all day."

"I get it. You're used to going non-stop all day, and this is the exact opposite."

I sigh. "Yeah, I'm not very good at just sitting. Or following directions." I cringe.

"I'd say you're doing just fine on that front. Arlo just wants to make sure you aren't vulnerable."

Willow comes to join us, and I look around and see we're the only ones here.

"Sooooo." She smirks.

"Ask away, Will. Get it out of your system." I slump back in my chair, knowing this was coming.

"How long have you been Arlo actually been dating?" She thinks it's a simple question, but it's anything but.

"Umm…" I struggle to find an easy answer.

"I'm just giving you shit. I'm not trying to know all the details. If you want to tell me, you will. I have a feeling things between the two of you are still … complicated." She laughs as Oakley rolls his eyes.

I bark out a laugh. "Understatement of the century." Is it more or less complicated that we're technically still married?

"We can go back to your workshop once I close here," Oakley offers.

"Nah, I'm just calling today a wash. I was actually thinking about how I can help with this whole situation." Oakley arches an eyebrow at me. "Even with whatever Arlo is doing right now, we don't have a warrant in order to actually do anything, correct?"

"Correct."

"So, what if we draw him out? Force Tyler's hand."

I see his mind working in front of me. He doesn't want to like the idea, but he does.

"Arlo will hate it." I wince at the truth of his statement. I know Arlo will hate it, but sitting here doing nothing isn't really my style.

"Yep."

"And you still want to do it?"

"Yep."

He sighs, and I almost cheer. I have him interested.

"What do you have in mind?"

"Can I chime in and say Arlo will absolutely lose his shit and this is a terrible idea?" Willow asks.

"You just did," I deadpan.

"I'm just thinking about how I took things into my own hands when… Well, you know, and things did not really go well." She's talking about Tennison. When she showed up, saving the day, but it also cost her a lot.

"Why did you go to that cabin?" I ask her.

"Rina…" Oakley scolds.

"No, this is important. I know it's hard to talk about, but why did you put yourself in danger? Why did you go there?" I ask again.

"Because I needed to do something. I needed to help Oakley. I couldn't just sit here and do nothing if there was a chance I could help." Her soft voice, a little shaky, makes me feel bad for forcing the issue.

But her answer is exactly how I'm feeling.

"And look how that turned out!" Oakley's raised voice echoes through the space.

"Listen, you understand Arlo's side of this. Willow understands mine. I need to do something, Oakley. Sitting here until the red tape gets figured out isn't doing me or you both any favors. What if I'm able to expedite things and end this?" I'm trying desperately to plead with his rational brain, but I'm not sure it's working.

"What if the worst-case scenario happens and you get hurt? I'll never forgive myself. Arlo will absolutely lose any progress he's made. As your friend—hell, as his—I'm telling you this is a terrible idea."

"We don't even know if it's actually Tyler. If I draw him out, get more information, we can at least determine if he's the bad guy." I throw my hands up in exasperation.

"Jesus fuck, you Hutton women are feisty and stubborn as shit," he grumbles. Willow beams like it's the best compliment in the world, and I have to hide my smile behind my hand.

"Does that mean you'll at least hear me out?"

"Arlo's going to kill me."

"I can handle Arlo."

"Oh, I bet you can," Willow singsongs before slapping her hand over her mouth. Laughter from everyone breaks the tension.

"Tyler was really upset when we ran into him. I technically ghosted him on our first date, and I think using that is our key. I can call him, apologize for being a bitch and ditching him, and then see if he wants a re-do?"

"I like apologizing but not attempting a re-do. You going out with him will give Arlo an aneurysm, and it puts you in too vulnerable of a position." Oakley pokes holes in my plan.

"What if we can ensure my safety?"

"And how do we do that?"

"Someone tails us?" I offer. Honestly, I have no idea. This isn't something I consider doing on an everyday basis, and I have a feeling Arlo and Oakley have better ideas on how to accomplish it. It doesn't mean I think we need to scratch my whole idea because I intend to do it, regardless of if they help me or not. Things need to change, and if that means taking them into my own hands, so be it.

Oakley looks up to the ceiling.

"I don't like it, but I understand your reasoning. I would need to include Arlo and probably the Rosedale Police Department."

"That sounds like it'll scream 'set-up'."

"You won't see us—hopefully. But going in there without any form of back-up is out of the question. Arlo will fire me." He smirks.

"You don't work for Arlo, so he can't fire you," Willow adds, and I'm going to have to build something for her for having my back.

"Whose side are you on, Trouble?"

"Uh, I'm on yours, of course." The breathiness of Willow's voice makes me roll my eyes. I don't want to know any of the kinky shit they get up to.

"Jesus, get a room," I mutter.

"We have one upstairs," Oakley says so smoothly as he keeps his eyes on Willow. "Shit, sorry." He has the decency to look embarrassed.

"Yep, we're never speaking of this again. So, I'm going to go call Tyler, and you can fill Arlo in on whatever you need to." I stand up and go to the opposite corner, using the distraction to my advantage. They can keep making googly eyes at each other while I get shit done.

I pull up the number after searching for a second and hold my breath as it rings.

"Rina?" Tyler answers on the second ring, with hope in his voice. He doesn't sound like the asshole he was at the bistro, and it throws me a little. I was prepared for hostility, and this is anything but. I hear Oakley attempting to stop me in the background, but Willow somehow stops him. I'm too focused on my phone call to see what's going on behind me.

"Hey, Tyler, I'm glad you picked up. I wanted to call and apologize for ghosting you on our date. That was an asshole move, and I'd like to make it up to you if I can." *Shit, that wording is going to send mixed signals, but it's too late to take it back.*

"You want to apologize?"

"I do." I leave it at that, hoping he takes the lead from here. This is already not where I thought the conversation would go, so maybe it's better to be on the defensive.

"Did that guy you were with do something? Did he put you up to leaving me?" His eager tone is confusing. He sounds like a teen hoping to get praise from his crush. It worries more than I'm willing to let on.

"He's..." I contemplate what to say. "Not in the picture anymore." The words, although what Tyler needs to hear, physically hurt to say. Arlo will always be in the picture, and even if it's a lie, it feels like a betrayal to say.

Silence greets my ear right as Oakley enters my line of sight and sits down opposite me. I arch my eyebrow at him as he mimes zipping his lips shut, letting me know he'll be quiet.

"Meet me Saturday for dinner. At the steakhouse." Tyler's demands refocus my attention, and I wince at what he said. I know I had this idea, but I wasn't fully committed to actually seeing him again.

"Umm."

"Make it up to me, Rina. Dinner, that's all I'm asking." I want to tell him he's not asking at all, but I have a feeling invoking his ire isn't a great option for me.

Oakley subtly shakes his head, apparently close enough to hear Tyler's side of the conversation.

"Saturday. I'll meet you," I say reluctantly, and instant regret laces my decision.

"You won't regret it. I can't wait until you're mine again." Then he hangs up.

My blood turns cold and drains from my face. If we weren't sure before, I am now.

"What the fuck, Rina?" Oakley whispers.

"I-I— Fuck, what did I just do?" I whimper as tears flood my eyes.

"What did he say at the end?" Oakley's voice is calm, but when I look up at him, I can see the panic just below the surface.

"He said 'I can't wait until you're mine again.'"

"Fuck, I need to call Arlo." Oakley stands up and starts pacing, but the front door opens as he does.

The bell dings, and we turn to see who it is. When Arlo stops dead in his tracks, I close my eyes and realize trying to play hero was the wrong move. There's nothing to do about it now, though, because knowing Tyler is my stalker means I want him caught yesterday. And this is the easiest way to do it.

"What happened?" he asks, looking between Willow, Oakley, and me.

Oakley turns his eyes toward me as if to say, *This is your plan; you tell him,* and even though he's right, I make a vow to never build him a piece of furniture for Grind Time for him throwing me under the bus.

"I called Tyler."

CHAPTER THIRTY-SEVEN
ARLO

"You did what?" I yell, any remanence of calm gone with three words. I turn my attention to Oakley and lose it. "You were supposed to watch her. You were supposed to make sure she didn't do anything stupid. How the fuck could you let this happen?"

His eyes flash with anger, but I couldn't care less.

"You've got to be fucking kidding me. I'm not a kid, Arlo!" Rina yells at me as she walks forward and shoves me in anger. I'm sure later, when I have time to reflect on this moment, I'll realize I'm being an asshole, but that time is not now.

"You sure as hell are acting like one! Why the fuck would you call him?"

"Because I'm trying to end this!" she yells. "Because I don't want Oakley to have to fucking watch me when you need to do something. Because I have a whole-ass business to run, and I want my normal life back!"

"This isn't the way to accomplish that," I growl.

"So that's why I'm meeting him on Saturday and getting real evidence, so we can end this once and for all."

It takes me a minute to register her words, but once I do, I stumble back against the side wall.

"Woah, easy there." Oakley rushes over to me and helps me sit down. My vision blurs as my chest constricts. I feel like I can't get enough air into my lungs, and my heart is beating too fast.

"Hey," I hear Rina's voice, but it does nothing to calm me. "Breathe with me. In; one, two, three, four, five. Out; one, two, three, four, five." I try to follow her directions, but the lack of oxygen is making me feel slow. "Again. In; one, two, three, four, five. Out; one, two, three, four, five. Good, that's good, baby." It's the fear in her voice that drags me back to the surface. Her eyes focus on me as she repeats her count, and I try with all of my energy to follow her words.

"Good, you're doing good. One more time." She guides me once again through the breathing exercise I've only told her about once, and my chest finally unlocks and I feel like I can get air again.

"Hi," I croak as the panic recedes.

"Hi." She still looks concerned.

"I—" I have no idea how to explain what just happened.

"Nope. No explanation needed. I'm sorry for causing it." She looks like she's about to cry.

I take a shaky breath and try to organize my thoughts. Looking around, I see Willow tucked under Oakley's side with worry on her face, and he looks a little shellshocked.

Fuckkkk. I hate that they all had to watch me like this. I hate that I'm not further along with my therapy to prevent an incident like this. It makes me feel weak.

"I'm sorry you guys had to see that. Is there any way I can borrow the apartment upstairs for, like, twenty minutes?" I owe them all a bigger explanation, but right now, I need to call my therapist so he can help me digest the information I just got from Rina.

"Of course. It's all yours. We're closed up, so just come down when you're finished and lock up. We'll head home, but call me later," Oakley says.

I nod my thanks to him, then turn my attention to Rina, who is still crouched beside me, running her hand along my thigh.

"Will you come with me?" I murmur.

"Of course." She stands and helps me up as we head up to the apartment Oakley used to live in. It's sparsely furnished, but there is a couch and that's all we need. I pull Rina to it and sit down with her as I pull out my phone and dial a number I've never called. I've never had to call him outside of our video appointments, and it feels like an invasion, even though he told me to call in times just like this.

He picks up on the first ring. "Arlo? You okay?"

"Nope. I'm a whole lot of not okay right now, Doc." Rina grasps my hand, and I give it a squeeze.

"Start from the beginning." He doesn't hesitate, and I have no idea if I'm interrupting him, but I get the feeling he wouldn't tell me either way.

"I'm trying to get leads on Rina's stalker and went to find some. When I got back from a little reconnaissance, my girlfriend informed me that she called the stalker and was meeting him on Saturday in an attempt to draw him out. I-I just panicked when she told me and had a full-on panic attack."

"Okay. Let's start with how you're currently feeling. Calmer? Do you need to go to the hospital for some medication?"

"Nope. Rina talked me through my breathing, and I'm feeling okay. Not great, but better."

"Okay, that's good. Do you want to talk through why you had a panic attack, or do you want me to help you come down from it?"

I appreciate that he's asking me what direction I want to go, but as I look up at Rina, concern written all over her face, I know I only have one answer.

"Why. I need to talk through the why."

"Okay. Your girlfriend made plans behind your back and when you found out about them, you felt like you lost control of something you previously held control of."

"It's less about behind my back, although my ... co-worker being involved and okaying it didn't help things, and it's more about putting herself in danger without thinking of the consequences." I look at Rina, and I can tell she's trying very hard not to refute.

"Good, keep digging on that line of thought." Dr. Ames likes to leave it open-ended when we talk. I'm glad he got me started, but figuring it out on my own with little pushes from him seems to be more beneficial for me to understanding things in the long run.

"This guy is escalating, and we don't know what his next move is. He seems impulsive and emotional, and that's usually a terrible combination when talking about a stalker. Rina creating a plan isn't the issue; it's the lack of back-up and support that bothers me more. I need her safe, and rashly calling up this guy and agreeing to meet negates that. I have three days to get back-up to try to expedite a warrant because we still need that to do anything and create contingencies to keep her safe." I sigh once all of it is out. Rina looks guilt-ridden, and as much as I want to comfort her, I need to talk through this all first. I'm glad she's here so she can see my thought process and understand why I freaked out. But at the end of the day, I need to figure out how to cope with stressful situations without crumbling, and that's the reason for the emergency therapy call.

"All appropriate reasons for your brain to go into overdrive."

"Maybe, but a panic attack isn't a response I can afford as sheriff. The only reason I didn't curl up in a ball on the floor was Rina counting my breathing for me. I couldn't even focus long enough to do it." It was scary not being in control, and I want to learn how to avoid it if it ever happens again.

Rina's hand slides into mine, squeezing it in silent support, and I couldn't be more grateful for her. I know I need to apologize for yelling at her, but she's giving me the time to sort myself out first.

"But you've never had a panic attack on the job before, correct?" Dr. Ames asks.

"I've only had one in the hospital after the accident."

"So, what does that tell you?" he gently leads the conversation.

I look over at Rina again and know the answer. "I panicked because it's Rina. I'm putting more weight into it when the reason I had such a strong reaction was because it puts Rina at risk."

"Good. I don't think you need to worry about how this affects your job."

"Okay, but how do I ensure this doesn't happen again?"

"You don't. There is no way to guarantee this won't happen again, but talking with Rina about why you reacted this way will help. Making sure you two are on the same page so she understands your feelings and concerns about her safety will ultimately be what lessens the chances of this happening again. I also think it's a good idea to step back when you start to feel the panic rise and do your breathing to bring some clarity to your head before you start talking. When you jump in with that initial reaction, you don't give yourself time to process everything. You're hyper-focused on the fear, and it's hard to see anything past that."

Everything he says makes sense. Will it be easy to adjust my natural inclination when it comes to Rina's safety? No. But if I want her in my life long-term, it's something I need to put the work into.

"Makes sense. She's the trigger," I murmur, still thinking about his words.

"Which makes sense when you look at the bigger picture."

His simple statement is an epiphany. The bigger picture is keeping Rina in my life; of course, her safety is a huge trigger. I know I won't be able to keep her in a bubble—Lord knows she would never allow that to happen—but making sure she understands my fears and concerns with her safety will allow her to help me alleviate the potential panic in the future.

"As always, you're the best, Doc."

"You do the work, Arlo. I'm just here to tap you in the right direction. You think you're doing better? I can put you on the schedule for tomorrow too"

"I'll let you know if I need another one before that. Thank you for taking my call with no hesitation."

"I gave you my number for a reason. I'm just glad you used it. That, in itself, is a huge step. I'm here if you need me again, but good job today."

"Thanks, Doc." I hang up and take a deep breath. Shifting so I'm facing Rina, I squeeze her hand. "I'm sorry."

"Nothing to be sorry for. I'm the one that should be sorry. I knew you wouldn't approve of the plan, and I did it anyway. I thought taking it into my own hands would make things happen faster, and I didn't think about logistics past that."

"I'm not very good at verbalizing my concerns, especially when it comes to you. I know I'm getting better, but fucking Tyler has me more on edge than I want to admit. It's not that I think your plan is bad; I just need to figure out how to let you do it safely. I will not jeopardize you for anything."

"I see that now. I was too caught up in getting from point A to point B as fast as possible and didn't think about what it would take to actually accomplish that. It's not as simple as going to dinner with Tyler and 'catching him'. We need to make sure everything's in place, so when you do take him in, charges stick and no one gets hurt. It was shortsighted of me." She sighs and leans into my shoulder.

"I want to get a plan together and cover all our bases, but I'd really like to go back to your house and hold you tonight. All of that can wait until tomorrow," I murmur against her temple.

"Done. Let's head out."

"Can you drive? I still feel pretty drained from the damn panic attack."

"Of course."

I shakily stand up, Rina supporting me the whole time as we head out after locking up Grind Time.

There's a lot of work to get done before Saturday, but tonight? Tonight, I'm going to hold my wife as she sleeps, knowing she's safe in my arms.

CHAPTER THIRTY-EIGHT
ARLO

Saturday comes too fast.

I'm a bundle of nerves, but I'm trying to stay focused on what needs to be done and not the potential problems that could arise. Nothing good will come from me stressing about the what-ifs.

"Great news," Oakley says as he walks into my office and sits down in the chair across from me.

I arch an eyebrow, waiting for him to continue.

"Usually, people get excited with good news, you know. Anyway, my guy on the Marshals helped the Rosedale Police Department obtain a warrant."

"Do I want to know what helped means?"

"Nope. You just get to be relieved there's a warrant in place. We can execute it while Rina and Tyler are at dinner, or we can keep an eye on them and see what information Rina can get before going in."

"And we have Rosedale's support?"

"We do. I'm in contact with one of their lieutenants, and he's just waiting for word on which approach we want to take. They've been really easy to work with. I think they're just happy to get a scumbag off the streets, one they didn't even know about." He smirks.

"It's probably the only reason they so readily agreed to work with us."

"That, and when a U.S. Marshal tells you it's a priority, people tend to listen." Oakley grins.

"You would know."

"How's Rina doing?"

I sigh. "She's acting fine and tells me she's ready, but I know she's nervous. We don't really have a concrete plan on how to get information out of him, what she should say, and where she should steer his movement and the conversation. Everything is open-ended, and I think she realizes that now."

"We don't know much about him, other than that he's unhinged, so I'm not sure we even can give her more than we've already talked about."

"Exactly. I don't like it, but I also see the merit in finishing this shit now."

"Can I give you some bullshit advice from someone who is also dating a Hutton woman?"

"I have a feeling you're going to tell me anyway."

"I am glad we're on the same page. Willow took things into her own hands with Tennison because she thought it would help me. She wasn't thinking about herself or the aftermath. Rina is the same way. Yes, it's her life that's being affected, but she's doing what she thinks is best for everyone. Waiting and being patient is not a specialty for them. Going along with it and not fighting it is a hell of a lot easier than standing in her way," he says.

"I'm not trying to stand in her way. I'm trying to keep her safe." If I sound defensive, it's because I am.

"I know you are. That's why I got Woodcroft to do some digging into Tyler."

"Your old partner?"

"Yep. I'm just waiting for him to call me back with the intel. I'm not sure we'll get a ton more information, but any can help Rina tonight."

"That makes me feel marginally better." And it does. I'm no less worried, but more information usually means a better outcome.

"Did you apologize to Willow again for me? I didn't expect to pull you away from Grind Time so often." Changing the subject eases my nerves.

"I promised her a solid month of not having to open when this is finished, and that seemed to appease her." His smirk lets me know that wasn't the only thing promised, but I'm not trying to hear about their bedroom activities.

"I'm shocked you left the two of them in charge of your shop." I chuckle.

"Yeah, that's why I'm leaving." He stands up, giving me a small salute.

"I'll be over in a few to get Rina," I call as he leaves. He throws up a hand in acknowledgment, then disappears out the front door.

Putting a call into the lieutenant in the Rosedale Police Department, I fill him in on Oakley's development and let him know I'll call him again once I get more information. We're hoping whatever gets dug up will help strengthen the case against Tyler. Since we already have the warrant, now we need more evidence.

I count my breaths before heading over to Grind Time. Rina and I had a long talk the other night after my panic attack. I told her my worries and fears, and she did the same. We mutually agreed this is the best option for locking up Tyler, but we both know it's not the safest approach and a lot can go wrong. Being able to understand each other and where our heads are at has helped my anxiety a lot.

The walk to Grind Time gives me just enough time to turn my focus on Rina instead of what's going to happen in eight hours.

"Long time, no see," Oakley chirps from behind the counter as I walk in. Rolling my eyes, I turn to Rina and join her at the table she's sitting at.

"How are you doing?" I ask.

"Good." She's too cheery, trying too hard to ease my mind.

"How are you really?"

She sighs. "Nervous. Mildly terrified."

"Understandably. You want to go for a walk?"

"Absolutely." She stands abruptly, walking over to Willow and giving her a hug, then drags me out the front door. "Where to?"

"My truck." I chuckle. This is stir-crazy Rina, and my idea to take a breather from everything makes even more sense now.

I drive to the one place to guarantee to calm us both down and distract us until it's time for her little get-together with Tyler. I refuse to call it a date.

I can feel her tension release as we pull up to the trail that will lead to the falls. She slumps in her seat and grabs my hand.

"Thank you."

"I think we both need this," I tell her, leaning over and pressing a kiss to the crown of her head. We get out of the truck and onto the trail, and the fresh air and smell of pine trees are a natural drug, pulling us both out of our heads and calming the worry vibrating through our bodies.

We hike silently until we make it to our spot and grab a seat on the large, flat rock on the edge of the pool of water.

"I'm nervous. This is all one big mistake." She breaks the silence first.

"You're a badass, and I think this is the best way to finish this once and for all."

"Quite the change of opinion there." Her head tilts to look at me with a smile on her face.

"I may not like this plan at all, but it has nothing to do with you not having a good idea or being capable of handling yourself. It's that he's unpredictable and none of us know what's coming. But I have complete faith that you will get this done like the boss you are and nail this asshole to the ground."

"That might be the sweetest thing you've ever said to me."

"Not true, and you know it. I happen to remember, not too long ago, when I was very romantic and told you exactly how I feel about you. That was the nicest thing I've said to you." I smirk.

"And so damn humble," she snarks.

Laughing, I grab her around the waist and bring her to my lap.

"I mean it, Emmerdeur. You are capable, and I know you'll do just fine. Oakley and I, along with the Rosedale Police, will be there as back-up, so you won't be alone. Just ... be safe and don't make any drastic decisions, okay? I don't think my heart can handle that."

"You know, I've been so hesitant with us. We're obviously great together, but the hurt and trust are hard to get over for me. This Arlo, though? The one that's grown and put in work to be the man you want to be? Makes it extremely hard to remember the Arlo from all those years ago and all the hurt he caused. It also makes it hard to be mad about still being married."

My breath catches in my throat. We haven't mentioned being married still since she found out, and now was not the time I thought we'd discuss it.

"The last six months have changed a lot for me. Everything with Tennison made me re-evaluate my priorities. And somehow, everything with Tyler has made me realize the man of my dreams has been in front of me all along. You've been patient, attentive, and yet stayed your perfectly grumpy self while I figured things out. I don't want to go into tonight with any regrets or wishes."

"Rina..."

"Let me, please." She adjusts so we're facing each other, and I see the depth of her emotions in her eyes. "I love you. Not the idea of you or what we had when we were young. I love the you that you are now, the you that loves me despite all my flaws. I love how you care about this nosy-ass town and act like you hate it, but you do it every single day with zero complaints. I love that you are taking steps to heal. I love that you loved me so much you tattooed my heart on your skin. I love you, and I want you to burn those fucking divorce papers," she says through watery laugher.

"As soon as this shit is over, they're gone," I whisper.

"Good." She kisses me. "I love you."

"I love you too." We press our foreheads together and breathe each other in.

I took her out here to completely step away from what was happening in town. Instead, a confession I never thought I'd hear from her lips again has me feeling confident about our future. Patting my pocket as we get up, I feel the box I've been carrying with me for a couple of days now with nothing but hope in my heart.

Sitting in the car with two other officers, not knowing what is going on in the damn restaurant, may give me a heart attack.

The good news is that Oakley's old partner found some interesting information about Tyler. He hasn't held a job in over three years and is currently living in a house he inherited from his mother. We're not sure where he's getting money from, but his social media boasts a high-paying illustration job and the lifestyle to match. He's full of contradictions, and it gives me even more surety that this is the right move.

Collectively, we've decided to let Rina lead things and see where it goes before executing the search warrant on his house. This gives us the best chance of getting a confession to ensure charges stick and have the highest penalty. There's a couple of plain-clothed officers inside, close enough to hear what's going on at their table, and they've been relaying information to us periodically. It's set up the best we can, and all things considered, we have a lot of bases covered. However, there is still a lot that's unknown, and that's what I don't love. Not with Rina in the middle of it.

"Brad just texted. Sounds like Rina is hinting at taking things back to his place," Lieutenant Kempe says as he looks down at this phone.

My fists clench hard, and I try to remember the objective. She doesn't want to go to his house. It's just a way to get us more information. If I keep that on repeat in my head, maybe I won't go bust down the fucking door.

"Why don't we just go search his place while they're at dinner?" the officer in the backseat asks. I didn't even pay enough attention to catch his name.

"Because she can get under his skin and figure out his endgame. She can get us more information needed in order to lock him away for the rest of his life. And there are other women involved, so getting as much information can help link more things to him as well." An exaggeration, sure, but the reasoning still works.

"We're aiming for evidence," Lieutenant Kempe adds.

"Riiight," the douchebag in the back says. I don't care if he agrees; his boss is telling him to do it. He doesn't need to ask questions.

"Heads up. Looks like they're walking out."

My head jolts up as I watch Tyler leading, more like dragging, Rina around to the parking lot. It takes everything in me not to climb out of the car and go after her.

"Brad says they're going back to his place." He puts the car in drive, slowly pulling out to follow them. We have officers in his neighborhood already, but they won't move in until we tell them to. Oakley is with them, and I'm attempting to keep him updated in between keeping myself in check.

We follow him at a close enough distance to keep eyes on them, but the entire drive to his house I have a bad feeling deep in my bones. It's no longer worry; it's a gut feeling that shit is about to hit the fan. The same feeling I had before repelling from the helicopter that broke my hip and back.

CHAPTER THIRTY-NINE
RINA

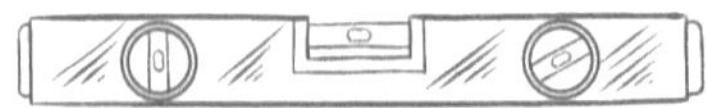

My stubborn tendencies may have taken things too far this time.

Planning this sounded easy. Getting information felt like a necessity, especially with other women in jeopardy. But as I'm sitting here attempting to eat a bite of my steak, I'm second-guessing everything.

Tyler's anger and aggressiveness from the last time I saw him are nowhere to be seen, but there's something lurking just under the surface. His smarmy smirk sends a tremor down my spine every time its attention is focused on me.

"Sooo…" I know I need to push conversation with him, but all I want to do is run far away and straight into Arlo's arms. "How's work going?"

"The usual, nothing exciting. I'd rather talk about you and why you ghosted me." *There's the aggression.* His tone is firm and annoyed.

"The man I was with, he's from my past and I needed … closure. There was some bad blood, and I wanted to hear him out, but that-that wasn't fair to you. I apologize." Do I sound earnest enough? God, I hope so.

He holds my stare for an extended moment, and all I can do is hold my breath and hope he believes me. Everything relies on this.

"Is he out of your life now?" His curiosity shines through his attempt at a bored tone.

It physically hurts me to give him the answer I need to, especially after our conversation at the falls earlier. "Completely out. It was just for closure, I promise."

He pops a piece of steak in his mouth, chewing slowly as he contemplates if I'm being truthful or not, I assume.

"Let's start fresh. I'd like to just forget about the last time we saw each other. I wasn't at my best," he says.

"We can do that."

"How's business going? Had any interesting requests lately?"

It's an odd question and very specific. I build furniture and that's not a question that's common, but it instantly brings the request for my dream bed to my head. Is he digging for that? Does he want my reaction to receiving that weird-as-fuck request?

"Umm, I had one that was kind of flattering." It wasn't, but if it gets him more comfortable opening up to me, I have to run with it. "They wanted me to construct my dream bed. It's not something I've really thought of, so I haven't gotten back to them yet. I need to come up with a plan first." I smile.

The small smirk on his face tells me I did well and fed right into what he wanted.

"A very interesting request. You'll have to keep me updated on the progress of that one." He takes a small sip of his drink, and I hold in the cringe that wants to break free. I've never been more aware that I rarely hide my emotions on my face and how hard it is to hide them right now.

"Absolutely."

He talks about mundane things for most of dinner, nothing too in depth, and I'm thankful because I'm trying to figure out how to broach the subject of getting in his house. I know that's where I'll get the most information, whether it's from what I see or from him being more comfortable in the privacy of his home.

There's a lull in the conversation, and I decide to go for it. If I have to sit here any longer and fake it, he'll catch on to my disgust and fear of being in his presence.

"Would it be possible to take this somewhere more private?" I go for sultry, although I'm not sure I pull it off.

He tilts his head as he looks at me. Right now would be a great time to be able to read minds, but unfortunately, I'm just a plain old boring human.

"Where did you have in mind?" *Damnit, he's not taking the bait as easily as I hoped he would.*

"Well, I don't live here, so we can't exactly go back to my place. Maybe yours?"

God, I hope that wasn't too forward.

"You want to come back to my house?" I almost fist pump at the excitement peeking through his question.

"I would love to. You know, get to know you a little better but not in such a crowded place." I subtly look around and realize that was stupid to say because it's a nice steakhouse. It's not overly crowded or obnoxiously loud. I'm really bad at this covert work, and I hope I don't fuck this whole plan up.

"Let me just grab the check." He makes a big show of pulling out his wallet and flagging down our waiter. I watch once he gets his card back and see him barely leave a ten percent tip. *What a fucking asshole.*

"Let's go," he snips as he shoves his chair back. His abrupt change in tone starts my heart racing. Adrenaline floods my veins, and I try to use Arlo's breathing technique to calm myself down. This was only the first step, the easiest step, and now I need to be the badass I always claim to be.

I start walking to my truck, but he pulls me in the opposite direction.

"Where are you going?" he sneers.

"To my truck? I was just going to follow you."

"I'll drive, and then when you want to go home, I'll drop you off back here or you can just grab a ride share." He doesn't leave me any options, and I have a feeling if I push this issue, he'll give up and I'll lose the chance to end this.

"Sure, sounds great."

The drive to his house is a mix of not shoving his hand off my thigh, as well as listening to him brag about all the jobs he's gotten recently. He name-drops some big animation companies, and I roll my lips together to stop myself from saying something sarcastic and ruining this whole thing.

We pull up to a fairly standard house for the area, in a nice neighborhood, and it just confuses me more. He brags about all his money and flashes expensive shit around like it's his job, yet this is the most average house on the block.

"I wasn't expecting you to want to come here, so excuse the mess," he says before he climbs out of his car and heads to the front door.

Well, in this case, chivalry is well and truly dead, I guess. Not that I'm surprised.

I shove my way out of his car and walk to catch up to him as he opens the front door.

The inside is like eighties floral threw up on all the textiles. The mash of patterns is nauseating and puzzling. It's nothing like I pictured when thinking about the pretentiousness that's Tyler. I expected a classic bachelor pad, all steel and leather.

"It's nice," I say cautiously.

"I'm in the process of remodeling. It was my mother's house, and it is desperately in need of a change."

"I see." I'm not sure how I'm supposed to respond, so I keep it neutral.

"Do you want a tour?"

Yes! I scream internally. "Sure." I keep my tone interested but calm.

He walks me through the main area, points out the obvious spaces, like the kitchen and dining room, before heading down a dark hallway. It's eerie, and I'm waiting for the jump scare. This is how all scary movies go, so I figure it's just a matter of time before I get hit with one.

"Spare bedroom, bathroom, office..." He trails off as we reach his office and starts to shut the door, which I find odd.

What I catch a glimpse of inside changes everything. My breath catches, and the blood drains from my face before I remember I need to continue the charade. Just seeing a wall covered with pictures of me, as well as other women, isn't proof. It will be once they execute the warrant, but I don't think it's strong enough. It doesn't prove anything other than him being obsessed. I need something to nail his ass, to ensure he ends up in jail and doesn't get to leave.

I clear my throat. "It's a very spacious house. No wonder you wanted to keep it."

He snorts. "I'd tear down the whole damn thing if I could, but free housing is free housing."

I nod, unsure of what to do next.

"And this is my bedroom." He walks into the room at the very end of the hall, and I reluctantly follow him. The smarmy look on his face makes my skin crawl, and with sudden clarity, I realize I'm all alone in his room with no clear way out if things go south.

Terror. Anxiety. Regret. All of them hit my square in the chest, and I wonder why I was so fucking stubborn and thought this was a good idea.

I look around aimlessly and slowly start moving my hand into my purse. Maybe if I can grab my phone, I can send an S.O.S. text to Arlo.

"Are you uncomfortable?" Tyler's voice halts my movements. "You wanted to come here; I thought this was what you wanted." The way he says it isn't friendly or understanding, it's sinister and full of anger.

"I-I—"

"You can't take it back now, Marina. You're mine," he sneers before he lunges for me.

CHAPTER FORTY
ARLO

"Arlo, man, I need you to calm down. She's fine, and she can always send us a message if needed." Oakley's words don't make a dent in my hazy, stressed-out brain.

We've shifted positions since we all arrived at the house. Oakley and I are currently in the back of Lieutenant Kempe's car.

"And what if she can't get to her fucking phone? What would you say if it was Willow in there?" I snarl. I'm taking everything out on him, and while I know I'll feel bad about that later, I know he understands where my head is at.

His silence let me know my point about Willow hit home.

"What if he did something to her and we don't know?" I whisper.

"She's tough and knows how to take care of herself. She'll fight like hell until we get to her if something goes wrong," Oakley reasons.

"We've got guys surrounding the place as we speak, looking for any sign they need to bust in. But we're hoping Rina can talk to him and get him comfortable enough to tell her his big plan, and how many women he's done this to," the Lieutenant adds in like it's supposed to be of any comfort to me.

My knee bounces as I count to five and do my breathing. Something that normally does a damn good job of calming me down isn't giving me the relief I so desperately need.

Static from a radio clicks on as the regular check-ins start. With every "all clear" and "in position" check-in, my leg starts to slow its chaotic beat.

"We should have just checked out the fucking house while they were at dinner," I grumble.

"From the room you saw, there are other women and it would be nice to know if there are more than just those. Once we take him in, I doubt we'll get any information out of him. Rina can get that information, but we have to give her the chance," Oakley says.

"This is bullshit. Rina is bait, plain and simple, and we had a shit plan going into this." I don't throw in the towel. If needlessly arguing keeps my head occupied, I'll continue to do it.

"Get it all out," Oakley goads me.

"Our plan wasn't great with Tennison, but this is fucking ridiculous. A five-year-old could come up with something better."

"Your girlfriend came up with the plan," he adds.

"And I told her it was a terrible idea!" I yell.

He arches an eyebrow at me as I slump back into the seat. I'm thankful he let me be a dickhead for a few minutes. I seem to have had all the wind taken out of my sails after getting worked up over things out of our control currently.

"This fucking sucks." I sigh.

"I know, and it's not my favorite plan either, but Rina's hard-headed and wasn't going to be talked out of doing something," Oakley says.

"You know she would have just done it behind our backs if we didn't agree."

Don't I fucking know it, and it makes my head explode to even think about.

Another round of check-ins sounds from the radio that spikes my anxiety. All I can think about is the worst-case scenario. Everything that could go wrong will inevitably go wrong.

I reach for the handle of the door before a hand on my arm stops me.

"Not a good idea," Oakley says.

"I can't just sit here."

"We've still got the all-clear. I have men in position, and they currently have eyes on Rina. She's fine," Lieutenant Kempe adds.

I rip my arm away from Oakley's and open the door.

The Lieutenant's stern voice hits my ears and freezes me in place. "If you go in there, I'll have you arrested for interfering with a police investigation. You have no jurisdiction here, Arlo."

He wouldn't, would he?

I look over at Oakley, who cringes. Shit. Apparently, he would.

"I'm not sitting here all fucking day," I say as I sit back in the car.

"I'm not asking you to. I'm asking you to take a backseat because my department is in charge, and you are too close to this whole situation. We've got it handled, but if you go barging in there, everything will be for nothing." His eyes meet mine in the rearview mirror, and I know he's serious.

I sit in silence for the next ten minutes before I'm on the verge of breaking again. My phone buzzes in my pocket, and I panic to get it out in case it's Rina.

When I'm finally able to get it out of my damn pocket, it's not Rina, but my doctor, Dr. Vincent.

I forgot I was supposed to be expecting a call from him. He wanted to do another scan after my last injection because I have had a constant twinge in one spot. I didn't think much of it, but he wanted to be overly cautious.

"Hey, Doc," I answer, hoping talking to him for five minutes will be just the distraction I need.

"How many times do I have to tell you to call me Brian?"

"Apparently one more," I joke.

"I'm calling because we got results back from your latest CT scan, and I have some concerns."

"What concerns? I've been feeling great overall." I'm confused. Everything has been going well, and I've been feeling like a brand-new man. One twinge shouldn't be cause for concern, right?

"Of that, I have no doubt. While I'm still seeing increased healing, it looks like the damage is more extensive than I originally thought. It was hard to tell initially because of all the swelling, but now that a lot of that is down, I'm not sure the injections are going to be the only treatment needed."

No, this was supposed to be the end of it.

"So, what are you saying?" I can feel Oakley's eyes on me, and I know he's hearing a good chunk of this conversation.

"I'd like to get you into some physical therapy and see if we can work on spinal traction, and your overall back and core strength. If, in a few months, doing that doesn't show significant improvement, we may have to extend your fusions."

"More surgery?" I can't believe I'm having this conversation.

"Nothing definite yet. I just want to prepare you in case the physical therapy is less effective than I hope it will be."

"Fuck."

"I know it's not what you were hoping for, and I am happy with what the injections have done so far. This disease can be unpredictable, and I just want to make sure you're ready to roll with the punches as we continue treatment."

"Thank you for that."

"I'm going to email you a couple of therapists I usually work with. Go ahead and schedule with one of them, and we'll continue injections while you're doing that."

"I can do that." As long as Rina doesn't put me in an early grave first.

"I'll touch base with you later. Sorry for the downer news."

"No problem. Thanks, Brian." I hang up and stare out the window. That certainly wasn't the news I was expecting when dealing with my back. Especially because things have been going so well so far.

The click of the radio check-ins makes my nerves want to explode. Too much is happening right now, and I don't feel like I'm capable of dealing with any of it.

"You okay?" Oakley's soft voice penetrates my overactive thoughts.

"No." I sigh. "But I will be, eventually. One thing at a time."

He nods, not pushing, and I'm grateful. An unscheduled radio check-in interrupts anything further we were going to say.

"We've got a problem. They're in the main bedroom, and he's getting handsy and pushy. It looks like he took Rina's phone, but she fought him over it."

I'm out of the car before I hear anything else and racing to the door. Lieutenant Kempe must be on the same page, finally, because I hear the commands of him telling his men to enter the house. A group of three men beat me to the front door, where they kick it in, and I shove my way through. I look around, trying to figure out where I am before I hear Rina yelling.

I sprint to the back room and find Rina standing over a cowering Tyler, yelling with conviction.

"How dare you think you can just take what you want! Especially a whole-ass person!"

CHAPTER FORTY-ONE
RINA

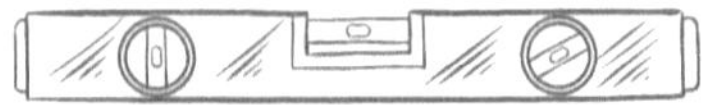

I panicked when he lunged for me, and I did the only thing I could think of. Ran.

It led me to the room with the pictures I saw earlier, his "office". I struggle to get the door open as Tyler chases me with shocking speed. I finally get the door open and go stumbling through it, landing on the floor.

"Now, now, Marina. Is that any way to treat the man you're with?" His sinister tone sends chills down my spine.

I scramble on the floor, bumping into the desk, which draws my attention to the room.

Pictures. Hundreds of them cover every wall in the room. A lot are of me, but there are a handful of other women on here too. "What is this?" I whisper, not even realizing I'm asking out loud.

"This is where I keep track of my women." He says it so simply, like it's normal human behavior to have creepily taken pictures tacked up in a room.

"Your women?"

"You thought you were the only one?" His laughter is cold but has an edge of hysterics to it. "You may be my favorite at the moment, but you aren't my only. One day, I'll have all of you here. Serving me just like you should be."

He's wistfully daydreaming about how he expects the women he stalks to just fall in line. How utterly delusional. But it's that thought that forces me to focus. If he's delusional, I need to use it against him or outsmart him. I can't be stuck in here with him because Lord knows what else he has planned. Hell, he may have a fucking dungeon somewhere, but I'm not sticking around to find out.

"How many are there?" Instead of asking about what he means by serving, I need to get more information about the other women. I'm not sure how easily the police can figure things out just from photographs, so the more I can get, the better.

"Currently? Six. There were a few other possibilities, but they fell through." He takes a step closer to me, a coy smirk on his face.

"Why did they fall through?"

"One I lost track of; another was engaged. She wasn't one of my favorites, so I decided to be gracious and let her go. There were two others who moved away. Following them felt unnecessary since I had the seven of you already in place." He steps to the side of the desk, grabbing something off of it, and I resist the urge to vomit all over his shoes. Although that may not be the worst way to distract him. He's holding up duct tape and an ominous leer, and no matter how much true crime I've watched, witnessing something like this in person is a whole different ball game.

"Ha-have you done this before?" I'm scared to ask, but I know we need to know if there are other victims.

God, I hate that word. I don't want to be a victim.

"When I was in college" —he crouches down to my level, almost caging me in— "I became infatuated with two girls. I followed them everywhere and just wanted to be a part of their life. I knew they wanted me to. They were friends and said hello to me a couple of times when they passed by. I followed them a lot, learned their patterns, but then summer break came and the next semester they were just gone." Anger litters his voice.

Good, they got away.

"And am I the first you've ... brought home?" I'm not sure if this is the right approach. It could tip my hand or make me sound interested in his life. I'm hoping against hope it's the latter.

"You kind of forced my hand, lovely Marina. I wasn't ready for you yet. But that's okay. I have enough ready that we'll make do." He holds his hand out, and I debate what to do. If I take his hand, does it lessen my chance to walk out of here? If I don't, does he flip his personality like Dr. Jekyll?

Fuck it.

I take his hand as we both stand up, and he forcefully pulls me out of the room and back into his bedroom. He shoves me onto the bed, and fear creeps up my spine. I don't know how many options I have here, and panic is starting to set in. I need a level head to get out of this, especially since I can't access my phone easily anymore.

He paces back and forth in front of me, and I calculate if I could beat him to the front door, but his height and speed would beat me every time.

There's tension in the air, heavy with uncertainty and fear on my end.

I'm not even sure who moves first, but I know that I don't want to be in here anymore. I don't want to know any more information, and I want to get the fuck out of here and to my husband immediately.

I tackle Tyler as he lunges for me. He wasn't going to get the better of me, no; I was going to take care of this once and for all. I have a life to live, after all. I hit him with all my force, my arms wrapped around his middle like a football tackle as I take him down against the dresser. I hear an awful thud, but I know it wasn't from me, so I don't care.

I have him cornered against the piece of furniture and the wall, and I think I hurt his arm when I tackled him to the floor because he's whimpering like a little bitch. Some macho man he's ended up being. Folds immediately when hurt. I'd roll my eyes if I wasn't so damn terrified and *angry*. I scramble to stand up, still blocking any chance of him going anywhere.

"How dare you think you can just take what you want! Especially a whole-ass person! Seven people!" I yell at him. He doesn't respond, so I nudge him with my foot, which has him sniveling.

"Stop! Please!" he sobs, and now I do roll my eyes. How fucking pathetic is he? A weak man with a superiority complex.

"What the hell were you going to do with me?" I hear people clamoring into the small room, but I hold my hand up. I'm not done here, and they can wait until I am.

"I-I-I—" he stutters.

"Spit it out. You've fucked with my life for too long, and I want more answers."

"I thought you wanted me. We saw each other a long time ago, and you looked at me like you wanted me. And I tried to get you to go out with me, and then you left with him." He sneers, looking behind my shoulder, where I assume Arlo is. "And it made me crazy. You were mine. All those other women are supposed to be mine too," he says under his breath. "Treat me like a king and love me the way I should be loved." He gains an air of his complex back, and it only makes me want to punch him.

"And do the others know about you? Have you left them little presents too?" I push. This is what we need.

He looks at me with hatred in his eyes, but he doesn't talk. I shove him again with my foot, careful not to give him the opportunity to grab me, even though he's now surrounded.

"Most don't know I've been watching them."

"And the others?"

"I brought them here," he murmurs, and I can barely hear him.

"Speak up. Did you do something to them? Did you take without giving a shit about them? Without *asking* if they wanted it?" I sneer. I feel like Arlo's going to have to pull me off of this piece of shit. "Did you go into their houses too when they slept? Go through their underwear drawer? Their dirty laundry and steal shit, like you did me?" My voice gets louder as I start to lose my patience. I'm shaking with disgust and on the verge of being sick. The realization of what's happening, what's been happening, is becoming overwhelming.

"Y-y-yes." He trembles with fear. I take a step closer to him and he curls in on himself, probably realizing he isn't getting out of this.

"You're a piece of shit. Using fear and manipulation to feed your ego because you can't get a woman any other way. You put on a persona and fake us out, and then strike like a fucking coward. So pathetic." I close my hands into fists and take a step back, right into Arlo's arms. I can feel him shaking, or maybe that's me. I can't tell. I grab his hand and drag him out of the house. I need out of here as much as he clearly does. Judging by the number of officers here, they'll take care of Tyler. I don't even care if I never hear what he did to the others. Honestly, it's probably better if I don't know. I'm not sure I'm strong enough to handle that at the moment.

Once we're through the front door, I sit down on the front step and urge Arlo to join me.

Relief like I've never known mixed with the adrenaline drop make me feel like I'm back in the hospital, waiting for news on Lennox.

"God, I fucking love you," Arlo breaths out with sheer awe on his face. "I was so damn scared when the officers noticed things were happening. I burst in there to find you telling him off while he cowers in the corner. Such a badass." He shakes his head with mirth.

"I don't even know what just happened," I breathe out. "What the actual fuck was that?! Also, don't ever let me pretend to plan an epic police shakedown because that was a terrible fucking plan! I'm not cut out for this shit." Tears start to well up in my eyes, and I know I'm very close to losing my shit. The comfort of having Arlo here makes me feel safe enough to just *feel* everything.

"That's what I was saying the whole time," he grumbles.

"You were right." I sniffle, trying desperately not to cry. I was a total badass back there, according to my husband. And now I'm close to a full-on breakdown.

My husband.

That's the second time I've thought that today. The realization jolts me from my almost meltdown. I know I told him to burn the divorce papers, but that feels very different from perceiving him as my husband. And yet, it's the most natural thing I've ever felt. Like building a dresser or hiking to the falls, it's like he's always held the title. Not because of paperwork but because we were always connected, always meant to be husband and wife, no matter what life threw at us.

"Hey." He wraps an arm around my shoulders. "You're okay. You're safe. I'd never let anything happen to you," he mutters against my temple.

"I'm okay," I attempt to say with conviction. All I want is to go anywhere but here and talk to him. "Are we able to go home?"

When he doesn't answer right away, I look up at him and see tension in his eyes. Sighing, I know we're in for a long night.

"I'm sorry. They're going to want statements. If they don't get them tonight, they'll need them another day, and I'd just as soon get all of this over with. They probably need to check you out too."

"I'm fine. They need to check Tyler out because he was crying like he broke something in there." I chuckle, but he doesn't join in.

"You could be in shock," he says quietly.

"Listen, I'm not going to pretend I'm perfectly fine after that, but don't micromanage my reaction to it all. I just want to put this whole thing behind us, getting these statements over with so we can go home and decompress with each other, and I can freak out in private." I'm rambling—I know I am—but I don't want to be here any longer than we need to be. The house creeps me out, and knowing that Tyler is only a few feet away is starting to get to me. Maybe this is shock, but I'm not going anywhere but home to deal with it.

Oakley walks through the front door, nodding to us both as he walks around us on the front steps.

"Lieutenant Kempe said we could go down to the police department and give our statements to one of the officers there. He knows how to reach Arlo and me if he needs more than that. He said as long as Rina doesn't need medical attention, we're good to go." He eyes me like he's waiting for me to lie to him.

"We're good. Do we have a car to take us there? My truck is still at the station," Arlo says as he stands up and then helps me to join them.

"Yeah, an officer is going to take us back."

We follow Oakley, no one saying a word. The entire drive to the station is the same, and I'm grateful because there is too much running through my head right now. What I do know is I'm ready to put this nightmare behind me and start the life I always wanted.

CHAPTER FORTY-TWO
ARLO

They separate us at the station, and I feel like I'm crawling out of my damn skin. I've been away from Rina too long, and I know everything that happened is going to hit her all at once. Because she's so damn stubborn, she'll hold it all in and wait until she feels safe to breakdown, and I don't want her to hold that in at all. I need to get her home.

"I think that should do it. Thanks for the co-operation. I'm sure Lieutenant Kempe will call you if he needs anything else," the officer who interviewed me for the last thirty minutes says. I didn't even catch his name, too focused on wrapping this up quickly.

I see Oakley sitting in the lobby as I'm walked out, but no sign of Rina.

"Is Rina not done?" I ask as I continue to look around like I somehow missed her.

"Not yet, and I'm about to give them hell. She shouldn't need to be kept that long. Take her statement and let her go. If they need more, call one of us," he grumbles, knee bouncing.

I'm so fucking glad he found Willow and started opening up to us all. His friendship and fierce support are something I didn't realize I was missing. I gave him a lot of shit about not having friends not all that long ago, but that was hypocritical considering my lack of friendships.

But everything's changed in the last few months. All thanks to the woman I will forever call my wife.

Oakley abruptly stands, and I turn to what he's looking at. Rina walking out in all her beautiful, stressed-out glory. She shoots Oakley a small smile before looking at me with eyes that scream to get her out of here. I can see the threads holding her together are barely hanging on.

She reaches us, cuddling into my side as I hold out my arm for her.

"Can we get out of here?" she whispers. I look up at the officer who walked her out, and he nods, letting me know we're good to go. I'm glad to have their approval, but they couldn't stop me even if they wanted to. Rina wants to go home, and I'll make it happen no matter what it takes.

Leading her out of the building, not taking my arm off of her, I walk the three of us over to my truck in the parking lot across the street.

"Shit. My truck is still at the steakhouse." Rina stops in her tracks.

I look at Oakley over her head, and he nods at my unspoken question.

"I'll drop Oakley off, and he'll drive it back to your house."

"You don't have to do that. I can drive home," Rina argues.

"Nope. I'll drive it back. You ride with Arlo." God bless Oakley for understanding my need to be by her side right now.

"Thank you." Rina nods in appreciation as we make it to my truck. Oakley jumps in the back, and I help Rina into the passenger side. The drive over to the steakhouse is fast thanks to everything being downtown. Oakley hops out after taking Rina's keys and waves to us as we pull out and hit the highway.

I'm waiting for her to take the lead on our conversation. I don't want to push her or say something that will trigger anything for her. I'm a mostly patient man, and whenever she wants to talk about what happened, I'll be here to hear every word.

It doesn't lessen my worry and uncertainty about what exactly happened in that house.

Her hand slides down my forearm and intertwines our fingers. It instantly calms the noise in my head, and I'm grateful.

"Thank you for having my back." Her small voice echoes in the cabin of the truck.

"Oh, Emmerdeur, never thank me for that." I squeeze the hand holding mine.

"I promise to never think I can pull something like that off ever again. I am not the badass I thought I was."

"You are more of a badass than you give yourself credit for, but I will tie you to the fucking bed if you decide you want to do something like this again." I glance over at her and see a small smile on her pretty face. She looks exhausted, but she also looks like the weight of the world is off her shoulders.

She scoots as close as she can to the center console before leaning her head on my shoulder, content to ride the forty minutes home in silent, safe company.

Pulling into her driveway, I didn't even realize this is where I drove us. It's where she feels the most comfortable. It's where I feel like home too, so it was a no-brainer.

"Alright, we're here," I murmur, not sure if she fell asleep or not.

She jolts up, looking around to get her bearings before her shoulders drop in relief. I climb out of the truck, walking around to open the door for her to find she's already out and walking to her front door. She opens it, still not saying anything, and I follow her as she walks back to her bedroom.

Without changing her clothes or stripping down to just her underwear, she collapses face first onto her bed.

"What the actual fuck just happened?" The comforter muffles her words, and I have to laugh at her response to this whole day. Only Rina wouldn't be completely freaking out. I'm sure she's shaken by what happened, but it's not breaking her. She isn't letting it take over her life or her happiness. And even if she does, if she has a moment where she needs to break, I'll be right by her side through it all, piecing her back together.

"What can I do?" Helplessness is still prevalent in my chest. I hope she'll tell me when or if she needs anything because right now, I'm not sure what to do to make things better.

"Ugh," she groans and moves her head to the side so I can hear her. "Food, probably a shower, and sleep. I'm open to the order of those, though."

I smile at her, amazed that she's mine. It's been a hard day, and somehow just being here with her, doing mundane shit like figuring out dinner, makes me so damn happy.

"I'll work on dinner if you just want to stay here and rest," I offer.

"Yeah, that sounds good. I'll lie here for a few minutes then help you," she mumbles, then turns her head into the mattress again.

Walking closer to the bed, I intertwine my fingers in her hair, pressing a kiss to the crown of her head before whispering, "I'll handle it. Just relax."

I'm going to have to call in a couple of favors, but it's worth it if I don't have to leave Rina right now. Pulling out my phone, I call Sal's diner.

"Sal's, how can I help you?" Kelly answers on the second ring.

"Hey, Kelly, it's Arlo. I was hoping you could help me. I need to see if someone can bring some food over to Rina's house. Is Jim or any of the Huttons there by chance?"

Kelly chuckles into the receiver. "Oh, man, I love that this is happening. Do you both want your usual?"

"That's perfect." I don't acknowledge her other statement.

"Let me put you on hold while I put this in really fast." I hear the click of her doing just that, and I hear a truck pulling into the driveway at the same time. Heading out to make sure it's who I think it is, I see Oakley climbing out just as Willow pulls in behind him to pick him up. I wave my thanks to them both as he quickly jumps in, leaning over to kiss her before she pulls out and they disappear as quickly as they came.

"Well, well, well, Sheriff. I hear you are in need of some food delivery," Old Man Walters says over the phone.

"Yes, sir, I am. Are there any Huttons, or perhaps Jim is there?" I ask again, praying someone has a car that can help me.

"There are, but I'll be helping you out today, son."

"I appreciate that, but I don't want to impose."

"Nonsense. You're at Miss Rina's place?"

"We are." It's easier not to fight him. I learned a long time ago, when I took over for him as sheriff, that he's as stubborn as they come and he will always get what he wants.

"Great. Looks like your food will be up soon, then I'll head that way. And Arlo?"

"Yes, sir?"

"I'm glad you finally grew half a brain and went after that girl again."

I freeze in place, rendered speechless by his words as he hangs up on me. I'm not sure if Rina and I were really not that sneaky back in the day, or if it was just his nature as sheriff to know everything that goes on in this town. Either way, he somehow knew of our history and managed to keep it to himself all these years. I'm grateful, but knowing how much time I wasted still kills me inside.

The rocking chairs on Rina's front porch are too inviting, and I want to give her some time to decompress without any pressure, so I sit in one as I wait for Old Man Walters to deliver our dinner.

My mind wanders to the future and what I want to do differently this time with Rina. Sure, we've recommitted to each other, but we're mostly still hidden away, still keeping so much a secret. All I want to do is shout to the world that Rina is mine, and I vow to make it happen. I think about the little box still in my pocket and start devising a plan I think will show Rina how much I love her.

The rumble of his old truck comes down the driveway, and I stand to go meet Old Man Walters. He rolls down his window as I reach his truck and hands me a huge bag of food.

"Miss Kelly says it's on the house." He winks. It suddenly feels like everyone in town has been secretly hoping Rina and I would get together, and I have to laugh at how our obvious discontent for each other didn't hide our feelings very well.

"I appreciate that, and you for driving it all the way here."

"I just wanted to give you some advice from an old man who just wants to see you happy. Hold on to her, fight her fights, and stand by her side. The two of you were destined to be together, and you both deserve all the happiness in the world. You both pushed aside your own lives in order to take care of other people, and as admirable as that is, it's your turn. I'm proud of you, Arlo. Now, stop living at the damn office and go love on your woman." He smirks.

"Yes, sir." I nod and hold out my hand to shake his. "Thank you. For everything." I'm not usually sentimental, but if he hadn't given me this job, I fear I would have been lost for far longer than I was. He brought me back to the town I love and the woman I was meant to be with, and in a way, I owe him so much.

"I expect a wedding invitation soon." He manually rolls up his window with a chuckle, and I shake my head at his blatant assumption.

It does reinforce my idea, though.

Walking back into Rina's house with our bag of food, I find her right where I left her.

"Hey, Emmerdeur, food's here." She groans, but rolls over, rubbing her eyes as she wakes up from her catnap.

"Tell me Kelly put a burger in there." She groans as she sits up.

"Why don't you find out, and I'll get us some drinks." I hand her the bag and grab some water for both of us before joining her in bed again.

She hands me a Styrofoam container, and I open it to find a club and fries, and I practically drool, realizing I haven't eaten since breakfast.

We demolish all the food in the bag without saying a word, both of us feeling a little more human after eating.

"Oh my God, I think that was the best burger I've ever eaten." Rina groans as she rubs her stomach, an action so cute I just want to kiss her. Instead, I grab all of our trash.

"How about I clean up and you jump in the shower?" I ask, trying hard to give her time with no pressure for anything from me.

"Thank you, that sounds amazing." She climbs out of the bed and starts stripping before she reaches the bathroom, and I have to bite my lip to quiet the groan threatening to come out.

She looks over her shoulder with a smirk, and I arch my brow at her in return. Little minx knows exactly what she's doing.

"Careful, Marina."

"I think I like living a little on the edge," she retorts, then starts the shower and climbs in once it's warm enough.

As much as I want to join her, I need to clean up and change her sheets. I know she's not focused on it right now, but having clean sheets that she didn't wear outside clothes on will help her brain settle down and hopefully help her sleep better.

I make quick work of throwing them in the washing machine and finding a clean set to throw on. Is it perfectly made? No, but it's clean, and I think that's what's important here.

I strip out of my clothes and walk to the bathroom, leaning on the doorjamb to watch her. Her head is on the tile in front of her as she lets the water sluice over her. The sound of my feet padding across the floor is the only sound before opening the glass door and sliding in behind her. My hand spreads across the expanse of her stomach as I pull her back against me. Her head tips back against my shoulder as she releases a heavy breath.

"It's over, right?" she murmurs.

"It's over. You did so fucking good, even if it almost gave me a damn heart attack."

"I think I gave myself one honestly. That room... The one with all the pictures. I think it may haunt my nightmares for a while."

"I'll be right here to hold you through it."

"This whole stalker thing has me questioning how I run my business." Her hand slips over mine, intertwining our fingers against her stomach. "Maybe cut back on deliveries or hire out to do them. I know this isn't a direct correlation to me doing deliveries, but it makes me nervous to think about something like this happening again."

"We can make a plan and figure it out. I can make deliveries with you, or if the company can handle it, you can certainly hire out. You don't need to decide right this second." I don't know if she wants options, solutions, or just to vent, so I'm trying not to barge in with my opinion on things that don't need to be settled right this second.

"I was really scared," she whispers.

"I know. I said I'd protect you, and I didn't. I failed you on many levels today." I don't realize how much guilt I feel until I say the words. I've been so focused on making sure she has what she needs, I never stopped to think about how little I helped her today.

"It was no one but Tyler's fault, and you know that. I was just so desperate to figure this out and catch him that I was willing to do stupid shit to make it happen." She turns in my hold, wrapping her arms around my neck. "I promise to try to not be a willful know-it-all and land myself in a fucked-up situation like that again."

"I promise to protect you so that you never have to think about putting yourself in a position like that again," I counter. And I mean it; this is something that shouldn't have happened in the first place, but I also realize I can't control the actions of other people either.

"You might need to set up an office in my workshop if you're bound and determined to protect me all the time." She smirks.

"Don't tempt me, Marina."

"You are very easy to rile up. It's super cute." She places her head on my chest, right over my heart, and we stand there until the water goes cold.

"Alright, let's get you dried and in bed so you can sleep off the stressful day." I drag her out of the shower, grabbing a towel as I do and drying her off thoroughly before letting her go find some clothes to put on. I make quick work of drying myself off and realize I have no spare clothes here. I don't really want to put on any clothes that were in that fucker's house.

"Hey, Rina?" I call out from the bathroom. Silence greets me, and I panic for no logical reason.

"Rina!" I call out as I rush into her room buck-ass naked.

I find her standing in front of her bed in underwear and a tank top.

"What's wrong?" I ask, confused as to what just happened.

"You changed the sheets?" Her voice is so small that I wonder if I fucked up.

"I did. Was that the wrong move?" "No, it was the best move ever." She spins around and jumps on me, wrapping her legs around my waist as I hold her up. She presses a gentle kiss to my lips before pulling back with glistening eyes. "Thank you."

"You are very welcome. I just wanted to make sure you got some good sleep tonight."

"Very thoughtful, my love. How about I throw your clothes in the washer so you have something to wear tomorrow, unless you want to do a very awkward walk of shame back home?"

"That's probably a good idea, but I'll take care of it. And it wouldn't be a walk of shame with you. Nothing ever done with you is shameful." I press a soft kiss to her lips before walking her to the bed and gently setting her down, making sure she's covered up before I grab my clothes and take care of them.

Once I return, she's fast asleep. I crawl under the covers and slide against her, wrapping my arm around her middle.

Today was messy and hard, but we endured it, and now it's time to live the life we always should have.

CHAPTER FORTY-THREE
RINA

I wake up overheated.

Attempting to roll over proves useless, as there is a heavy limb over my stomach. When I peek over my shoulder, instant comfort hits my soul.

Everything from the past twenty-four hours runs through my head, and I know I should probably be more freaked out, but the only thought I can focus on is what Arlo and my future looks like.

Last night gave me a glimpse, and I want more. He let me have space last night when I needed it. He didn't push me but supported me. And he changed my sheets when he knew I didn't have the energy to do it, even though it bothered me. The little things he does mean everything to me, and now I'm determined to create a life together that we both love.

If the events of last night and what happened to Lennox don't show the glaring reason to not let the past rule you and to hold on to the good things with both hands, then I'm not sure what will.

Life is short and uncertain. Having Arlo in my life makes me happy, and I feel like this is the life I should be living. A dream I gave up on so long ago is now in the palm of my hand, and I refuse to ever let it go again.

Shifting slowly, I turn to face him. He looks calm and so fucking beautiful. It's almost painful. My anger toward him all these years was out of hurt, yes, but also out of self-loathing that I couldn't find a way to keep him. On some level, I blamed myself for failing in our marriage.

Last night made me aware of how quickly everything can change. Holding on to the past and pushing Arlo away is no longer how I want my life to be. I want to support him the same way he's supported me. I want to help him heal and work through his injuries, and remember small details that bring a smile to his face.

My fingers barely brush against the scruff along his jaw. His lips are so tempting that I don't even bother to restrain myself. Leaning forward, I press a soft kiss to them, savoring the way they feel against me. When gentle pressure pushes back against me and his arm tightens around me, I know he's awake. I pull back and let him wake up a little more.

"That is one hell of a way to wake up." His sleep-roughened voice is so fucking sexy I could jump him right this second.

"Thank you," I whisper. "For last night. You have no idea—" I suck in a breath, trying to hold the tears in. My emotions are on a hair trigger, but I want him to know how I'm feeling. "Last night, you let me process and still took care of me without smothering me. You understand me on a level no one does, and I meant what I said about burning the divorce papers. Stay married to me ... please." I whisper the last part and hope that we're both on the same page.

The smile that blooms on his face could bring light to the darkest days.

"No takebacks," he murmurs before kissing me again. This time, it's not soft and sweet. No, he's claiming me, marking me as his.

He rolls us so he's on top of me, never releasing my lips. His tongue trails against my bottom lip, and I greedily open for him. My legs wrap around his waist, heels digging into his ass, desperate for him to be closer.

He rips his lips from mine, looking down at me with concern in his eyes.

"Are you sure you're okay? I won't ask again after this, but I need to make sure you're okay after yesterday."

"Will I probably want to talk through everything at some point? Yes, but right now, if you don't fuck me, I will actually scream."

"Well, I would never want to leave my wife unsatisfied." He leans back on his knees and slides his hands up my thighs, gripping my panties in his hands and ripping them from my body. If I wasn't so hung up on him calling me his wife, I might care that he just ruined a pair of my underwear, but right now? An overwhelming feeling of rightness sits heavy in my chest. *His wife.* All that I've wanted since I was eighteen was to be this man's wife. Through all the years, I never put effort into finding anyone else because, deep down, I always knew it was Arlo or no one.

His thumb finds my clit, circling it softly to give me just the hint of pleasure, but I need more.

"You're so fucking wet for me already, Emmerdeur." He groans as he notches his cock at my entrance. He doesn't thrust, just sits there as he teases my clit.

"Arlo," I groan, arching my back.

"That's right, beg me." He adds pressure, making me moan.

"I need you inside of me, please," I plead.

His thumb dips down to where his dick is, gathering my arousal around him, and it's something so erotic my clit pulses as his thumb returns, getting me worked up and right at the edge.

"I'm so close," I whimper.

"I know. You're right there, aren't you? I can feel you pulsing and clenching against me. Do you want to come?"

"Yes!" I scream. I need more, and the fact that he's teasing me and withholding it from me is making me crazy.

Right as I'm about to crest, he slams into me, triggering my orgasm instantly.

I'm floating in pure pleasure. Every nerve ending is hypersensitive, and he holds still and lets me ride the wave.

His groan finally pulls me out of my haze, and I open my eyes to see his head tipped back, the tendons in his neck taught with restraint.

"Holy fuck, Rina," he breathes.

I take advantage of his distraction and sit up on my elbows before shifting my hips and flipping us so I'm on top with him still inside of me.

His hands grip my hips as his eyes pop open in shock. Heat and need reflect back at me as I look down at him with a smirk.

"My turn." I put my hands on his chest and shift my hips back and forth. Starting slowly, I want to tease him and make him wait, just like he did to me.

His hands grip my hips tighter, but he doesn't take control. He breathes deep before sliding his hands up and taking my tank top with him. I didn't even realize I still had it on, but he makes quick work of it, making sure I'm fully naked as I ride him.

His hands return to my hips as he smirks at me. "Show me what you've got, Marina."

Circling my hips, I search out the spot that shoots me to the stars. Once I find it, I tuck my feet underneath me and start to bounce on him.

"God, you feel good," I moan.

I keep my rhythm, determined to take the lead and give him the best orgasm of his life, even if it kills my thighs. His hands help me along when my pace starts to falter, and he starts panting. I can feel the tingle in my lower belly, but I don't want to come yet, not when he's this close.

He seems to sense my struggle because he uses his core strength to sit up, shifting my ass as close as it'll get to him. Face to face, it's more intimate and our pace slows considerably. I'd be upset, but the intensity and closeness heighten everything. My arms wrap around his shoulders as we grind together.

"I love you," he whispers, pressing his forehead to mine.

"I love you too. I'm sorry it took this long to get back here."

"We both were stubborn," he adds, shifting his hips deeper.

"Fuck, you feel good." I close my eyes and focus on how he feels.

"You're my wife, Marina Hutton. Forever and always."

"Steel," I moan as I open my eyes. "Marina Steel," I tell him.

I never took his name when we got married initially. There was a lot going on and we were keeping things quiet, so it just didn't happen. But I wanted to. I dreamed of the day I could be Mrs. Arlo Steel.

Arlo's eyes clench close and his teeth grit together, jaw popping. "You can't say things like that if you want this to last longer," he growls as he opens his eyes to look at me.

"You like the idea of me being Rina Steel? Yours for the whole word to see?" I smirk as I swivel my hips. I'm so close my legs are tightening on his.

"I fucking love it. Seems like you do too, judging by how wet you are. Are you going to come for me? Come with me?" He grunts as he thrusts. Well, as much as he can in this position, but it's enough to send me over. My clit grinding against his pelvis, mixed with his movement, sends me spiraling. I vaguely hear him moan as he pulls me as close as I can get to him.

There isn't an inch of space between us. Every bit of skin is touching, and it somehow still feels like I need to be closer. We collapse into each other, panting and catching our breaths.

"I'm going to need this as my wake-up call every morning," he says seriously.

Laughter bubbles up out of me. "I'd never get out of bed and work if we started every day like this."

"How about just the weekends?" he counters.

I sit up and look him in the eye. "I think we can make that happen."

"So, we've established you're my wife. How far are we taking this? Living together immediately? Working up to that and enjoying breakfast in bed on the weekends?" He asks the second part to bring a levity to his question. He still doesn't want to push me but does want to know what all of this means.

"Well." I smile. "Your house is pretty small. And my workshop is here. It would make sense for you to move in, right? Sell your house and turn this into our home?" I want him to know I'm all in. He could move in tomorrow, and I wouldn't bat an eye. I can't imagine sleeping alone after the last few months together.

"You're serious?" he asks in shock.

"A thousand percent."

He shifts, reaching over the side of the bed, fumbling with the night-stand. When he comes back to me with a familiar box, I don't think my smile could get any bigger.

"Is that what I think it is?"

"Marina Steel, will you continue to be my wife? The person I love more than anyone. Who I want to wake up next to every single day and never take a single moment for granted." He opens the box, revealing the small diamond ring he got for me all those years ago.

"Yes, holy shit, yes!"

His kiss takes me by surprise, but no words are needed. We're doing this for real, and we'll never have to be without each other again.

CHAPTER FORTY-FOUR
ARLO

It's been a month since our lives changed for the better.

Tyler is sitting in jail and won't be getting out for a very, very long time. I moved into Rina's house three days after everything happened, and we haven't looked back.

But today? It's time to give her something she's always wanted but never made a fuss about.

First stop on the long list of shit to get done is a long talk with Ledger. Pulling up to the house he shares with Ainsley, I'm nervous. I never repaired our relationship from when we were kids, and I regret that. And now that Rina and I are married, I don't want what I did hanging over us. I want to be a real part of the family, not someone he has to put up with.

Knocking on the door, I shift on my heels and wait until the door opens.

"Arlo, hey." He looks confused, and I can understand why.

"Hey, man, can I come in?"

"Umm, sure." He moves aside to let me in, and I follow him into the living room.

"What's up?" he asks.

"I want to clear the air. When I left, I didn't just hurt Rina; I hurt you and lost one of my best friends. I never really tried to fix that, and I would like to do so now."

"You can't really fix something that happened fifteen years ago," he says.

"You're right. But I'm hoping to marry Rina today, and it would mean a lot if there wasn't any bad blood between us."

"You're hoping to what?" His eyebrows almost reach his hairline.

It's not that we've hidden that we're married, but we also haven't thrown it out to the world as this huge announcement. All the Huttons know we're legally married now, but no one expected us to have an actual wedding, especially Rina.

What he also fails to realize is that Ainsley, also Ledger's fiancée, has been helping me plan the whole thing and is getting Rina ready for this elaborate plan today. And if he's clueless, that means she took secrecy seriously.

"Umm, Ainsley helped me plan the perfect wedding for Rina. She's helping me get her there today, and I would really love it if you were there to give her away."

"Holy shit, who are you right now?" he asks with wonderment.

I chuckle at his shocked question. "She deserves it, man. I'm just trying to do right by her and make up for the past."

He eyes me for a long minute. "When you left, I lost my best friend. When you came back, it was like we were never friends to begin with."

"I know. Because of everything with Rina, I handled things with you terribly. I didn't know how to be your friend when your sister was the woman I loved but I broke her heart. I thought you were all better off without me here. And then I got hurt, and I just shut myself off to everyone, not just you. I fucked up a lot of things, but I'm working on it."

"You never needed my forgiveness, you know. I knew there were things that happened to you, but I just wanted you to feel comfortable talking to me—or hell, anyone—about it."

"I get that now. I was ... stubborn." I scoff. "Really fucking stubborn. But I'd like for us to be friends again, whatever that looks like to you."

He holds out his hand, and I eagerly shake it.

"We're good, man. So, what's this about a wedding?"

Relief hits me hard. Ledger's always been a good guy, but he had a lot of responsibility back in the day. He's different now, and I'm grateful for easy forgiveness. I fill him in on my plan, and he quickly agrees to walk Rina down the aisle.

He walks me to the door, hugging me once we're there.

"Welcome to the family. I'll see you later, I guess."

I clap his back, clearing the emotion from my throat.

"Thanks, Ledge. Now, I've got to go see a man about a ring."

The drive to Rosedale gives me time to reflect on how much has changed. Therapy is going well, and although I go less often than before everything with Tyler, I've kept it up. My back is slowly getting better. I started physical therapy, and it sucks so badly. After every session, I come home, collapse on the bed, and try not to cry from the pain. Rina's taken to helping me into a super-hot bath with Epsom to lessen how long I'm down for. Her support has been instrumental in continuing through the torture that is physical therapy. Besides that, the twinge is lessening, so we'll see what things look like in six months.

I've never been happier with my life, and it's all thanks to Rina.

Pulling up to the jeweler, I step out and hope that the ring is ready. She's been wearing the original ring I gave her, but I wanted to surprise her with not a replacement but an addition to represent our future.

"I was just about to call you," the owner, Jack, says as I walk in.

"Oh, yeah?"

"I was just getting your ring ready. You want to take a look?"

I nod and walk up to the counter. An infinity band sits on a padded mat, and I gingerly pick it up. A thin line of baguette cut diamonds span around the small band. It's simple but classic, and something that won't get in the way of any tools Rina needs to use while she works.

"It's beautiful," I breathe as the reality of the day hits me hard.

I'm finally giving Rina the wedding she always dreamed of, the one she always should have had, and I can't fucking wait to shout it to the world.

"Shall I wrap it up for you?"

"That'd be perfect, thanks." I wait while he makes it pretty before I make the trek back to Bluebell Falls.

My phone rings when I'm about fifteen minutes away.

"Sheriff," I answer.

"Hey, so we may have a problem," Ainsley frantically answers.

"What do you mean?"

"Well, I'm at your house trying to get Rina ready, and she refuses to leave her damn workshop."

"She shouldn't even be working today. What the hell?"

"She said she needs an hour to finish up her project, then she'll be ready for whatever nonsense—her words, not mine—I need. Does that leave us enough time?"

"It's cutting it close as hell. Can you send an S.O.S. to the gossip crew and tell everyone to bump back an hour? My only worry is people showing up and ruining the surprise."

"I'll just call my dad, and he can make sure the town knows. Consider it done."

"Thank you. I've got some things to pick up, then I'll head that way. I'll try to give you an hour to get her to your house."

"Perfect. I'll see you in a little bit!" She's excited, and I'm glad she's helping me out with this. I don't think I could have pulled this off without her.

As I get into town, I know I need to kill some time, and I find myself parked in the driveway of Uncle Charlie's old house.

I think he would be proud of me and the man I've become. I didn't always feel that way. There were many years that self-loathing took over, but I finally feel content. I wish he was here to see this, though. He always loved Rina.

"Thank you for everything, Uncle Charlie," I whisper before leaving and getting the rest of the things I need to make this wedding happen.

Ainsley texts me with the all-clear, and I head back to our house where Ledger, Oakley, and Lennox, of all people, are waiting for me.

"Well, this is a surprise," I say as I climb out of my truck.

"Ainsley said you probably need help, so put us to work," Ledger says.

They help me grab the cake that Kelly made as well as a shit-ton of flowers I secretly got from Ledger's nursery thanks to Ainsley. Kelly is bringing food when she shows up later, so at least I don't have to worry about that.

In a matter of two hours, we have an archway built and covered in flowers, and the only thing left is minimal decoration inside for when everyone comes back here and then changing into my suit. Setting up the ceremony spot won't take long, and thanks to the guys' help, it'll take no time at all. The three of them take the flower arch and tell me to take a minute to myself and they'll make sure things get set up properly. All I need to do is meet them there.

Changing into my suit is quick after I shower. As I sit on our bed, I take in this feeling. When we first got married, I didn't feel nervous. I felt invigorated. Now, nerves tickle my chest and I have to call on my breathing technique to calm myself down. I'm not worried about Rina not wanting to marry me. We're definitely past that, but I'm nervous that she doesn't want the whole wedding with all our friends and family there to celebrate. Maybe she wants it to be just us.

Shaking my head, I remember that I know her, and as much as she says she's fine with how things are, there's a part of her that wants the big wedding and the celebration.

The only thing I want is to make sure all her hopes and dreams come true, so this is happening. I just have to shove my nerves down.

Grabbing my suit jacket, I put it on and stand in front of the mirror. Patting my pocket, I double-check that I have the ring, then take a deep breath.

"Go marry the love of your life," I tell myself before spinning around and making my way to our spot to wait for Rina.

CHAPTER FORTY-FIVE
RINA

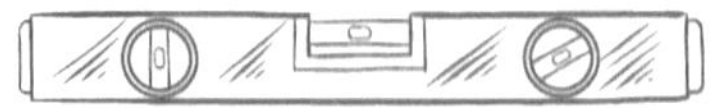

Ainsley is very suspicious right now.

She hovered over me as I finished up a personal project, and now she's dragging me to her house for God knows what.

"What the hell is happening right now?" I ask for the fifth time.

"Just shut it and let me do what I need to do." She hushes me again. I throw my hands up as we pull into her driveway.

I follow her inside, where she leads us to her bedroom, and it just makes me more confused.

"Put this on." She tosses me a garment bag. I wearily open it up and see a cream dress, and I immediately throw it on her bed.

"I'm not wearing a dress. I'll put on dress pants or something."

"No can do. Put the damn dress on, Marina." She glares at me, and it's not her joking around glare; it's her "do as you're told, or there will be hell to pay" one.

"I'm here! Sorry I'm late!" Willow calls from the front door after it slams.

"We're in my room!" Ainsley yells back.

What the fuck is happening right now?

"Shit, sorry. I was writing again and lost track of time," Willow huffs as she busts into the room, carrying her own garment bag.

"Is this some kind of talent show? Why are we all dressing up?"

Willow looks at Ainsley, who just smirks.

"Fine. I'll play along, but if this ends up being stupid, I'm leaving." I go to grab the dress, but Willow stops me.

"Hair and make-up first."

"No." I go to reach for it again.

"Trust us. You'll want hair and make-up done."

"You know I hate everything about this. Surprises are not my friend."

"We know, but this one is worth it. We wouldn't steer you wrong," Ainsley says.

"She" —I point to Willow— "absolutely would steer me wrong. Why don't you ask her how many books she's killed me off in?" I arch my eyebrow.

Willow snickers as Ainsley turns to her. "You haven't killed me off, right?"

"Umm, no, of course not!" Willow says a little too forcefully.

"Damnit. I thought I was in the clear," Ainsley mumbles.

"Well, this is fun and all, but if you want to do my hair and make-up, your window is passing. I only have so much patience for getting dolled up." I grimace even thinking about a layer of make-up I'll need to take off later.

In a half hour, the girls curled my hair and pulled it up into a soft up-do, and put very light make-up on me. I'm grateful it isn't more, and I have to admit they did a damn good job. I don't look like a woodworker; I look like a woman getting ready for a date or something.

"Okay, put the dress on while we change, and then we'll be ready to head out."

"I need to tell Arlo I'm going to be late for dinner," I absentmindedly tell them as I pull my phone out and shoot off a quick text. What I really wanted was to set up the bed that I finally finished before he got home, but it looks like that's not going to happen.

I look up to find them both staring at me. "What?"

"Nothing! Put your dress on!" they both say as they move to separate areas to get ready.

Something is going on, but I know these two and they won't tell me anything until they're damn well ready.

Pulling the dress fully out of the bag, I admire its beauty. I don't wear dresses, but if I did, I would want to wear something like this. It has thicker straps with a fitted bodice covered in subtle jewels. The bottom is flowy enough that I don't feel constricted, but it falls to the floor in a soft wave. I walk over to the full body mirror and turn back and forth, looking at all the angles, shocked to find a version of me I consider beautiful. It's not that I don't love my looks normally; it's just not something I put effort into. This feels like an elevated version of me, and I love it.

"Shit, it's even better than I thought it would be," Ainsley says with a sniffle.

"Holy gorgeousness, you look amazing," Willow echoes.

"Thank you. I assume I have you to thank for it, so high-five your-selves."

I turn my attention to them and find them in knee length dresses, in different shades of blue but not the same style. They go together but they don't match, confusing me even more.

"You both look beautiful," I tell them.

"Thank you. We have two more things for you before we head out," Ainsley says cryptically.

Willow brings over a shoe box and pulls out a cream pair of hiking boots, and I have to laugh. At least they aren't trying to cram me into heels. I'd break an ankle for sure.

They help me lace them up so I don't wrinkle my dress, and then Ainsley goes to her dresser and grabs a small box.

"We wanted to get you something that you could wear and remember today." She hands me the box, and I carefully open it to reveal a stunning pair of earrings that have a main stone that looks like diamonds surrounded by smaller blue stones. They're small and not overly showy, and perfect.

"I love them, but I can't accept these," I murmur as I run my finger over them.

"Yeah, we're not doing that. Put them on, and let's go!" They both have smiles on that light up their whole faces, and it's infectious. I may not know what we're doing, but I'm starting to get excited about it. I am still distracted, trying to mentally calculate when I'm going to have time to put the bed together and if I can keep Arlo out of the house until I do.

We climb into Ainsley's car and make our way to a familiar area. I start to get suspicious when we park at the trailhead that leads to the waterfall.

"Guys..." I can feel my heartbeat racing.

"Follow us, please," Ainsley says with a knowing smile, and the pressure of incoming tears hits behind my eyes.

It takes us fifteen long minutes to get to Arlo and my spot, but once we're there, the tears start to fall.

Every single person in Bluebell Falls creates a semi-circle facing the falls. On the flat rock that Arlo and I frequently lounge on is an arch covered in wildflowers, with the man himself standing underneath it.

A sob breaks free as I cover my mouth in shock. I can't believe he put all of this together. Ainsley and Willow quietly go to join the masses when another presence walks up next to me.

"Can I walk you down the aisle?" Ledger asks, and I don't even care if I'm ugly crying because this is exactly what I've wanted since I was a teenager and never thought I would get.

Arlo has made every single one of my dreams come true, and I don't know if there are enough words to articulate how I feel right now.

Overwhelmed seems to be the largest emotion, though.

"Of course," I say, trying to pull myself together.

He holds out his elbow, and I hook my arm in his as we start walking down the split in the crowd. I don't take my eyes off my husband, and when I'm close enough, I see his eyes glistening with tears.

We step in front of him, both of us smiling like lunatics when Ledger releases me and claps Arlo on the back.

"Take care of her," he says with a smile.

"Always," Arlo says, taking both of my hands.

Ledger walks away, and we're left to face each other.

"What did you do?" I whisper, still in shock.

"You deserve a real wedding. You deserve the world knowing how much you're loved," he says simply.

His words melt me on the spot, and I lean forward to press a kiss to his lips.

A throat clears in front of us as I look up to find Jim Mathews clasping his hands, smiling.

"I believe we have to do the vows first." He winks.

Everyone laughs as my cheeks heat and Arlo shrugs.

Jim continues with a very short and sweet ceremony, which is exactly what I would have wanted, and when he says, "You may now kiss the bride," Arlo takes control in my favorite kind of way. He dips me down, holding me close to his body, and kisses the hell out of me. I'm glad the girls just put lip gloss on me because it would have been ruined.

Cheers and claps surround us, making me laugh against his lips.

"You are fucking amazing, Mr. Steel."

"All you, Mrs. Steel. I hope I did okay." He picks me up, and we stare at each other like it's only us here.

"You did... I'm speechless. This is more than I could have ever imagined."

"I love you so damn much." The awe in his voice makes me want to strip him right here and show him my appreciation.

"I love you. I don't know how you pulled this off." I shake my head.

"Lots of help. Speaking of, let's make the rounds, and then everyone will meet us at our house for the reception."

He kisses me once more before pulling us off the rock and over to our friends and family. The well wishes and happy conversations are not something I thought I needed, but damn does it feel good to know we're supported.

I see Lennox off to the side, and I let go of Arlo's hand to talk to him.

"You didn't have to come," I tell him.

"I wouldn't miss your wedding for anything, even if you are a pain in the ass." He winks.

"It wouldn't have been the same without you, so thank you. Are you coming back to the house?" Am I overly hopeful? Yes, but I'm concerned by his need to stay at home all the time.

"Not this time, sis." I can tell he's sad about it, but I also won't be the one to push him.

"Door's always open for you, Lenny. And I have something that's almost done for you. I'll drop it off next week, yeah?"

"You didn't have to make me anything." His cheeks are tinged pink. A shy Lennox is one I haven't seen since his adolescence.

"Well, tough, it's almost done, so say thank you when I deliver it and brag about how awesome the piece is."

He chuckles at that and gives me a hug before he wanders off down the trail.

"He'll be okay," Ledger's voice sounds from behind me.

"I'm not so sure," I mutter, more worried about Lennox than I was when he was released from the hospital.

"Come on, we'll worry about him tomorrow. Today, your husband is waiting for you."

I turn around and find Arlo looking on with concern, but I shoot him a small smile and make my way to him.

"He okay?" he asks, wrapping his arms around me.

"I don't know." Leaning my head on his chest, I watch as our town files out down the trail, leaving Arlo and me to our moment of quiet.

"You are quite the secret keeper, sir."

"There's one more surprise," he says.

Reaching into his pocket, he pulls out what looks like a ring box but doesn't open it.

"I wanted you to keep your original ring because I know it's sentimental to you, but I also wanted to get you something that symbolizes our new future. It's not an upgrade, just an addition." He opens the top of the box, and I suck in a breath at the infinity band in front of me.

"Arlo…"

"It took me too long to get to this point. I know we're not apologizing for the past anymore, but I want you to know that I will love you to the ends of the Earth and far beyond that. You are my heart and soul. Thank you for loving me just as much."

"Jesus, are you sure we can't kick everyone out of the house? You are not allowed to say things like that and not expect me to jump you." Emotion clogs my voice.

"Sorry, Emmerdeur, you'll have to wait a little longer for your orgasm tonight." He smirks, and I rise up on my tiptoes to kiss him again.

"Take me home. Let's feed everyone and then kick them out. I have a surprise for you too."

"Alright, I kicked everyone out. What's this surprise?" Arlo asks, sliding his arm around my stomach and yanking my back against him.

"You ready to get a little sweaty?" I ask.

"Hell fucking yes!" he says eagerly because he has no idea what he's in for. I grab his hand and make him follow me to my workshop.

"Recreating fun times? I like it," he jokes.

I don't respond; instead, I pull him to the back corner where our brand-new bed sits.

"It took me longer than I thought it would. I promised you a new bed when we moved in together, and I'm about a month late. Sorry about that." I smile. "I also had intended to move it into our actual room before you got home from work today, but you kind of spoiled that plan."

"Rina... This is stunning." He runs his hand over the natural walnut I built the bed out of. The headboard is a live edge slab with the most gorgeous striations. The rest is a fairly simple build, but the headboard proved to be one hell of a challenge.

"I know I didn't get your opinion on it, but when I saw this slab, all I could see it as was our bed."

"Is it cheesy to say I'm so damn excited to own a Rina Hutton original?"

I laugh at how adorable he is. "Honestly, it makes me feel way more important than I am, so let's run with it."

"Okay, let's change and then figure out how to get this inside." He rubs his hands together.

"Nope. When you take this dress off, it will be so you can give me multiple orgasms. I have two pallet carts that will hold the entire length of headboard. We just need to slide them under it as we disconnect it, then roll it over to the side door."

It sounds simple, but it'll take a bit of work to maneuver it in the house. The good news is we don't have to carry the heavy ass slab of walnut.

"This is not the wedding night I had in mind," he grumbles as he starts to roll up his sleeves.

"The faster we get this assembled, the faster you can show me what you had in mind there, Mr. Steel."

"Grab your carts and let's go."

An hour and a half, a rip to Arlo's shirt, and a bottle of champagne later, we're standing at the foot of our new bed. We didn't even put bedding on, just threw the mattress on top and decided that was good enough.

"It looks good in here," I observe. I barely get the words out before Arlo shoves his hand in my hair and turns me to him, kissing me like he's been starving for me.

We break apart, and he cups my jaw. "I'm going to spend every day worshiping the ground you walk on and making you so damn happy with our life."

"You're doing one hell of a job already. Just keep loving me," I say against his lips.

"Forever, Emmerdeur."

EPILOGUE
RINA

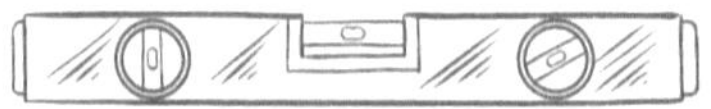

*T*wo weeks later...

Arlo and I are getting ready for family dinner when my phone rings. When I see Willow's name, I don't hesitate to answer.

"What's up, sis?"

"I need help." Her panicked tone sets me on edge, and I make eye contact with Arlo, who furrows his eyebrows as I set the phone on speakerphone.

"Arlo's here. What's going on?"

"Lennox went for a hike and fell on one of the harder trails. He called me, downplaying everything, but Rina, his leg is definitely fucked," she whispers.

"What the fuck?"

"Where are you guys?" Arlo says at the same time.

Willow tells us the trail they're on, and I look at Arlo with concern. He matches my gaze. Both of us know the trail that Lennox was hiking is too advanced for someone who hasn't gotten a ton of physical activity while healing and had really deep cuts on his legs.

"We'll be right there, Will. Is it bad enough that we need to take him to Rosedale?" Arlo asks.

"I think taking him to Doc Grant first is a good idea. I don't know what actually happened, so maybe he can at least give us an idea first and tell us we need to go to Rosedale," Willow says quietly.

"We're headed out now. I'll text Ledger and let him know family dinner is on pause."

Arlo takes over the conversation while I slip on some hiking boots and a hoodie before we head out to the truck.

It takes us ten minutes to reach where they both are, and when we walk up to them, Lennox looks too pale.

Arlo jumps in with his first aid knowledge and has Lennox answer some basic questions while I pull Willow to the side.

"What the fuck was he thinking?" I hiss.

"I don't know. I think we need to have a family discussion about how to help him because he knows better than to come out on this trail when he hasn't done more than hike to the falls. And it's fucking freezing today. It's like he doesn't care what happens to him."

"Can y'all help me get him up? We're going to hobble to the truck," Arlo calls out to us. It's a damn good thing we're only five minutes from the trailhead because there's no way we'd be able to get Lennox to the truck otherwise. We'd have to call in search and rescue, which he would have fucking hated.

It takes all three of us to get him up and to the truck. The whole time, Lennox doesn't say a word. He's pale and a little green, so I know he's in pain, but even prompted questions get no reply.

When we finally reach the doctor's office, everyone in the family is there to meet us. Arlo gets Lennox set up in the room before coming out to the small waiting room with the rest of us.

"We've got to do something for him," Ledger says.

"We told him we'd give him space to figure it out," Willow says weakly.

"That was before he messed his fucking leg because he tried a trail he wasn't in shape for!" I throw my hands up.

"Marina…" Arlo warns.

"No. Are we going to just let him be self-destructive? Hide away in his cabin until he's no longer someone we recognize? We have to help him."

Ledger drops into one of the visitor chairs and puts his head in his hands. Ainsley sits next to him, running her hand along his back.

"Have we failed him? Should we have done more after everything happened?" Ledger asks.

"We didn't fail him. We were giving him the space to figure out how to heal. Now, we need to step in because the path he's going down is … scary," Oakley murmurs.

"He's going to hate this," Willow adds.

"What choice do we have, though? Are we just going to let our brother downslide and get worse? He's only come to family dinner a handful of times since being in the hospital and rarely says anything in our group chat. At what point do we step in, even if he'll be pissed about it?" I ask.

The six of us think on my words. We're all adults, and none of us want to step into Lennox's life and make him do anything, but if we are truly this worried about him, then what other option do we have?

A throat clears behind us, and we turn around to see Dr. Grant with a weary smile on his face.

"I just wanted to update you. He tore his quadricep, and there's nothing I can really do here. I can't tell how bad the tear is, so I can't tell if he needs surgery, but my best guess is he does. I splinted it, and he'll be fine until he gets to the hospital. I also gave him some pain meds, even though he was refusing. I know this injury is painful as all get-out. He'll need physical therapy and possibly look into a counselor or therapist. He's very closed off and isn't telling much beyond the basics of what happened. I also called ahead to the hospital, so they know to expect you."

"Thanks for getting that splinted. We'll get him in one of trucks and get him to the hospital." Ledger takes charge.

Dr. Grant nods and heads back to Lennox as we attempt to figure out a game plan.

"Okay, so Oakley and Arlo can help me get him in the truck. Do we all want to head over there or just a couple of us?" Ledger says.

"I need to put food away, so if you guys go ahead, I can head there shortly after," Ainsley says.

Willow and I agree to help Ainsley while the men take Lennox right away.

The men nod, standing up to go help Ledger as us women hang back.

"I'm worried about him," I say.

"I am too, but I don't want to force him into things and push him away further," Willow says.

"What if I put an ad on the employment site we use for Bluebell Landscaping and see if we can get someone to check on him and help with his physical therapy or regular therapy? With the tear, he'll be down for a while, but maybe we can get a jump with physical therapy to get him stronger," Ainsley throws out there.

"He's going to hate that," Willow says.

"Maybe we need to worry less about him hating us and worry more about getting him through this hard time. So far, giving him time and space has not proven to help," I say.

"Fuck," Willow groans.

The sound of crutches on the floor, followed by multiple boots, makes the three of us look up as we watch Lennox struggle to get to the front door. I make eye contact with Arlo as he subtly shakes his head.

By the time they get him into Ledger's truck, I'm exhausted at the thought of intervening in Lennox's life.

"Hey, Emmerdeur, you okay?" Arlo asks as I stop in front of Ainsley's car.

"I don't know. I know we need to help him, but I can't help but feel this will push him away even more. I just hope, eventually, he sees that we just wanted to help and not hold that against us."

"Between the six of us, I think we'll be able to figure out things without overwhelming him. Let's worry about his leg and then go from there."

"I can't believe he tore his freaking quad. What else does that poor guy need to be hit with?" I sigh.

"It's totally fucked up, but maybe this is the eye-opener he needs."

"I hope so."

One thing I've learned recently is that you have to be willing to change. Opening yourself up to the possibility that life isn't what you thought I'd be is a hard pill to swallow. But looking at Arlo, I know real happiness is possible.

I just hope we can help get Lennox to that point.

ALSO BY

The Catalyst Series

<u>The Beginning</u>

Meet the women of The Catalyst Series a decade before the series takes place!

<u>The Detour</u>

Bea and Riggs

<u>The List</u>

Penelope and Andy

<u>The Case</u>

Larkin and Theo

<u>The Vacation</u>

Jane and Pierce

Bluebell Falls

<u>Second First Impression</u>

Ainsley and Ledger

<u>For the Thrill of It</u>

Willow and Oakley

Be sure to join my newsletter to stay up to date on new releases and all other things me!

http://www.samanthamthomas.com

If you enjoyed What You Broke, please think about leaving a review! I would be so grateful to you!

Review Here

ACKNOWLEDGMENTS

Thank you for sticking around for my rambling!

Michelle- Could this book have gotten done without you? Probably. But would it have been any good? Hell no. I am so grateful a random Facebook post brought us together. I can't imagine bothering anyone else every single day with the most random questions. Our friendship is perfection. I wish I could express how much it means to me, but we're a special kind of unhinged that only we understand.

Emi- Thank you so much for everything! You've helped turn this series into something truly special and I'm so grateful!

Nina- Ma'am... you are a rockstar. You've helped me more than I could ever express, and I am so very grateful to have found you. You're stuck with me now. No take backs.

KATE!- (yes, this needed to be yelled) I am so in love with these covers. You took my barebones idea- so basically nothing- and turned it into something so gorgeous. Not to mention all the amazing fictional brands you've created too! *Chefs kiss*

Kait- I can't even classify you. You're more than a sounding board, more than a beta reader, more than a hype girl. You're one of my best friends and I can never tell you how much you mean to me! You never fail to make me laugh and one day, we will be in the same damn city so we can promptly cause all kinds of trouble.

Joscelyn- Girl... I don't think I could finish a book without you. Between late night chats, alpha/beta reads, whatever we're calling it now, and just being a friend when this author thing gets hard, our friendship has been a bright spot in my life.

To my readers, ARC readers, street team- YOU ARE WHY I DO THIS! Seeing reactions, hearing how much you love these characters that just sprung from my wild brain never fails to be AMAZING! Truly, it's like I'm watching you talk about someone else when I see reviews, or comments about my books. Thank you. None of this is possible without you. Thank you for going on this wild adventure with me.

Hubs- Always last, but certainly not least. When I started writing this book we were talking randomly about some small details within. It clicked in my mind how very Arlo you are. Or how very Arlo is you. Not the grumpy, asshole Arlo, but the small gestures, always going above and beyond Arlo. The always going the extra mile in your words, just to make me happy. You do that every single day and I'm so grateful to do this crazy thing called life with you.